CORNER STONE

THE KING

MICHAEL PAUL

Publisher: Michael Paul Author LLC

Cover and text illustrations by David Provolo.
Designed by David Provolo.

Library of Congress Cataloging-in-Publication Data is available upon request.

ISBN: 978-1-7371660-6-1 (hardcover)
ISBN: 978-1-7371660-8-5 (paperback)
ISBN: 978-1-7371660-9-2 (e-book)
ISBN: 978-1-7371660-7-8 (audiobook)

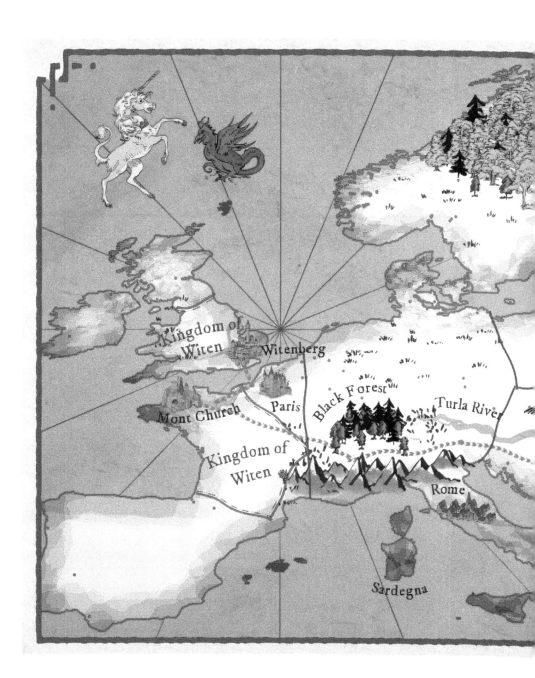

for Robyn Campbell

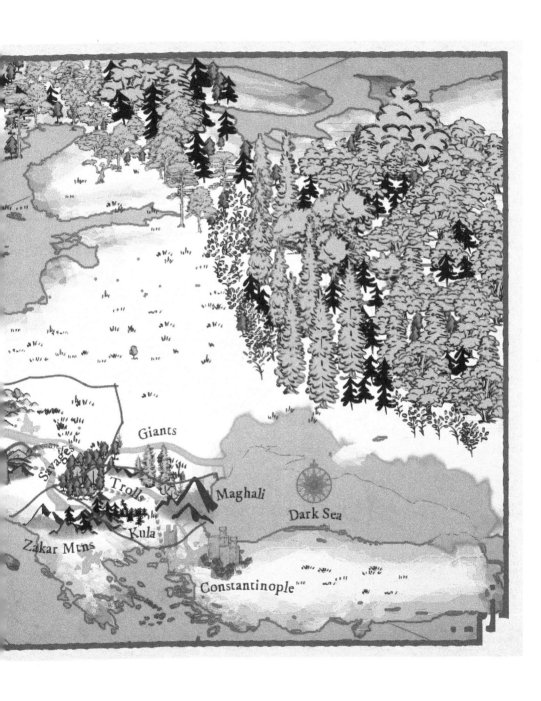

Giants

Savages

Trolls

Maghali

Kula

Dark Sea

Zakar Mtns

Constantinople

TABLE OF CONTENTS

TABLE OF CONTENTS

PROLOGUE

Valentine's Day 1192

Love or Freedom?

This question was written on playing cards Matia had stashed around the bell chamber.

He quietly removed the master woodcut that protruded from his pocket and felt the words and symbols that ran slowly beneath his fingertips. In one symbol, he saw in his mind's eye a cross, a circle, and a flower, combined to make the cornerstone.

The wind rushed and whistled around his hood, and his warm breaths created a fog. He hid behind a gargoyle in the belfry and pulled his hood more firmly over his salt-and-pepper hair.

He waited.

A door shot open. *A Watcher*, he thought.

Shivering, the Watcher adjusted his wool earmuffs and put on leather gloves. A pendant fell from its thong around his neck, but the Watcher promptly bent and lifted it from the dusty floor and put it in a pocket within the folds of his tunic. After checking the candle clock, he told his hands, "Quick, then slow."

The Watcher raised his hood and pulled the rope.

Sharp strike, sharp strike, sharp strike.

Ring up. Wait.

Matia's heart leapt as playing cards fell from the lip of the bell and rode the wind through an opening into the courtyard. For years, he had covered his ears, the sound forever burning in his mind as a reminder of the murder.

But tonight—tonight, restoration began. The clergy would interrogate, the ruling class panic, and the peasants play.

Long strike. Full circle.

Hundreds of cards shook loose from their hiding places in the bell chamber.

Four rings signify the hour.

The sound of joy rang out in his heart as the cards snowed upon the Watcher.

Include, transform, transcend, Matia thought.

Around the roof and down the staircases he hurried, body aching, bloodied hands painting red the center pole.

He remembered the saboteur's last words: "Mati, oh, Mati, why do you always seek to rebel against me? Our plans are for the greater good."

He fled the tower, and the grotto door clicked shut behind him.

Matia looked back, but a shadow had vanished into the cool dampness of the stone cathedral.

"Oh, Mati," the hunter called in the flat, dry tone of a clerk. "You can't hide from us."

Matia's heart thumped against his rib cage. It fought for space in his chest with the air stalled in his lungs.

The hunter reappeared and darted around the stone columns. "There you are," the hunter said, relieved. "You're proving to be quite interesting."

Escape seemed possible still, but marking the cornerstone symbol was more important. It was a message for her, a symbol that pointed to the mysteries of the stone.

PART I

THREE DAYS LATER

CHAIR

Miah wrote several notes, paused—exasperated—and muttered, "Stupid—no." Scratches covered the writing, and he drew the figure in action. *Perfect,* he thought. Beneath the bench, he opened the chest, stowed the prototype carpenter-hero in its proper place alongside diary entries, playing cards, a blanket, and a collection of light-warriors, wizards, Watchers, dragons, goblins, Giants, Savages, and Trolls.

Miah took a couple of deep breaths, drawing in the heavy tang of wood, to get back to his proper work. He measured the ninety-degree angle and grabbed his saw to make a cut. With a hammer, he pounded the last nail into the chair; it would be ready before the cardinal's visit to St. David, the town cathedral.

He swept sawdust from the chair and set it in the center of the shop. Miah stood tall and proud as he imagined hundreds of villagers admiring the chair in a packed cathedral.

Across the carpentry shop, his father tapped his pencil on the table he was building. With weathered, sticky hands massaging a grizzled beard, Elfred scanned the shop, then groaned and grabbed his lower back when he bent to examine the chair.

Miah walked closer and grabbed Elfred's arm, noticing the gooey residue of sap coating his father's fingertips. "Chopping again with Alf?" asked Miah. "Mum will say something."

"Yes, Son, I know. But we needed more wood before we travel."

"Travel?" asked Miah.

A satisfied smile trailed across Elfred's face. "We've been invited by the royal council to deliver the chair."

Miah released the arm and hugged his father, rubbing his chestnut cheek against his father's powdery sawdust stubble. Linseed and wax scents mingled in the air, and he inhaled all he could of it with eyes closed as he moved about the shop.

"Careful, Miah."

"Thanks, Dadde," Miah said and opened his eyes, "but I know where everything is."

With a deep grumble, Elfred inspected Miah's work. "I'm proud of you, Son. Remember Pythagoras and prime numbers?"

"Of course, Dadde . . . you taught me, remember? That would be prime numbers two, three, five, seven, eleven, thirteen, seventeen—shall I continue?"

"No, no. I believe you."

"When we go to the king's village, can we find a gift for Marianne?" asked Miah. "I know of a large stall in the market that has many toys and dolls."

Elfred's bushy, blond eyebrows raised, and his royal-blue eyes brightened. "Dolls, Miah? Isn't she a little old for that?"

Miah glanced to the chest that held his own figurines and shrugged. "I don't know . . . what do girls like?"

Elfred grinned and said, "Miah, hand me the rag." He looked over his son and asked, "Time you started to shave, isn't it?"

Miah clacked the hard soles of his recently grown-tight shoes on the floor as he crossed the shop to snatch the rag.

"I believe I'm becoming a man," he said, rubbing his chin. "That is probably one reason I think she's the greatest." Miah tossed the rag with a grin. "Catch, Dadde!"

"Good throw," said Elfred as he snatched the rag from midair. "Come on, help me polish off the staining. Take the other rag. We need this spotless even before we seal." Two fingers jabbed the rag into the jar of tan stain as he continued: "You've thought Marianne was the greatest since you were eight. But now you've moved on from playing games and noticed she's a girl."

"Dadde . . . ," Miah dragged out as he dipped his own rag in the jar. His nose wrinkled and his voice cracked as he applied the fragrant stain in tight, small circles on the arm of the chair.

Elfred chuckled and slapped his knee.

"I don't like her like that," said Miah. "We're just friends."

"Well, let's talk about it soon."

With pursed lips, Miah blew onto the chair and rubbed until it sparkled. "Perfect, Dadde," he pronounced. He took both rags and under-handed them onto the bench.

"Come on, Son—let's finish the chores and go home for dinner."

"Wait, wait," Miah said and polished again with the cuff of his sleeve.

"It's good, Son. There's no need to rush or perfect it. Even the finest wood has flaws."

"Yes," he said and dabbed a bit more stain on one spot. "But this is for the church."

From the workbench, Elfred grabbed birch paper marked with Lord Harold's latest decrees. "Take this, Miah, and snip and rip, and spread the pieces across the cowshed yard."

"Yes, Dadde." Miah pulled iron scissors from a drawer and cut the paper into smaller pieces until they could fit in his pocket. Before exiting, Miah swept the shop floor like a hand pointer meticulously reading a document word by word.

"All clear," Miah said and shut the door.

They walked briskly beside the village creek and water mill, then up the hill towards their cottage home.

Atop the hill, a short and hot-tempered bailiff was dragging a peasant, probably to the ecclesiastical court. "Working on a holy day, me see," the little man said as he grimaced and hauled the filthy peasant over a clod of earth.

"I could say the same thing of you, Asser the Short," replied Elfred.

"Aye, Elfred of the Wood. But me bosses are a weee bit holier than yours."

The peasant coughed, and Asser yanked him. "No listening to Master Elfred. Lock it."

"Dadde, why is he covered in dirt?" Miah asked, concerned for the beleaguered peasant.

"Your son?" asked Asser, extending his stubby hand as if he wanted to pat Miah on the head. "How old are you?"

Miah stepped back and said in a feigned, deeper voice, "Thirteen."

"Aye, me see," Asser replied hoarsely. "Curly, brown hair, almond eyes, dark skin, large nose and lips . . . Hmm . . . much different from your father."

Elfred wrapped an arm around Miah's shoulder. "From his mother's side. And someday, he'll make Master and replace me as president of the Carpentry Guild."

A laugh rose from the peasant, and Miah followed the man's eyes to the dark clouds rolling in. Another laugh erupted from the man's slobbering mouth, and the peasant's wild eyes searched the sky. "He's coming, he's coming!" he cried.

"Witen off!" Asser yelled with his fist raised. "Quit gawking and pull over your hood."

A whoosh blew leaves around, and free-roaming chickens scattered for cover.

"Not the full shilling," Asser said in low, scratchy voice, "didn't have the full shilling." He twirled the knotted braids in the gray-flecked amber tufted beard that covered only his chin. "Peddling in black medicine, me measure."

The peasant started to turn over, but Asser placed a boot on his back and added, "Ever since the archbishop died, Witenberg has gotten woody."

"Must be your bosses, Asser, causing the trouble," said Elfred, and Miah watched for the lines of bitterness in his face and the shuffle of steps that came when his father commented on politics.

"Many holes, aye—corrupt as the king."

Elfred extended a hand towards Miah. "Son, give me the paper."

Elfred took the stack of pieces from Miah and threw it towards Asser, who opened his arms to catch what pieces he could. "For your bum," said Elfred.

Miah pulled Elfred's arm. "Can we go?"

"One moment, Son."

Smiling, showing a front tooth partially missing, Asser put together a couple of the pieces and read. "Not enough pictures," he said, then laughed, "but me can make out." He ripped the paper made from the bark of birch trees and flung the pieces to the wet dirt. "This rubbish isn't fit to wipe me bum. That me agree with you, Master Elfred."

Elfred's boot buried the paper deeper into the mud. "We must be getting on home, Asser," he said, nodding to their house nearby.

"And me to court, Master Elfred. Good day." He tipped his forest-green flat cap and reached down to yank the peasant again.

Elfred and Miah came to the cottage Elfred had insisted they build themselves rather than press peasants into service. Their home was different than neighbor lords' lofts and the merchants' manors in the village. It had an oak framework of uneven timbers cut by hand, though Elfred had tried to make it as straight as possible. Miah and his brother had thrown many of the failures into the firewood pile.

Miah's mother stood outside the loafing shed where the cattle took shelter in uncomfortable weather, for next to it was her annexed kitchen. Her cheeks were flushed from cooking dinner, and odors of wet dog hair, manure, and onion soup wafted through the air.

Sarah shook her head and chided, "Working again on a Sunday, Elfred?" He did not respond, breezing past Sarah and disappearing into the open door of the cottage.

Miah picked his way over piles of cow manure and grabbed a pitchfork inside the barn.

"Leave it, Miah. I'll do it later," Sarah said crossly, so Miah followed his father into the house and sat at the table with his brother, Alf, and their grandfather, who shook his head and pursed his lips.

"Shut it, Martin," said Elfred.

"I hope you working this much brings in more money," Sarah began as she appeared in the doorway. "I could use your help with the cleaning—we don't want our children to get sick—especially in this cold." She looked through the door, across the meadow to the church, and said to Miah and Alf, "You will join me tomorrow for Mass."

"But—but, Mum!" Miah cried. "That's not fair. Another Mass? We already went this morning. Dadde and I are taking the chair to the castle tomorrow."

"I won't hear of it, Miah. You and your dadde can leave promptly after your appointment, then you can join me."

DELIVERY

The sun rested on the horizon as Elfred and Miah guided the mule and wagon, loaded with the chair, across the bridge and bumped it along the cobblestones in the king's village. Miah, who usually wore a simple tunic, had donned his best clothes and cap for the palace visit. Elfred had instructed him on proper etiquette before they departed.

Down an alley, the wagon rolled past a stumbling cleric amid broken bottles and frosty breaths, and past a pair of sunken eyes glaring from underneath a heavy blanket. Two young women approached the wagon and lifted the cloth covering the chair.

"Stop," said Elfred. "This isn't yours."

"Please, please," one begged, "we just want food."

Elfred calmed the mule and halted the wagon. Glancing at the marks on their wrists, he reached into the wagon and lifted the lid of a box inside.

"Here," he said as he broke bread and handed it to them. "Now leave us be."

They sat on the cobbles again and covered themselves with a single cloak. After devouring the bread, they stroked their cats' heads and promised them, "Next time, next time, next time, we'll save some for you."

Miah knelt and stared at them. One cradled her cat and sang. The other pulled a vial from her coat and dripped a drop into her mouth.

"Let's go, Miah," said Elfred, and they continued on their way.

The carriage bounced from the alley and rolled onto smoother, better-packed stones, and suddenly they saw up the alley to where the castle loomed on the hill beyond the gate they would reach in moments.

"Papers," demanded the guard dressed in purple, black, and blue. "It's earlier than your appointment, Master Elfred."

"Yes, I know, but the wife . . ."

"Kicked you out?" The guard chuckled.

Elfred nodded.

"I understand. I understand." He signaled another guard. "Fetch the chamberlain. Right this way, Master Elfred."

The guard turned to Miah and said, "Always use proper customs and courtesies when addressing the king and his court. Better yet, stay quiet."

The castle was far more crowded this day than usual, so the iron gates had been closed, but the guards moved aside to let them pass. One section of the gate rolled on a rail to the side and another raised and lowered.

A large clang and Miah knew they were inside the castle grounds. He looked around in wonder, having never seen it from the inside.

"Don't forget to salute, Miah," said Elfred.

Two large doors swung open, revealing the torch-lit dark passageway within the stone tower.

Miah stood straight with his chest out, mentally practicing his tribute for the king, until a man dressed in white, with golden buttons all the way down his coat, greeted them. He embodied the very essence of prosperity. Miah's eyes raked over the man, taking in every stitch and button and lingering on the large silver key worn by the master chamberlain.

"Welcome, Master Elfred, and son, I presume," the man said. "Sentinels, place the chair inside and wait for my instructions."

"Thank you, Chamberlain Vere," Elfred replied, rummaging for the papers with the king's seal and handing them to the door sentinels, who inspected the wagon and everything in it and wheeled it ahead of them farther into the castle.

Into the warmer grand space they were ushered, and Miah gazed in wonder at the marble central staircase directly ahead as it wrapped around a stone pillar to the first and second floors. They passed beneath banners decorated with three lions and into an arched space whose walls were lined with portraits of the republican heroes who had been replaced by the king. In the middle of the ceiling, a chandelier blazed with a rainbow of candles. Below their feet, various geometric shapes were etched into the marble floor, and the slight breeze in the space flooded lemon scent all around them.

"A mark of the queen," said Chamberlain Vere, a finger to the side of his nose as he noticed Miah breathing deeply. "She enforces a daily cleaning." He glanced towards the central staircase, where men were huddled around the wagon, and he motioned to Elfred and Miah to stop.

"Master Elfred, wait here with the sentinels until I return. A few moments." Then he glided across the hall to meet the three men beside Miah's chair, which had been unloaded from the wagon.

"Dadde, who are they?" Miah asked in a loud whisper.

"It looks like our glorious sheriff, the honorable Lord Harold," Elfred said tartly, "and the smaller man with the sword is the earl marshal—he's named Stewart and is commander of the royal army."

"And the man with the long coat who bounces on his toes?"

"He's a priest I haven't seen before."

Suddenly a boy entered the hall from a corridor and sauntered past young servant women cleaning. He puffed his chest and brightened as he recognized Miah. He ran right over and punched Miah in the shoulder, chanting, "Little Miah, little Miah, the privy is amazing. But it's too grand for you."

"Stop it, Harry!" cried Miah with a defensive swipe of his arm, but the other boy had already taken Miah's cap and swaggered to the grand wooden chair.

Miah was speechless, but Elfred took action, turning to the guard beside him at motionless parade rest in his tricolor uniform and purple beret.

"Excuse me, Sentinel," said Elfred. The guard did not respond. Louder, Elfred said, pointing out Harry, "Sentinel—that boy in the chair."

The sentinel's white-gloved hands moved from behind his back to his sides, but the rest of his body remained still. Across from them Harry had plopped on the chair, squirming, ensuring Elfred and Miah saw him rub his bum on every inch of the seat.

Elfred fumed and stepped forward, but the sentinel stretched out his hand. "No." But Miah ducked under the forbidding arm and ran to the chair.

"Get off my chair, Harry!" he ordered.

"Or what, little Miah?" Harry stood on the chair and put on Miah's cap. "I'm Miah. I'm king of my carpentry shop," he declared.

"Give me my cap."

"Get your dadde to fight for you," Harry said with a smirk.

"My dadde? What about your dadde?" Miah about-faced and walked to the huddle and stood behind Lord Harold, who was shaking the priest's hand.

The priest leaned into the handshake and extended his long, thin fingers. "I am Father William," the man said, then his face scrunched and his mouth opened, but no words came. Eyes narrowed, he squeezed until the words spat out: "P—p-lease—p-lease—pleased to meet you. I'm sorry. I'm sorry. The archb—bishop's death ..." Through his pointed, slender nose, he inhaled long and exhaled longer. "The B—the B—Father Virdis's death. The abbot appointed me to investigate. I've come to meet the court."

They paused and Miah tapped Lord Harold on the back. "Lord Harold," said Miah.

"One moment, gentlemen," said Lord Harold and turned around. When he saw it was just Miah, he whispered with a snarl, "Leave, child." Then he turned back to the men.

"A priest?" continued Lord Harold. "Shouldn't someone from the court investigate?"

Miah pressed into the huddle, weaving between the men.

"Leave, child," said Lord Harold again.

"No, no—there is nothing more to be said here," said Chamberlain Vere. "Gentlemen, the court sends regrets, but the king is not here. He orders you to return tomorrow to review security protocols."

Chamberlain Vere put a hand out to the visitor's arm. "Father William, stay for a moment. The queen wants to meet you." From his pocket, Father William pulled out a charcoal pencil and sat on a bench. He wrote in a large, thong-bound notebook.

Lord Harold strode over to Harry and hit him across the head.

"That's what you get for embarrassing me," he said, and looked towards Elfred, who had a blithe smile painted across his face. Lord Harold dragged Harry by the collar past Elfred, then across the marble. Harry tried responding, but his voice kept cracking.

Finally, Harry pushed through words in a deeper voice, moaning as his father dragged him towards the door, "But, but, Dadde, I want to know why *he* is here."

"His dadde is probably complaining about the king again," said Lord Harold. "But, Son, I'll be watching them."

Miah smirked, and Harry mouthed at him with a finger raised, "Witen off, bastard."

"Thank you for your service to the kingdom, Master Elfred," said Chamberlain Vere. "The king and cardinal will be most grateful."

"Where will the chair go?" asked Miah, his curiosity overcoming his manners. "Where's the king?"

"The king is not here. The chair will be placed in the palace central hall for the cardinal when he visits. Then we'll move it to the cathedral."

Elfred waited for payment from Chamberlain Vere. He waited awkwardly for several minutes, then tried different approaches: asking politely, asking repeatedly, and then demanding. However, after twenty minutes of this, it was clear Chamberlain Vere could not approve the transaction himself.

"I will most earnestly request the king's clerk send payment to your household as soon as possible," Chamberlain Vere assured him.

"The court officer told me I'd be paid when I delivered the chair."

"Circumstances have recently changed, Master Elfred." He looked up and called across the floor, "Sentinels, escort them out."

"Wait, wait!" shouted Queen Rachel as she swept onto the landing of the staircase, accompanied by ladies-in-waiting. "Chamberlain Vere, I order you to halt."

The Chamberlain turned. "Yes, Your Highness."

"I want to give our guests a gift," she said, "for bringing the chair."

Miah's mouth dropped open at the queen's elegance in her lavender dress, which swirled several marble steps below her feet, her olive skin glistening as she glided down the stairs.

Sliding one hand across the new chair, the queen said, "Like my father—so much attention to detail." In the hall, she said to the priest, "Father William, wait here until I'm finished with Master Elfred. Master Elfred, I want to show you something."

"Yes, Your Highness." Elfred bowed.

"Thank you for coming," she said, sounding quite delighted. Coupled with a wedge of light that fell across her face, the gentleness of her words irresistibly drew Miah into a love he couldn't describe.

"Of course, Your Highness," answered Elfred.

She ran a hand through her thick, shining brown hair, tucking it behind one ear. "And who's this dapper young man?"

Elfred nudged Miah. After two sharp elbow strikes to his chest, Miah closed his gaping mouth and bowed. Rising, he said, "My name is Jeremiah, Your Majesty."

"Jeremiah. I like it. Jeremiah the Wise."

She placed a small, golden ball into his hands and held them together with her own warm hands. "Balance, Jeremiah the Wise. Remember balance."

She took the ball again and dropped a silver pendant into his palm. "This is our kingdom's symbol: three lions, to signify duty, honor, and kingdom." She lightly squeezed Miah's hand and said, "Protect this, Jeremiah."

He uncurled his fingers and inspected the tiny cursive writing etched into the silver.

She stood and addressed Elfred. "I know, Master Elfred, it is just a small token of our appreciation, but I assure you—you will be paid."

"Thank you, Your Highness," said Elfred with his mouth drawn in lines of endurance and solemn recognition.

"Before you go," she said, "I want to show you something."

She sped them past statues of previous kings and tapestries showing the royal family tree. She stopped at the Kingdom of Witen map draped on the wall, traced her finger over the four duchies and eight counties as she summarized the kingdom's history.

Elfred pointed to the map and said, "We once elected dukes, lords, and counts as rulers, but now the king appoints."

"Correct, Master Elfred," she said. "You are well versed in the kingdom's history. And teaching your son—brilliant." She paused and held a warm glance towards Miah. "Peace started to crumble when various kings grew the kingdom beyond its original footprint and exerted more control centrally in the capital."

She walked them to Chamberlain Vere and said, "Thank you for visiting." Her voice came pleasant but with a dash of some emotion Miah couldn't name.

She shook Elfred's hand, then offered a hug to Jeremiah.

Jeremiah started to bow, but Elfred motioned with his head and said, "It's fine, Son. Go ahead."

She hugged him and, for a moment, his heart rejoiced, but his mind mocked him that hugging a queen was unusual and odd. Joy then ebbed into subtle restlessness and a strange desolate feeling.

They bowed, and the queen left to meet with the priest. Then Chamberlain Vere escorted them outside to their mule and wagon, and they climbed up to ride out of the king's village.

Once on the bridge outside of town, Elfred said, "The queen is a magnificent woman."

"I like her too, Dadde. She is happier than Mum."

Elfred yanked the mule's reins and both blew lips in unison, glaring at his son. After a pause, he said, "Your mum is a special woman, Miah. She is selfless and loving, but she is under great distress."

"Distress?" asked Miah.

"Someday you'll understand, Son. Padre's remembrance Mass for the archbishop is not today—it's on Wednesday. She got the days mixed up."

Miah grabbed Elfred's wrist and pleaded with his eyes.

"Yes, Son, you will still go to the Mass."

INVESTIGATOR

William rocked heel to toe in his wooden-soled shoes that matched his thirty-three-button black cassock, and he carefully parted his brown hair to the side and slicked it down so it would stay.

Appointed to investigate the matter two days after the archbishop's death, William was still pondering his new responsibilities as he gathered his notebook and a bundle of things he didn't have time to stuff into his satchel, then met the abbot in the narthex of the cathedral.

"How was the castle, Brother . . . I'm sorry—" Abbot James stopped abruptly. "*Father* William?"

"Yes, Father Abbot. It was as expected," William carefully noted, uncertain whether his conversation with the queen was confidential.

"I'm sorry—old habits are hard to break. Your first time to the castle?"

"Second, Abbot James. The first since law school."

After six months at Rose Abbey as a monk, with the encouragement of Archbishop Virdis, William had left the order for cathedral and law school. He had hoped to rekindle his close friendship with Virdis when he returned a month before, but the archbishop was away—on mission, as the monks called it.

"Here is a room for an office." The abbot held out a hand of welcome, and both entered the simple space.

"Your most important investigation," James said slowly, intently. "As you know, the abbey is restless since the archbishop's death on

Friday—I request that you please hurry with your initial findings before the funeral next Sunday."

"Yes, Abbot James, I will certainly hurry, b-but"—he paused— "but I will be thorough." He shook the abbot's hand. "The archb-bishop deserves a fair investigation."

The abbot handed him the keys to the cathedral and grotto and stood in the doorway. "We'll be watching, Father William. Report to me before the cardinal arrives on Thursday."

The door closed.

William dropped his things onto a desk and unrolled a large piece of parchment and then reached deep into his bag for something he had packed first. It came out slowly in his shaking hand—it was a small painting of the archbishop. He lit a small candle and placed it in front of the painting.

"Now I can begin," he said.

After pinning the parchment to the wall, he dipped a feather into ink and wrote the words *Who, What, When, Where, Why,* and *How,* each word below the one before. He checked off this task on a list in his notebook and went to the next.

"Possible motives," he said, then mumbled, "suicide, murder, accident," as he wrote.

Two knocks sounded on the door.

"One moment!" he called.

Three more.

"One moment—is that you, Father Abbot? Back so soon?"

From the other side of the door, a voice responded: "No, this is Chamberlain Vere. I've come to meet you."

William got up and opened the door slightly, and he extended his long fingers to meet the man's hand.

"Chamberlain Vere," William began, "I thought I had the cathedral to myself."

Both men stood with their backs straight, sizing up one another, as rigid as the corpses in the sarcophagi of the cathedral. Vere shook

William's hand firmly, the movement of his body matching the distinguished formality of his clothes. Vere's thinning hair left bare a large central spot, the only part of Vere's body that wasn't precisely at its best.

William glanced at the notebook in the chamberlain's hand and asked, "You need to take notes?"

Vere brushed imaginary dust from the book. "The king asked me to meet you and see how your investigation is proceeding."

William curled his fingers and rested his fist against his mouth, his thoughts focused. "Very well. You can watch, but I won't delay for you. I am only just getting started. We'll begin at the crime scene." He turned back to the table, where his own notebook rested, and picked it up with the charcoal pencil. "Follow me." He closed the door and turned the key he'd just hung in the small collection on his rope sash.

They passed through the sanctuary and beside the baptismal font, stopping at the cathedral's tree, an evergreen Virdis called Levan. Planted under a glass dome to allow it to grow, commemorating the bishop becoming Archbishop of Witenberg, the tree's upper branches were more than ten feet high. Twigs and pine cones crunched underfoot.

William dragged over a chair. As he climbed onto it, he noticed a symbol carved into the tree: a circle with a line down the middle.

He drew the symbol in his notebook, then said, "The abbot said the Night Watcher found the archbishop's body hanging from this tree."

"The Night Watcher?" asked Vere.

"The name of the brother who cleans the cathedral at night. Before Lauds, he woke the abbot with the news."

"Perhaps a suspect?"

William shook a branch and focused on the light pouring onto the floor from a side chapel. Then the vision began . . .

Come on, dance and live, Father William!

Like a tall reed, he began to sway atop the chair.

Very good! That's it! The violin bow behind the music moved quicker, back and forth. His swaying increased, and a foot slipped from the chair. He grasped the branch and woke, shaking his head.

"What's the matter, Father William?"

William stepped down off the chair, his wooden heels clacking on the marble. "Nothing. What did I say about questions? I don't know. Maybe. We're gathering evidence. Haven't you been here?"

"Yes," Vere said with a faint air of mockery, "but I'm not well versed in church matters. What else did the abbot say? About the Night Watcher?"

"Since you're taking notes, Vere, mark down that I want to meet that brother." He bent and picked up a twig that he snapped distractedly. Then inspecting the floor more closely, he found red dots, then looked even more carefully, following the trails of pine needles and smashed cones.

Multiple paths, he thought, and jotted something in his book. *Something else*, he noticed. He went to the baptismal font and dipped in a finger. Returning to the trail, he knelt and wiped a dot of deep crimson with the drop of water clinging to his finger.

"The b-blood."

A cold wind blew in, and his hand froze and his jaw locked with tension. Where had Vere gone?

A door clicked shut. The sound of footsteps on the marble came back to the tree.

"Do you need a break, Father William?" asked Vere.

"What were you doing?"

"Oh, the door wasn't closed all the way—curious thing—"

William's face brightened, and he swiftly retraced Vere's steps back to the door and examined the handle. The wooden latch was broken.

"I didn't do that, Father William," Vere called across the cathedral as he walked over to join him. "It was like that when I entered."

"It's not broken, Chamberlain Vere. This was intentionally cut." William pushed the heavy bronze door open, and he stood outside underneath hundreds of small figures carved into the stone wall climbing above them to the spire. He stepped away from the building to see better and lifted a hand to shade his vision from the sunlight poking through a heavy cloud deck.

Vere joined him.

"The archbishop never locked the doors," said William. "The cathedral was meant to be open at all times—for prayer."

"There's a *but* coming," said Vere.

"But the abbot wanted the cathedral as a sanctuary, another fortress in Witenberg. He wanted it to be a refuge for commoners in times of trouble. He wanted a way to lock the doors from the *inside*."

Vere laughed. "So, the archbishop had the latch cut."

"I need to talk to the abbot too."

"Are you gathering that the archbishop was murdered?" Vere asked, suspicion in his voice.

"The b-b- the bishop, I'm sorry," stammered William. "The archbishop was full of life. I don't believe he killed himself . . ."

"Did you know him?"

Know? How well can you really know someone? he wondered.

Like armor, his body stiffened, and he closed his lips in a tight line, his whole being moving one ungreased piece at a time. The words came flat: "Yes, I knew him."

Then he lurched forward and said with a wave over his shoulder, "Back inside."

"Wait," said Vere and pointed to the fountain. "Is this another baptismal font like the one inside?"

William smiled and walked over to sink his hand into the cold water. "The archbishop was a bit of a showman and loved discussing light and dark. Reserving baptisms for sunny days, he invited family and friends outside, here."

"Outside?"

"Yes, but the congregation inside could still *watch* the baptism."

"I'm not following," said Vere.

"Camera obscura. Something he learned from his Eastern friends."

Vere squinted and rubbed his chin.

"Follow me inside, and I'll show you," William said with a wave.

Once they were in the cool shade of a portico, William pointed across the church to a side chapel. "We go towards that light." He unlocked the door, swung it open, and light swallowed Vere.

As he basked in the warmth, William went around the room and pulled ropes to close the curtains, which quickly sent the room from light to dark. William pulled the ropes again, and light reentered.

"Look this way," William said, and waved.

Vere's gaze followed to where William gestured. "I don't understand. Where are you pointing?"

"On sunny days light tunnels through this small hole, where the curtains don't block it. Now close the curtains and wait a few moments, watching that wall."

William left the chapel and outside, dipped his hand into the font, blessed himself, and mouthed the words. He ran back inside, opened the gate, and pulled the curtains. Darkness turned to light.

Vere stood there with his mouth hanging open. "How'd you do that?"

William bounced in place and asked mischievously, "Do what?"

"Against this blank wall, Father William." Vere's hands rubbed the wall. "I saw you make the sign of the cross, but upside down. And I saw your lips move. Then it vanished."

"Camera obscura, Vere—science. Like I said, the archbishop was truly a remarkable man."

"Did that magic get him killed?"

William ignored his question and added, "And the hole size can be further widened or closed up."

"What do you mean?"

"The smaller the hole, the sharper the focus, but the smaller the image. It's the reverse if the hole is larger—bigger image, but fuzzy."

William closed his eyes and bounced on his toes, then he swayed like a reed as warm sun soaked his bones through the windows. "Light.

The archbishop was light. He didn't kill himself."

The sunlight cast shadows around the room, and darkness partially covered Vere's face.

"But did you really know him?" asked Vere grimly. "Most have a dark side, Father William."

A cold breeze threaded a brief chill between them, but William remembered what the queen had shown him.

"Didn't the archbishop have the stone?" Vere continued. As soon as the words escaped him, he gasped and covered his mouth with a hand.

"So that's the reason you're here?" William challenged. "To find out about the stone? Does the king even care about the man's death?"

Vere flushed even across his balding dome.

"Your assistance is no longer needed today, Chamberlain Vere," William said.

Vere yanked his collar and said, "Very well, Father." Uncomfortably, Vere closed his notebook and put it inside his fancy-buttoned coat.

William followed him down the corridor with his eyes until Vere had gone outside, mounted his horse, and begun galloping towards the castle. Then he returned to his office and drew symbols of three suspects to the wall with a charcoal pencil: a lantern for the Night Watcher, an apple for the abbot, and an obelisk for the king.

He sat and stared at the painting of his friend, and his pencil tapped and tapped the table. Looking around this spartan office, from white walls to bare floor, he was reminded of the abbot—by the dampness. Images from seven years before appeared in his thoughts.

✦———✦

That day he had eased a few books from under his armpit to the desk and dropped his bag on the bed to look around at his new quarters. William, a twenty-two-year-old fresh from university, had just joined the order as a monk assigned to Rose Abbey. He clicked open the buckles of his satchel and drew out the neatly folded habits to place them into a cabinet.

Abbot James filled the doorway of the room and pushed the book with the abbey's code of conduct into this newcomer's sunken chest. "Read this and understand. We need men like you here to enforce our rules. And join us tonight at midnight. The archbishop will celebrate Mass in the chapel."

+ ——— +

A bell gonged, and the tapping—and William's reverie—stopped. "The chapel," he muttered. He grabbed the keys, opened the door, locked it behind him, and sped across the courtyard to the cathedral. He found the key to the chapel and turned it in the lock. The dampness of the small octagonal room contrasted with the warm vibrations he'd felt during that first night with the archbishop. He sank onto a chair and closed his eyes.

+ ——— +

Empty chairs and the man in a simple white tunic practicing his violin had accepted him among them. William had faltered: "I'm sorry. I came for Mass. Am I early?"

The man William came to know as Mati stopped midnote, turned the next page of sheet music, and grinned. "Brother! Welcome to rehearsal. Please come. Come in. We've got an hour. Please join me. I am Father Matia."

He waved William closer. With colorful enthusiasm and what William would learn was his customary zeal, the man enveloped William with a hug. Mati placed both hands on William's shoulders and said, "Good to see you, Brother. Welcome. I hear you're new."

William melted at the gleam in Mati's eyes. He fell in love. He searched for something to brace himself on but stumbled. Mati helped him to stand.

"You can write, can't you?" Mati asked. "Can you help me? I'm crafting something that's been on my heart since university."

With wide eyes, William said, "Yes! Yes, I will help."

"Good. I'm practicing my favorite song, 'Benedetta Maria.' Please join me."

A cold breeze blew, and the door slammed, dissolving William's dream again. His open mouth shut, and his body that had relaxed with such comforting memories snapped into a straight posture and he looked about him.

The pencil and notepad had fallen onto the floor. "The investigation," he said. He bent and noticed dark dots on the marble.

The sense of dampness returned and thickened in his throat and stomach. The trail of dots led out the chapel door. He felt the handle and discerned hard flecks upon it. With a fingernail he scraped at it, and blood shavings sprinkled to the floor. He followed the trail to another door, where a spiral staircase wound and narrowed upward. Slivers of light peeked through the window slits and threw shadows onto the stone steps.

In random patterns, blood dotted the stairs. William went up quickly and then quicker, up the steps, narrowing and narrower. His thoughts were spinning, his arms grasping the stone columns to steady himself. His heart hammered, and he heard his feet pound up each step.

Each few steps revealed more blood, and his thoughts constructed a fight and a chase. His foot landed on yet another step, but this time he stepped on something else and his foot went out from under him and he tumbled, his lower back and butt hitting the steps hard.

He cried out. Pain thrashed across his back as he lowered himself against the smooth stone and started to slide, small balls of something on the steps propelling him faster. He extended his arms to brace himself, but he crashed his face and chest into a column.

With pinching fingers, he brought one of the balls closer to his vision. "A rosary bead," he said. Glass. He picked up more and more beads and dropped them into his pocket. Around a curve of the staircase, light reflected from something else.

He pressed the silver rosary centerpiece into his palm to inspect it, then flipped it over. On the back, cursive writing read, "Ave Maria."

"The archb-bishop," he said, his face hot with realization, his back stabbed with pain. "This was Mati's."

He groaned to his feet and quickly climbed up the stairs to another door. He searched his pocket for a key, but his hand on the door handle could feel that it was loose. The door creaked open, and a fresh breeze cooled his face. He pressed into the cold, biting wind of the tower and found himself under an archway. Below him were Rose Abbey, vineyards, the River Isis, the town of Witenberg, and the castle. He followed the winding ledge around the roof of the cathedral to a door and spiral staircase that exited down to the narthex.

"Back where I started," he grumbled. The excitement diminishing, his pain grew, and he hobbled to his makeshift office. Along the way, he saw something he hadn't noticed when he inspected with Vere. There was blood not in a puddle or specks but in a shape like a print.

Grimacing, he started to bend over to examine it but opted to squat gingerly instead. The shape was the outline of a boot and something else. "A flower? A hand?" he asked himself. The fingers weren't slender but short and rounded. He thought of the large flag draped over the castle wall, the kingdom's symbol. "It's not a human hand. It's a lion's paw!"

He drew the symbol in his notepad and pulled from the dried blood a purple fiber that was stuck to it.

In his office, he inked check marks next to the crime scene and chapel boxes, then started looking for something. He rummaged through the drawers and searched the floor of the office, but it wasn't there, either. He left the office and locked the door. Window by window, beside each candle in the cathedral, he searched.

"I know," he said finally. Forgetting his pain in his hurry, he trotted out the cathedral, over the cobblestones into the abbey, then ran upstairs to his room. From his closet, he pulled a wooden tinderbox and brimstone matches.

He turned to leave, but the tall abbot stood in his doorway, just as he had that first day seven years before.

"Back so soon, Father William?"

NIGHT WATCHERS

The habit lengthened the already-tall abbot, who balanced his large head and thick mustache over thin lips. "Back so soon?" repeated Abbot James.

The slightly pungent odor of the tinderbox grabbed William by the nose, but apple and cinnamon fragrances from the abbot's cider mug masked the worst of the sulphur.

"Yes, Father Abbot. But p-p-" He lowered his head and tried to escape. "Please excuse me. I have more work to do."

James's arm extended and blocked the door. "Can't you just feel the unease in this place?" he asked.

He walked past William into the room and surveyed the bare floor, white walls, and bed in the corner. He stopped at the window and looked out beyond the river to the castle on the hill. "Have I ever told you my dream?" he asked. He sipped from his mug, then licked the cider, leaving some sugar coating parts of his mustache.

William set down the box and matches on the desk and slid to his bed. "I don't know, Father," he said distractedly while looking around the room. "Remind me again."

"To be archbishop one day," James said evenly, in a grave tone of finality. He stepped from the window and pulled the chair from behind the desk and asked, "May I?"

Before William nodded, the abbot sank his large frame into the small wooden chair.

"Ever since I was a child, I have dreamed of being Archbishop of Witenberg, ruling this kingdom with my family—my cousin as king, he ruling temporal matters and I guiding the flock in spiritual matters."

William gathered the books on the bed and stacked them on a shelf. "Wonderful, Father Abbot. Perhaps someday you'll become archbishop."

"Yes, but I can't have this restlessness. We need order in the abbey and order in the kingdom—otherwise, chaos will rule, and we can't control what they believe."

Leaning forward in the chair, with deliberate slowness, as if to underscore the meaning of the gesture, James asked, "Do you understand?"

"I think so," William said, orienting his body away from the other man.

"I don't want any secrets between us, Father William."

"I understand, Father Abbot."

"I need to trust you, that you can complete the—"

"Father Abbot," William interrupted, "I understand. I will complete the investigation. Can you stay and answer some questions about Archbishop Virdis?"

James sat back into the chair. "Yes, of course—ask."

A knock made them look up to where a gentleman usher, clad in a red coat, stood in the doorway. "Abbot James, Chamberlain Vere requests your immediate visit."

James catapulted out of his chair. "Perhaps that hope of mine will come sooner," he said to William, then guzzled the last of the cider.

"Yes, one moment, Usher," he said to the other man. "Father William, we'll discuss things later. For now, continue your investigation. The cardinal will expect a thorough report."

"One question before you leave," said William. "Where is the Night Watcher?"

"The Night *Watchers*, you mean?" he said, emphasizing the name. "That silly name they call themselves. There isn't just one, Father William. They all live in the abbey basement. You may find some sleeping—the others are probably in the fields." With an upraised hand, he was out the door and down the hall behind the usher.

———

Down the front staircase and out the door William went, with the tinderbox and matches in a pocket and his notebook and charcoal pencil in hand. He followed the trail around the abbey to the vineyards, where some brothers were working. Most were preparing the beds for spring planting. He went to one man who wore a wide-brimmed hat and a wider frown, his broad fork plunged deep into the soil, and asked, "Excuse me, Brother. Where are the Night Watchers?"

The man lifted his head and blurted, "Oh, you startled me, Father William." He rested against the broad fork and stroked his mustache.

"The Night Watchers?" the man asked incredulously. "You haven't heard that name? For the order of brothers? Weren't you here for a few months before you left for cathedral school?"

"I didn't know they were an order," William said defensively. "Nor do I know what they do except clean the cathedral. I thought monks belonged to abbeys."

"I guess they didn't teach you in school," the man uttered. "And probably buried in the books—or with him."

"Excuse me?" asked William.

The man's lower back cracked, and his leg jerked the broad fork, knocking it over.

"Virdis is dead, Father William. Why aren't you sad? We know you spent much time with him."

William tugged his collar. "I don't know what you mean, B-B-Brother."

"Maybe you should look inside yourself first, Father William. Maybe your sin, your secret, caused his death. We all know it."

My secret?

Knots formed in his stomach, and he rocked on his feet while the knots twisted within him. "I understand you're sad, and I am too, but

I will find the murderer. Tell me about the Night Watchers."

The man pointed to the field. "They work together. Towards the end."

Across the vineyard, they looked like boulders. These men had smaller frames than most of the brothers, but with wide, hunched backs, and many had small, flat noses and eyes that slanted upward. All had beards.

"Night Watchers," he called, the closer he came, "can you help? I'm investigating the archbishop's death."

One brother turned, showing his hat that read: *Jesus is my boss.*

"Sneaking up on us, are you now?" the man said, with his eyes squinted against the streaks of sunlight. "And what you got there, in your hands?"

William gulped, caught off guard by the bluntness of the hat, then said, "Your boss is my boss."

"Is he now? Pray to him to help you." He extended a stubby arm for a handshake.

The man's hand was as rough as a rock, and pieces of something dotted his beard. "I'm the leader of this group. Name is Brother Adolphus. The other brothers call me Fuss because I'm such a gentle fellow." He smiled and showed grape skins scattered across the teeth he had left. "Let me show you the little operation we have here."

Fuss led William past the vineyards and pasture and through open doors into a wooden barn. William caught a sniff as smoke billowed from the roof.

"The Order of the Night Watchers has been around for centuries across the kingdom. We take an oath to defend churches. And we maintain the bell towers and the clocks, clean the churches, and more. When not in prayer, watching, sleeping, or eating, we make wine."

Outside the barn, brothers dressed in long coats were placing barrels from an ice pit onto tracks and rolling them forward. Fuss licked his lips, then said with a sly smile, "I can almost taste the wine, just the tiniest hint."

Waves of sweetness and fragrance crashed over them as they moved through the barn. "Stinky Feet!" Fuss yelled. "Get out of there!" A team of brothers were stomping grapes, clapping hands, and chanting, but Stinky Feet had jumped into a barrel to join them. Fuss pulled Stinky Feet by the hood and told him to wipe clean the smile and the trail of red juice that dotted the planks.

"Stinky Feet is our cork master," said Fuss. "He manages the team of brothers that makes corks for the bottles. Let me show you."

Past the barrels, they came to large cauldrons of boiling water.

"This is Cracky," Fuss said. "He maintains the fires and cauldrons." Ash smudged the man's large nose, mouth, and ears, and he coughed from the smoke during the introduction. William's gaze made his way from the wide feet and thick ankles to slumping shoulders and dark, deep-set eyes.

"He's one of our best workers," said Fuss.

"Does everyone have a nickname?"

Fuss laughed. "You have much to learn about the Night Watchers. We all prefer our names to the title 'brother.'"

William pulled Fuss aside, behind the shelves of bottles. A brother was popping corks with a tool. "Listen, Brother—I mean Fuss," William said shortly. "Thank you for showing me, but I don't have much time."

"I know, Father William. We've been expecting you."

The grape stompers stopped, lifted themselves out of the barrels, and untied the sackcloth tied around their legs and feet. They gathered in a circle around Fuss and William.

"We want to help you find the murderer, Father William," said Fuss. He pointed to his hat. "As Jesus is our boss, we will do everything in our power to help."

"Good, good," said William. "I want to start with the Night Watcher who found Archb-bishop Virdis the morning of his death."

Fuss beckoned Stinky Feet and handed him a bunch of keys. "Take him to the bell tower. Pius is there now."

"Oh, I can find it myself," William said.

"We're the only brothers who have keys to the bell tower, Father William," said Fuss.

William jammed a hand into his pocket and jangled keys as he discerned why the abbot didn't disclose this detail earlier.

But the door was unlocked, he thought.

Stinky Feet's beady eyes sparkled beneath bushy eyebrows that knit into one. He took a comb and brushed cork from his beard, then nodded to show William he was ready.

"Don't you need shoes, B-Brother?" asked William.

"Please?" asked Stinky Feet.

"I mean, Stinky Feet, don't you need shoes?"

"Nah, need these to breathe, Father." He bent and combed cork from his foot hair. Once finished, he jammed the comb into his long, mangy mane. He looked him over and laughed. "No cork in the Lord's house, Bouncy."

William's lips pursed, and he found sandals hanging from a wall. "At lease take these for when we go into the cathedral."

———

When they entered the building, William held up a hand.

"Wait a moment, please. I need more kindling." William entered his office and hurriedly circled the apple on the wall and wrote in his notebook, "King's cousin. Possible motive—wants to be archbishop."

He locked the office door, and they went to a door near the altar.

"Everyone has a nickname?" asked William. "How'd you get yours?"

Stinky Feet stopped and pulled one foot to his nose and laughed. "Ain't it clear as mud, Bouncy?"

"For you, yes, but Pius? That sounds like his real name."

"Nah, this will be clear. And you ask many questions." He shook his stubby finger. "And that is why you be the investigator." He awkwardly galumphed along the cathedral hallway to the bell tower door by the chapel. Stinky Feet opened the door and started on the first stair, but William remained.

"What's got your throat, Bouncy?" Stinky Feet asked.

William examined the door, mouth gaping, then retraced his steps. He was certain he had seen a lock on the door in the morning.

"Nothing—it's nothing, Stinky Feet. I assumed we needed keys for the bell tower."

"We do if we enter from the ground floor—outside," Stinky Feet said with a faint tone of mockery in his voice, "but someone wanted to come *inside*."

"Oh," William said sheepishly, "no need of shoes."

"Right, Bouncy. My hair keeps my feet warm."

They bypassed rosary beads on the spiral staircase and pushed through the door to the rooftop.

"This way, Bouncy."

They turned left and went under an arch, and the path narrowed. Up steps farther than William had gone before, around a gargoyle, Stinky Feet pulled the loop of keys from his pocket and unlocked the iron gate.

A man hunched over with a wool blanket wrapped around him rustled when they came closer. "Pius!" Stinky Feet yelled and picked up a bottle of wine that lay sideways at Pius's feet.

Pius was buried into a book and startled, then removed his wool earmuffs and grumbled.

"A quiet one, Bouncy," Stinky Feet said and took the book. "A romance novel, Pius? Again? Fuss said no mo'."

"Well, gotta have something to keep me busy for twelve-hour shifts." Pius went to the candle and said, "Move, Stinky Feet."

The candle had burned to the next mark, and Pius rose, put on the earmuffs, and grabbed a rope.

Sharp strike, sharp strike, sharp strike.
Ring up. Wait.
Long strike. Full circle.
Fifteen rings signify the hour.

Pius pushed a stick to the clock face that clicked the dial to the next quarter mark.

William looked at the book and pulled out a bookmark.

Love or Freedom? he read. "I'm Father William," he told Pius. "I'm investigating Virdis's death. What is this paper?"

"I found this poem stuck to a bell the night of the archbishop's death."

"May I have it?"

"Get me another bookmark, and you can have it."

William tore a piece from his notepad.

Stinky Feet read the poem and said, "A good one for the novels you like, huh, Pius?"

"The abbot told me you found Virdis?" William asked as he jotted notes.

"Yes," Pius said. "Found him black and blue, hung from the Levan tree."

William's Adam's apple dropped with his stomach.

"Why did you leave your post?"

"A man has to pee, Father William. Too much wine."

His hand stopped taking notes. "Were you drunk, Brother Pius?"

Stinky Feet laughed. "Him, drunk?"

Pius's forehead crunched. "I've been on bell-tower duty for a year, Father William. Penance for my lust. The wine and books have helped."

"Anything unique about Virdis's body, something that you noticed?"

"Blood on his face, but the hood was pulled up. And I ran as soon as I figured it was the archbishop. Ran to the abbot to tell him."

"And what did he say? How did he react?"

"He was asleep, so when I pounded on his door, he grumbled and cursed at me. I remember his owlish eyes."

"Did he act surprised or sad or angry?" William leaned in and emphasized his words: "Or, like he knew about it?"

A chilly breeze blew through the tower, and Pius wrapped the blanket around his shoulders. "I don't know. I don't know. He was asleep. He thanked me and asked me to return to duty. When I asked him the following day, he told me they performed a funeral and buried him that night."

"They?" William grabbed the edge of the blanket. "They!" he said angrily. "Who else was there?"

Stinky Feet pulled at William's sleeve. "Easy, Father. Easy."

"Ask the abbot, Father William."

His teeth clenched, and the chill cut to his bones. "I'm sorry, Pius—thank you. Is there anything else you can remember from that night?"

"The archbishop was buried in the crypt. We can go there."

"Virdis is buried in the crypt?" asked William. A gurgle from his stomach shot to his heart, and he grabbed his left breast. He took a few deep breaths.

"Show me."

"Very well. Stinky Feet, manage the ropes while I'm gone."

They spiraled down the stairs and into the corridor behind the altar area of the cathedral, then came to a wooden door behind the altar. Pius grabbed the latch by the lion head and pulled, inserted a key into the lock and turned. The door creaked open, and moistness filled the spiral staircase. They stared into the darkness.

"Do you have a tinderbox?" asked Pius.

"Yes," William said and removed it from his pocket. He struck flint over tinder until it sparked. He gently blew—nothing. He blew harder—nothing, and the spark died. He struck harder.

"Father William—stop. It's too damp here. We'll need to strike in the treasury."

They slowly descended the granite spiral staircase. Water trickled from the ceiling and splashed onto William's nose. Like after a downpour, an earthy, musty smell hovered in the air, but a hint of rotten eggs settled on his lips. Pius stopped at the bottom, and William heard droplets dripping into water.

"Take my hand, Father William. We'll go around the fountain through the grotto and into the treasury. The air is drier there."

Pius extended his other hand before him and thumped into something.

"What was that, Pius?" William asked, hearing something clicking back and forth. He rocked back and forth on his toes until settling into a gentler bouncing.

"It's locked," said Pius. He jangled keys with his fingers until he found the right tooth pattern. He inserted the key into the lock and turned.

"There are candles on the wall. I'll grab one."

"Tell me why we didn't take a candle from the bell tower?"

Though they were in near complete darkness, William could make out a hint of a smile curving within Pius's beard. "Our own adventure, Father William, our own novel. Don't be afraid."

Inside the treasury, the air hung about them drier, with fewer odors. After several flint strikes and blows, the tinder ignited. William lit the brimstone match and candle and used the damper to extinguish the flames in the box.

Lighting candle by candle as they went, the pair followed a tunnel that led to the treasury. In glass cases were various kingdom treasures: sculptures, tapestries, books, jewels, gold and silver chalices, and the finest embroidered priestly vestments. At William's feet was a blood trail, and kneeling, he found it was scattered with strands of brown hair and purple fibers.

Who wears purple? he wondered.

The blood trail led to a larger stain in a corner. He bent and stuffed into his pocket a pinch of the hair and fibers.

"There must have been a fight, Pius. Why were they fighting?"

"Probably over the kingdom's most cherished treasure."

"How do you know?"

They went to the center of the treasury. An iron gate squared a waist-high marble pedestal protected by glass with a forest-green tint. William stepped closer and saw an opened chest with a broken lock.

"The stone, Father William," Pius sad sadly. "It's gone."

"The lock," William said and pointed. "Who knows the combination?"

"Only the archbishop—maybe higher," said Pius. "We have keys for the gate. That's it."

As thoughts crossed William's mind, he caught Pius examining him, like he was reading a novel.

"Virdis didn't want sentinels roaming the church's treasures—that's what we're for, Father William. Plus, only he knew the combination."

They heard a slow creak.

"What was that?" asked William.

"The wind, perhaps? It's drafty in here. We should leave soon and lock the place. We can come back tomorrow to see the crypt. It's getting late, and my shift is almost over."

William rubbed his arms. "You're right. Stinky Feet is probably cold." Pius took one candle, and they blew out the rest as they left through the tunnel again.

A louder creak echoed down the twisting space.

Then came a cough. Another cough.

"Did you hear that?" asked William, his voice softer.

Step by step, crack by crack, noise came from the stairs.

"Stinky Feet?" they asked. Another crack popped—this time louder. At the bottom, the man yelped.

"Who is replacing you on your shift, Pius?"

"I don't know. Who's there?" Pius shouted.

William stopped and lowered himself into a crouch. He found bits of wood on the floor in the weak light flickering from the grotto.

A hunched man with a beard stood beside the door.

"Cracky?" asked Pius. "Is that you?"

The man nodded. He opened the door and handed William a pendant. "Father William, I believe this will interest you . . ."

MARIANNE

Elfred's expression remained stony as they tied the mule and wheeled the wagon into the shed and went into the shop.

"What's wrong?" asked Miah.

"Nothing, Son," Elfred said, shaking his head slightly. Scratching his stubble, Elfred roamed the tidy shop. "There it is," he said. "Miah, help me lift."

Against the wall was a table Elfred dusted off, and Miah helped him lift it onto a work bench.

"Just needs a few more nails and your usual polish," said Elfred. He was thinking about something as he counted with his fingers and uttered, "This should hold us over."

"Over what?" Miah asked. "I'm confused. Who's this for? Someone wealthy?"

"A lord's wife, I believe." His face relaxed, and through a thin-lipped smile, he said, "A real good polish will do."

Miah's fingers ran along the back of the unusual construction.

A lord's wife, he thought. *Maybe, maybe it's for—Marianne! She would love this.*

Elfred stowed his hammer in his belt and said, "It flips up to hold a canvas."

Heat flushed to Miah's cheeks as he thought about Charlotte's daughter. His musing was interrupted by a sharp whistle and a finger jabbed into his side with a "Hey, you! It's been a long time since we were playmates, hasn't it?"

He turned to the once-familiar voice and dropped the polishing rag. "Marianne!" he croaked, then leaned towards her with out-stretched arms and hugged her, taking in the scent from the honey-suckle twined into her long, wavy, amber hair. Then he pulled back to look at her and lost himself like a stargazer navigating the constella-tions. Just as he inspected his woodwork, he checked every inch of this beauty for imperfections. Numerous brown freckles across her nose and cheeks contrasted with her otherwise-fair skin.

None, he thought. *No imperfections at all.*

He grabbed both her arms again and said, "I've missed you."

Silence.

He was crestfallen. *Just what I thought.* He turned away and swiped at the table with the rag.

"Me too," she said.

Oh?

"Why are you here?" he asked.

"Came to see my table. How much progress have you made?" She looked around in the shop. "Where is it?"

Miah furrowed his brow in surprise and looked towards Elfred, who was chuckling in the shadows.

"Dadde! You didn't tell me Marianne was back in town, and this table was hers. I mean, I had an idea, of course, that it could be for her, how pretty it is, how you and I worked on it and the chair, the chair for the cardinal, and this for someone, I had no idea who, but someone, and—" he rambled until stopped by grunts.

At the sound of axe blows, the three of them left off discussing the table and went out of the shop. Outside, Alf, four years older than Miah and well-muscled, drew all their eyes as he landed the broad axe into the oak one last time for the afternoon. The lumber was riven in two, and he wiped his brow and threw the pieces into the pile.

He looked up and rambled over to Miah to put his arm around his neck. "Hey, little brother," he announced comically, "there's your girlfriend." His clothes were suffused with the fragrances of cut oak and pine, a combination of caramel with his sweat and the clean, elevating residue of the sap.

Miah's cheeks turned rosy as he stood there helplessly, half-choked. "She's not my girlfriend! Go away!"

Alf looked at Marianne and pointed at Miah. "Moody one, isn't he?"

Miah squirmed out from the hold, but not until Alf released it, and Miah then pulled Marianne by the hand back towards the shop. "Come back in."

"Fine, fine," she agreed.

He dragged her to show the finer details of the recently polished white-oak wood, pointing out the appealing quarter-sawn grain markings, smooth-cut edges, and the numerous rings indicating its age.

She slid her fingers over the wood grain and stared at the intricate patterns carved into the wood. "Miah, it's breathtaking."

"It's not perfect—we made a few mistakes, but . . ." His voice trailed off and he quietly said, "I didn't even know it was for you."

"Miah," she said with a sigh, "it's breathtaking."

"See the rings?" he asked, brightening again. "A few hundred years old at least. The tree is from the grove."

Elfred stood up from where he'd squatted to pound the hammer a few more rounds into the flattened nails and said, "As old as the republic, a republic long gone."

Miah ignored the comment and pushed his shoulders back, chest out and chin up like he'd seen Alf do, as Elfred had commanded he hold himself in the palace. He continued: "It should be finished tomorrow."

"Fantastic," she said. "I can't wait. See you soon." She whirled to leave the shop.

"Soon?"

She looked back over her shoulder. "Meet me at the river Saturday at sunset. I'd like to hear about your apprenticeship . . . and maybe we can walk back here to see the finished table."

Miah remained fixed on her exit, frozen in a staring grin.

Alf said from the doorway, "Miah, wipe the drool from your mouth."

Miah waved him away and went back to inspecting the table. *For her it must be perfect.*

"Do you want help?" Alf asked with a smirk.

"No."

"Isn't this the first time you'll be alone with her? Saturday?" Alf pulled a wooden sword out of a straw dummy hanging from a rafter and gave it a final thrust.

With a scrunch of his forehead, Miah said, "I don't need help. Go back to practicing killing. Trees, men—it makes no difference."

Alf puffed his chest and stood tall. "I will be a knight one day, going on adventures across the kingdom."

"You want to be a pawn of the king?" Elfred asked, lifting his eyebrows.

"Dadde, becoming a knight is an honor and a privilege, the highest order of freemen."

"Once an honor and a privilege, Alf. But knights have forgotten their ultimate master—they're no longer free, but bound to kings and lords, men who have no check on their power except their own whims on any given day."

"Maybe *I* will help restore the old guard, the honorable class," said Alf proudly.

"Don't get wrapped up in glory, Son. Self-defense is one thing, rescuing others another, but conquering lands to add resources to the kingdom is different—and wrong."

"We have a right to defend our outposts when attacked by savages," said Alf with an edge of sharpness in his voice. "Their way of life won't work in our land."

Sucking in his breath, Elfred scrubbed his knuckles over his scratchy, unshaved jaw, gripped the hammer too tightly, and slammed the final nail of the day. He released the hammer, and it fell to the ground with a thud.

"This won't get settled here, Alf. Sons, your mother is calling—so let's get on over to the house for supper." He left the shop.

Alf knelt and inspected the table. "So, how long again until you see your girlfriend?"

Miah briefly stopped polishing and put his hand out for the adze.

Alf grinned with mischief and said, "Exquisite craftsmanship."

Miah carved at a small imperfection with the curving adze. Wood splintered and shavings sprinkled to the floor.

"Leave me alone," he grumbled.

Alf began prowling through the shop.

"Quit, Alf—stop touching my things." Miah put down the adze and followed him. "Why are you still here?" he pressed. "Why don't you go help Mum in the kitchen? Or go slice another pig's neck, you savage."

Alf oinked, then oinked again and said, "Savage? No—provider and protector."

"What are you looking for?" asked Miah. "Stop messing with my things."

Alf rummaged through the chest, scattering the fresh woodchips from his belted woolen tunic across Miah's pristine workbench. He picked up one by one a belt hammer, a groping-iron chisel, and a measuring gauge, fondling each before Miah plucked it from his hands and placed them all back where they belonged.

"Oh, Miah, look!" Alf exclaimed. "Your old dolls!"

"Figurines, Alf. You played with them too not so long ago."

Alf removed the dragon and light-warrior and asked, "Who'd win in a fight?"

"Stupid question, Alf. You know the light-warrior would win. He's faster and wiser, and he can summon lightning."

"Yes, but the dragon is stronger and can take more hits. Legends say just one look into the dragon's eyes will terrify a knight so much that he can't move. Frozen solid in fear, he'd be."

"It's a legend, Alf. A legend. The light-warrior has the power to defeat the dragon. His light blinds."

"Let's fight," said Alf, holding out the light-warrior in one hand and the dragon in the other. He opened the dragon's mouth and attacked the light-warrior with it.

"Alf! I don't want to play right now."

A leg broke off the light-warrior and fell to the floor.

"You're never careful, Alf!" cried Miah, stooping to retrieve the leg. "Look what you've done."

Alf put the figurines back in the chest and continued to search. "I don't know, Miah. The legends say how much damage dragons have done."

Alf found what he was looking for—wrapped in a rag. It was a girl figurine carved from cherry wood. He stroked it and sniffed at it. "Oh, like red wine. What do we have here? For Marianne?"

Miah slid across the sawdust and punched Alf in the gut and opened his hand to take it. "It's nothing. But give it to me."

Alf punched back harder and ran, carrying the carving with him.

Miah chased him to the cottage and right to the kitchen table for dinner, both of them quietly slipping into the benches as they had so many times over the years.

"Mum, tell Alf to stop making fun of me," Miah complained, and when Sarah turned her head away, Alf punched him in the arm. Miah returned the punch with a kick to Alf's shins.

"Give it to me, Alf," said Miah.

Alf fumbled around in his pockets. With a creeping flush across his cheeks, Alf whispered, "I'm sorry, Miah. It must have fallen out during the run."

Miah kicked his shins harder, shoved the chair, and punched Alf again.

Alf groaned with feigned pain. "I'm sorry, Miah," he said in a tone that might be mockery. "I'll make it up to you. I'll go to the castle to see your chair."

Miah crossed his arms. "Fine. Do that."

Sarah stopped stirring the pottage with the wooden spoon and turned. "Boys, are you done fighting? I'm tired of hearing it. All you do is fight and argue. You sound like your father."

"Right, honey," Elfred said from the doorway as he brought in a pail of fresh milk. "They raise only smart, sophisticated arguments, I'm sure." Elfred tried to kiss her on the cheek, but she turned away. "What are they arguing about this time?" he asked.

"The boys fight like Elfred?" asked Martin. "Elfred can fight?" The old man laughed. "Your father's fists have never met another man's jaw, boys. He plays with wood and complains about the king." To his daughter he added, "You'd have no issue with money if you'd married a knight."

"Not now, Dad."

Miah squirmed. His grandfather Martin, a former knight with an unhealed broken nose, reveled in his past glory between snorts, always taking opportunity to belittle his son-in-law.

"Help, Sarah?" asked Martin. "Don't you need help? Shouldn't he offer his lady help?"

She snapped her wrist at Elfred and said, "Out for two eggs, please." Her husband obeyed and disappeared.

Martin showed Alf the knight's patch on his sleeve. "Someday soon you'll earn this, Grandson."

"Duty, honor, kingdom," chanted Alf. "A few more weeks, and I'll be a knight."

"And probably go on worthless campaigns," said Elfred coolly as he stepped back into the kitchen and carefully placed two eggs on a cloth at Sarah's elbow.

Miah let out a loud sigh, and Martin shouted, "And there it is! I knew you didn't want Alf to become a knight."

Elfred lowered his head and clasped a cup. "Martin, now is not the time."

"At least one of your boys will continue the family tradition."

"Dad!" Sarah plated his food with vegetable pottage, dark bread, and cheese—he could do without the egg. "Take your food and eat outside." She stared until he grumbled his way from the kitchen.

"Boys," she said, stepping over to smack their hands away from the bread. "Get your paws off the food until we pray."

Miah lowered his head but peeked at Alf through one eye while he began. "Thank you, Father, for this food . . . Alf, quit looking at me. Mum, Alf won't stop looking at me."

"Alf, quit looking at your brother. Miah, finish, and then Alf will go."

"Thank you, Father, for this food. God is good, God is great."

Alf folded his hands. "Bless us, oh, Lord, for these our gifts which we are about to receive from thy bounty, through Christ, our Lord, Amen."

"Was that hard?" asked Sarah.

Miah twirled his spoon in his bowl.

"What is it now, Miah? You don't want your vegetables? Why aren't you eating?"

"Alf keeps making fun of me for liking Marianne."

"Miah and Marianne sitting in a tree . . . ," sang Alf.

"Alf, please," said Sarah. "Why won't you help me here, Elfred? So, you like Marianne, Miah. She has always been nice, but you're too young to think about girls. Focus on your apprenticeship. How's that going?"

"One day I'll be on the throne," declared Miah. He straightened and folded his arms before him.

"King Miah the Curly Head does have a nice ring to it," said Alf. "*I* will bring honor to this family by becoming a knight. Girls will love me even more." He stood and pretended to stab Miah with a sword.

"Enough, boys," said Sarah. She kicked Elfred under the table and mumbled at him.

Elfred got the hint and said, "Enough, boys."

After a few bites in silence, Sarah asked, "So, honey, any updates on payment?"

"No. No word from the palace."

She released a long breath. "Elfred, we have only a pittance in reserve. What will you do?"

"I'll go to the treasury tomorrow and ask for payment again. I'm sure a king's representative will come to the quarterly guild meeting next week if we don't have it before that."

Sarah bit her lip and stirred the pottage in her bowl. "Boys, give me your dishes, then go to your room."

Elfred finished his last bites and stood.

"Elfred, stay here," said Sarah.

———

The brothers sat on their straw beds, and Miah covered his ears. Alf practiced sword thrusting, and Miah thought of Marianne and the missing figurine—anything to block out his parents' arguing. But it didn't work.

"Sarah, we will be fine," said Elfred.

"That's what you said years ago, before you built this house."

"Our home, honey."

"But we still owe money to the merchant guild master and his lenders, and your business has fallen away."

"It will be fine. Don't worry about George of Bath. Why do you always worry?"

Sarah raised her voice. "Always, Elfred? Always? Why do you insist on being so different from everyone? Our house . . . your politics."

"You married me because I *was* different."

"Yes, but . . ."

"But what?"

Miah heard something drop to the floor.

"Give me that, Elfred. I need to clean."

"Can I help?"

"No, I will clean by myself."

Elfred slammed the door and banged his head against the wooden timbers just outside.

Martin laughed and snorted from the porch. "She's as stubborn as me, Elfred."

Miah, in consternation, buried his fingers in his hair and rubbed his temples with his palms. Then, hearing it quiet beyond his room, he snuck into the corridor and out the back door. He headed straight to the riverside, where he knew his mother's favorite wildflowers grew.

Miah was kneeling by the river with a fistful of flowers when he heard hoofbeats and looked up. There was the capital sheriff, Lord Harold, out on horseback patrol.

"Isn't a little late to be this far from your dadde, Miah?"

"I'm fine, Lord Harold," Miah replied, looking up with a reassuring smile. But before he could say more, the sound of raised voices carried over a nearby ridge.

Lord Harold kicked the horse and sped away down the road to approach the village from the other side. Miah tucked his bunch of flowers into his tunic and followed across the grass. As he crested the hill, he saw a throng of the villagers below, and they seemed to be circled around Elfred. He ran headlong down the hill and splashed across a creek.

The plump baker was pointing a baguette towards Elfred and said, "Quiet, Master Elfred. Go back to your shed and play with your wood—you probably enjoy that more than your wife."

"You are one to speak, you yeasty, beef-witted maggot-pie!" shouted Elfred, a fist in the air.

Miah gulped and ran up to the men, out of breath. *It's no good when he gets like this.*

"Everything alright, Miah?" asked Elfred, looking quickly down at his son and then back at the threatening baker.

Lord Harold trotted into the commotion from behind the blacksmith's and asked, "Are you bothering your neighbors again, Elfred?"

Elfred pushed Miah behind him and said, respectfully, "No, my lord—just a friendly argument."

"Carry on, then, Master Elfred"—he looked up and around at the whole crowd—"but no more noise tonight."

"Yes, my lord," said Elfred, wiping spittle from his mouth, and the villagers mumbled assent as well.

Lord Harold spurred the horse and laughed at the power he held over his underlings.

Elfred spat towards Lord Harold and grumbled, "He's a pribbling, motley-minded coxcomb who spends more time dressing than does his goatish, flat-mouthed, canker-blossom wife."

"Careful, Elfred," said Martin, who had come out to see about the commotion. He was suddenly the voice of reason among the rest of the villagers.

Miah reached into his tunic for his bunch of flowers and selected just one. He handed the rest to Elfred and said, "Dadde, for Mum."

"Thanks, Son. Now onto bed," said Elfred.

Miah took the several steps to their home. Before closing the door, Miah heard his father apologize to the baker.

PADRE

arah and Alf called for Miah to join them as they walked through their neighborhood of straw-thatched huts. Miah waved from the ridge above the town and scampered across the grid of wooden ramps, leaping over gullies, jumping onto a downed tree. He finished a dozen paces ahead of Sarah and Alf.

"What took you two so long?" Miah joked as he kept pace beside them in the crowd approaching the church that was more chapel than cathedral. Its circular design and open-air interior were different than most cross-shaped churches.

Once through the doors, he felt his body wrapped in incense, and candlelight brightened each nook and cranny of the structure. Miah stood on his tiptoes to look for Padre, but the church was packed. All were standing, turned towards a painting of Mary holding her Son.

The Litany of Our Lady began in Latin, and villagers prayed to the Holy Mother for blessings. Once the litany was concluded, the congregation knelt, and Padre opened with the sign of the cross, tracing from his forehead down his long, white beard to his chest and then across from one broad shoulder to the other. He interlaced his fingers and rested his hands on his round belly.

Miah waited for it on the edge of the chair—the chin tilt and slow, rising smile. Though he was the shortest person in the room, Miah's energy made him grow taller inside once he made eye contact with this giant force in his life.

"Thank you all for coming," said Padre. "It is a somber day but also a celebration." He cued the violinist.

In slow strokes, the sound of a Marian melody reverberated around the chapel, soaking through Miah's ears down into his chest as Padre began singing. After Padre belted the last lyrics and the violinist extended the final note with a long bow pull, the priest wiped away a tear.

"A beautiful rendition for a beautiful friend," said Padre. "I remember the first time I met him, many years ago—I was the second among brothers to enter the cathedral chapel for vespers."

Padre hunched his shoulders and wrapped his cloak tightly around his shoulders. He closed his eyes and tucked his chin. His left arm went out, and his right moved back and forth. "Archbishop Virdis—then just a priest—tucked the violin under his chin and played," said Padre. "He and the violin became one. When he finished the intro, he stood taller and sang with a rich, husky voice, without strain. His eyes were mostly closed, and his facial expressions moved freely with his voice."

Padre stopped moving his hands and rested them on his belly. "He told me I was invited to join him at rehearsal whenever I wanted." Padre called an altar boy to bring him a flask of oil. Padre blessed the oil, poured it into bowls, and distributed them to several men and women. "As the archbishop modeled the rite for us, we will receive healing."

Miah left his chair with Sarah and Alf and joined the longer queue before Padre. Congregants were folding their hands and lowering their heads. The fragrance of rich oil warmed his nostrils as the priest applied it to him in the sign of the cross. "Receive the Holy Spirit, Miah."

Padre's bald head lowered and rested against Miah's forehead, long enough for Miah to hear him say, "God loves you, Miah. God will always love you."

A warming sensation flooded Miah's veins like warm apple cider coating his throat on a cold day. His glow followed him back to his seat, and his mother smiled at him.

The healing ended, and Padre asked the altar boy to retrieve the bowls. He then invited everyone outside for a meal. "And a pint if you're interested," he said with a wink.

The chapel began to clear, and "Padre!" exclaimed Miah, as he ran through the church and into a hug from the big man.

"Miah! How are you, Son?"

"I'm great. Father and I were able to deliver the chair to the castle on Monday." Padre released Miah and extended arms for a hug with Sarah, who had caught up with them, Alf trailing behind. "And how are you, Sarah the Strong and Alfred the Brave?"

Alf dismissed the question, but Sarah welcomed it. "Good to see you, Padre," she said. "That was a lovely celebration."

"Thank you. I haven't seen your family in a long time. I've missed you. Will you stay for the festival? We're serving the archbishop's favorite—fish, pasta, and cheese, drizzled with olive oil—we spared no expense."

"Certainly," she said, "and I'm sorry, Padre—we've just been busy. But why have you done this ceremony now and not after the cathedral funeral?"

"He was more at home in the intimate settings," Padre responded.

Trumpets sounded, cymbals clanged, and drums pounded. With a smile, Padre said, "The fun has begun. Follow me through the meadow to the house. Miah, I have a gift for you."

Goldfinches fluttered from the bird feeders as Padre led the three around his garden and into the rectory. He untied his cloak from its metal brooch Miah so admired—the shape of a bunch of lavender—and placed it on his bed in the side room. The family followed him into the room, where small paintings of Padre's family and friends filled the wooden desk, and Miah looked about in wonder.

The priest pushed papers and wooden figurines to the side, looking for something, and as one manuscript fell to the floor, Miah knelt to retrieve it. The heading read: "Love or Freedom."

What does that mean?

"Oh, thank you, Miah, but I've got it. Please excuse the mess."

Miah couldn't resist digging an elbow into Alf's side. "See, Alf, even Padre has figurines."

Padre stuffed the manuscript into a fold of his cassock and shuffled the jumble on the desk. "Ah, I found it." He handed a small wooden cylinder to Miah. "A puzzle for you."

"Thanks!" said Miah, and he fiddled with the smooth shape, finding one end open. "What is it?"

"A scytale. There's a strip of parchment inside with a message. Try to decode it."

Miah dropped to the wooden floor and concentrated on the symbols on the parchment until he'd deciphered them. He looked up in triumph, announced that it said "AMDG, whatever that means," then stood and looked for something else of interest. He touched a painting of Archbishop Virdis and Padre, then handed it to his mother.

Padre dropped his head a little. "My favorite memory with him—he presided over my friend's wedding."

"I'm sorry for your personal loss," said Sarah and handed the painting back to Padre.

"Thank you." He turned it over and wiped his nose. "He'll be missed."

Sarah touched a tentative finger to Padre's shoulder. "Padre, I didn't realize how close you were to him. Could we come with you to the funeral?"

"Yes, certainly. That would be a comfort."

"And please join us for dinner one evening this week," she added.

"Mum," said Miah in a loud whisper. "Not Saturday. I have plans."

She looked at him in surprise.

Alf laughed. "He's meeting Marianne, Mum."

Padre winked towards Miah. "I'm busy Saturday night, but I can visit on Sunday before the funeral."

QUEEN

Queen Rachel snapped awake, a sheen of sweat hanging on her brow.

The king was still sitting up in bed beside her, like he had been when she fell asleep.

"One moment," Richard told her and sketched more lines onto what looked like a map. "Then I'll blow out the candle."

Pain bubbled from her stomach to her chest, and a groan burst from her, fast and short. She rubbed her lower belly as a stream of thoughts flowed through her mind, the residue of her dream but more so years of keeping a secret from her husband that now she was considering revealing.

She felt an intense desire to laugh and cry—as she had laughed at the news from her midwife, as she had cried when she told her friends—but she knew that if she did release these emotions, the thing she feared would hold her, would not release her this time, and she would invite years of passive aggression until he accepted her betrayal. Rachel drew back and, for a moment, kept her lips closed tight.

When the moment was over, when laughter of joyous defeat of him only sounded within, she accepted his past neglect and wondered when she could tell him the secret. She curled up beside him, absorbing his warmth and blinking as cold sweat dripped into her eyes and she alternately shivered and felt waves of heat pass over her.

"Hold on, Tulip," said Richard. He placed his drawing on the side table and shoved their large, long-legged puppy off the bed. Reclining next to her, he wrapped his muscular arms around her.

He combed her soaked, curly brown hair to the side, felt her forehead and said, "You're drenched. It feels like a fever, but it's breaking."

"I've had a terrible dream."

"Tell me what's wrong, Tulip."

The words came starchy as he glanced at the map, unable to drag his attention from it, but she found comfort in his size and strength. That solid presence had been revealed by his tight-fitting tunic when she'd first seen him eighteen years before. The young prince had rescued a sixteen-year-old damsel in distress in a field of flattened, yellow tulips. And when he'd drawn closer to her, she'd been captivated by his piercing blue eyes.

"Drought, famine, people storming the castle, fighting, and something about a stone," she said. "I woke as soon as some official gathering started, and elders were speaking."

She tried to prop herself up on her wrist, but it collapsed under her as stabbing spasms like forked lightning slashed beneath her abdomen. Grimacing, she placed pressure on her belly with her hand, but the cramps were too great. She tossed the sheets and hobbled in bare feet across damp stone to the lavatory.

"Tulip, did you say a stone?" Richard asked and reached for the drawing.

Wincing, she tried to speak, but dry heaves forced her to hunch over the basin to retch. She felt her face going white and clammy. The thought of pregnancy crossed her mind, but she shuddered and shook her head. She hadn't seen dark or red bumps on her cheeks—*It must be something else*, she told herself. She rinsed her mouth and returned to the bed, slid underneath the sheets as the pains subsided, and turned her head away from Richard.

She cleared her throat and said with a slight bite in her voice, "There was more to my dream."

Luta barked. "I know, Luta," he said. "Your mum is dreaming again."

Rachel opened her arms, and the puppy jumped back up on the bed. Rachel massaged Luta's ears, and Luta panted contentedly, with a mix between a moan and a growl. "People were chasing the stone because of its supposed magical powers," she said.

Richard sat up abruptly in bed. "Who had the stone?" he asked, grabbing her shoulders from behind. "That stone is extremely important."

Through a groan with a returning pain, she said, "I don't know."

"Did the archbishop have it?"

"The *murdered* archbishop, you mean? Why aren't you more concerned about how he died, anyway?"

He swung his legs off the bed and went to the map. "The dead archbishop, Tulip. We don't know it was murder."

"Something isn't right," she said. "The missing stone and the dead beloved archbishop."

"He wasn't loved by *all*. In fact, the cathedral chapter will select *my* nomination for the next archbishop, someone friendlier to the kingdom's policies."

Her hand went inside her silk robe to place pressure above her hip bone where one pain was still stabbing at her. She mumbled, "Unless Rome interferes."

"What did you say?"

Challenging Richard was an art form—knowing when and how far to push while smoothing his edges. She had already broken through his defenses with her petulant tone about the stone. Going back would signal weakness, but she had a move to play.

She coughed, then spoke louder: "We should investigate the death. But why do you still care about the stone?"

His fingers uneasily drummed the map in a chilled, dark wave that landed several strikes against Constantinople. "Rachel, you know how important the stone is to me."

"Yes, I'm quite aware of your strange obsession with it. You found it before your brothers did."

His neck tightened, and he clutched his head, his fingernails digging into the flesh. "Not now, Tulip."

She sat upright in the bed. "I know you believe the stone."

He pulled at his hair. "Not now, Tulip."

"Honey, you proved yourself to your father."

His hands snapped together like a mouse trap, and he came back to the bed and climbed in. "I think you'd better lie back down, Tulip. Your forehead was quite warm."

"No, Richard."

Luta growled.

His fist clenched as he slid away from Rachel. "Shut it, Luta, or else." He threw back the covers again and stalked to the doors, opening them to walk out onto their balcony.

Rachel got out of bed and tied her robe and eased her feet into her slippers. Luta nosed into her leg and led her outside. Rachel's gaze followed the falcons swooping from their castle perches until the gleaming dawn on their wings faded as they flew out of sight. She took in the entirety of the castle complex, protected on either side by walls and the Rivers Isis and Tamesis: the castle and its central courtyard, the lower levels of quarters for the court, the watchtower, the chapel, the royal training grounds and stables, and her vineyards.

Richard reached out for her hand, and she took his fingers but promptly released them and stood alone.

"Remember?" he asked.

Silence.

A knock came from the bedroom door inside.

He tried again to reach out for Rachel, and Luta jumped to nip at his hand.

"Easy, girl," said Rachel. She interlocked her fingers with his.

He raised her hand to kiss it but flinched when he saw her purple wrist. He tried to kiss her cheek, but she pulled away.

"I'm so sorry, Tulip. Please forgive me," he begged. "I love you."

Averting her face from his gaze, she felt the thickness in her throat balloon until it burst and a tear splashed onto the floor. She wiped her eyes with the back of her free hand.

"Yes, my love, I do remember your love," she said. A few moments passed and then she added, "Why must you return to the Holy Land? Go to Jerusalem *again*? Another Crusade?"

"That hasn't been decided yet."

"Will you leave our family again?"

"That hasn't been decided yet. And—"

Another knock sounded on the door.

"Richard, we have no business invading a land very different from ours, though with noble intentions to unify under one God."

"Tulip," he said irritably, "for the third time, that hasn't been decided. But if war is the decision, the pope will bless it."

"The Church desires more power—more than the conversion of souls," she rebuked.

Another knock sounded on the door.

"My servant, bringing my food and medicine," explained Rachel.

"Right," he said tightly, "and I've got things to do before I'm late for Court. How can I fix this?"

"Confess. Confess, Richard. Confess to a man you dislike."

"And who is that?"

"Cardinal Conti."

Voice rising, he released her hand and said, "That impatient, calculating, controlling tyrant?"

"Strong, strategizing, and ambitious—like you."

He tenderly kissed her forehead. "I love you, Tulip."

"Tell me when you've confessed, Richard."

Luta followed Richard to his cabinet room, barking until he finished dressing and left through a private door into the hall.

Rachel walked to another hall door and opened it to let in her maid.

The maid took in the scene, then began by wiping Rachel's forehead with a cool rag.

"Thank you, Elena," Rachel said.

"This will help you sleep, Your Highness"—Elena handed her a vial. "And please remember to eat your breakfast."

"I will. Thank you."

After some food and a morning nap, Rachel's stomach calmed. She put on a robe and walked to the lavatory.

"Don't look, Luta."

Luta angled her head, then stretched out on the stone tiles. Rachel slipped from her robe and poured water from a jug into a bowl, then dipped in a sponge and squeezed it against her brow. Cold water soaked onto her forehead and dribbled down her cheeks. Then down both arms, across her chest, then she dipped again and held the sponge over her stomach.

"It was the right decision," she told herself. She finished washing off the rest of her body and dropped the sponge to the floor. Luta hopped up to fetch it, but Rachel grabbed the sponge and squeezed its remaining water onto Luta's head. Luta yelped a little, and Rachel smiled. "Oh, you know it feels good, girl."

She found clean undergarments and a light tunic, then she sat in a chair in front of her armoire and called past the lavatory into the maid's room. "Elena, I am ready."

Section by section, Elena smoothed tangles from Rachel's hair with a flat brush. She grabbed the sections and pulled one over another, crisscrossing until she had formed a braid. Rachel tilted her head and flashed a smile, her dimples making two dark spots in the polished stone vanity mirror.

"He will love this, Your Highness," said Elena, as she wound fresh flowers into the braid.

From the cabinet room down the hall, Rachel heard the unloading of bags and Richard dismissing Chamberlain Vere, then sounding his footsteps back to their rooms.

"Thank you, Elena," said Rachel with a friendly, dismissing wave of her hand, and Elena took the brush and went back to her room.

Richard pushed through the hall door into the bedchamber.

"Welcome back, honey," Rachel said. "How was your meeting?"

"Not now, my Tulip."

"I see how it is—good talking to you, like always."

"What did you say?" He went around the room looking for something. "Do you know where it is?" he asked, opening his side table drawers. "My Les Andelys castle drawing."

Papers shuffled and he closed the drawer with a thunk. "Never mind—found it."

"Where are you going?" she asked. "And where is Chamberlain Vere going?"

He kissed her forehead, and her lips pressed together slightly. "To Durham, to check on John the Short," he said.

"Him again?" asked Rachel. "Your younger brother is not a threat to the throne."

"He's not, Tulip," Richard said dryly, "because I *do* check on him."

"But when I return, we'll have a new market on the cathedral square." He rolled his wrist to hold out a hand as if presenting something to her on its surface. "So please prepare."

"And Vere?"

He ignored the question and breezed past her into the hall again, shutting the door and murmuring a warning to someone outside.

Under her breath and with arms crossed, Rachel said, "Have a good trip, love. I'm drinking with friends."

A young female voice shouted from outside the door, "Mama! I need you!"

"Hold on, Isabella," said Rachel.

But without knocking or waiting, their sixteen-year-old daughter barged into the room.

Just like her father.

Isabella's servant Klara stood at the door until dismissed.

"Mama, can we please go by the carpenter's house tonight?"

"Not today," replied Rachel. "Maybe a day next week."

"Tomorrow, then?" Isabella held her mother's hands with hopeful persistence and dreamy eyes, begging like Luta when she wanted leftovers. "But Maa-maa"—she stretched out the name—"I don't even remember the last time we went."

"Fine—fine, Isabella."

"Thank you!" The girl hugged her mother. "I especially want to see Alf when he practices his swordsmanship. He's so strong."

"Women and their love of men's blades," said Rachel, remembering an earlier time when she had known that love, when she first fell for Richard. A simpler time. "No power," she murmured, "no thirst for power, no fear of losing power."

Pirouetting, Isabella asked, "What'd you say, Mama?"

"Nothing, Bella. Carry on."

"Mama . . . please. Bella is a little girl's name. No Izzy either. I'm a woman now. Isabella." She twirled her brunette braids and closed the door behind her, lighter in step as she went back down the hall with Klara.

As queen, Rachel had a wide range of options for her dress for the day; her closet dwarfed many peasants' huts. Rachel looked for the right ensemble, something different from the daily show-and-tell: too many women preened in their tunics, wearing too much powder of varied colors, flashing expensive jewels. After pushing aside many different dresses, she settled on a black, maiden-hooded dress. But something was missing.

She sat at her armoire and opened the top drawer. She moved several scarves until she found her favorite—crimson with pink tulips, and adorned with calligraphy.

The silk hugged against her hair as she slowly wrapped it around her head. Once covered, she placed hands to her framed face and meditated upon her mother's love for her in this gift to her young daughter in Constantinople. More memories of home flooded through her mind, interrupting the dressing ritual. Finally, the memories stopped as she tied the scarf. No one would be able to tell she was queen. The black hood and bright head wrap peeking out of it contrasted with her chocolate eyes and camel-brown skin, which darkened when tanned but always stayed smooth and soft to the touch.

Wisdom is a gift of age, she thought. *No regrets.*

In the bottom of the drawer, below the scarves, was a knob she twisted to reveal a secret compartment. Inside were letters from her mother and letters she had recently written to Richard, to her daughter and son, and to Father William. She brought them out and with the candle on her dressing table, sealed each one with a circular stamp and stowed them back away, keeping out the letters for Father William.

Rachel shut the drawer and emerged from the lavatory into her private room, where Elena and another maid were sewing.

"Elena, I'm going out for a bit. If the chamberlain asks." Then Rachel stopped.

Elena rose at the pause. "Yes, my lady?"

"Never mind. Carry on with the quilt. If anyone requests me, please make appointments for later in the week."

Elena winked. "Don't have too much this morning—remember your stomach."

Rachel covered her mouth and bit the bottom lip, but her cheeks shined. The opportunity to sneak from the castle unnoticed for wine with friends put a bounce in her step.

"Did you eat?" asked Elena, glancing at the cloth-covered tray that had held Rachel's breakfast.

The queen pulled up her hood and wrapped the cloak tighter about her. "Yes, thank you."

From the hallway, she skipped like a girl down each step on the stone staircase to the ground floor. Breathless at the bottom, she turned to see behind her and craned her neck. Soldiers guarding each rampart and arrow slit stopped the watch during shift change, and she had timed it just right.

She hurried along a trail past a building housing the court's living quarters and into the forest until it opened onto rows of twining grapevines. She climbed to a building atop a hill overlooking the queen's vineyards. There, two men were rocking on the porch, one with a wool blanket over his legs.

"You're late, my lady," Padre said as she climbed the stairs. He handed her a glass of wine mixed with elderberry juice.

Rachel looked beyond him to the Witen chief. His tunic displayed multicolors like a peacock's and bore symbols of his family embroidered around the hem and sleeves. The slightly elevated bridge of his nose gave him character and accentuated his overall patrician bearing.

"Lord Charles, good evening," said Rachel. "And Padre, always good to see you."

She lowered her hood and collapsed into the third rocking chair, holding the glass aloft to keep from spilling it.

After a few sips, she said, "Our first meeting without Mati."

"Seven years," said Charles, "since I met him. A colorful chap."

"Very much unlike you," quipped Rachel. The muscles of her face moved briefly in soundless laughter. "I was so nervous when I confessed to him."

The weight in her chest vanished with the first glass of wine as the sun rose higher and burned off the late morning fog. She yawned and shivered. Rachel could not help grabbing at her abdomen again, moaning as the clenching came, and covering her mouth to hide her reaction.

"How are you, my dear?" asked Padre.

"I'm fine," she said. "Pour me another, Padre."

He took her glass and filled it from the flask. "Are you sure you want another glass?" He held the glass he had just filled.

"Yes. My stomach has been bothering me recently—but it's not a child," she assured herself in a murmur. "We were careful. Plus, I'm older." Then louder she said, "I've never thanked you enough, Padre, for comforting me when I lost them."

"You'll see your unborn children someday."

After a yawn, she said, "I'm thankful to be alive."

Padre handed her the glass and looked straight at her. "My dear, you made the right decision to try again," he enunciated gently.

She lifted her hand to hide her chocolate eyes that had softened and brightened. "Thank you, Padre." She winced and shivered at another pain. Her chest heavy, she regretted that she had not told Richard about their son, now almost a man. *Maybe I should tell him.*

But not yet.

"Take this." Padre stood and placed the blanket over her shoulders.

Light bounced off drips from the morning fog and she caught its sparkle in a tear poised at the top of her cheek.

"Pardon my manners," said Charles, "but our business . . ."

"Yes, of course," Rachel said and shook off a memory of Jeremiah's birth.

"Now is the time," concluded Charles. "Jeremiah must be trained."

"Too early, Charles," countered Padre. "He isn't ready."

"When will he be ready?" asked Charles.

"But Padre," Rachel interrupted. "You will tell me, right? When he is ready?"

Padre nodded. "He needs to finish his apprenticeship and grow in maturity."

"Fine," said Charles shortly. "But we need to meet periodically to review the plan."

The three rocked and sipped quietly for a while, their silence cementing their purpose.

After finishing his glass, Charles asked, "What do we know about Mati?"

"Our beloved friend," mused Padre. "He was loved by all. My brother in the faith, and more priest than archbishop," said Padre.

"And we still know so little," said Rachel. "He had just returned . . ."

"Do you know who killed him, Your Highness?" asked Charles.

"No, no, I don't know, Charles, but Mati was a threat to many."

"He was an ally in the cause," added Charles. "The Crown has grown too large, and religion and kingdom are too close."

She pulled the letters from a pocket and showed them to Charles and Padre.

"Are you sure you want to include him?" asked Charles.

Padre smiled at the official stamp. "Very clever, my lady. I can tell you've thought this through."

"I met him recently when he was at the castle," she said. With the rim of her glass resting on her bottom lip, she felt the lemon and pear scents rise with faint honeyed notes and mild tartness to twirl with her thoughts and calm her hesitation. "Yes, Charles, I'm sure. I trust him."

"Shall I give it to him, then?" asked Padre, holding out a hand for the letter.

"That's too obvious," Rachel answered. "I'll find a moment to meet him in his office we gave him."

"Review next steps in the plan after your meeting?" asked Charles.

"Yes," she replied. "Look for our signal. When the purple flag rises atop the castle, meet me here the following night at sunset."

MARKET

Naturally introverted, Rachel preferred quiet nights at home with family, wine, and sweets. But being queen had its perks, and she was infatuated at first with her title. The love affair ended quickly, however, and she had been numbed by the loss—two decades away from the family and culture she had left for Richard.

Her heart burned when she touched her mama's letter, but then she forcefully swept her hand across her chest and leg to flush the pain away. She stuffed these letters for Father William into a leather handbag.

She put on a ruby dress with beige floral trim and long, voluminous sleeves that ended in angled, draping fabric, the volume of the skirt enhanced with a full petticoat. Her hair flowed over her shoulders, and the knotted crimson scarf flowed down her bosom.

Just so.

She went to Isabella's room and knocked.

"Ready, Isabella?"

Klara opened and clasped her hands to her chest. "She will be ready soon, Your Majesty."

Isabella danced around the room, tossing multiple dresses to the floor, rummaging to find the perfect outfit.

"There it is," said Isabella. "I think Alf loves blue. You know—because of his Norse heritage."

She slid into a baby-blue twill dress with a trim in a Viking design. She had plumped up her bosom with a wool undergarment, and brown suede knee-high boots made her taller.

"Is that necessary?" asked Rachel. "Come on, let's go."

"Absolutely, Mama," said Isabella, while smoothing some of Rachel's lotion over her unruly brown braids she had unfastened, raking her fingers through the tangles. Then she leaned over and shook the hair until it was fully free.

"He will love my curls." She fastened on a matching blue head scarf, making sure to display some of the curls, and wrapped a cloak around herself. "I'm ready, Mama. Thank you so much for waiting— and for taking me."

"Let's go," responded Rachel, businesslike. "I want to visit the new cathedral market first. It's on the way."

Elena and Klara quietly followed mother and daughter through the castle and to the waiting royal carriage.

Down the hill, across the bridge, and through the city gate, their carriage stopped as the incline flattened into a stone courtyard. The cathedral and Rose Abbey were a few paces to her left, and the city with homes, shops, the court, and the Witen assembly building was a longer walk to her right.

A footman opened the door; immediately, commoners recognized the queen and rushed to help her exit the carriage. Isabella rolled her eyes, and Elena and Klara tried to block them.

"Let them come," said Rachel.

All classes sought her hand and ear, but she spent more time listening to sinners' sobs and confessions—they felt she had more than just political authority. *An opportunity*, she thought, and listened to several, offering comfort, before noting Isabella's growing impatience.

"Thank you all, but after hearing so many confessions," Rachel said, "now is the time for *me* to go to confession."

The crowd laughed, and they bowed in unison as she gave them a final farewell. "Elena and Klara, I'll be back. Take Isabella shopping—I'll find you both soon."

Introducing the plot to save the kingdom to a stranger was risky, but her intuition was usually right. *No—it's always been right,* she told herself. She had a history of stomach pains when faced with a dilemma, but her gut quieted after she'd made the weighty decisions. It was the anxiety leading to the decision that aroused the monsters inside.

Once William was chosen as the investigator, she had to meet him. He wouldn't know why she had hugged him at the palace the day they met, but she knew. And she knew that, at a later date, he would remember the feeling—love, acceptance, and trust.

+———+

The cathedral was bare, save for pigeons and the priest. William was locking his office door and turned at the sound of her small heels clicking against the marble. *He notices things.*

"Father William," Rachel said. "We meet again."

His notebook under an arm, he transferred it to a hand and bowed. "Your Majesty—a surprise."

"Do you have a moment?"

"Of course." He gestured for her to sit on a bench and pulled out a pencil.

"Can we go somewhere quieter, Father William?" She inclined her head towards his door as wings flapped through the cavernous arches above them. "Like your office."

The bells sounded for half past eleven, and he raised his head to note them. "I'd love to, Your Majesty, but I must be carrying on."

"What I have to tell you is about the investigation, Father William."

"About the archb-bishop's death?"

A long silence lingered, and Rachel wanted to spill everything there, confess what she knew about Richard's half-brother Rohad, her history, the stone, and her list of potential suspects.

"Or about the stone?" he asked.

"No." She raised a trembling hand and pulled the knot of her scarf. "But about information that may help."

"My apologies, Queen Rachel, but I'm late for an appointment with the abbot and cardinal. Can we meet later?"

"I understand," she said and pulled the letters from her handbag. "Please take these. One is for you and the other is for the cardinal. If the cardinal asks, tell him it's from your source."

"Yes, Your Majesty."

"Thank you. If you have questions, there are instructions in your letter about how to contact me—in private."

He placed the letters in his thong-bound notebook, then bowed. "Thank you, Your Majesty, but I must go. I will read them in the abbey—and contact you later."

She watched him push through the door and run onto the court-yard. When the door shut, she exited a side door and looked for her daughter.

Elena, Klara, and Isabella hadn't left the first tent yet. "Look, Mama, there's Marianne!" cried Isabella. "And her mum."

Charlotte and Marianne spun from table to table with arms full of clothes. The daughter was a petite version of her mother—both had amber hair, blueish eyes, and hourglass figures.

Marianne strolled past Isabella and stopped abruptly at the table beside her, as if she had had a sudden epiphany. "I'll give you one penny for that," she said imperiously to the merchant.

"But, my lady," the man said and lifted the turquoise ring to the light, "this is far more valuable than a penny."

Marianne crossed her arms and raised her voice: "Two but not a penny more." She walked away. "Come on, Mum. To the next booth—this is a joke."

"Three," he said.

She about-faced and examined the ring. "Cut that in half and you have a deal."

His lips pressed together, and he waved a hand to Isabella. "Next customer."

As Isabella stepped forward, Charlotte curtsied. On the upswing, Rachel noticed her rosy cheeks as she said in the faintest tone of mockery spread over the smooth notes of her voice, "Your Majesty."

"Hello, Lady Charlotte," Rachel said, braced for bitter griping from a lord's wife.

"It's so nice of our queen to grace us with her presence at this inaugural market."

Rachel entertained a caustic response, but she dismissed it with a small shake of her head, then she saw George of Bath's burgundy hat two booths down.

"Stay beside me, Bella," Rachel said and pulled her away from the table.

"Mama! No, I'm not a child." Isabella retracted her hand and walked towards the crowd.

Marianne turned to look towards Charlotte, and at the snap of her mother's fingers, Marianne's eyes brimmed with tears and she began to cry, loud and then louder. She pounded the table and moaned, "The first market, and you try selling garbage at this price?"

A crowd had gathered around the table, and Elena and Klara shielded Rachel from the onlookers pushing to see a show.

"Fine, fine, my lady—one-and-a-half pence," said the merchant. He wrapped the ring in a small sheet of birch paper and handed her the package.

After a flip of her hair and a pirouette, Marianne bowed. "You're welcome, sir, for the customers." She dropped the coins into the man's hand, then unwrapped the ring and let the paper flutter to the ground. She slid the gem onto her finger and shoved her hand at Isabella. "That's how it's done, Bella."

Isabella huffed and said, "I'm going to Alf's house," and she ducked through the crowd.

"Bella," called Rachel, "Bella, come back." She watched Isabella's baby-blue twill dress blend into the crowd. "Elena and Klara, please go after her."

"Yes, my lady," they said.

Charlotte lifted a bag of her purchases and said, "We are so thankful that the king agreed to this market, particularly since he's away." From the side of her mouth, in a higher pitch, she added, "Leaving *you* in charge—quite a stir, if you ask me."

In one ear, Rachel overheard clerics selling church offices, and in the other, Marianne laughing.

Charlotte grabbed a flag and pointed to the image of the merchant guild master portrayed on it. "My husband told me George of Bath here pressured the king to have a market on the church square." Her tongue clicked on the roof of her mouth as her head wobbled. "Seems the merchants have more power than does the king or the church. What has this kingdom come to, Your Highness? The archbishop died. Now, church offices are sold on the church square."

What has Richard done now? Rachel wondered. "I'm sure it was for a good reason, Lady Charlotte." Rachel stood on tiptoes to look for Elena's and Klara's blond curls.

"Good day," Rachel said and excused herself to follow.

A few steps ahead, she spied the light-blue dress and then saw George's elaborate, rich, silk Venetian suit—with a dueling sword at his side—appear through an opening in the crowd. Black leggings matched his black corset. *Always the dandy*, she thought.

Rachel quickly tied up her hair into a bun and lengthened her stride.

Isabella followed George to a booth. *Why?* Rachel thought. "Oh, I see," she said and shook her head. George was introducing Isabella to a tall, barrel-chested, brown-bearded, courtly groomed prince.

Rachel caught up to them at the booth and avoided an introduction by breezing through a rack of dresses and scarves.

From his sleeve, George pulled a head scarf and slid it over Isabella's neck. She wrapped it around her head as Rachel had done so many times. He smiled and bagged a similar scarf.

Rachel stepped up to them and said, "Thank you, George, but we can't accept these."

"Mama . . . please," Isabella said and blushed.

In a velvety smooth voice, George, the merchant guild master, turned around and said with a bow, "Queen Rachel, you have impeccable timing." He caressed his luxuriant white beard and offered his hand to Rachel. She hesitated as her eyes moved over his face, dark-blue eyeliner contrasting his powdered face and ruby lips, though his teeth showed yellow. His soft-butter fingers with polished nails took her hand to his lips for a kiss.

"I was hoping you'd come so you could meet Robert," he murmured.

Rachel looked to the man beside him, and her eyes locked on his striking blue eyes. For a moment she froze, remembering her first meeting with Richard. She broke her gaze and listened to George's introduction.

"This is Robert the Bearded—a warrior with glory from Jerusalem, a prince in Anjou, cousin of Phillip, whose sympathies align more closely with Richard's line. He's a strapping specimen for your bloodline and male heirs, my lady."

Robert winked and bowed. "An honor, Your Highness."

"Nice to meet you," said Rachel.

"You have a lovely daughter," the man said, "as beautiful as you."

Rachel caught herself running a hand through her hair, almost loosening the bun.

"Thank you, Sir Robert, but—"

Rachel abruptly turned as Isabella accidentally bumped into someone in the crowd.

A sword clanked against the cobbles, and the boy Alf suddenly lay on the ground.

"Oh no!" cried Isabella. She stood stiff in alarm, and her ears and cheeks flashed red. "Oh no!" She knelt but fidgeted and covered her face with her hands. With weakened voice, she said, "I'm, I'm sorry, Sir Alfred."

"Good to see you, Alfred," said Rachel.

After a quick rise and bow to Rachel, Alf's eyes darted and connected with Isabella's.

"My lady," he said and kissed her hand. "I'm not a sir yet. But one day. Thank you. A week from now I'll be eighteen, and graduated from the academy."

Cheeks blushing deep crimson, Isabella, like a parrot, stammered repeatedly in a higher pitch, "I-I'm sorry, I'm sorry, I'm sorry."

He held her hand. "I'm fine. I'm fine. It's fine." He looked around and glared at George and a winking Robert.

"Were these men bothering you?" he asked, brows furrowed.

"No, no, they're fine," Isabella said and played with the scarf still around her neck. "George gave me these gifts."

George extended a fishy hand, and Alf took it but promptly released it as he sneered at George.

"I'm sorry, Alfred," said Rachel, "but we must go."

"But, Mama, this scarf!" Isabella said. "And Alfred, what about Alfred?"

Rachel pulled Isabella's hand. Over the whining, Rachel told Alfred he could see Isabella another day.

As the queen's carriage departed, another carriage rolled into the courtyard.

CRYPT

Cardinal Lothar Conti of Segni exited the carriage with his staff. Like geese flying in formation, the entourage moved through the crowd with the red cloak as its captain.

Late to the meeting with Abbot James, William apologized and excused himself to wait outside in the market for the thirty-two-year-old cardinal to come into view, looming over his staff, which included a short, balding man with a round belly and carrying bags.

Most people dispersed to make way. William weaved through the crowd as some ducked beneath the table full of merchandise as the cardinal passed.

Conti marched towards one booth as if on a mission, and men scattered, their coins rolling along the pavement. At first glance, the contrast between the women in the booth was stark. One concealed her shaggy hair and muddied face, and the other flashed gold ornaments and ruby jewels, leather shoes and close-fitting silk garments. Conti coughed at her perfume.

"You make quite a pair," he said, "to run—apparently—a good business." With gloves on, he picked through various cosmetics, silk embroidery, gold bracelets, turquoise rings, and gold hairnets.

"Let me guess," he said to the disheveled one. "You invoke pity? Or rather, you seduce the poorer customers?" Turning to the fancier harlot, he added, "And you, you take the man's weekly wage?"

"What of it?" rebuked the harlot. "Free will, right? Isn't that what you preach?"

Conti laughed, then immediately retorted, "Like the Church

fathers have said, if we eliminated you from society, everything would be polluted by lust. So, you are a social necessity. But where is your procurer?"

"I have none; since the archbishop died, I run my *own* business."

"There is a better way," Conti said and pointed to the cathedral.

"And you're my judge? You don't know my life, my struggles."

His laugh hung in the air. Conti left the table and went towards Abbot James standing outside the abbey door. Conti ducked behind his bald porter to avoid James's sneeze, but he failed and watched the spray land on his sleeve. He cringed, wriggled, and looked for the door to escape the encounter, but James kissed his ring and both cheeks.

William observed, laughing to himself at the cardinal's discomfort at the miasmas and humours swirling about him.

Unhinged and with haste, Conti plucked at his eyelashes, excused himself, and skittered into the abbey.

William rubbed a hand over his left breast to ensure the pendant was still in his coat pocket. After a curt nod to James, he looked below the abbot's sharp jaw for the first time and saw the pendant hanging from a gold chain around his neck. He then walked into the abbey and joined the cardinal and the brothers sitting around a large table in the dining hall, James following behind.

Conti stood before the brothers and made some excuse for his refuge to the abbey—something about a weak bladder.

Some of the brothers leaned forward, elbows upon the large oak table. Some winked and shared looks. They were all riveted, though, waiting with hushed breaths. Some tapped their feet nervously or overlapped their fingers and pretended to pray. One was so nervous he sneezed.

Conti glided his hands through his thick brown hair and stroked his shaved chin. William observed that the man's gray eyes underneath thin eyebrows appeared older than his years, and tired. His voice came low, cold, and deep—deep enough to fill the dining hall from end to end.

"Brothers," he started, with a finger in the air, "we will—"

"Cardinal Conti," interrupted Fuss.

"Yes, brother with the hat."

"Weren't you here a few weeks ago?"

"Yes, yes, I was." He paused and lifted his finger again. "We will rid this house of evil. We—"

A hand raised, and Conti tapped a foot impatiently. "What is it?"

"Why were you here then?" asked Fuss.

William furrowed his brow and opened his notebook to a page with the same sketch he had on his office wall. He flipped through the pages until he found the queen's letters, and his fingers ran over the seals colored in purple wax: a circle with a line drawn down the middle. *The same shape as on the tree?*

What does this mean?

"Brother," Conti began again. "I'm a new cardinal and have been traveling across the kingdom to visit each archdiocese. Now, as I was saying, we cannot tolerate the murder of priests, less so of archbishops—rather, potential murder. The search for justice is your highest priority."

"But Witenberg twice?" asked Fuss.

A smile appeared, forced, and Conti knocked the table with a bishop chess piece. "Brother," Conti said.

"Please?" asked Fuss.

"What is your name?"

Fuss stood and lifted his chin. "I am Brother Adolphus, elder of the Witenberg chapter of the Order of the Night Watchers. It's our duty to protect the church. We want to know why our beloved archbishop was murdered."

As the cardinal and abbot turned their attention to the brothers sitting in the back row stomping their feet, William pretended to take notes. He broke the seal to his letter with the pencil. He unfolded it and read:

Love or Freedom? What will the kingdom choose? Meet me in the king's scriptorium.

Where is the scriptorium?

The pencil scratched the page and scribbled a wavy line. William tapped the page. *How is she involved?* He wrote in Rachel's name and connected a line to the king. *Inspect his room?*

He rubbed the seal on the letter addressed to the cardinal, wondering what Rachel had written.

"The case hasn't been solved yet," continued Conti. "But"—he moved around the table—"are you accusing me of something, Brother Fuss?"

"Just curious, Your Eminence, why the king's cousin, our abbot, is next in line for archbishop?"

"Do you believe in obedience, Brother Fuss?" Conti asked and walked towards him. "Tell me, Brother, what does your hat say?"

Chest out, Fuss tightened the hat over his large forehead. "Jesus is my boss."

"And in the hierarchy, who is below Jesus?"

"The pope."

"And who next?"

Stubby fingers stroked his beard. "I know where you're going, but we're not perfect."

"Yes, of course, but with proper discernment and agreement by the College of Bishops, the pope's rulings are directly from God."

The foot stomping stopped, and Brother Fuss bristled. Conti completed his circuit of the table and returned to the front.

"Obedience, brothers. We are all called to obedience. I nominated Abbot James after the archbishop died, and I believe"—he looked to William—"he has appointed a very capable, qualified investigator."

The cardinal nominated the abbot, William wrote and drew a line connecting the abbot, king, and cardinal. After finishing the line, he smiled. "Thank you, Your Eminence."

"At half past noon, Father William will give me and Abbot James an update on the investigation."

Arms crossed, Fuss huffed. "Can I come too?"

"Brothers," James interjected, "the cardinal has a busy schedule during his visit, including, as you know, the archbishop's funeral on Sunday."

James dismissed the brothers, and William, with notepad and birch papers in hand, walked past the open door to the abbot's study and stopped at Mati's room. After a quick pivot to ensure no one was looking, he stole in, then quietly shut the door. Though he had quickly checked the room without the abbot's permission the day he was appointed, emotional pain had deterred him from a more thorough search.

Bright light from the window showed Mati's simple office: a wooden desk, two chairs, a crucifix, and a large painting the archbishop had told William he'd bought from a Gypsy in Rome. In its foreground, Jesus hugged the bride and groom. In the background, children played while Mary supervised, guests refilled wine jugs, and revelers danced.

As he explored the room, he listened for the creak of the abbot's door. The stale air sank heavy against his skin like the weight lodged in his chest, so he cracked open the window. The glass panes screeched against the wood casing. His shoulders hunched, and he heard the abbot's voice a few heel clicks away in the corridor: "I know he's late—I'll find him, Your Eminence."

With breaths tugging at his throat, William sped to the door and heard footsteps going the opposite way.

Quick, he thought. *Anything else?* The bed hadn't changed. The closet looked the same. The desk. The drawer. He hadn't searched the desk during the first visit.

He ruffled through birch papers and parchment in the drawer. Another purple seal. A letter addressed to him. *From the archbishop?*

Forgetting the window, he exited with the letter in his pocket. The tickle in his throat became a laugh as he flashed a quick, private smile. Hands behind his back, shoulders relaxed, he waited against the wall outside the abbot's door. He touched the smooth tips of parchment in his coat pocket and fantasized about what Mati had written.

"There you are, Father William," said James, gesturing towards his office door. "Come in."

"Father William," said Conti, also gesturing towards the door, as if it were his own office, "please come in."

James moved into the office, and Conti took the abbot's desk chair.

"Please sit and show me what you have found," the cardinal said.

From his pocket, William pulled out a small bag and handed it to Conti. "Your Eminence," he began, "the hair, cork, and purple fibers in the bag point to the archb-bishop's murder. I believe there was a fight, and I will confirm that once a Night Watcher takes me to the crypt to look at his body."

Conti examined the evidence and looked to James. "Thank you, Father William, but that will not be necessary."

"Not necessary, Your Eminence? But why?"

"We are celebrating his life soon, and his family will be here tomorrow. Do you really want to see his body? What will you learn?"

"I don't know, but I'd like to see him."

Conti dug into his pockets and slid a bishop chess piece across the desk. "What do you think, Abbot James? You saw his body, correct?"

"Yes, my lord, and the Night Watcher's testimony confirms what I saw too. I agree that he was murdered."

"Your Eminence," added William, "I have interviewed many in the abbey. And I have a letter for you."

Conti relaxed his shoulders. He tapped the bishop against the desk to punctuate his monotone question: "Where did you get the letter?"

William's lips pressed together into a slight grimace. "A source, Your Eminence," he said.

Laughter burst from both the cardinal and the abbot. "A source?" cried Conti. "Did you miss my obedience lecture earlier, Father William?"

William's blinking increased.

"Who is your source? The archbishop himself?"

William opened and closed his mouth and said, "No, no, he's not the source." He felt the spots of red begin on his cheeks and slowly expand to paint his whole face. Conti stared sharply into William as if he were breaking a lock and entering his soul.

After prolonged, uncomfortable silence, William began to bounce on his toes. He noticed it and stopped but then stammered and confessed. "The archb- . . . archb-bishop and I are, I mean, we were friends. But he wasn't the source. I loved—"

Conti leaned back into the chair, judged William with squints, and jotted a note.

"R-rather, I loved his dreams," continued William, "his plans to unify the realm the right way, through love and community."

"That's enough," said the cardinal. "Please give me the letter."

William opened to the correct page in his notebook and handed Conti the letter.

Conti opened and read. "Who is your source?" he asked.

The bread from breakfast tightened into a ball in William's stomach. His nose wrinkled. He yearned to put a hand to his inner breast pocket and rub the seals. He had kept to himself his undelivered letters to Mati and the queen's letter to him.

"Holy Father, I can't compromise the source."

"Very well, Father William. I need to pray and think. You are dismissed."

William scurried to his room. Once inside, his lips curved into a mocking smile of childlike triumph.

With back pressed to the door, he opened Mati's letter. The page of parchment torn in two with a perfect tear went unnoticed. He licked his lips, and his attention skipped to the juicy parts.

He read aloud. "My dear brother in Christ, you have been most gracious and attentive to me . . ."

Yes, of course.

"For fun, play with this homophonic cipher: use key phrase 'Ogdoad, Live the Eighth! Baptismal Crosses.'"

I love puzzles. Oh, yes, I know, a substitution cipher.

"Ogarc ca acomc o mioahrceab!"

He hurriedly opened his notebook and drew a grid. He tried various substitutions. *This is taking too long.* After lining up the correct combinations, he solved the code. *Repetition, alas!*

"About to start a revolution!" he exclaimed. He leaned back in the chair, satisfied at solving the puzzle, and continued reading.

"Thank you for the debate. Keep our conversations private. The king and cardinal cannot know yet that the plan is from me."

William scrambled to his feet. "He hasn't addressed the other topic," he said aloud. He combed through the rest of the letter. It ended at a torn edge with "I'm sorry, but I need to address one matter, my friend."

No salutation. No signature. Unlike Mati.

Or, he wanted to leave me in suspense.

Frustration boiled to anger. He stuffed the letter in the back of his notebook, then marched to the abbot's office, where James was pouring apple cider into Conti's mug.

"Back so soon, Father William?" Conti asked with narrowed eyes. Behind his steepled hands, it was clear an intense malice was slowly rising.

"I want to know who was at the burial with Abbot James," demanded William.

"I told you I need to pray and think, Father William."

"When can I interview you and Abbot James?"

"Father William, I am meeting with the king soon. Please make an appointment with Abbot James."

James widened his stance. "Yes, certainly, you can make an appointment, but I can answer now. I was there with some of my staff. We prayed in the crypt and buried him in his sarcophagus."

Conti stood up and guided William to the door.

"No one else? Where was the king?" asked William over his shoulder.

"Look at the treasury visitor logs. The archbishop had always asked everyone to sign their names and write a petition so that he might pray for those who visited the stone."

"Father William, go rest," Conti ordered and opened the door.

William stomped through and let the door slam in his wake—just enough of a bang to register one final protest. Back in his room, he grabbed a candle and its holder and the brimstone.

Down the central staircase and through the kitchen he went, then lowered his head and trooped to the basement. On the wooden door, at about chest height, was fastened a brass knocker in the form of a hooded man with a large ring in one hand and a lantern in the other. *The symbol of the Night Watchers,* guessed William.

He knocked once.

Nothing.

He knocked again.

Nothing.

After a third time, the peephole slid open and a voice came through: "Who goes there?"

"This is Father William."

"How do I know?"

"Can't you see me?"

"Come closer."

"Ugh," said William. Rocking in place, heel to toe, he stomped one boot on the step. "I'm leaving."

"That won't work. I can see you. Come closer."

William leaned in and squinted one eye. A man wearing a hat stood behind the door.

"Fuss, open the door. You know it's me."

"We don't respond to the knocker. Grab the rope on the wall and ring the bell."

After the bell rang, the door opened, and Fuss waved with a wide grin. His cap was on backwards, yet *Jesus is my boss* was written on the back.

"Welcome, Bouncy."

"Was all that necessary?" asked William and walked into the Night Watcher's room. The glow from candles lit the low, arched stone ceiling.

"All in good fun, Father William."

Several brothers sat around a table playing cards in the common area. Down the long windowless hall were two rows of bunk beds and a man with a single eyebrow over both eyes. A string of unclear purpose hung from the ceiling and ran the length of the room. Against a wall were pinned many hats of various shapes and colors.

William smiled and gestured to the hats, asking, "Yours, Fuss?"

"You know it. Made in the city by the same weaver who makes our shoes."

"And what is this?" William examined the cone of parchment tied to the string. He cocked his head and lifted one eyebrow.

"Watch." Fuss spoke softly into the cone and waited for a response.

"Please?" asked Fuss. "Speak louder, Pius." Fuss shoved his ear deeper into the cone, and he said, "What? I can't hear you. What? Oh."

Fuss chuckled. "Pius says he wants his bookmark. And Stinky Feet wants to say hello."

William bent forward, his mouth slack.

"The Night Watchers are into magic, Fuss? You send voices through vast chambers?"

"Another gift from the archbishop," Fuss said proudly. "Go ahead, speak into it, then put an ear to it."

"Stinky Feet," he started and tilted his head.

"Bouncy!" exclaimed Stinky Feet. "You looked like a cat bouncing when you entered our quarters."

"Can't be—no." He inspected this strange toy and flicked the string.

At the opposite end of the corridor, he could make out a brother waving from the shadows. He began walking that way, and the farther he walked, past some brothers in bed reading, the colder it got. The familiar odor of feet, dirt, and cork became stronger the closer he came to an open door.

"Bouncy!" repeated Stinky Feet. He jumped up from a bed and pushed his short, stubby hand out for a handshake. "What brings you this way?"

"Uh, good to see you too, Stinky Feet. Nice toy."

Stinky Feet ignored the hand and hugged William instead, who relaxed once Stinky Feet let go.

"Not a toy, Bouncy. Another archbishop invention."

"Interesting. Well, then." *That does sound like him*, he thought. Arms crossed, and he said, "I need to visit the crypt."

"Any particular reason?" asked Fuss.

"Just something I need to check. Can I have the keys?"

"We will go with you," said Fuss.

William started down the hall, but Fuss said, "Wait a moment, Father William. Let me check on the brothers. This way." Fuss led William and Stinky Feet out a door and towards the barn. They walked into the sound of stomping twice, popping once, a clap, and a song.

> Here we go, down the road,
> a cork for lovers, a cork for brothers,
> new wine flows, new life shows.

Each brother on bottling duty stomped his feet, popped a palm against his mouth, and finished with a clap. The spigot opened, wine poured into a bottle, and the bottle flowed down the line. A brother corked the bottle, then placed it in a box.

"In this well-oiled rowing machine," Fuss explained, "the coxie steers the operation, changes songs when morale sags, and maintains proper speed of the cloth conveyer belt by manning a wheel." Then he applauded and cheered: "Well done, saints!"

William hadn't noticed that Fuss had swapped hats; this one read *Saints*. He joined them in song, then rang a bell. The coxie stopped the wheel.

"We have good news, saints," said Fuss. "Father William asked me and Stinky Feet to help with the investigation."

A finger to his mouth, William attempted to speak, but the brothers cheered. The coxie stomped his foot twice, and the song began again.

"I didn't say you could help me, Fuss," said William.

"Sure you did, Bouncy. When you asked us to visit the crypt."

A comb stuck straight up in the midst of Stinky Feet's tangled, thick hair. "Always be brushing, Bouncy," he said and grabbed a hat and coat from Fuss's office. "It be cold in the crypt."

"Where's Cracky?" Fuss asked the coxie.

"Since he wasn't making corks today, I believe he joined Pius to sit atop the bell tower."

For a moment, William thought about the pendant. When he'd asked Cracky why he had it, Cracky had said he found it in the church courtyard during his slow, painful walk from the abbey to the cathedral for bell-tower duty.

But that didn't make sense, William thought. *Why would someone leave something this valuable—a gold piece—on the ground for so long?*

"The Night Watchers take our duty very seriously," said Fuss. "Stinky Feet and I have joined your investigation team."

My team? William rubbed his temples.

"Let's go, team," said Fuss.

"Listen, Fuss," said William, trying to keep pace with the surprisingly fast walker, "if you are—and I didn't agree, but if you are to be part of this team, you are not the boss."

"Of course not, Bouncy. What does my hat say?" He must have forgotten he'd changed hats.

"*Saints.*"

"My other hats."

"Yes, they say *Jesus is my boss*, but in this investigation, I'm the boss."

"Yes, suh, Lord Bouncy," Stinky Feet said and climbed the hill and yelled, "Beat you both to the crypt."

As he watched Fuss's short legs motor rapidly ahead, William heaved a long sigh. "They didn't teach us this in law school." Around the abbey, up a hill, he jogged with them to the cathedral. After lighting candles, they walked through the grotto and treasury.

"Be careful, Bouncy," said Stinky Feet. "Watch your step."

Black iron gates blocked a stairwell in the corner of the treasury. Fuss descended and unlocked it for them. "Hold onto the railing," he said. Pillar by pillar, Fuss lit each candle, throwing a white glow on stone demons. William's eyes followed the slope of the arched ceiling to paintings of angels above.

"For dramatic effect?" asked William. His hand touched the demons in the shadows.

"The way the lights hit them?" asked Fuss.

"Yes—some faces are lit, whereas for others, it's their bodies. But each angel painting above—we can see all of it. Amazing." He found candles in places unexpected: on short pillars, tall pillars, holes in the wall, on the stone floor, and hung from the ceiling. Each holder had a covering, each shaped in angles to throw light in different directions.

"A symphony of light and dark," said Fuss. "The archbishop designed the lighting."

"And the angels?" William's neck craned as he walked.

"Yup, the archbishop asked us to repaint," said Stinky Feet.

One angel was defending with sword and shield, another giving away a sword and shield, one attacking with a spear, one speaking with a book in hand, one playing an instrument and singing, one hugging another, and one standing with a shoulder turned.

"That last one," William pointed, "is interesting. It's like he's ignoring the demons."

"Ah, hard to do, very hard at times, Bouncy," said Fuss.

Stinky Feet checked each sarcophagus. On the fourth one, he stopped and said, "I believe this is the archbishop's."

"How do you know?" asked William.

"It says so. That there, Bouncy, a plaque."

Something doesn't feel right, William thought.

"Why is Virdis buried here?" he asked. "The other coffins were kings."

Kneeling, William smoothed his hands over the stone coffin, the last image of the most handsome man he had ever seen popped into his mind: thick salt-and-pepper hair pulled into a ponytail, a sparkle that glittered in his dark eyes, high cheek bones over olive skin, and the slightest of dimples.

But it was the quiet confidence, the energy he radiated, the presence he created, the stillness—the love that captured him. And the hug—a soothing, bury-your-face-deep invitation into the shelter of his shoulders as the hair from his beard tickled your cheeks, the warmth from the soft jacket he always wore, the unconditional love he returned as his muscular arms wrapped you, held tight, and let you release all your pain—the kind of hug a large dog with a soft coat might give. It could have lasted a short time, but the feeling was eternal.

Like a stone dropped into a creek, a wave formed inside William's stomach and vibrated through his chest to his throat—the taste was sour. He immediately stood, but as the blood rushed to his head, he wobbled and swooned.

"Easy, easy, Father William, I got ya." Stinky Feet caught the falling investigator. William stabilized and refocused on the coffin.

Without a body sculpted into the stone, William thought that something was off. "I don't think he's in here," William told Stinky Feet. *What is the abbot hiding?*

With a shoulder push, William nudged the lid. "Help me, Brothers."

The stone lid slid, but no odor came.

The space below was empty.

"Now what?" asked Fuss, undaunted by the eerie sensation that wrapped William in its tendrils.

"There must be something—some clues," William said, coming

back to the matter at hand. "Look on the floor, the ceiling. Is there another exit?" William searched the room. "Abbot James told me he and his staff were here for the funeral."

William went to the coffin again. Inside were purple strings. He thought about the fight scene, the rosary beads, the chase, footprints, and purple fibers by the tree. Under his breath, he said, "Got you. You killed Mati." Louder, he told Fuss, "We missed this."

"Please?" asked Fuss.

"These purple fibers. Tell me, who wears purple?"

"Clergy during Advent and Lent."

"Yes, but, who else wears purple? More often? Daily?"

"The king does!" proclaimed Stinky Feet.

"You're not saying you think the king did this?" accused Fuss.

William rushed to the visitor log, a thick, bound book of parchment. He flipped it open to the date of the archbishop's death.

There were no recent signatures, but two symbols showed: a lion's paw and a circle—the carving in the tree. His fingers ran back, and the same symbols were stamped over a few pages.

"Why would they sign it, Father William?" asked Fuss.

Was Mati here? The king?

"Do you know what this means, Fuss?" William pointed to the page. "It's the same symbol we saw on the tree."

Fuss tightened his hat. "No, no, I've never seen this. But"—Fuss looked closer at the symbol—"the same shape is right there."

Beyond the coffin was another room, blocked by circular iron gates. "I don't suppose you have a key for this room too, Fuss?"

"Afraid not, Bouncy. But we could get in anyway."

Stinky Feet ran to the stairwell, let out a roar, and charged towards the gate. Airborne, both feet out, he kicked through and broke the gate.

Fuss laughed. "Well done, Saint."

They followed the tunnel to a wooden door that opened to steps and an earthy smell. High reeds and trees formed another tunnel out in the open.

William brushed dirt from his tunic and observed where they came out of it. The vineyards and cathedral rose in the distance behind them, and he could make out two Night Watchers in hoods atop the bell tower. "Shall we?" asked William.

Lighter in step than his two short-but-sturdy companions, William seemed to glide as softly as the swaying reeds in the wind. Dirt became stone, and he walked over something with an arch—a bridge! Stone became dirt again, yet reeds blocked their peripheral vision. Ahead, the reeds became shorter and shorter.

"You won't believe this, Brothers," said William.

Stinky Feet and Fuss crossed the same bridge and stopped. William shimmered like the sun reflecting off the water behind them. They were at the back of the castle. Hidden from view in the front, the castle complex extended several leagues with walls and towers of varying heights.

The road led to a door and a sign that read *The King's Scriptorium.* *The queen's note!*

"I didn't think the king could read," said Stinky Feet. "And another scriptorium? Different from the abbey?"

The door handle didn't budge, but William had all he needed. The puzzle pieces connected—*Case closed*, he believed.

"The king killed Virdis," declared William.

WITEN

William read the agenda posted outside the theater before he entered for an emergency Witen session. Past sentinels blocking entrance for peasants and commoners, he pushed through the doors with an air of distinction, as if he were in a university commencement ceremony.

Onstage, Charles of Desford appraised the converted Roman theater. The Witen Chief's peacock tunic was not out of place in the assembly, for also dressed in their finest apparel, barons, lords, and counts mingled and chattered gossip until the gavel slammed. Charles' long, thin legs nearly buckled, and his noticeable nose almost touched the floor during his deep bow to the crowd. King Richard and Queen Rachel sat in a private balcony overlooking the stage.

I'm sorry, Your Majesty, he told himself. The motive wasn't clear, but the clues pointed to the king. He was confident Mati hadn't killed himself—*he couldn't, he wouldn't*. Maybe the king was afraid of Mati? Of his power, his influence?

Abbot James, the king's cousin, wants to be archbishop.

Mati didn't approve of the king's wars.

It all seemed so clear.

William's arms hung loosely at his sides in a position he took at the margin of the theater. This was not a place usually open to him, but he was as relaxed as in his meetings with Mati. It wouldn't bring him back, but getting this closure would alleviate William's pain and stitch up the wounds Mati had begun to heal.

Charles opened the session. "Gentlemen, His Majesty has asked us to debate the state of the kingdom. Per Witen rules, you have two minutes on stage to give your account. After each has spoken, I will conclude and open the floor to general discussion."

Charles sat in his chair with the hourglass at hand. According to custom, the eldest capital lord went to the podium first. Charles flipped the wooden three-legged hourglass stand, careful not to damage the winged base.

Most of the speakers strolled to the stage to display their wealth, then flattered themselves in their speeches, taking more than the allotted time and rambling on. All in the theater became drowsy at the droning.

After the last lord spoke to complain about loss of rights and influence, William walked onstage, knelt beside Charles, and whispered into his ear. After several approving nods, Charles stood and said, "Gentlemen, tempus fugit. Thank you for your accounts. Though we may differ in opinion, we all know how to complain about the king."

The theater filled with laughter.

Charles smiled and continued. "We must not waste time, however. We know the republic has declined, and I was just informed about a damning indictment, another chink in this great kingdom's armor, another sign that we must restore our old ways. We will forgo open debate and listen to a guest speaker. Father William, your turn."

The crowd quieted, and William commanded center stage. "Lords, I come to you with a grave charge. A week since the archb-bishop's death, we don't know why he died. Some believe it was suicide—others believe murder." He lifted the pendant in his hand.

"As the abbot's appointed investigator into Virdis's death, I vowed to pursue every lead and follow the evidence."

After a deep breath, he continued. "I didn't want to believe suicide. How could a man so full of life and energy kill himself?" Above the crowd, in the balcony, he caught the movement as Rachel elbowed a drowsy Richard, and a warm sensation ballooned in William's belly. "But the evidence points to murder," he said. "And one particular piece of evidence needs to be presented to this b-body."

He lifted the pendant and walked with purposeful swiftness across the stage, displaying it to them. "Gentlemen, this is a gold pendant with our kingdom's symbols, the three lions. Only one person in the kingdom has this, only one person in the kingdom wears this, only one person. And that person sits right there."

He pointed up to Richard. Stuttering, he accused: "King Richard, King Richard, come, come to the stage and de-de-fend yourself. Why did the bell ringer f-find this pendant on the cathedral courtyard the morning of the archb-b-bishop's murder?"

The Witen hushed, and like a military rank on parade, turned in crisp unison to watch the king. Each member grasped the knobs they used to bang for voting aye or nay. After a few strikes of discord on the wooden benches, the rhythm rose in intensity and settled into unison until Richard reacted.

"Oh, Witen," he grumbled and rose from his seat and turned to the stairs down to the main level. Like a gladiator entering the arena, he went to the stage and raised his arm to silence the crowd. The corner of his mouth drew a little backward, exposing his teeth, and the muscular tension formed a distinct furrow on his cheek and produced a strong wrinkle under one eye.

He hissed and snatched the pendant from William. "This—this, Father—Investigator? Whoever you are? Are you accusing me of murder? Of *murder*? With this evidence? Where are your two witnesses? You're right—this is a grave charge, but a worse crime in our kingdom is accusing someone without evidence. Are you certain you want to do this?"

Sitting in the first row, Lord Harold shouted, "Maybe Father William should go!"

King Richard flipped the pendant into the air and let it fall, rattling on the stage like a child's toy. With his large boot, he stomped it once, twice—paused for dramatic effect—then slammed it with all fury.

"This, *this* is your evidence?" He lowered his massive frame into a crouch, then lifted and rubbed the broken pendant until gold flaked off and snowed onto the stage. He unfastened the family pendant around his neck and thrusted it into the air.

"A fake, gentlemen, a fake. I only wear *real* gold, not imitation."

Frozen, William cowered when the king hurled the pieces at him. They thudded against his chest and fell to the floor.

"Out of mercy," Richard said to all assembled, "I grant the chief his wish to hold session, and this is how you ungrateful Witen thank me? By accusing me of murder?"

He grabbed the chain, marched towards William, and shoved it into his chest.

Lord Harold struck his knob on the railing before him. "An embarrassment to the kingdom. Time to go, time to go, time to go!"

Richard held up a hand to quiet his supporter. "I know of only one other institution in this kingdom with that much wealth, with real gold, and stingy enough to only paint it on—the church. Where were you, Father Investigator, the night of the archbishop's death?"

William tried to speak, but he stuttered as badly as a wagon off its wheels. He fled the stage, running past Lord Harold and out the door, then out in the street he sprinted through an alley. Shadows flew up before him, and women with hissing cats ducked underneath their blankets. Once the darkness passed, they pointed their fingers and cursed, "The sickness!"

William kept running, running until he stopped in front of the abbey and staggered to catch his breath, bumping into a Night Watcher.

He shuffled backwards, lost his footing, and fell onto the steps, then sprang up and ran to his room, fumbling with his key and then slamming the door behind him with a gasp, hoping he wouldn't hear them. But the sound struck like a pounding headache.

Sharp strike, sharp strike, sharp strike.
Ring up. Wait.
Long strike. Full circle.
Sixteen rings signify the hour.

DEFENSE

Bells from the cathedral rang and rang. Richard covered his ears and coughed.

Rachel's hand instinctively ran through her hair, but she sat still without showing emotion. However, her stomach rumbled. *No, William,* she thought.

Lord Harold stood and said to the assembly, with his back towards the stage, "We need a new investigation, Witen. Clearly, the church is biased."

"We want to know where the king was!" shouted a man in the theater.

"The bell ringer claimed he bumped into a tall man!" yelled a shorter man from the other side.

Richard sought a signal from Rachel where she sat in the balcony, but she mouthed, "No, do not tell them."

"Again, as flimsy of evidence as are your spines," spat Richard. "Come here on stage and accuse me, you cockered, half-faced popinjays. All those taller than John the Short, that is—wait, all of you are taller. And you don't need to accentuate your manhood with a codpiece like he does."

John the Short, surrounded by ladies, rose and yelled, "Listen to this clotpole we have as our king. It's no secret how many whores have lifted your flap; time and time again, no son has come. Poor, poor Rachel, I apologize for Richard; it's not you, my queen. It's him."

Richard looked towards Rachel. He unfastened the family pendant of three male lions with the inscription of *duty, honor, and kingdom* and removed his purple cloak.

Rachel covered her face with a hand to shield the likely outburst from Richard, but Richard remained still. He then paced with unusual calmness and stopped at center stage.

What is he doing? Rachel thought.

A lord declared, "Silence from the king! John the Short has won this battle!"

Before slow claps built to thundering applause, Richard's chin dipped to his chest, but he managed to say, "My brother is right— we've had trouble. But I will not allow you to disparage the queen."

"Not the queen," John the Short said. "Brother, I'm mocking you."

Richard scratched the back of his neck and stared at his feet. Then, lifting his head, he grinned at his wife. "Where was I the night of the archbishop's death? I was with Queen Rachel."

Rachel squirmed, assuming he would divulge the sordid details of his infidelity.

"Stars twinkled and mist sprinkled," Richard began. "We had a fight, but how many married couples don't fight?"

Rachel's hands squeezed her thighs, and her chest tightened. What had she asked him? *Who is knocking at this hour? One of your whores?*

"Crows mocked my fright and flight from fight night; they trolled in full rolls," Richard waxed poetically. "Oh, the bells, the bells, the bells!"

A tingle shot across her chest and zoomed down her arm. Her wrist ached. *Rachel, no, don't open the door. Rachel, no, don't hurt her! He grabbed my wrist and yanked, leaving a bruise. I fell to the floor.*

"Their rhyming and chiming etched time and crime in my mind. Oh, the bells, the bells, the bells!" Richard cried. "The swinging and the ringing pounded my crown. Their clamor and clanging banged at me."

John the Short whined, "Don't buy this show, Witen. He's not sorry."

Richard lowered himself to his knees and prattled, "Too ashamed to speak, I slipped and stumbled on the wet apex of the bridge, but I found no words to release. But, oh, the bells, the bells, the bells! I straightened up and sprinted—to fret alone in my castle privy. The bells tolled."

Wincing and rubbing his chest, he begged, "Rachel, please forgive me. These ghouls still patrol my soul in the city. Please, forgive me."

The Witen were silenced—a single cough echoed through the theater.

Holding her wrist, Rachel rose from her seat.

"Don't buy this act, Rachel. He's not sorry," shouted John the Short.

"Yes, I forgive you," she said in a firm voice.

Knobs struck the benches.

"I am not a perfect king," Richard said firmly, "and this kingdom has had its challenges, but I will rise to overcome them. And with God's help, we will have a son!"

Knobs pounded and pounded the seats until the sound deafened the theater.

When the Witen had quieted their pounding, Richard asked for their blessing to march east across France, the Holy Roman Empire, and Hungary and annex Bulgarian territory to support the pope for another Crusade. "Our souls!" he chanted. "Rescue them. Save them!"

Richard smiled, stood, and strode over to Charles. From where she sat, Rachel could read Richard's lips, as she had many times before. "Do not embarrass me again, Charles. We will not have a Witen session for the foreseeable future."

Rachel hurried down to join him on stage, and they kissed for all to see. He told her quietly that he had confessed to the cardinal.

"Did you mean what you said?" she asked.

"Yes, Tulip, with all my heart."

She wanted to believe him, but she couldn't let go of the pain, of the hole in her heart from his frequent infidelity. *I did it myself once,* she rationalized. *For the greater good . . .*

"I must leave you alone for now, my love. I must prepare for war."

She frowned. "Yes, of course, Richard."

They held hands and walked off stage, but Rachel looked over her shoulder, and Charles gave her a reassuring grin.

✦————✦

Hours later, Rachel joined Padre and Charles rocking on the vineyard terrace, watching the setting sun. "Thank you for meeting me again this evening," Rachel said with a slight coloring of regret in her voice. "I'm sorry . . ."

She raised her glass of wine to her nose, where the aroma flooded in and opened up, giving its best as the blend of grapes flowed in, starting strong, and finished gently on her lips. The nectar fogged over the nagging pull that her intuition might have been wrong—perhaps she shouldn't have trusted William. She didn't know him well but knew he was determined to find the murderer because of his love for Mati.

"Yes, Your Highness. No regrets. You made the right choice."

"Thank you, Charles. I need time to think before we strategize."

"Of course, my queen," Charles said reverently.

"I'm sorry for the show this afternoon."

"It's confirmation. He's a hard man to love, but your duty to the kingdom is admirable."

"I do love him, Charles," she assured him, "but power has corrupted him. We will implement the plan. My son will become king one day."

Padre placed his hands atop Rachel's and said, "Mati approved and would continue encouraging you in this direction if he were alive."

She drank again. The word "alive" contrasted with her gut feelings of remorse and emptiness and disgust—from the night she had snuck into his bedroom, drunk off wine and high off poppies.

Fourteen years ago. He didn't know who she was at first, but she knew who he was. Preserve the bloodline and provide a legitimate heir to restore the kingdom, she had rationalized. The seduction didn't take long. Though his vision was blurry from the wine, he had recognized the confidence and aura she carried as Prince Richard's wife. The other girls in the room scurried when she entered—they knew who she was.

Her womb was fertile, but the midwives blamed her for miscarriage after miscarriage. Infuriated at having no son, Prince Richard wielded passive aggression, offering backhanded comments and direct blame that fatigued and drained her.

Pain ripped through her even stronger than the wine, and she placed pressure down low to relieve the tangle of anxiety.

They had gotten lucky once, and their daughter Isabella was a tremendous blessing.

She drank again and thought of Jeremiah. "I will see him tonight," she said confidently, her voice seeming to gain life with each syllable.

"How's your stomach, my dear?" asked Padre.

"Better now"—she pointed to the glass—"because of this."

"Would you like company in your quest? We may catch them finishing dinner."

The rocking slowed and stopped. "Thank you, Padre, but tonight I wish to venture alone."

"You are a tough one to persuade, my dear. Aye, but let us drink one more before retiring for the evening."

She twirled the rest of her wine in the glass and lowered her nose to it. Hints of lemons, lime, and apples spiraled upwards over the grape.

"I haven't thanked you enough for protecting him."

"Part of the plan. Always has been," Charles reminded her. "When should we begin training him for the crown?"

"I've tried convincing Richard to relinquish some responsibilities to the Witen. He won't."

"Though much of our power has diminished over the decades, we reserve the right to propose a new king under certain circumstances. We helped your husband come to power over his brothers."

"Yes, King Henry wouldn't have recognized the older half-brother as the legitimate heir. Richard may have grown to love power over the years, but Rohad would have been far worse."

"I can't imagine him ruling the kingdom," said Charles. "He's terrible now as a duke. Maybe Richard should move him to a duchy farther away."

The temporary comfort of the wine lost its magic. Rachel's mood and then her shoulders slumped.

"I'm sorry, my dear," said Padre.

"No, no, I remember that night. I sought forgiveness from you for the sin I was about to commit, to cheat on Richard and try to conceive with Rohad."

Clouds covering the moon broke, and the small mountain range came into view. "A sign, gentlemen," she said. "Time to depart."

"I understand, madam. I bid adieu, my dear." He kissed her right hand.

"Oh, stop it, Padre."

"Good night, Rachel."

She lowered the glass and stood. "What—no customs and courtesies from the Witen chief to your queen?"

"Not when she's drunk!" retorted Charles. "Seriously, are you in condition to walk alone tonight?"

"Yes, thank you. I'm fine. I'll take a horse."

They hugged each other farewell.

She went past the vineyard to the stables to mount her favorite horse. His ears perked and he flapped his lips in disgust. "I'm sorry," she said and rubbed his chocolate-brown chest. She brushed the copper mane from his eyes and confessed to him as she put the bridle's crown over his ears: "Part of me wishes I hadn't done it."

That stupid stone—power.

She placed the saddle on his back. Gloves went on, and she led him out of the barn. Looking past the bridge in the darkness, she wasn't watching and her boot missed the stirrup on the first attempt.

Come on, Rachel.

She pulled her hood tight and climbed onto the horse, then grabbed the reins and gave a kick. Over the bridge the wind whipped at her, and like her jabbing stomach pains, droplets pricked her cheeks.

I wanted him uncorrupted by power.

Though cold from the ride, her body remained warm and flushed from the wine. But the wine could not fill the empty pit in her stomach nor quench the longing to be reunited with her son. His visit to the castle elated her for hours, until Richard returned from France and dampened her mood.

He needed to live a normal childhood.

She kicked harder, and the horse sped over the main route through pastures and fields.

It was the right decision.

Her blood galloped, though the horse slowed to a trot once in the village.

Lights—his black-and-white house.

She wrapped the reins around a tree at the edge of the pasture.

"I won't be long, I swear," she told the horse.

She slowly walked, considered, and went the most indirect route around one row of homes, around the church, past women at the well, then towards his house.

What if they see me?

Holding a pendant just like the one she had gifted to him, she paced and breezed by their front window, briefly glimpsing a table.

She reversed her steps. *Stupid,* she thought. Spotting a tree, she clung to the trunk and spied from behind it. She could make out the family setting the table for a late dinner. Talking. Laughing. Teasing— Alf hitting Miah, stealing a figurine, running, parents shouting.

"Oh, a head full of hair and skin like mine," she blurted and immediately covered her mouth.

She sniffled and could not hold back—her cries echoed through the trees.

The mother passed by the window and checked for intruders.

Unconditional love.

Rachel beamed, yet tears strolled down her cool cheeks.

Always protective.

Sarah the Strong.

Rachel hid behind the tree until the shades were pulled. Back on the horse, she relived the interviews with various women at the village well once she had decided to conceive.

Always she had concealed herself in a veil, so the women didn't know. As soon as she met Sarah, her intuition decided: this was right. The conversations were humbly honest, the encounters effortlessly loving, and the heart and soul proved pure through the eyes.

Sarah didn't know the woman's name, but she knew he was her baby the day the woman put his swaddling basket at the doorstep.

DIFFERENT

Sarah counted coins at the kitchen table before supper.

Elfred mumbled, "Counting our money again?"

"I heard that, Elfred. We'd have more if you didn't spend it all."

"I spend it on the shop—it's called an investment."

"An investment that hasn't paid yet, Elfred. That chair was expensive to build."

Elfred called for Miah to come to him, but Miah stayed in bed. His fingers followed the etched cursive writing on the queen's pendant. The language was odd, with different letters than he knew, and strange markings.

"Our kids are probably tired of your whining," said Elfred.

Sarah laughed. "My whining—it's been your whining about the king that caused our taxes to increase. Lord Harold and his thugs ensured the last pittance was paid."

Miah snuck from the house with a flower in hand from his mother's vase. With a sense of urgency, he walked to the creek. Most trees were barren, yet single buds sprouted. With legs dangling over the bank, he skipped rocks along the surface.

Mum and Dadde often fight, he thought. He plopped a larger rock into the water. *Stupid money. Am I to blame?*

He recalled Mum's words—*An expensive investment that hasn't paid off*. The sun sank beneath the trees, and the gray sky turned darker.

"Where is Marianne?" he asked aloud. "She said sunset, right?"

His legs moved back and forth more rapidly.

He placed the flower beside him and launched more rocks, then fiddled with the others in his hands.

Where is she?

He stood, then heaved up a log and toppled it into the water.

A pain shot across his left arm, so he massaged his left breast. Clouds broke, and the sun vanished beneath the horizon.

She's not coming.

He leaned back and hurled a rock as far as he could, hurting his arm with the throw. Down the grove, through the breaking mist, he made out several figures. One had red hair, another long amber hair—a couple.

No! his mind screamed. He palmed another stone.

Am I that bad? Him over me?

Miah pictured the nearest tree was pinned with birch paper having Harry's face drawn on it. He aimed for the imagined forehead, pulled back, and threw the stone. It went high.

He tried again, but the second rock missed terribly.

The two released hands, and she hugged the boy and left with a wave to the rest.

And at the same place we were supposed to meet!

He ripped the flower petal by petal, then started up the hill towards home, hurrying to bypass the red-haired, pimple-faced monster and his friends.

The chubby thirteen-year-old boy—Harry—ordered an underling to bring a lantern closer. He scooped a large stone from the creek bed. "Look, knaves, the bastard." He threw the stone at Miah's feet, but it bounced and hit his left calf. Miah turned, and in the moonlight, Harry shone in brilliant malevolence.

"Why'd you do that?" asked Miah.

Harry's boys came closer and taunted Miah. A couple of kids came close to pull his long, brown hair, while others brushed off his sawdust-covered tunic and the rest examined his blistered hands.

"A carpenter is barely better than the peasant filth you call friends.

But not as good as a lord's son," said Harry.

"Leave me alone!" hollered Miah as he pushed them backwards.

"Look at his hair! His dark skin!" they taunted. "A bastard son! *Who* is your dadde?"

They circled him and gawked like he was a rare animal caught for experimentation. Their pale, pinkish skin and light hair was common to most in the village.

"Enough, boys," said Harry, suddenly reasonable. "Move away." He pulled a figurine from his tunic. "Look, Miah, what I found, after your stupid brother dropped it." Harry circled Miah and said, "I thought about giving this to Marianne tonight, but"—he stopped and smooched several kisses—"but my lips were a better gift."

His followers chuckled, grabbed Miah, and held him tightly. Miah tried to wrestle free but could not. They locked his arms. He screamed, but the sound didn't carry over the hill. Harry stroked Miah's cheek with the figurine and whispered into his ear, "Stay away. She's mine. My dadde says so. And he's the sheriff—so you must obey. Now tell me you'll stay away."

Miah refused.

There was more stroking and more whispers. Miah still refused, so Harry tried a different approach. "Look at you. Why would she want a bastard? Have you seen your reflection in the creek? Completely different from your parents. *An outsider.* You're not like us. Say it."

Again Miah refused.

"We'll release you. Say it. Say you'll leave her alone."

Miah refused once more and screamed louder.

"Fine!" barked Harry.

Harry used both hands and banged the figurine against a tree until she broke into multiple pieces. He returned to Miah. "Here, have your precious Marianne." He dropped the pieces of the figurine at Miah's feet.

Miah screamed and kicked Harry's thigh, but the fat kid barely reacted. His gang pulled Miah's arms backwards, and Harry walloped him in the gut.

"A kiss from Marianne, bastard." He kissed Miah on the cheek.

Miah's body convulsed violently as if he were attempting to vomit up a foreign object or sickness. Miah's lips pulled back to bare his teeth. The guttural roar sounded to all of them like the wolves that sporadically roamed the village, so they taunted Miah with howls to the moon.

Alf sprinted down the hill, yelling, interrupting the boys before they landed more blows on Miah.

"Let's go, whiflings," said Harry. "We'll suggill him black and blue another day." The boys released Miah and ran.

Miah's energy fully depleted, he writhed and twitched erratically while scrambling to recover the pieces of Marianne. Then he collapsed onto the rocks as Alf arrived. He looked at the pieces.

Miah slumped in pain from the beating and absolute defeat. Alf slung Miah's arm across his shoulders and helped him up the hill, past Lord Harold sneering and saying, "Just boys being boys."

<hr/>

There were few words at dinner except for one question. "Why do I look different?" Miah asked, raising his eyebrows in disbelief already at what they might say. His parents claimed he resembled a distant cousin, but Miah forced himself to ask the question a second time.

Sarah relented and told the truth: "A young woman left you with us when you were a newborn—I promised I would care for you as if you were my own. And I have."

Martin stuffed his mouth with his food, as usual; Sarah stared at the tabletop; Elfred twirled his food uncomfortably; and Alf kept saying he was sorry.

Miah ran to his room but soon heard Sarah's footsteps and a knock.

"Leave me alone, Mum."

"I'm sorry, Miah. Can we talk? Maybe sing your favorite song?"

"Leave me alone, Mum!" shouted Miah.

"Miah, Dadde and I love you very much. We know your natural mother loves you too."

"How do you know?" he asked with a razor-sharp bite in his voice. "She dropped me off like a package. And what about my father?"

She didn't answer.

Miah stood against the door until he heard Sarah's footsteps retreat to the kitchen.

"Let him be," said Elfred.

+———+

He lay on his bed and pretended to sleep when Alfred entered the room. Later in the night, once assured his family was asleep, he escaped to the shop. In the darkness, he found his figurines and played out the battle scenes. The dragon destroyed each opponent.

STONE

The sound of footsteps in the stone corridor increased in intensity, then stopped outside William's door. Two knocks indicated the arrival, and eight rings from the cathedral bells signaled the hour.

William's mind raced as he crossed to the door. *How could I have been so wrong?* He had reviewed his notes, examined the evidence again and again—*all clues pointed to the king*. But he didn't have a clear motive. The queen's note mentioned the king's scriptorium. *What is important about that?*

Seemingly timed to coincide with the ending bell bong, the final pound came just before William opened the door to the former Abbot James, the new Archbishop of Witenberg.

Dressed in black cassock with a double-breasted overcoat, James wore a gold pendant hung from his neck. He stood there wreathed in the scent of warm apple cider that was bitter to William in the wake of his thoughts. But he gathered himself together.

"Congratulations, Archbishop James Eames III," said William respectfully around sourness that filled his mouth. He went back to his task, folding his clothes and packing them neatly into a suitcase.

After conducting a final room inspection, the archbishop handed William a letter. "From your friend," he said. "We found it in his room the day after he died."

"And his other belongings?" asked William.

"We're leaving all in place—his room and your office, for the new investigator. The cardinal and king agreed that someone without bias—potential bias," he corrected, "should investigate. Someone outside the clergy."

The bitterness in his heart flared, and acid burned deep in his throat. He dry-heaved, and pinches of pain squeezed across his chest, like his muscles were tightening into a noose—a noose he had created.

"Perhaps wait to open the letter until you are in Rome?" said Eames. "It's warmer there, and far away . . ."

"Thank you, but I can manage." He stuffed it into this coat pocket.

"Leave your bags here until after the funeral. You will leave here for Rome in Cardinal Conti's carriage."

William dropped his bags and skulked past Eames into the corridor. His body tightened at the reminder of his demotion, but perhaps a few years with the cardinal would help him solve the case, he hoped.

"I'll see you at the funeral, Archbishop."

"Aren't you forgetting something, Father William?"

William handed his keys to Eames and made the slow walk from the abbey to the cathedral. *Strange*, he thought as he looked up to the clock tower. The funeral was not for an hour.

His steps quickened, and then he sped into the cathedral. It was empty. For a last time, he tried the handle to his office, but it wouldn't budge. *A positive memory may help*, he thought, so he walked to the side chapel.

He stood in the same spot where he and Mati had practiced singing "Benedetta Maria." The satin of violin strings, then Mati's voice with his in perfect harmony resonated in his ears. He could taste the richness of the voice in his own mouth: roasty and creamy, with heavy hints of honey.

In this state of relaxation, he spied the open grotto door. Candlelight snaked up the spiral staircase, inviting William down.

Past the statues of Mary and David, his steps quickened with his heartbeat as he heard someone else. *Someone is wearing sandals*, he thought. The light guided him to the treasury. The door was open, and he heard a voice. A boy's voice, with the cracks of adolescence?

116

"I assumed the grotto would be closed for the funeral," the boy said. He was not tall, but he looked older than he sounded. In a corner against the wall, the boy knelt. An older man in a tunic stood behind the fenced glass case and said, "I thought he planned to return it?"

At the sound of the creaking door, the boy rose suddenly, then he stood still in fright. "Who goes there?" asked the older man.

"Who are you?" asked William as he teetered on his toes. "And you?" he asked the boy. "How'd you get in? This place is off-limits."

As the man said the grotto door had been open, William remembered he had forgot to lock it after returning to the cathedral from the scriptorium.

"I'm Padre, the priest from Our Lady parish across the river. This is Jeremiah."

The boy relaxed slightly, yet tension stressed the shape of his mouth as his head turned impatiently.

"You can't be here. We need to leave."

"Why were *you* here?" asked Padre.

"I'm Father William, the investigator . . ." He paused and lowered his head. "I was the investigator for the archbishop's murder. Has anyone else been here?"

"We didn't see anyone," Padre said sheepishly. "I wanted the young man to see the stone before the funeral."

The boy kept shooting furtive glances towards the door and said glumly, "I hoped to see it."

William ushered them through the treasury into the corridor and through the grotto. "Many people are after the missing stone, Jeremiah." *And I will find his killer*, he thought.

Upstairs, William found people had begun to fill the cathedral, and he sat in a chair beside the Night Watchers. Padre and the boy walked to the rose-window side of the church and waited. Across the aisle, the boy stared at a lovely girl sitting beside her mother—they had a shared beauty.

Though he wanted nothing more than to scream and curse and launch the pain in his stomach onto her, Miah remembered the broken figurine and his years of dreaming about her. The pain temporarily vanished as he saw her amber curls and numerous freckles. She smiled at him, and he forgot about the rejection as the funeral Mass began.

Or was it me? he wondered. *Did I hear correctly? The right time, the right place? Maybe it was my fault?*

Cardinal Conti climbed the wooden pulpit and rested. He removed a cloth from his pocket and wiped his hands and mouth exactly three times.

After watching the ritual of the man waiting, moving his hands, waiting, moving his hands, Miah became restless.

"Mum"—he tugged her sleeve—"I need to use the privy. I won't be long."

"You can wait until after the homily, Miah."

Miah sank into gloom and accepted his fate.

"Brothers and sisters, we come here today to celebrate the life of a truly wonderful man, almost a brother to me," started the cardinal. Each word carried the same level of flatness and speed. "His warmth, his laughter, his smile, his love for you and the church truly impacted each of your lives. He was a living reflection of God's love. We also come to bury him and celebrate his life."

I don't believe much of this—don't think he does, either, Miah thought.

Conti paused and readied to raise his voice. "It troubles me, however, brothers and sisters, that the archbishop was not everything we believed he was."

The congregation rumbled, and many now straightened in their chairs. Those half-asleep awakened. Miah also stirred but in another way. He fidgeted between calming his urge and tugging Sarah's tunic.

"Fine—go, but be quiet," she whispered.

Miah escaped from the chair and sped down the side aisle. Into the privy he went, then poised himself over the hole in the board.

Over the insistent stream and then the trickles, he heard some of the sermon.

"The archbishop, as you know, had recently been preaching homilies contrary to Church doctrine . . ."

Then came the loud, from-the-diaphragm sigh.

"Homilies encouraging you to disobey the teachings of the Church, to find your own path and relationship with God . . ."

With his bladder empty, a smile lagged across Miah's face until he rearranged his tunic and hosen and rested in the relief.

"If you are not on guard, a lion from the forest will attack, a wolf from the desert will ravage, a leopard will lie in wait to tear you to pieces—because your rebellion is great."

Miah left the privy and the door slammed as he heard the cardinal pound the pulpit and shout, "The devil is real! Repent or go to Hell!"

As he came back from the privy, he heard people gasp, and some covered their mouths. The archbishop paused for several moments, until everyone stood.

Perfect opportunity, Miah thought.

"We will remember the archbishop as a kind, loving man, but we cannot forget he attempted to upset the Church order. We are trying to unify the entire kingdom, and more importantly, save people's souls."

As the last of the congregation stood, Miah ran down the aisle and opened the grotto door. He took the stairs three at a time and ran to the treasury. He foraged through discarded pilgrim tunics and broken rocks.

Where is it?

There!

He tossed the tunics and dug the stone from its hole in the corner behind the treasury door. It was smooth and rolled around in his hands. He took it near to a candle.

The stone glowed in the light, but it glowed of itself too. Footsteps sounded in the hallway, and he quickly stuffed the stone into a pocket.

"What are you doing? Weren't you in the privy?" asked Marianne.

She has been watching me!

With glossy eyes, he greeted her.

"What were you doing?" she asked, leaning closer and inspecting the candle.

The stone warmed his hand in his pocket.

"What do you have?" She tried to dig her hand into his pocket.

He turned a shoulder. "Oh, it's nothing." High on the energy from the stone and from her, he kissed her cheek.

She slapped him and cried, "Miah! Come on, let's go back to the church."

Miah rubbed his cheek, smiled, and took her hand. In the grotto, they stopped. "Wait," said Miah.

He peered from behind the Mary statue. The priest he had just met was there, pulling his hood over his head. He lit incense and said, "Dragon's milk."

Dragon's milk?

Pine, Arabic sandalwood musk, and amber smoke covered his body in a fog. William unfolded something he had pulled from his pocket. It was a letter.

"N-no," he stuttered.

Marianne buried her head into Miah's chest in fright as they both watched red blotches scatter across William's pale-as-cream skin. William convulsed in terror and tried to speak, but his throat clogged.

The letter escaped his grasp and floated in slow motion to the stone. In a fury, he removed all the letters in his pockets and shredded them. He shivered violently and clenched his hands, with flared nostrils and bared teeth.

Miah felt one of his hands clutch his stomach and the other protectively brush Marianne's curls. "Don't look," he told her.

William threw out his arms.

Miah took Marianne's hand and guided her away through the grotto. As they wound around the spiral stairs, they heard the booming voice: "No, no, l-l-longer. No longer! I'm no longer Father William! Stutter, go to Hell!"

MARCH

"Aren't you saying goodbye?" asked Elfred from the doorway of the shop.

Miah continued to move figurines across his workbench. "I already said goodbye to him," he said tonelessly.

"Let's go, Son," said Elfred.

Miah dragged himself to open the chest and stowed away all the figurines but the dragon.

"Stupid war," he said under his breath.

Outside the shop, soldiers were marching and singing songs while onlookers clapped. The rhythmic pounding of boots matched the repetitive knocks of woodpeckers against the trees.

Alf led his squad to the grove and stopped near the water mill. The formation clicked their heels to attention, then relaxed to parade rest. Miah and Elfred joined Sarah atop the hill and scrutinized several groups of young men eager to fight for unification.

The Church had blessed the mission to fight for heathen souls. King Richard had bypassed the Witen a day after the archbishop's funeral; the kingdom approved with voice votes—parades in each city, lords rallying their villages, and clergy preaching conversion to their parishes the ensuing week.

Except Padre. He disobeyed all authorities.

Miah wandered the grove, looking for his beloved priest. He came to a tree where something caught his eye among last fall's leaves—a piece of the Marianne figurine. His heart ached briefly, but then he remembered the stone.

Miah took the hill and ran into the house, where he unwrapped the cloth and held the stone.

"At least I have this," he said, his voice desolate but with notes of wonder and pride. Alf's rescue popped into his mind but vanished as soon as he heard the horn.

He stepped outside the house.

The war had begun.

Formations broke, formed two lines, and marched to the sound of drums. Rampant blue lions sailed high on academy graduates' flags.

Before the people dispersed, Lord Harold sounded another horn. He announced that King Richard had appointed his office as the new investigator, and his staff would commence the search for the stone.

As his parents watched for Alfred until he vanished among the tangled miles of trees and hillsides, Miah snuck to the shop with the stone in his pocket. He considered hiding it in his chest among his figurines but then had second thoughts.

With no one looking, he dug for the secret box buried in the ground only he and his father knew about, a box that hid a key to the shop. There he could keep the stone safe.

PART II

SIX YEARS LATER
FEBRUARY 1198

BROTHERLY ANGER

As Jeremiah dipped a thin brush into a small pot of black dye, the fragrance of something floral entered the shop. And then she did.

"I heard your dadde will speak again at the guild council," said Marianne. "What will he complain about this time?"

In light brush strokes, he painted curly whiskers onto the dragon's cheeks. "Can't you see I'm busy?"

"Aren't I making your day, little Miah?" she said gaily.

"You know I go by Jeremiah."

"Oh, Jeremiah, huh?"

She leaned against a pillar, and over a raised shoulder she gave him a sideways glance. She raised onto her toes to reach a light-warrior figurine, but it was beyond her fingertips.

The brush fell from his fingers, and he kicked the stool over as he jumped. "Stop touching my stuff," he said, suddenly beside her and aware of the thin, flat slippers she wore. "And why aren't you wearing boots?" He noticed he was a head taller.

Her floral scent covered him like a warm blanket. His stomach fluttered, but his tone remained flat. "Can you move, please?"

She broke eye contact, drooped her gaze down, then directly up again to lock onto his eyes. Stepping aside, she said, "Oh, I'm sorry. A big boy, Jeremiah. I see, from all the toys around the shop."

She pulled out a stool and sat at the bench beside where he had been working.

"These are for children," he said gruffly and stood the figurine upright.

"All of them?"

He opened his mouth, but no words came. He appraised her. "Your hair is longer. And new clothes from the market? Still rummaging about in Harry's pockets, are you?"

"You're just jealous," she said and lifted a small piece of wood full of curving lines.

"Jealous of what? His money? His fiery hair? His unibrow?"

She raised her brows. "Funny—hilarious, *Miah*. Seriously, this piece of lumber reminds me of something, but I can't remember."

"Too much mead again last night with one of your boyfriends?"

"Jeremiah, stop messing around."

He snatched the piece of wood from her and smoothed a finger along its lines. "This is scrap from the chair I made for the cardinal. Very proud of it."

"Rather, very prideful. The last time you and I were in the cathedral treasury together? At the archbishop's funeral? You mustered the courage to kiss me, though only on the cheek." She hopped off the stool and roamed around the shop, playing with tools and turning her head to ensure Jeremiah followed.

"It was a fine kiss for a thirteen-year-old boy madly in love," he said.

"Yes, so innocent. I was surprised by it and have wondered why you haven't pursued me again."

"Pursue you again?" he exclaimed. "You've been all I've dreamed about these past few years . . ."

"Besides the carpentry business and my brother," he added miserably. Many long nights he had spent in the shop to avoid the house and the pain of hearing Alf wail at the nightmares that roared through his mind after he returned from the War of Unification.

"Yes, it seems you only think about wood." She pushed her hips forward at an angle and put her weight on one leg. With one hand against a wood pile, she used the other to twirl her amber curls.

He slammed the wood into the ground. "Stop. You know he

deserves our care. Alfred displays no physical scars, but mentally he returned different."

She straightened and said, "You're right. I'm sorry—just trying to lighten the mood of this place." She went to him and cupped her hands over his. "Since Alfred's return, this place hasn't been the same. Gloomier. There were casualties, Jeremiah, but not many. And the war did unite the kingdom, far and wide."

"Is that what your lord tells you?" he snapped.

She removed her hands. "I'm not a simple artist who enjoys pretty things, like you. Yes, before the war, we were many scattered fiefdoms, each duchy and county ruling on its own without direction from the king. We've added a duchy next to vital land—Constantinople and the Dark Sea."

"The king planned the war and used fear to drum up support for his death campaign," he said.

"I've had enough of this nonsense." Her sudden about-face kicked up sawdust from the floor.

Through coughs, he added, "Many men died, Marianne, and women and children became widows and orphans."

"I'm leaving, Jeremiah."

"Good—have fun at the mead ball with Lord Oaf."

"He and I aren't going, thank you very much. We're going our own ways for a time."

Without thinking, the impulse came: "So you need a date?" he asked faintly, expecting a "no" but hoping for a "yes."

Her slippers slid on the sawdust, and her hands braced against the door. She turned and studied him, and her slightly parted lips opened to show her teeth. "Yes, Jeremiah, I will go with you. But don't get any ideas."

Through the open door, Jeremiah saw Harry and Lord Harold had been watching. They kicked at their horses and rode away.

Jeremiah had been a loner. He could not see any of the other girls—he dreamed only of Marianne. And here was an opportunity.

The remaining workday was unproductive, except for drafting on birch paper the feelings he'd had for her over the years. It didn't take long to write. He was inspired, and the words flowed in less than an hour, but he basked in the thoughts the rest of the afternoon.

Agitated by it all, Jeremiah trotted to the house and babbled the news to his father too fast, so that Elfred couldn't understand the jumbled words. The young man's cheeks were still flushed, his eyes wide and glowing, and Elfred offered a handshake as more appropriate than a hug.

"Congratulations, Son. Marianne has become a fine young lady. But I don't want you to get hurt."

"Dadde, this will be different. I have one evening to impress her."

Elfred scratched his full beard and tapped an index finger against his lip. "You'll need folk dance lessons, but Mum can teach you. You'll also need a horse. I'll ask at the meeting to help with that."

Jeremiah stepped back in to embrace him.

<hr />

That evening Jeremiah and Elfred walked to the large building beside the water mill. Made of wood from the local forest and stone from the nearby quarry, the meeting house was the place for villagers to discuss local town affairs, make decisions, and drink. And when the guilds met, as the carpenters did this night, they included artisans who had traveled from elsewhere in the kingdom. Elfred took his stand in front of the fireplace, and Jeremiah sat.

The usual ceremonial activities commenced, from the beginning prayer, to pledging allegiance to the kingdom, to recognizing visitors. "Thank you for joining us to do the guild's business," began Elfred. "I know many of you traveled a good distance to come here. I hope you're enjoying our delicious beer and mead, made close to the castle."

"Tastes like the king's arse!" shouted one carpenter.

"Yeah," yelled a master craftsman. "Does his scite fertilize the hops, and his urine add a little something to the water?"

"I'm certain the abbey beer is made from the same ingredients," a third man said.

"Enough," said Elfred. "We all have balls."

All hooted and hollered, their discontent dampened—at least temporarily. "Let's get on with tonight's agenda. I will first recognize my son."

Elfred summoned Jeremiah to the stage. "As you know, this is my last meeting as master. My son has become a master craftsman and was duly elected as the new guild master. It is time for his installation."

After Jeremiah recited an oath, Elfred placed his hand on Jeremiah's left shoulder and raised his pint of beer to signal the praise could begin. "Hear ye, hear ye, Jeremiah. Huzzah!"

Guild members raised their mugs, then slammed them on the long, wooden tables before finishing the contents.

Jeremiah returned to his seat.

"I'm proud of you, Son," said Elfred. To the guild, he added, "And my son is also going to his first mead ball."

As guild members softly pounded the tables in support with their mugs, Elfred asked them to fund a horse for a night. They responded with another slam of their mugs and a passing of a collection basket.

With his chin high and in a strong stance with his chest out, Elfred made eye contact with individuals across the room, rather than gazing vaguely at them all.

"I know many of you are tired of current economic conditions. Many of us supported the king in his attempt to unify the kingdom. I know the considerable cost of—" Elfred stopped abruptly and slumped. After a moment, he regained his posture and confidence. "But this hasn't stopped us from supporting the king, and, for that matter, the pope. They desired kingdom unification under one king and one God."

Some men nodded, some looked down and shook their heads, and some stared impassively, waiting for whatever would come next.

"However, like many things in life, the pendulum has swung too far, and the king and pope have too much control over our lives. Our money has devalued, and despite promises of security, we have unrest in the outlying regions."

"All true, all true," called out a man near the front, "but what will we do about it? The guild's influence has waned over the years as the king's knights and dukes have grown in power. The carpenter class has lost our voice."

"Right!" slurred a drunkard. "Our class has suffered, paid higher taxes, but the merchant class hasn't."

"That's because the merchant guild master is the king's right-hand man," yammered an older man.

"Yeah! Bollocks to George of Bath," griped a carpenter. "Master, let's take care of ourselves."

A drunk man stood and yelled, "Witen *you*! Let's ally with the king. We need help in the farthest regions. Money has dried up, and we need more for investment."

Elfred placed his hands on his hips and offered his solution. "We have two choices, brothers. We curry favor with the king and his court or work against the king to return power to local levels."

The room silenced. The men looked at each other, looked at their empty mugs, and looked at Elfred. "Like at all meetings," Elfred said, "we'll vote on a direction and decide the strategy after we choose. We'll adjourn and come back at half past the hour to vote."

Elfred sat down and reclined into his chair without giving his own recommendation.

Though he was more focused on the ball than any of the politics, Jeremiah observed a combination of anger and fear in the hall, no doubt a dangerous mix when combined with alcohol. *Common sense will disappear with the ale.*

An hour later, Elfred stood with the announcement. "We've tallied the votes, and by a margin of two to one, we will continue supporting the king."

Elfred turned to gesture towards Jeremiah, urging him to stand. "Our new master will work with you over the next few meetings to plot our strategy."

Elfred left the stage with a shrug of his shoulders. "Your turn to fight, Son. Let's get your horse tomorrow. Let's go home."

———

The two men dragged themselves wearily into the darkened house and into bed, then in the morning they rented a horse from the village stables, did their usual chores, and set to their work of the day before there was any opportunity to discuss the events of the previous evening.

A light wind carried a roasting pork aroma to the shop as the men left that afternoon. As they walked past Sarah rotating the pig on a spit, she called out, "Help me in the kitchen, Son," and pointed through the open door to the cupboard. He dragged his feet as he had always done, and she noted, "You may be the guild master now, but you are still needed about the house."

Trying to take on his dual roles with some grace, Jeremiah set the table as he waited for his parents' conversation.

Elfred escorted his wife inside and shut the door, then stood beside Sarah at the thick veneer countertop as they'd done for years. His own position as guild master didn't make him too important to help, Jeremiah noted, even when they were angry. His parents stood close to each other while preparing the family meal, but with enough eye rolls and silent treatment to freeze the entire kingdom.

"What's wrong, Elfred?" asked Sarah.

"Oh nothing, sweetheart."

Elfred sliced carrots, but the knife kept missing.

"I know when you're upset," she said and opened a palm. "Let me have that."

The blade dropped, and Elfred watched it spin a few rotations on the table.

"You stop speaking and turn to your work when there's trouble," she said. "I haven't heard a word from you all day. What happened at the guild council?"

"Yes, you know me too well"—he smiled and kissed her, a fast peck—"but I don't want to discuss politics at supper."

She lowered her head and stared with penetration, and Jeremiah took it all in.

"The guild decided to support the continued centralization of the king's power."

"And how will this affect the business? Our money? The children's inheritance?"

"You'll be fine with your knight," quipped Martin as he snorted up from a doze, leaning in his chair against the hearth.

"Not now, Dad," she said forcefully. "Mind your business."

Elfred pressed thumb and finger into his eyelids and then down his cheeks to his chin. "We are fine, honey, but I'm afraid there will be more war. The guild thinks war benefits business because there will be more customers with the expansion of the kingdom."

He turned to where Jeremiah was shelling peas in a bowl Sarah had left on the table for him. "Son, this will all be yours. " He laughed grimly.

The door opened with simultaneous friendly knocking, and Padre entered.

Sarah pulled her long, brown hair into a bun, brushed carrot shreds from her blouse, and walked over to hug Padre. "So good to see you, Padre."

"Good to see you too, Sarah the Strong. Your radiance always brightens my day."

"That's only her freckles blinding you, Padre," Elfred said, his voice coming tired and dreary.

Trailing Padre, Lord Alfred and his wife, Lady Thèrèse, carried their four-year-old daughter, Maren, into the house.

"Grandpa!" Maren said gaily and leapt into his arms. "See what Mumma did to my hair."

"Very pretty," Elfred said, with more life in his voice. "Show your grandmum too."

"Son, so good to see you!" Elfred called. He looked about for a small task and set the cutting board and knife on the table. "Please take over."

Alfred slowly lowered himself to his childhood spot on the bench and took the knife. Soon it wobbled, and Sarah calmly removed it from his hand and said, "Get the pig instead, Son."

Alfred left the kitchen and soon returned with a great tray and the good-sized pig and set it on the table.

"Good to see you, Padre," Alfred said without emotion, as if his little family hadn't followed the priest into the house just minutes earlier. "I don't believe I thanked you for the prayers before I left for the war." With vacancy in his eyes, Alfred seemed to have been transported somewhere else. He added, "Probably saved my life."

"You're welcome. But not me—God. Thank Him."

A sudden twitch of anxiety, a look that preluded panic, creased the outer corner of Alfred's eyes, but Padre placed his hands on the younger man's shoulders. "It's fine, Son."

From where he sat quietly shelling the beans, Jeremiah observed it all.

Alfred snapped to the present and abruptly released himself from Padre.

Thèrèse took his shaking arm and said, "Let healers help with your memories."

Alfred's shoulders tightened against her, and he seemed to shake something out of his head. "Where's Jeremiah?" he asked, coming back to himself.

"I've been here since you arrived, Alfred."

"I'm sorry, I didn't see you. Were you playing in your room?"

Jeremiah, never able to stand his ground with Alfred, got up and blustered past his brother. "Funny, Alfred. Funny." He ignored the others and went to his room.

"Jeremiah," called Sarah. "Don't be gone long. It's time to eat."

"A few moments, Mum."

Jeremiah sat on his bed and unwrapped the blue cloth holding the stone. Its light mesmerized him and drew his fingernails into its crevices. He palmed it, but its warmth quickly faded, and the smile it had brought to him sank into a frown. He carefully wrapped it again and hid it under his bed.

"Smells brilliant, Mum," he said, returning to the kitchen. "Hello, Padre," he said with a bite in his voice. The priest hadn't even acknowledged him when he came in. "Where have you been lately?"

"In the outlying capital parish, Jeremiah. I've invited you several times to visit, but you've never showed."

Jeremiah avoided eye contact and said briskly as he sat at the table, "Too busy with work."

"Miah . . . ," said Alfred.

"Jeremiah," he rebuked him sharply.

"Jeremiah," repeated Alfred, his voice sincere and earnest. "Each time we visit, you sneak away—to your room, to your shop . . ."

"Because of work," he replied and shot a look of venom towards Alfred. *He knows just where to dig at me.* "Hi, Maren. Hi, Thérèse."

Maren stared at Jeremiah with wide eyes and went up to touch his face as if he were a stranger. His heart softened, but Thérèse promptly pulled back the girl's hand from her uncle.

Jeremiah had always found an excuse to avoid them, so his niece didn't even know him.

Now twenty-four years old, the once-immature Alfred who mercilessly teased his brother had raised a family. On numerous occasions, Alfred had invited Jeremiah to his home, but Jeremiah declined and continued to hold a grudge.

"Jeremiah, apologize to Alfred—now," Sarah said firmly.

"For what?"

"Your coldness to Alfred and his family."

"Coldness? Alfred calls me a boy's name. He left me, and he's been gone so long, he doesn't even—" he said tensely, stopping. He fiddled with his hands. But inside, bottled-up anger bubbled to the surface. "Never mind. Can we eat?" he asked.

The family joined hands, and Padre blessed the food.

"So, your father told me about Marianne," said Sarah to Jeremiah while cutting the pig. "And a horse? A big day—your first mead ball."

"Mum," he said with a break in his voice, "can we not talk about it?" He looked towards Alfred, searching for the slightest mockery. Alfred's eyes glittered wickedly but briefly, then he stopped Maren's hands from grabbing at the pig.

"Congrats, little brother," said Alfred in bored amusement, as he cut the pork into smaller chunks for his daughter and plated bread for her.

"Dadde," whined Maren, "I don't want the bread."

"You've had it before, Maren."

"But I don't like it now, Dadde," said Maren and stood on her seat.

"If you don't eat all of it," said Jeremiah irritably, "you won't get as much when you visit next time."

She put hands on her hips, bobbed her head side to side, and said, "That's fine."

"Maren," said Thérèse in a saintly voice, "please sit and eat. When we get home, you can play with your dolls."

"Yes, Mummy," she said obediently and sat down to her food.

"Bribing the princess, I see," said Jeremiah, his voice low, threatening, "so she gets what she wants."

"You're the one to talk," said Alfred quickly but stopped before saying the word.

"My figurines, Alfred? Or, rather, my *dolls*?" said Jeremiah coldly and left the table.

"Jeremiah, come back," said Sarah. "Elfred, get him."

Through a snort, Martin said, "Yes, Elfred, fetch the real princess."

Jeremiah went in and shut his bedroom door, crouched on the floor, and grabbed the stone underneath the bed. Then he stormed out of the house and barreled down the hill to his shop.

"Jeremiah," shouted Alfred from atop the hill, "come on, I'm sorry. Can't we just eat?"

"Leave me alone," snapped Jeremiah. He slammed the shop door.

"What's wrong with you?" came the voice through the door a few moments later. And then Alfred opened it. "You always do this! Running away!"

Jeremiah sat at his workbench and fiddled with his figurines. "Leave me alone, Alfred. I don't want to talk."

Alfred stood at the door resolutely with his arms crossed. "What's wrong?" he asked casually.

"You don't care—go to your family."

"I'm not leaving until you tell me."

Jeremiah swiveled the chair, the bottled-up loneliness brimming from his body. "For years, you fought a stupid war."

Alfred's hand trembled, and his voice rose in an air of righteousness. "Stupid war? What about the kingdom, the greater good? Heathens converting to Christianity?"

"By force and blood," retorted Jeremiah. "You saved others, but you left me behind."

"That's why you haven't spoken to me? Mad at me for leaving?"

"I needed a brother!" thundered Jeremiah.

Alfred's hands clenched into a fist. "Always about you. What about visiting your niece? You're a ghost to her. When was your last visit? I want you to come back and apologize to me openly—to both of them."

Jeremiah's head jolted back. "For what? Calling you out? Your glory, Alfred? Wrapped in a cloak of glory? Pleasing the corrupt, power-consuming king? The guild just voted to give the king even more power."

Alfred's wrist snapped down with an accusing finger. "Miah, stop."

Elbows on the bench, leaning forward, Jeremiah ordered in a low growl, "Stop telling me what to do, Brother. Glory only paints others red."

"Miah, stop."

"No. Why fight, Alfred? For glory? You got that in battle. Duty? Is that it? Duty to the Crown, to honor? Duty destroyed you before the war," Jeremiah said in disgust. "Oh, Isabella," he said lightly with a strong bite in his voice.

Alfred moved into a fighting stance. "Don't go there, Miah."

Raising his voice, Jeremiah said harshly, "You chose duty over your true love. You didn't fight for her."

Red as the scorched pig, Alfred marched towards Jeremiah with hands out to throttle him.

Jeremiah shifted and clutched a hammer. As he raised the hammer in the air, Elfred thundered through the door.

"What's going on?" he exploded. "Jeremiah, put the hammer down!"

"You know what, Miah?" said Alfred, safe with their father's presence. "I'm glad Harry broke your Marianne doll." Laughing scornfully, Alfred continued, "And you a fighter? How many times did girls reject you? How many times did I protect you?"

Elfred slammed his fist on the bench. "Enough, Sons. Enough! I've had enough. We *will* enjoy the meal, like we used to years ago."

"I'm not hungry," said Jeremiah defiantly. "I'm staying here."

"Apologize to each other," said Elfred urgently.

Their extended silence signified truce.

"Fine. That will do for now, but I want you to formally apologize in my presence this evening."

Alfred stomped away to the house, and Elfred followed.

From dusk through the night, Jeremiah sat at his workbench in dim candlelight, fondling the stone and dreaming of the mead ball. When Alfred and his family departed, Jeremiah waved farewell from a distance.

SCRIPTORIUM

William looked up at the clouds blanketing the sky as he swung his wooden-soled shoes from the carriage door and dug into familiar dirt.

In the dampness of winter, the sight of the cathedral startled him, like jumping into cold waters and recoiling at the immediacy of the sensation. He recalled his last visit six years ago when he had read Mati's letter and its forceful condemnation of a man's love for a man. This devastated him to his core, an essence he felt couldn't change.

The carriage departed, and William took the path that led him to the Night Watchers' front door.

He stroked each side of his mustache in an upward curl. His tufted beard showed gray in spots, and his hair was longer. But he was still himself. He knocked.

And knocked.

"I remember now," he said. He pulled the rope, and the bell rang. The door opened, and a hat greeted William, the man hidden below it.

"Saint," said Fuss with open arms. "Thank you for answering our call. We've missed you." After a brief hug, Fuss continued. "And not a moment too soon. We need you to investigate."

William dropped his bags and draped his coat over an arm. "I'm sorry, Brother Fuss, but that's not my assignment. Remember, I was stripped of that duty."

"What were you doing all this time in Rome, then?"

"Writing. Here . . ." He handed him a note. "From the Curia for the abbot. The pope has ordered all brothers to cease from their duties and become scribes."

Fuss's huff sounded like he was gargling water. He drew in a dramatic breath and said gallantly, "If the pope has ordered."

William looked down the narrow hall. The Night Watchers' room had become packed with beds—almost double the normal occupancy.

"We will be obedient," said Fuss. "But—only some of us. Follow me."

"Where are we going?"

"To your bed. But first"—Fuss stopped him—"remove your shoes. We can't have the sickness again."

William lowered to a knee and untied one shoe, then the other, and held them out.

"Take a rag," Fuss pointed. "We clean daily and walk around here in just our leggings."

"Sickness? What sickness?"

"A few brothers died of a sickness several years ago. So did many in the city. A terrible time after the war. So many suffered." He removed his hat and parted the flattened remaining tufts of hair. "Many men came here."

"Even Stinky Feet got shoes?"

"Yes, I ordered him to. Speaking of shoes, have you had yours for a bit?" asked Fuss, inspecting them. "Time for a new pair?"

Though the heels had lost some binding, William said, "No, they're fine—but, maybe a new shine."

"You will go with Stinky Feet when he visits the city. For a well-dressed man like yourself, you will get new shoes to match."

The once-familiar scent of dirt and wine wafted in through the open door. As he walked down the hall, William's chest felt heavy, so heavy that his soul felt like it was sinking down his torso, down his legs, and down to the stone floor and into the abbey's foundation. His body urged him to rock back and forth on his toes, but he had learned to quiet this habit while in Rome.

They stopped at a bed.

"I'm sorry, but the top bunk is yours."

William threw his bag and coat on the bed.

"And the shoes?"

"Put them next to the chest on the mat. After you've settled in, meet me in my office."

William shivered and unpacked his belongings into the chest. Neatly folded tunics were stacked one on top of the other. The bound notebook he had used for the initial investigation thudded onto the floor with the pope's manuscript. He still didn't know the killer, despite the assistance he'd given to Cardinal Lothar Conti of Segni, now Pope Innocent III.

William had left Witenberg with Conti, eager for Rome and its warmer, sunnier days. But more so, he wanted an escape.

He poured his heart into Conti's manuscripts on misery, human nature, and governance. Working with legal scholars and theologians, he drafted, composed, and edited. After years of close collaboration, he mustered the courage to ask these men about Mati's time in Rome and his unsuccessful bid to become a cardinal. The man he once knew materialized, a man that hadn't changed in Rome nor in his assignment to Witenberg.

William formed hypotheses, investigated, and gathered evidence, but the picture developed blurry. When the puzzle pieces connected to Conti, the current pope, he stopped answering questions. Too busy, he said. Finally, William was reassigned, and he had returned to Witenberg. Rather than hold a grudge against Mati, he had vowed to find Mati's murderer.

+———+

"What is that?" asked William as he walked into Fuss's office. "A new look?"

"For you, yes. Not for me. Let's see how it fits." Fuss removed the wide-brimmed black hat from his head and gave it to William. "Fits perfectly."

He ran his hand over the felt and cocked-up right side. *Genteel* came to mind.

"I don't think this is me, Fuss."

"Certainly, it is. And you will wear it as you investigate."

"Listen, Fuss," said William as he placed the hat on the desk, "I'm not investigating. I'm a scribe now."

"Tell me about Rome," said Fuss, arms crossed and shoulders back against the chair. William thought he saw his ears perk up.

Drawn to the rounded puffiness of the determined Fuss, William felt images of a fight resurface. The heaviness that had rolled into the abbey floor lifted and caught at his tongue. He wasn't going to share his feelings for Mati, nor tell of the bias the abbot—now archbishop—had accused him of, nor reveal the feelings of rage he'd had when he had read Mati's letter.

Now that he was back at the abbey, something came clear—something didn't make sense. In his gut, in his heart, he wanted to believe—no, he did believe, that Mati wouldn't have used damning words against the likes of him.

Who wrote the letter, then?

Maybe I should investigate, he thought. *Why did this never come clear to me in Rome?*

"You know you want to investigate," said Fuss. "You can scribe part of the day and rejoin the old team." His voice went up in a hopeful rise of pitch at the last words.

William's tongue untwisted and his jaw relaxed. His whole body became light, weightless—so weightless that his soul seemed to rise and rest at the low, arched ceiling. He was floating, swaying like grass dancing in the wind, like reeds—

Reeds! He remembered the king's scriptorium and the queen's meeting spot.

"I wondered if she found anything," said William.

"*She*, Father William? What are you talking about?"

His neck flinched in a spasm, and he caught himself before

revealing too much. "A woman I met in Rome, Fuss."

"You're right," he said, changing the subject by taking up the hat. "I do want to investigate. But what about the king's investigator? Where is he? Did he find anything?"

"No. I heard he reexamined the same evidence you found, but he couldn't prove anything. After a few years of searching relentlessly, combing the villages and capital, Lord Harold and his men didn't find the stone. With no stone and no leads, the king dismissed him as investigator. There has been replacement after replacement with no further clues. The case has gone cold."

"And the archbishop?" asked William.

"Eames told the congregation the stone hadn't been found because of people's rebellion. The city needed to repent."

"Sounds like the pope," William uttered, but Fuss heard him and agreed with a nod.

"Correct, but we can be assured the Holy See has a team looking for the stone."

Fuss stood and beckoned. "I have an idea. I'll show you your new office—a place a little warmer."

They put on galoshes by the door and walked to the winery. "I don't understand, Fuss. I've already been here." They bypassed the front door, and Fuss pointed to a brick arched entrance nearby. Fuss pulled the handle, and the round door swung open. "Haven't you noticed the winery was built on a hill? This is the ground floor. The ice pit, where we keep the fall's harvest, is beneath the floor."

William's attention was immediately drawn to rows of pillars that never seemed to end.

"I thought you said it'd be warm, Fuss."

"It will be."

Fuss led William across the central corridor and stopped at a large furnace and a brick pipe. "The pipe goes to the first floor and connects with the chimney. The same fireplace extends to the one in the winery."

William's memory flashed to first seeing Cracky's ashen face contorting as he bent to place kindling on logs underneath several cauldrons. He had not seen where Cracky had gotten the fire starter.

"We're not all hot air, Father William. It wasn't the wine nor the singing and dancing that heated the winery. It was this. And now, this is yours—to build your hall for writing, for your scriptorium."

William paced the corridors, outlining tasks in his head, building a mental list of supplies, and inspecting the room for flaws. "Yes, this will work," he said. "You mentioned a trip to the city?"

"Yes. Let's find Stinky Feet and give your note from the Curia to the abbot. He'll approve, but we will ask him for money to build the scriptorium."

"Do we tell him about the investigation?" asked William.

"No," Fuss said sharply, "it's wise to keep this between you, me, and Stinky Feet."

＊———＊

"What's the matter?" Stinky Feet asked as they left the abbey and moved towards the city. Leaving the cobblestone plaza, Stinky Feet led William past the cathedral and narrow alleyway that opened into a street and the city's bath house.

"Nothing," William said distractedly, thinking through the possible reasons why Fuss had told him to keep the investigation a secret. "It's good to be back."

He took in the changes to the city. It was busier than he remembered, vibrant yet shaded with a different color than Rome. Time seemed to move faster than Rome and Witenberg of six years ago. The city teemed with newer people he didn't recognize.

Several women with bags accompanied an older man in a burgundy hat. A woman with darker skin and a nose ring held a long glance towards William as she held the door open long enough for the man's entourage to enter the bath house.

Interesting, William thought, and he made a mental note about the woman's appearance.

After a long trek, the passage opened into the heart of Witenberg. William continuously reviewed his list of items to purchase against the money supplied by the abbot after he'd handed over the papal order and explained the need for a scriptorium.

This feeling was new to him—the euphoria of spending others' money. As a middle child, he had scrapped and begged for food in a large family that seemed not to care about him. His father, a count in lean times, had nevertheless kept aside money for his schooling. William blossomed in the school, but under the surface of his success, he longed for loving parents instead.

As is often the case, the bag of coins in his hand temporarily masked memories of an absent father and critical mother.

"You're not good enough!" Clarina would say. "Work harder!"

"Yes, Mother. Yes, Mother," he would respond. He learned to calculate his responses; otherwise, she reprimanded him with paddles. He tried to find refuge in his father, but the count traveled much, on courtly business. Consequently, William retreated to controlling what he could. He found rules, he made rules, and he chided other children if they didn't follow the rules. Once of reading age, he perused legal texts. There was comfort there.

And there was comfort in the busyness of Rome and the Holy See—and now of Witenberg.

The city's main plaza buzzed, spidered with a web of activities. From second-floor balconies, parents yelled at their kids running around the central fountain. Merchants wheeled their carts with bales of cloth, and vendors stood behind stands of food. Pop-up tables from the cathedral courtyard had been moved to the city center and resembled an army encampment preparing for a siege. Poles flew, men moved, and orders barked out among them.

"Looks like a festival is coming, Bouncy," Stinky Feet said and clapped his hands. The air hung warmer, enclosed in the square space, the wind blocked by the buildings. William's stomach rumbled as carts rolled past him, knocking loose the cobblestones.

"Let's find food, Stinky Feet."

The two bought roasted turkey legs and devoured them. But William was still hungry. He went to another table.

"Need to wait for the water to boil," said the vendor.

"Aye, sir," said Stinky Feet and picked raw potatoes. "Just cut them up, and we be fine." From his pocket, Stinky Feet pulled a jar of homemade spices. He sprinkled the dried herbs onto the potatoes.

After a crunch, Stinky Feet smiled, showing green blotches scattered across his teeth. He threw an arm around William and pulled him closer. "I'm glad we're friends, Bouncy."

The little Night Watcher breathed a combination of a mild grassy smell—slightly pungent, peppery, with a blowback of meaty turkey.

"You're a unique brother, Stinky Feet," said William. "And I noticed you have shoes! Well done, well done." He slightly curtseyed and tipped his hat on the cocked side. But then he stopped abruptly and cleared his throat.

What am I doing? he thought. "What's gotten into you, Stinky Feet?" he asked.

"Please?" asked Stinky Feet as he licked his fingers.

"Your hair is trimmed, and parted too?"

"Of course, Bouncy. For my lady." His broad shoulders pulled back, and he strutted across the courtyard to a shop.

"You have a lady? But we need to buy so much," he said and looked over his list. "Candles, desks, books, bookshelves, ink wells, penknives, quills, and parchment. Oh, and paintings. The room was so drab."

"We have all that money? And no cart? How do we get them back? We just looking today, Bouncy. But you need new shoes and clothing—surely you do."

The white-plastered two-story building looked different than the other plain rectangular buildings with shed roofs in the square. With brown trim on the pillars and around the windows, the building's brown thatched roof rose from five angles to form a point at the top.

Stinky Feet pushed through the door and bowed. "My lady," he said and rang the bell.

At first glance, William saw streaks of silver in an older woman of elegance. A long, tightly wound ponytail fell down her back. She turned, and he locked into translucent green eyes, light with hints of blue but frosted like the windowpanes. The smoke-colored eyeshadow blurred her set of three laugh lines that curled like her lashes. The contrast of light with dark hitched his breath momentarily, and he tripped over his feet, knocking over boots and books lining the shelves.

"Stinky Feet," she said with a rolling of her tongue in sweet melody that ended in a noticeable crispness, as if she held him responsible for William's stumble. The confidence and calmness reminded William of his mother as she chastised him for leaving things out of place.

"I'm sorry, madam," William said and scrambled to fix what he had tumbled before his mother—no, this woman, yelled at him. The boots were returned to the correct shelf and the books to their proper order. His first instinct was to run. So he stepped towards the door, but Stinky Feet grabbed him.

"Bouncy, where are you going? I want you to meet my friend, Smoky."

"Oh, quit, Stinky Feet," she said. "You know that's just my nickname."

She moved around the counter in a slim-fitting lavender tunic belted at the waist. Her movements were effortless as she glided silently, and the transition from a firm handshake to a brief, warm back rub melted the tension William felt. "My name is Inanna, Anna for short. It's a pleasure to meet you." In more light, he saw her blond hair and eyes that were a shade darker than he'd seen at first, hazy like sea waters.

As he softened, William's concerns floated away with the white-capped Mediterranean waves in his daydream. He had left his hillside house in Riomaggiore for the sea, but his duty in life dragged him back and crashed like the guilt-dripped misery paddle his mother wielded when William strayed from doctrine.

"Souls must be saved," she would say. "If not, Hell awaits. And you will save sinners—including yourself."

His shoulders firmed. "Madam"—he bowed—"my name is Father William. I work with Stinky Feet."

Out of the side of his mouth, Stinky Feet said, "Nah, we be friends."

"Very well," she said and straightened into a professional posture. "How can I help?"

"Give him the treatment, Smoky."

She took a measuring tape and pulled at the string that held it. "Stand still, Father William. And please remove your hat."

As she measured his torso, arms, and legs, he noticed her black boots. A round, stylized flower design started on the toe cap and continued up her instep.

"I see you like my boots," she said. "I got them from a shop in Bavaria—"

"Where we first met," Stinky Feet said, finishing her thought.

"Yes," she confirmed. "A single rose becomes several," she said, and hiked her tunic to show embroidered roses on the shafts of the boots. "But if you don't like roses, we have other designs."

"Thank you, but I like my shoes just fine, madam." As he wandered the shop with her, reviewing different designs for his clothing, she arched her eyebrows at the sound of his loose heel base flopping against the sole.

"Tell you what," she said. "I'll throw in the boots for free. I can tell you need a new pair. Look around while I work up a pattern for your uniform." Her ponytail swung sharply like a whip when she vanished behind the counter.

Stinky Feet clapped. "What a deal, Bouncy."

"I don't know, Stinky Feet." He dragged out his words as he examined several designs. "I like my low-cut shoes. And these are too high. And too fancy for a priest."

"Come on, Bouncy, receive a gift. They are free. Despite our vows, we're allowed *some* lavish things. Feel the bottom," he said as he held out a pair.

William's fingers walked down the smoothest, softest leather he had ever felt. "Almost spongy," he said, "and I like the tread design, the same as the shaft."

"Try them on."

Like sinking into sand, William felt the cushion inside absorb his sore arches and soften his steps. Though he kept his slight bounce, his posture relaxed, and his back wasn't as stiff. "It feels like I'm floating."

William slid across the wood floor, shuffled his feet a bit, and spun on his toes, almost dancing.

Stinky Feet stood on a stool and grabbed an arm and twirled it over William's head. This was the most fun he had since Mati had taught him folk dancing. *The archbishop. That man again.* His heart sank, and his shoes planted flat into the floor.

"I'll take them, Anna," he told her as she hung several coats and trousers on a rack. "B-but, we must be getting on. I have an investigation to run."

"An investigation, Father William. How exciting." Her cloudy eyes cleared and glowed with a different purpose. "This one, then." She pulled out black trousers and a smoke-colored knee-length coat.

"Wool for the winter," she said, and removed the inner piece, "and lighter material for the summer. And it's a match—the same pattern as your boots. Excellent choice, monsieur."

To finish the look, she wrapped two checkered scarves over his neck. "One for the winter and one for the spring."

"How much?" William asked.

She looked at Stinky Feet and shook her head. "No charge. Stinky Feet and his brothers are our best account. Come back tomorrow to pick up. Your clothes will be ready after noon."

"And we be buying more shoes soon, Anna," said Stinky Feet.

William knocked the counter with his knuckles and said, "Thank you, kind lady." With a flourish, he rolled the hat up his arm to his head and tipped the cocked side to say farewell to Anna.

‹———›

After that day's buying and several more trips to the city, William, the Night Watchers, and the other brothers returned with carts full of items for the new scriptorium. William directed the copying operation and designed the division of labor. Some readied the parchment for copying by smoothing and chalking the surface, others copied the manuscript text, and others illuminated.

Meanwhile, in his private office, William pinned a large piece of parchment on the wall. He prepped his notebooks with sections for evidence, interviews, and checklists. Thumbing through the pages, a word he had written in the margins several years before popped out.

Child.

A sign from Mati? "He came not to abolish the law but to fulfill it," William read. Below the underlined text, there was more cursive handwriting.

"Become like a child . . ."

A child—that word again.

A teenage boy came into focus in his memory—kneeling in a corner. From the treasury, with a priest.

Why did the boy leave his chair during the funeral?

Like an itch that nagged until scratched, William wanted to see the grotto where a boy and girl had scurried to exit.

Where is the stone? Where is the carpenter's son?

"No," he said, "can't be." But he had carried an object in his hand, up the grotto stairs—something luminescent, an object that glowed.

Did the boy have the stone?

MEAD BALL

Jeremiah shivered at the creek's bank but was distracted by thoughts of picking flowers for Marianne. She loved honeysuckle, and he loved the aroma too, so he added it to the bunch.

Once the flowers were decided, he hastily removed his tunic and undergarments and threw them onto the rocks. He tiptoed into the creek with his right hand covering his private parts and his left hand grasping the bar of beige soap.

He sank into the frigid waters, the full immersion immediately heightening his senses. He daydreamed about the potential night he might have, and that inured him to the cold. "She will love the letter!" he shouted as he burst up out of the water.

From the corner of his eye, he spied a naked couple frolicking downstream. They saw him, pointed, and laughed. They should have been embarrassed too, but only Jeremiah blushed to warm his frozen face. Crouching low in the water, he scrubbed harsher and quicker until the wood smell dissipated.

Once he got home, Jeremiah saw Elfred waiting to present him with a gift. "Son," he said, "these garments have been handed down from my father and his father and his father before." He gave the young man a golden cloak decorated with the symbol of the family: a rampant blue lion facing left, standing with forepaws raised and tongue out.

Jeremiah lowered a hand from his chest and softened his eyes. "A keyhole? A key on it too?" He remembered retreating to puzzles and the stone as a child when hurt.

"Yes, Son, for my magus, the solver of puzzles."

Jeremiah wrapped the cloak around his shoulders like a cape.

"Remember," Elfred said, "the key to a woman is a caring heart. Forgiveness too."

Jeremiah went to his room. After removing his tunic, he pulled woolen hose over his feet and up his legs. Under his bed, he grabbed the stone and stuffed it into his undergarment pouch, then donned a long-sleeved, three-button-placket wool shirt with two front pockets that fell beneath his thighs. He fastened a leather belt, then slipped into boots and secured the golden cloak with a brooch shaped like a key.

He was average in height, and not far from full grown, so he had little prospect of getting taller. His dark complexion and very dark and curly hair stood out, though, among the fair inhabitants of the village.

He had had no chance with the girls when Alfred was single. Tardy with words, he always thought of the witty thing to say too late, whereas Alfred could merely stand speechless, and women would come to him. He envied Alfred's nonchalance and ease with wooing women—as fluid as wielding his sword.

Jeremiah hadn't ridden a horse since he was a child, but he would make this count. He transferred the stone from his pouch to his shirt pocket, then in one smooth motion, he ran and jumped on the horse's back, recalling the move that had come so easily when he was a child. He lifted the reins, clicked his tongue, and urged the horse to walk. He smiled at the shifting shadows as the clouds slid across the sun's path on this beautiful day. The weather was perfect: clear skies and sunny with a cold breeze.

He waved farewell to his watching parents and rubbed the horse's shoulder.

His movements are fluid and loose. He's happy with me.

Marianne's home was close, and he rode there like the wind. Jumping to the ground, he wrapped the reins around the door post.

Her mother opened the door. "Hello, Jeremiah." Lady Charlotte looked him over. "Why, you are rather dashing, I must say."

"Thank you, madam. Is Marianne ready? The ball starts soon."

"Yes, she will be down shortly."

A few heart-pounding moments later, the most beautiful woman he knew walked into the room. Wearing a simple white dress with embroidered lilies, sprinkled with honeysuckle, and a daisy crown covering her curly, amber hair, Marianne glided effortlessly towards him.

"Hello, Jeremiah."

"H-hello," he stumbled. He pinched himself and tripped as he extended a hand to help her out the door.

"The line on the floor gets me too, Miah. Like my dress?"

He swallowed a few times and maintained wide eyes.

Did I blink?

"Yes, very much so. I like it," he said.

She accepted his sweaty hand.

With a firm grasp on Jeremiah's shoulder, her father said from behind his thick mustache, "Bring her back here by eleven, Son."

"Yes, I will," Jeremiah replied. He avoided Lord Atticus' glare and instead his eyes darted from the coat of arms to swords to the shields hung from the wall.

Outside he helped Marianne mount the horse behind him, and eternity blinked. They rode together in slow motion as he yearned to capture every moment of what he had dreamed for so long.

The dance celebrated the town's prosperity and welcomed in the unofficial new year. Though spring had come early, winter's chill filled the air. A fire blazed along the center of the ballroom and at each end, smoke following the sloped ceiling, colliding with incense rising from a metal thurible, a priest was swinging on a chain.

This was his first mead ball, and Jeremiah assumed it would be a more formal affair, since his father gifted him such fine garments, but this gathering was nothing like he'd imagined, and he looked around with his mouth hanging open. He expected ladies of influence and gentlemen of regard in regal attire; instead, the room was colored with a rainbow of diversely dressed people.

All are welcome here, Jeremiah thought. Men dressed as women in skirts; women dressed as men in tall boots and long, many-buttoned coats. Some wore shoes, but most went barefoot. Some had shaved, but most flaunted their leg, armpit, and facial hair. All had smiles. The village was letting loose.

Jeremiah sniffed himself. The washing seemed like a waste; because he was clean, he noticed the difference. The place was filled with the normal, nasty body funk of any village market day. The stink lingered on the wooden floor and wooden walls. He escorted the delicate and sweetly scented Marianne past men rubbing herbs over beaver felt codpieces, and he couldn't help jerking back in revulsion. "What's that smell?"

Marianne laughed. "Cumin, mint, and dill, mixed with the lovely perfume of body odor. Beaver signals an open exchange."

He closed his lips tightly, knowing he was forming dimples on each cheek. "And how do you know that?"

"Just something Lord Oaf told me," she said lightly while interlocking arms with him.

Jeremiah walking in with the village's prettiest woman instantly increased the chatter among clergy, a handful of Witen politicians, and several lords. Vapors of frankincense, rosewood, and myrrh mingled with the garlic and moldy funk from their pores and the bitter drunken hot air blowing from their mouths. One said, "How did *he* get her?" and another, "Why is she here with *him*?"

"Let's get a drink," Jeremiah said, with a caress of the stone in his palm in his shirt pocket—for fortune. He grabbed her hand and led her to the large wooden barrel of mead against the rear wall.

Two busty women with name tags signifying they were folk dance regulars stumbled into Jeremiah before they dipped the ladle. They smothered sloppy kisses on both Marianne's cheeks, even as Jeremiah stood right there. Olga struggled to speak, but not Helga.

"If this isn't the lovely Marianne, and she's with this ugly chap!" Helga slapped his arm and almost knocked him over.

"Hi, Helga," Marianne responded with crossed arms. "Didn't know you fancy drink."

"Only when it's free and flowing. Of course, I know how to get it for free." She licked her teeth and offered a hand for a dance.

Jeremiah refused and whispered to Marianne, "Gross—what man would be with this gap-toothed woman? Won her fair share of bar fights, I bet. How do you know her?"

"She and Mum were childhood friends. Mum took one path, and Helga took another. Got pregnant at an early age. Man left her."

"I'm sure for another beauty."

Marianne hit him and said to Helga, "It was good seeing you. I'll tell Mother you said hello."

"Missing out," Helga said, pirouetting and fluttering to her next target.

"Let's get food," said Jeremiah. They moved to the large table adjacent to the mead. "This is amazing," he said at the sight of boar, turkey, goose, and duck. "Now I know where our tax money goes."

"Come on," she complained. "Can't you enjoy the evening without making some comment?"

"You're right, you're right. Care to dance?"

"Let me get a cupful of mead first," she said lightly. "You go ahead and eat."

After eating, while Marianne sipped at her mead, Jeremiah removed the golden cloak, placing it on a chair.

"Too hot?" she asked.

"Yes. Time to dance. Take my hand."

They sought another couple and introduced themselves. People formed three columns, grouped in sets of four. "This dance is a local favorite, unique to the capital but growing in popularity in adjacent duchies," one of the couple told them. "Just follow the caller."

As the caller described each step, Jeremiah's warmth surged. "Gird your loins," he jabbered to her.

"What?" Marianne asked and released her hands.

"Silly, stupid," babbled Jeremiah. "Never mind—see, I was talking to . . . never mind. This will be fun." His eyes zoomed in on hers. "Follow these eyes—or else beware. You'll get dizzy."

"Aye, maddo," she teased. "Am I at the right dance?"

The fiddle bows furiously danced across the strings in harmony with the flutes. Most dancers spun out on the floor with the traditional opposite gender.

Jeremiah followed the caller's instructions but improvised with multiple twirls, lifting and dipping Marianne between his legs. As they danced, occasionally switching partners, Jeremiah noticed each dancer had a look of radiance more than a smile, the look of youth and early morning. Presence was joy, pure as a baby's laugh.

Jeremiah flinched and avoided eye contact when he parted with Marianne and danced with a man taking the female part, but the anticipation of running into her arms—seeing joy radiate from her face as she glowed like an angel, basking in the firelight—melted away the temporary discomfort of grasping hairier hands.

After a few rounds of spinning with other partners, he spun back to Marianne. He extended his hand and asked, "Care to dance again, love?"

"Why—aren't *you* confident?"

He observed the dance caller wearing a short, colorful tunic but having broad shoulders, a deep voice, and thick, hairy legs. "A woman or a man?" he mused.

Smiling, Marianne hit him and leaned into his whisper.

Her darting hands tickled him. She drifted away in a tipsy swoon but caught herself and kissed him. He kissed her back, but they quickly separated after tasting one another's salty lips and tart berry breath.

"Come on, let's sit for a bit," he said. He led her to the table and poured them both cups of water. "Are you all right for a moment? I need to use the privy."

"Yessss," she slurred.

Past the door, Jeremiah thought he saw someone he recognized.

The man was slender, with a pointed nose with a flat bridge fanning out, resembling a sail from the side. He had his back against the wall. But he had a tufted beard. And a hat. And what looked like coal ash smudged over his face. His facial hair grew beyond the chin and jawline, and the neckline was clean. The trimmed mustache curled upwards reminded Jeremiah of fancy woodwork in the cathedral.

He moved on and walked outside. Orion's belt shined. He rubbed his hands to warm them while searching for the outhouse. There it was—the unique advertising of Lord Harry's face on birch paper. After taking care of business, stumbling slightly, he bumped into Harold the Younger.

Cupping the other young man's shoulder, he said, "Lord Harry, good to see you. I didn't realize your pinkish face with orange high-lights was painted on all the outhouses in town. Have you inspected each outhouse?"

"Piss off, bastard. And don't touch my fiancée," he threatened with a scowl, poking a finger at Jeremiah and squeezing his bushy, red eyebrows into a V shape.

Waving his hand to dissipate the foul, drunken breath, Jeremiah asked, "Fiancée? What are you talking about?"

"Oh, she hasn't mentioned me? Well, ex-fiancée, but I'll get her back."

"No, not at all. Why do you care? She's with me tonight."

"We'll see."

Harry pushed Jeremiah aside and slammed the outhouse door behind him. Jeremiah ripped the poster of Harry's smug face from the privy and stomped back to Marianne. He showed her and tore it in two.

"Your ex-fiancé is quite the gentleman. He's also a piece of scite, both literally and figuratively."

Marianne squinted. "Harry's here?"

"Yes, I saw him outside. Why didn't you tell me you were formerly engaged?"

Fiddling with her mug, she said, "Because it wasn't relevant. Besides, why would I reveal that on a date? And we really haven't talked in a few years. You've always seemed distant from me."

"Because I loved you!" he blurted.

After moments of awkward silence, he said, "You intimidated me. Why would a beautiful girl want an ugly man like me?"

"Ugly? You may look different than most men in this town, but you aren't ugly. I like your darker complexion. But your lack of confidence right now isn't appealing. Be present with me." She held his hands.

But he couldn't let go of the thought of the lord.

Why was the engagement broken off? No matter. Be with Marianne.

"You're right," he said. "I'm sorry. Let's dance."

They danced for a long time, and while he enjoyed each minute, occasionally he watched for Harry and the mysterious man. "I need a break again," he said and watched her continue with the folk dance, another partner for her taking his place.

He filled his cup with water and sat. While Jeremiah was skimming a flyer advertising an adjacent town's market, the mysterious man glided over and placed his hand on one of Jeremiah's knees. "Have you seen my sheets of music?" Then he was gone.

Jeremiah craned his neck to watch Marianne dance. He loved it when she turned and blew him kisses. The slender gentleman caller with the long face came around again and this time placed both hands on Jeremiah's knees. Fingers massaged his legs and slid upwards to Jeremiah's waist and started feeling into his shirt pockets. He felt the stone and asked the question again: "Have you seen my sheets of music?"

"Get away from me!" Jeremiah scolded, suddenly realizing he was being pursued. He jumped up and held the stone and ran to Marianne and impulsively kissed her passionately, right there on the dance floor.

"Whoa," she said. "Not so fast." After listening to his story, she laughed and kissed him.

Jeremiah kept pondering—the eccentric gentleman caller reminded him of someone from the archbishop's funeral.

The music stopped, and Harold the Younger sauntered onto the stage with ale in hand. "Let's give a big round of applause for tonight's band, The Geezinslaws!"

The crowd clapped, hooted, and hollered.

"Thank you, Michaela," Harry said, with a generous gesture towards the man-woman.

"Huh—I guess he's a woman," Jeremiah said to Marianne.

"And a mighty fine dance caller," replied Marianne.

"Now's the time for the roast and grog," Harry said. "This tradition goes back centuries to celebrate the past year. The protocol has been posted on the walls. You're free to call anyone to the grog bowl for any offense of the king's rules. But you must rhyme as you make your accusation."

Jeremiah watched Harry mix clear alcohol with unknown other liquids and foods. Chunks of something dropped into the concoction.

"I call little Miah," said Harry. "Jeremiah, Jeremiah, you stole the lord's bride, but I must confide, she chose a man who can't hit the hole or more, sprinkling when he tinkles, spraying wildly over the outhouse door. Now you must drink, but be careful the drink doesn't spill on the floor."

With a hand, Marianne covered her mouth to laugh at Jeremiah. She smiled when Harry winked.

Snorting, Jeremiah sneered at her and at Harry's buffoons joining their lord in pointing and giggling. He lumbered onto the stage, half saluted with his left hand, and rebutted. "Oh, Harry, your face is plastered on every outhouse in town, changing many frowns, sensing their lord is close when expelling waste. Tonight, because of this ball, you may be a hit, but in my book, you'll always be royal scite."

Laughter erupted, and heat flooded Harry's cheeks. Neck tightened and fists clenched, Harry turned to his father. Lord Harold the Elder stood against the wall near the stage and nodded. From his coat, a young liege took out a bottle he opened and headed for Harry.

Jeremiah grabbed the ladle, filled the mug full, turned around to face the crowd, raised the mug, and declared, "To this glorious mess." Unable to drink it all, he choked on chunks of food. Liquid dripped onto his forehead as he tipped back the mug and drank again.

Harry laughed and proclaimed, "Jeremiah can't hold his liquor! Miah the Little!" To the liege, Harry said, "Thank you, Squire."

The mug slammed onto the table, and Jeremiah scowled. With three steps forward, Jeremiah looked to Marianne, but she kept her eyes fixed on Harry, on his golden tunic, ruby ring, and fiery hair. Harry asked, "Will you muster the courage to drink from the king's chalice, *little* Miah? Show my fiancée how strong a man you are!"

After a burp and a cough, Marianne stopped smiling, hid behind a mug, and sipped water. When Jeremiah sat beside her, she turned away.

"Fiancée," he growled low under his breath. With lips curled, he leapt from his seat and stormed to the stage. His glare locked onto his target, overlooking Harry's sleight of hand that poured something clear into the chalice.

Jeremiah snatched the cup, tilted his head, and finished in one gulp. He stumbled back to Marianne. As others marched to the grog bowl, he noticed how different his skin looked—from everyone's. He disheveled his hair, stood, and interrupted each of the poets calling offenses against their friends.

"Sit down, bastard," yelled Harry. "You're no fun! No one wants to hear your rhymes. Listen to the wonderful sounds. All groans!"

Fidgeting, Marianne looked around the room. "Jeremiah, take me home. I'm not sure what's happened to you, but I don't like it."

"You don't like a man with confidence? Don't you like arseholes? The lord plays a fine one," he slurred.

She crossed her arms and watched him try to untangle his feet from his stupor stomp. Jeremiah toppled over but caught himself soon enough to brace the impact with hands and elbows. After the fall, she demanded, "Take me home."

Jeremiah began to recover, with the pain overpowering the drunkenness. He stretched, guzzled some water, and said, "Yes, I'm sorry. I'm not sure what's come over me. Let's go."

He shoved both hands into his shirt pockets, then patted his chest. "One moment," Jeremiah said and swept the table with his eyes, then his hands. "I forgot something."

Harry returned to the stage and said, "Ladies and gentlemen, the toast of the ball departs. But wait! What's dropped from the bastard's pocket? A letter. Oh! A love letter!"

The crowd shouted, "Read it. Read it!"

Realization punched Jeremiah in the stomach.

"Harry, you stole that from me. Give it back now."

The letter unrolled. "Dear Marianne," began Harry.

Jeremiah built to a sprint.

"Oh, how cute, a troubadour. Blah, blah, rhyme, blah, love, Your Miah." Harry fanned himself and held the letter to his chest. "How romantic. This must be true love."

Jeremiah sprang onto the stage and pounced on him. They wrestled and rolled. Once free, Harry smooched at him and whispered, "Remember the last time we were this close? And I broke your precious doll, bastard?" He threw the letter into the fireplace. Jeremiah dove to retrieve it, but it vanished.

He watched it burn.

Marianne screamed, "Jeremiah! Let's go. Let it go."

Muscles flexed, and veins appeared. Jeremiah shifted his weight, slightly squatted, and tucked his elbows in. His rear foot pivoted towards Harry as his torso twisted inward and his left hand shot out to protect his chin and temple.

As Jeremiah belted the same guttural roar he'd roared in childhood, Harry blinked rapidly. Jeremiah's right hand wound up and punched straight through Harry's jaw and cheek. Harry's head and neck jolted, but his feet froze. In slow motion, he fell backwards onto the stage and blacked out.

For a moment, Jeremiah stood shocked, speechless. Men rushed to the stage, and Jeremiah ran. He ran outside and into the first privy he saw. He quickly removed the stone from his shirt pocket and stuffed it into his undergarment pouch.

The door slammed open.

Lord Harold grabbed Jeremiah by a sleeve and pulled him to the ground.

"Take this filth to the king's prison," blustered Lord Harold to his men, "and throw him into the dirtiest cell."

"Yes, Sheriff," they said.

LOVE OR FREEDOM

The mead ball had been a perfect opportunity to investigate while overhearing the unguarded conversations of the drunk. However, after the boy—now nearly grown—had entered the dance hall, William focused on that single target. He had paced the perimeter of the floor, unsure how to confirm whether the boy had the stone.

This was new to him—never had he approached a man. Though the boots evened out his stance, his habitual rocking habit slightly returned. Beads of sweat soaked into the band of his hat, and his stomach tightened. When the music started, his memory flashed, and he bolted for a drink.

He knew how to proposition, but he needed steeling for that.

Despite his vow of chastity and his clothes of a cleric, men would call out for Father William when he walked from his residence to St. John Lateran for meetings with the pope.

Some of these men were teasing and funny, others outright aggressive. William had laughed one day while at lunch with a friend, when a slender man sitting at a table nearby rose and slowly bent over as he passed, long enough for William to notice and understand. But the ultimate pickup happened once when William was listening to a concert, sitting on the periphery of the crowd. A man had approached William and ran his fingers up William's legs from the knees to the groin, resting there.

Lighter in step from the drink and the encounter that had yielded knowledge of the stone, William floated from the dance hall to the scriptorium. He hurried down the corridor, past the hunched backs of men copying manuscripts at their desks, and into his office. With a ruler, he drew lines on the chart from the king to the archbishop. Though the king had been acquitted, William had questions.

I'll use knowledge of the stone to get closer to the king, he thought. What did the archbishop know? The chamberlain? Chamberlain Vere had led William to the Night Watchers, suggesting their involvement, but they were on William's team. He crossed out the Night Watchers and added a question mark beside Vere's name.

The quill pen tapped against his upper lip. He stared at the king's symbol. "The king," he said. "Has the queen told him?"

A knock came to the door. Two knocks banged from the ceiling. "One moment," said William and closed the notebook on his desk, concealing Rachel's letter. A louder knock came to the door, and two more from the ceiling.

"Come in."

"Master," said Stinky Feet, "it's time for the nightly huddle." Stinky Feet plopped on a chair beside the desk. "Impressive. I like what you've done with the wall."

Three more knocks came from the ceiling.

"Where is Fuss?"

"I don't know, but we can call him. But you better answer the cup—three knocks on the floor above. Something is important."

The smile that had softened William's cheeks vanished, and his temples throbbed—an acute pain of needles poking in a tight, circular pattern. He let out a heavy sigh, and the corners of his mouth drooped. "Why did we install this again?" He put an ear to the cone of parchment tied to the string and listened.

"Father William! Father William!" came the muffled voice.

"Yes, Fuss, I'm here."

"About time you answered. Three bangs—it's important, Father William. Where were you?"

He fiddled with the string but answered, "Investigating. But I'm back for our meeting. Why aren't you in my office?"

"Because I've found something. Come to the winery and meet me at the furnace."

"Be right there." William grabbed a notebook and pencil and rushed to the door. "Let's go, Stinky Feet. Ring the bell and dismiss the brothers to the abbey. Tell them we're stopping early tonight. Fuss has something important upstairs for you and me."

Like a set of dominoes, one by one, light from each desk candle extinguished, and the brothers single-filed out the round door, got their boots, tied their laces, and walked to the abbey. William and Stinky Feet climbed the hill to the winery front entrance.

"How fun," Stinky Feet said as his bare feet skidded on the wet grass.

"Where are your shoes?"

"Right. One moment. Why didn't you leave yours at the door?"

The darkness hid his reddened cheeks, and the crisp air focused his scrambled thoughts to find an excuse. "I was in a hurry . . . to get to my office and write something down. P-plus," he managed, "I'm thinking of asking the queen about her lemon cleaning solution."

"Is that why her name was on your wall?"

William pulled apart the wide sliding doors, and he went in. "Hold on," he said. "Almost forgot again." He sat and removed his boots. In the back corner, he saw a light. "This way."

Expecting a hat, the closer he got, William saw instead the top of a man's head. Kneeling beside the furnace, Fuss was arranging pieces of something.

"Find a clue?" asked William.

"I found fragments of a scroll in the hearth. Look."

William brushed close beside Fuss and noted his nighttime purple robe. "No hat tonight, Fuss?"

"Not when I randomly inspect the winery, Bouncy. But"—he turned and lowered the candle to his breast—"I had Anna sew the robe, for just such occasions."

Stinky Feet plopped to his butt and wiggled closer to the puzzle pieces. "I think we need more light, Bouncy."

"Good idea. But first—I want to inspect."

Fuss handed the candle to William, and William searched the hearth. "Fuss, did you find fragments anywhere else?"

"No, just the hearth."

"Can you show me where precisely?"

Fuss huffed and lowered to knees and pointed to the fireplace floor. "There," he said. "I found them beneath the ash pile."

William ran a finger across fire-cracked stone, ashes, and chunks of copper. "Parts of the cauldron leg," said William. As he examined them, two items long and brown caught his eye—a strand of hair and a string. He pulled them with his pencil and held them closer to the light.

"Does anyone else inspect?" asked William.

"No, just me," said Fuss. "I randomly inspect so the Night Watchers stay disciplined in their chores. What are you getting at?"

William quickly dismissed the strand as belonging to Fuss's short tufts of hair patted tight by his hats.

"And you've just seen these tonight?"

"Yes, of course—the hair caught my attention, Father William," Fuss said with a faint bite in his voice. "And then I dug and found the fragments."

"Unfortunately, we can't determine the date of these fragments then. Fuss, collect them and come to my office."

Back in the office, William lit more candles and placed the hair, string, and scroll fragments on his desk.

The hair was longer and darker than William initially thought, and the string looked of leather or suede.

"From a glove," said William, and he immediately thought of gloves used for the cauldron.

"Cracky manages the cauldrons, correct?" asked William.

"Correct," said Fuss, "but Night Watchers rotate duties."

"True," William said, dejected.

After a pause, he added while assembling the fragments, "Whoever burned this did so in a hurry."

"How do you know?" asked Stinky Feet.

"If he wanted to burn the entire parchment, he would've waited until it was only ash. But we have larger fragments, some with charred corners. Like he was ripping off pieces and throwing them into the fire."

"I know," said Stinky Feet and rearranged some pieces. "Two legs and hooves on the left side. A tail? Wings? On the right side?"

As letters formed, William's heart skipped a beat at the sight of *L*, *O*, another *O*, and *M*.

William pulled out drawers and rummaged, the parchment crinkling. "This," he said, unrolling one and holding the corners. "The same as the parchment that was on the cathedral bells the night of the archb-bishop's murder. P-Pius showed me."

"Love or Freedom?" read Fuss. "A unicorn fighting a dragon?" He reached across the desk and crumpled the tough, flexible parchment into a ball and threw it against the wall.

"What are you doing?" exclaimed William.

"I told Pius not to read any more novels. He'll be on watchtower duty for the foreseeable future." On the throw, Fuss's robe belt loosened, exposing his pale-as-cream rounded gut. Higher on the trail from his belly button towards his hairy chest, William saw a darker patch—ink.

A mark?

Fuss gargled a bit and quickly tied the robe. "No one wants to see that."

William went around the desk and uncrumpled the parchment. "Fuss, we should interview Pius. This is a clue."

"Whoever burned this was angry, ripping piece by piece, but he was in a hurry. Was he caught? Or thought he'd be caught?" asked Fuss.

"Precisely," William said, and pinned the parchment to the wall.

"The church, Bouncy?" asked Stinky Feet. "You placed that beside the archbishop."

"It reads theological, like something from the Church," William answered. "You're right, Stinky Feet. The hierarchy? An archb-bishop? Or . . . ?"

Over a yawn, Stinky Feet said, "Or a cardinal."

"Or a pope," added Fuss.

Stinky Feet yawned again, and Fuss said, "Stop yawning, Stinky Feet. It's making me yawn."

"I'm sorry." Stinky Feet stretched and covered his mouth. "The pope has that effect on people. And the copying. It be making us weary, Bouncy. Misery, the devil, suffering, Hell . . ."

An ache abruptly arose from William's lower left back and carried down his leg.

Fuss shivered his shoulders. Through a short gasp he said, "Obedience through force."

"Maybe we should call it a night and focus on this tomorrow," said William. "Until tomorrow night . . ." He shut the notebook, gestured for them to leave, blew out the candles, and locked the door. Once inside the abbey again, they all removed their shoes and walked to their beds.

Often William considered sleeping in his office, but Fuss would have disapproved. Something about the camaraderie of the brotherhood, he would have said. But rules were rules, and William understood. Lights out after Compline and mandatory Lauds and Prime in the cathedral. Unless given permission by the abbot, William had to attend all events by the canonical hourly schedule. This meant his normal investigative period was the few hours between liturgies in the morning and afternoon or between sunset and dawn.

He despised being late and having to change clothes beside his brother's bunk; however, with the latest clue from Fuss, William could interrupt his neighbor's sleep. His long legs skipped a few rungs on the wooden ladder, and he climbed into the top bunk.

The coat protected his back from sharp straws poking through the cloth, but he was too warm. He tossed and turned to his bunkmate's low-pitched, harsh grunts. The snore carried in a rise of three, vibrating in higher pitches on each inhale, like the sound of frogs at night.

He closed his eyes, but the words *love or freedom* scrolled left to right in a continuous loop across the dark canvas of his mind. At some point he fell asleep, but he awoke to three bells ringing. His temples pounded, as if his mind continued to plan his next moves while at rest.

Find Rachel, his mind insisted. *Ask about the scroll. Tell her about the stone.* He covered his face with the hat, but this suffocated him and the cough that tried to escape. The place was still; even the snoring from below had quieted.

Should I go? he wondered. *Need noise, though, to cover me.*

On his back, to his left side, then right side—no position calmed him. He sat upright and nearly hit the string hung from the ceiling. *Stupid*, he thought. *But it was* his *invention.*

"Easy," William told himself in a whisper. He removed his socks, and his bare feet carefully gripped each rung until he was on the cold, stone floor.

Think. Think.

He looked around.

He pulled some loose straw from his bed, then crushed it into finer particles and sprinkled these onto his bunkmate's chest. After a slight heave from the sleeper, William froze, head pivoting in all directions. Under his breath, he whispered a prayer and sprinkled more straw. *Just enough to stir him up.*

One low-pitched grunt came.

Then another.

And a third.

Then—clockwork. The snoring continued in sets of three, loud enough to be normal.

Some stirred in their beds, and William leaned against the wall.

After some turned over and fell back asleep, he tiptoed down the hall.

Did the cup move?

No, it was the wind, he assured himself from the open door.

He slowly pushed the door until he heard a soft click. On the click, with his pulse pounding, the first strike came.

His chest tightened, muscles contracting, ripping like a cord against him.

Sharp strike, sharp strike, sharp strike.

Ring up. Wait.

Long strike. Full circle.

Four rings signify the hour.

"Just the bells," he said, short of breath.

He waited until the Night Watcher would have sat down again.

"Time to go," he whispered. "I have a few hours."

After hurrying to his office to grab the keys, he entered a cathedral side door and made his way down through the darkness, past the grotto, into the treasury, and into the crypt.

Nothing had changed.

He groped along the wall, using the sarcophagi as a guide. Expecting to move straight through the tunnel, he was startled when something blocked his way.

No! "What's this?" he said aloud.

Large and square, made of wood, it seemed to be a box—a door! He wrapped his arms along its side, but it was too large to take measure of. He pulled, and it nudged a bit. "Witen me," he said, "I should've eaten more in Rome."

He pulled again, but he didn't hear the sound of sliding wood.

Rather, the faintest of cracks popped in the silence.

A few moments went by, then more popping came. It came louder as boots thudded with each step on the other side. But there were no other sounds—no breathing and no voices.

He gave another heave and pull—*Got it!*

He slid through the tiniest of openings and sprinted farther through the same tunnel he had walked through six years earlier. With each step, water droplets splashed against his back.

He heard a whooshing sound at each step.

Is someone chasing me? The air blew colder. *Almost there.*

His speed kicked up wind and leaves or debris on the tunnel floor. Shallower and shallower, his breath shortened, but he made it to the door at the end of the tunnel.

No one was behind him.

He exhaled deeply in the open air and trekked through the reeds to the king's scriptorium. The doorknob didn't budge, and there was no keyhole. However, there was a box with five push keys, small circular knobs.

Great. How do I get in?

The watchtower loomed behind him like a shadow, its voice ticking and tocking, reminding him he didn't have long. He read the letter again. His fingers ran over the purple-inked seal: a circle with a line down the middle. "Love or Freedom?" The note read. "What will the kingdom choose? Meet me in the king's scriptorium."

Tick.

He flipped the letter. "Clean. Heat. The archbishop's favorite color, number in sum."

Tock.

"Clean? Heat? What does that mean?"

Purple?

Beads of sweat trickled into his eyes.

Tick.

He mopped his brow and punched several numbers.

Nothing.

Tock.

Tick . . . bells rang. One. Two. Three. Four. Five.

Must go.

PRISON

The next night, Jeremiah awoke to the scurrying of rats underneath his blanket.

What's this? Where am I?

He sprang off the straw bed and he tossed the blanket away, reeling with dizziness and the horrific squeaking. He put his hands out and felt a stone wall. His head throbbed. He picked at something on his forehead, and blood oozed over his fingertips.

"The stone," he said. He scrambled down, crawling along the floor as rats found their hole in the wall.

Where is it?

His hands jammed into his shirt pockets, then his undergarments pouch, then he searched through the hole in the wall until he found it.

Whew.

"Hello, hello, anyone out there?" he asked. "Where am I?"

"You're in the king's prison, you fool," said a deep, raspy voice from the adjacent cell. "Quiet or they'll force more medicine down your hole."

Jeremiah swallowed and scratched his neck, remembering the bitter, burning feeling the herbs had left in his throat. "What am I here for?"

"Don't you remember? You're the talk of town for almost killing Lord Harold the Younger. Least that's how me understand what little news we get in here."

Jeremiah rubbed his temples. "Killing him? What?"

He clutched the stone; his fist didn't unclench until enough negative thoughts hammered his head that to attend to them, he released the stone.

It fell to the gritty floor.

Jeremiah slumped. The night with Marianne had been magical until the grog bowl. "I don't get a trial?" he asked, twirling knots in his hair.

"Not in this current kingdom," said the man. "You assaulted a lord. Zero tolerance."

His cheek pressed against the bars, and Jeremiah leaned to inspect the dirt floor in the dim hallway. "But they don't have the complete story!" he spoke louder. "Harry isn't innocent. Has anyone visited?"

"No, me measure. Me've heard the guards laugh over you being in here for a long time."

A long time.

Jeremiah wrapped his fingers around the cold iron bars. Releasing them, he palmed the cool stone and juggled various scenarios in his mind. After a pause, he asked, "What'd *you* do?"

"Killing a peasant is one thing, but assaulting a lord is quite another."

"You killed a peasant!"

"Aye. Me didn't mean to kill him. It was an accident. Me approached him about rumors he was sleeping with me wife. He punched me, me punched back, and the bloody codpiece grabbed his heart and died. Fat bastard probably died of eating too much."

Jeremiah sighed. "We're both in here for trying to protect our women."

He circled the small cell, bypassing rat pellets. "So, no trial. No visitors. I'm stuck in here to rot. What's your name?"

"Asher, but my friends call me Ash or Asser. Yours?"

"Jeremiah, but my friends and family call me Miah. But that's a boy name. I prefer Jeremiah."

"Me think Jerry is better."

"I won't respond to Jerry."

"Good night, Jerry." Asser laughed and went to sleep.

＋———＋

Several hours later, early on Sunday morning, Jeremiah softly said, "Asser, Asser, you awake?"

There was no response so Jeremiah raised his voice, then scooped up and threw rat pellets into the adjacent prison cell. "Asser, wake up."

He showered more pellets.

"What is it, you fool?" said Asser bitterly. "Stop throwing rat dung. Me's awake. Awake."

"Good. I have a plan to escape."

"Yeah, you have a good plan? Like punching Harry to win over your girl?"

"Yes, Ass." Jeremiah kicked dirt near the rats' hole. "Do you have a hole at the bottom of the wall, next to your bed?"

"Yes, Jerry," he said. "Rats occasionally go in and out of there. They carry food, though me not sure where they get it. Must be from outside."

"Exactly. I think the hole connects to outside the prison, but I'm not sure where it leads."

"What do you want? We have no tools to dig out. Plus, the guards will hear us."

"No, we can't dig out of here. I'm a carpenter and would consider building a tool to escape, but I don't see any materials."

Jeremiah thought, touched his mouth, and squinted in dim candlelight to discern the parchment nailed on the corridor wall. He smiled.

"Wait—a carpenter?" asked Asser. "A carpenter from Witenberg? Who's your father?"

"Elfred. Why?"

Hands slapped knees, and laughter bubbled from the adjacent cell.

"What's so funny, Asser? You know him?"

"Elfred of the Wood—the best carpenter and best nickname. Wood . . ."

"Very funny, like I haven't heard that a hundred times. And now I guess it's my name—Jeremiah of the Wood—I'm the guild master—or was."

Asser's neck and eyes strained to attempt a peek through the bars. When he grasped Jeremiah's identity, he burst out laughing again, suddenly with the frequency of a goat's bleating. "You were his skinny son! Me remember—me met you and your dadde on me way to the court with the peasant."

"Father, Asser," Jeremiah said coldly. "Yes, I remember."

"And you knocked out a lord?" Asser banged his head against the bars and belly laughed.

"Keep it down, you fool."

Mid-laugh and mid-breath, Asser forced out, "Maybe, maybe, me'll call you Woody. No, even better. Will call you woodpecker. No! Pecker!"

"Shut your hole, Asser. I have an idea. We need to distract the guards." Jeremiah knelt to the floor and fingered the dirt as he considered ideas.

Asser would call the guard. "After all," he said, "Me was a summoner before the capital sheriff found me."

"A summoner?" asked Jeremiah.

"Yes—called people, mostly peasants, to court to pay fines for church crimes: perjury, simony, heresy, and adultery."

"Adultery?" asked Jeremiah, surprised. "Really?"

"Of course," said Asser with a huff. "That was the most fun—catching the cheaters out for a romp—normally with a member of the clergy. But they were never guilty—they had money. Caught me own wife too. Embarrassin' for her, but the fat peasant's lord, me discovered later, was also sleeping with me wife." He paused and said, his voice plain in tone, "So here me am."

A few minutes passed and a guard with a big belly waddled by their cells, trailing a nearly impenetrable fog of urine, vomit, and stale beer.

After the guard shift change, Asser shouted, "Please, please come here, guard! Me want to lodge a formal complaint about the rats in me cell."

"A formal complaint?" chuckled the guard. "You think this is a bath house? Fine, give me your complaint." He pretended to write it but then spat in Asser's face. "There, that's your verdict."

After wiping off the saliva, Asser rattled the bars.

"You may want to clear the rat dung," advised Jeremiah. "You must smell it daily. Wouldn't it be better for you if this was cleaned up?"

Jeremiah flung a handful of dung onto the guard, making a dire direct hit on his nose, cheeks, and mouth.

"Why you little bastard. I'm going to teach you a lesson."

Fumbling, the guard pushed against the iron bars until the door opened. Jeremiah wound and walloped him in the head with the cloth-wrapped stone.

The guard stumbled, fell—knocked out.

Jeremiah unrolled the stone to stuff it into his undergarment pouch. It was ice-cold, and he jerked away, dropping it and watching it bounce a few yards down the hallway. He scampered to retrieve it and placed it inside his shirt pocket.

"Great hit, Jeremiah!" shouted Asser.

"Shut up, Asser—quiet." Jeremiah removed the guard's keys and unlocked Asser's cell.

After Asser scratched his chin stubble, he spoke. "We need to leave before the other guard wakes. Get your stuff." As he began moving, it became clear how small he was—his short body covered by a gray tunic didn't match the deep voice or shoulder-length silver locks; he was shorter than Jeremiah and had small, child-size hands. And his small feet chugged along in slow motion.

Three in the morning, and most in the castle would be asleep, Jeremiah hoped. His life had taken quite a turn recently. A criminal and a fugitive, he didn't know where to go, except to his parents' house for clothes.

They got out in a courtyard, found the stable and stole two horses, then fled across the bridge. At the village creek, they halted. "Let the horses drink," Jeremiah said and gave Asser the reins. "I need a moment."

Jeremiah left Asser at the creek and walked to the carpentry shop. From the buried box, a secret shared between father and son, Jeremiah bent and dug for the key. He pushed the shop door open and walked into its darkness. Reds and browns were black but visible in the moonlight, and the familiar sweetness of wood clung to his nose.

He slid a hand across the workbench, scooped sawdust, and dropped it into a pocket. From memory, he skirted his father's boots by the door and maneuvered around tools hung from the bench and ceiling.

"Everything has a place," he mumbled, "except me."

In the corner, covered by a dirty rag, hidden from Alfred, he found them: his figurines. His heroes—the dragon, the light-warrior, and the light-warrior's separate leg. And Marianne's figurine. Broken in pieces, yet it was held together by rabbit-skin glue.

With a shaky hand, he took a final grip of his tools, and as he closed the door, a final whiff of musk. He locked the door, and his mind sealed the memories shut. He returned the key to the box and smothered dirt over its hiding place. He was leaving his refuge, his sources of escape.

Rejected.

Now he had an object more durable, more lasting, one that wouldn't break his heart—the stone.

"I'm ready, Asser. Let's go to the house."

Jeremiah headed up the hill, Asser following with the horses' reins in his hand.

The house lock was just for deterrence—he wriggled the handle and nudged the door open.

Asser tied the horses' reins to a porch railing and followed Jeremiah inside the house. Midway through the kitchen, Asser knocked something off the table. It thudded to the floor, and Jeremiah heard shuffling from his parents' bedroom.

"Who's there?" said Elfred.

His father's silhouette appeared against the wall. He had what looked like an axe in his hand, and Sarah stood behind him. "Who's there?" repeated Elfred in sharper voice.

"Hi, Father. It's Jeremiah."

"Oh my, oh my. It's you, my son." Elfred dropped the axe and hugged him.

Jeremiah's body remained straight and rigid throughout the embrace, then he pushed the man away. "Father, please. Not now."

"Weren't you in prison? What are you doing? And who's this?" asked Elfred breathlessly.

"My prison mate."

Elfred scratched his beard and covered his gaping mouth. "Son, you escaped prison."

"I don't have time to explain. We can't stay here. The king's men will be after us soon. For your safety, please don't tell them I came here."

Frozen, Elfred took Sarah's trembling hand. "Son, I don't know if I can lie. They'll find out soon enough."

Jeremiah felt his eyes enlarge, and in the dim light, he felt the demons tormenting him in a way that must be visible—it surely was, to judge from the looks on his parents' faces. He shuddered, then almost crumpled as his mind briefly flashed to the playful, carefree days as a boy in Dadde's carpentry shop. But one demon whiplashed, reminding him these weren't his real parents.

They had lied to him.

"Father, give me my inheritance," he commanded. "I'm practically dead anyways, and I may never see you again."

Releasing Sarah's hands, Elfred placed both on Jeremiah's shoulders. "Son, you don't have to run. I'm certain there's a logical explanation."

"It doesn't matter," said Jeremiah firmly. "Lord Harry poisoned me, but this can't be proved. Nobody would believe me, either. I shouldn't have responded to his instigations, but I did. It was my choice to assault the prison guard, but I had to, to escape. I'll be running the rest of my life."

Elfred left the kitchen with his hands covering his face, and Sarah came closer to Jeremiah. "My son," she said with sniffles. "Don't do this. This is your home, your family."

Without words, she locked her watery eyes onto his stare for an eternity. She broke contact first and held his stony body until Elfred returned. Jeremiah fought the memories and warmth and recalled the day he learned he was adopted.

Who am I? he thought. *I don't know.*

Jeremiah turned away. "I'm sorry, Mum. I can't stay here. I must go."

"Son," said Elfred, "I've considered it. We won't force you to stay. I put your inheritance and clothes in the bag. Say goodbye to your mum."

He lifted leaden arms and gently wrapped his arms around her.

Elfred stepped forward for a hug, but Jeremiah turned away. "Father, I'm sorry, but I have to go. Goodbye." He ensured there would be no further eye contact when he grabbed the bag and blew by Asser and out the door.

Asser stood in the doorway with his mouth open and listened to the sobs from inside the house. After several moments, Jeremiah summoned him in a monotone voice: "Are you coming, Asser? Or do you plan to stand there all night?"

"You could have thanked him. Your dad gave a bundle to an enemy of the king. Congrats is in order." Then he seemed to consider the situation and shook out his shoulders. "So, where are we going?"

"Adopted dad, Asser," said Jeremiah icily. "I don't know. But we can't stay here."

GROUSE

They hid for hours until Asser remembered where to head. Through the night they rode east, and dawn brought them out of a dew-dampened forest. Ahead in a meadow was a wooden shed smaller than a barn.

They halted and tied the horses to a post outside the shed. Asser lifted a large rock and hammered at the latch. The rusted brass loosened after several blows, and the shed door squeaked. A few more pulls, and it groaned, stuck on something.

"Jeremiah, help me."

They tried to open it, but failed even together until Jeremiah spotted what looked like a skirt and pulled at it. The door freed and swung fully open. He picked up the fabric and examined it. "What's this?"

Asser blushed. Grabbing it and taking a whiff, he said, "Nothing— we should toss it." It caught on the wall, revealing some stains on the fabric.

He snatched at the skirt, but the shelf came away with it.

"Asser," rebuked Jeremiah, "do you always break things?"

"Aye; me'll repay later." A small bed and crumpled clothes lay in the corner. "Smells like home," said Asser, stepping onto the straw. "Grab the king's saddles—we'll swap them with the saddles in the shed."

Jeremiah took the best saddle from the horse he'd ridden and carried it into the shed, then went out for the other.

"Should we change our names? And our appearance?" asked Asser. "You said you are a carpenter, like your father? Jeremiah of the Wood has a good ring to it."

179

"No nickname, Asser. No Miah either. Just Jeremiah. What about you? Tiny Hands, or Smalls, or Asser the Short?"

Asser replied with forceful punches and deep voice, "Nice try. But no. Me'd approve Master Ash or Asser the Large."

"But that wouldn't be true, Asser."

"Cute, Jerry. How do you know it's not true?"

Jeremiah smiled. "Where should we put these—under the bed?"

They pushed them far back and stuffed the clothes in front to hide them.

"Ever gotten marked?" Asser asked as he found the other saddles.

"No. My father would've killed me."

"Come on, it'll be fun." Asser started out of the shed with another saddle, and Jeremiah followed with his saddle.

"No, I'm not doing that, Asser."

After saddling their horses, Asser bolted the shed door, and they began to walk in the direction he indicated.

"The horses?" asked Jeremiah.

"We're not going far. Her house is this way."

"Her house?"

"Yes, Gwyn is an old friend—me refuge until me was caught. Me wife ratted me out to the capital sheriff, and me had no place to hide except this country woman's house."

Jeremiah stood in place as Asser walked towards Gwyn's isolated stick, straw, and mud house. "Are you coming?"

"I'm not sure about this, Asser."

"Are you scared?"

"No, I'm not scared," but his voice came out strained.

"Don't you worry, young Jeremiah, son of a carpenter. Me measure it's only a destination for weary wanderers searching for sarcasm, a shave, or coupling with a witch."

The same laugh Jeremiah had heard from him as a child burped from Asser and matched the frequency of the bleating from the goats wandering her yard. Asser pushed on, but then he raised a stubby finger and stopped.

"Me know. What about the stone in your pocket? She'll accept that as payment. You seem to have special care for it."

"Oh, this?" He pulled out the cloth-wrapped stone from his shirt pocket, glanced at it, and promptly put it back and pinged his gaze from tree to tree. "It's nothing," he insisted, "just something my father gave to me. And what should I give it in payment for?"

"You need a new identity, Jeremiah. Once a carpenter, now a fugitive. Unless you prefer to be called a criminal."

"No."

"Fine. Whatever money you have in your inheritance bag, offer some to her. She'll give you a mark equal in value."

"No mark, Asser."

The events from the past week blurred in Jeremiah's mind. With upset stomach and tight chest, he reminisced the days with Dadde in the carpentry shop.

"Maybe, maybe something small," he said, pinching his thumb and finger together.

"Great. She won't hurt you."

They came to the front porch. Asser knocked at the door, and a woman in her thirties answered. Her enlarged ear lobes, marked arms, and multicolored hair drew Jeremiah in. His parents would have accused her a witch.

"Well, if it isn't Asser Smalls. It's been a long time." She paused and said, "Since the Witenberg sheriff found you, right? Found you standing outside my door?"

"Aye, but me not small, Gwyn. Women love me personality."

Shaking the skirts of her dye-stained dress in merriment, she said, "You were standing outside my door, and all you thought to say was . . . excuse me"—she coughed and lowered her voice to mock Asser— "was 'me was outstanding.'"

"Yes, not me most clever line."

Laughing now, she continued. "And you confessed, you confessed you killed one of my customers with your hands? With your *tiny hands*?"

She walked her fingers up his thigh, grabbed a hand, and compared it to hers. A strong sweep of her arms pulled Asser into her chest.

Smushed, he said, "Me was drunk off your liquor, Gwyn. But one punch to the fat bastard's heart did the trick."

Tiptoeing up to meet her lips, Asser wrapped his arms around her to hold on, and they smooched.

Jeremiah yelped a little at the impropriety and wondered, *Where am I?*

"Aye, aye," she said. "Small in stature but not elsewhere. Please, come in."

Once through the door, into the kitchen, she stroked Jeremiah's long, curly hair and asked, "And who's this handsome fellow?"

Clearing his throat, Jeremiah said, "Hello, madam. My name is Jeremiah. I hear you ink bodies."

"Oh, that's why you're here? You didn't come for my knowledge of kingdom affairs?"

"She is a bit sarcastic like me, Jeremiah. But you'll get used to it."

Jeremiah looked for another exit. Plants spilled from the windowsill into the sink, next to vials of unlabeled liquids of varied colors. Lavender steamed into the air.

"So, you're here for marks, Smalls?"

"For Jeremiah, yes, but not me. Me need a haircut and new clothes."

"I gave your clothes away, but I'll look. Thought you were in prison."

"Me was."

Asser sank into the chair. "Completely off," he directed. "And clean-shaven. Me tired of the beard and gray hairs."

+———+

Once cut and shaved, Asser asked, "Can you cut his hair too? He has a tiny problem—needs a new look."

Removing a whetstone from its sink bath, she chuckled, "Tiny problem, Asser?"

"Funny, Gwyn. Seriously, he needs a cut."

"So stiff, Ass," she said coolly. "I will." Pointing to Jeremiah, she said, "Sit. This won't take long"—she lifted his curls in her hands—"though it seems a shame."

"Thanks," said Asser apologetically. "The sheriff again—trouble with him."

"Why?"

"We broke out of prison."

She burst out laughing. "You and little Jeremiah escaped?"

Jeremiah removed the stone from his shirt pocket, slid it discreetly to his undergarment pouch, moved it around to the right spot, and said, "I'm stronger than you think, Gwyn."

Asser and Gwyn slapped their knees and snickered.

"What?" asked Jeremiah.

"Your pocket. It's in an odd location," said Asser. "You sewed a codpiece, a tiny pouchy, into your drawers?"

"Yeah, quit dinking around with your thing," Gwyn said through her laughs.

"Oh," Jeremiah said sheepishly. Drawing his knees together, he turned his head a fraction to avoid the light reflecting off the knives on the table.

Gwyn sharpened a small blade against the whetstone's course side, and Jeremiah plugged his ears against the screech like rusted saw teeth on iron. Then she honed the blade on a brass rod.

When Gwyn was done cutting away the thick hair he'd worn so long, Jeremiah did not know what to make of himself.

"So handsome," said Asser, dragging his voice in a mocking high pitch. "It's nice to see a boy becoming a man. Come here." Asser moved towards him and landed a kiss on his cheek.

Jeremiah wiped away the kiss and escaped outside, past a large iron pot sitting atop a fire. He stopped and reveled in the woody smoke aromas with the hints of sweet molasses.

"Home," he muttered, "smells like home."

He slumped back towards the house while combing his short hair with his fingers. *I've aged.* "Now a mark," he said aloud. *Can I do this?*

"So, what'll it be?" she asked Jeremiah when he came back inside. "An animal, a symbol, perchance a picture of your parents?"

"Definitely not a picture of my parents." His body vibrated in the chair with shivers as a chill passed through him. "Let's start small. How about a hawk or an eagle? I've always loved birds."

"Or a witch?" piped Asser. "You see her saucing broom in the pot?"

"Oh, quit, Ass. Don't worry about a thing, honey," she told Jeremiah as she massaged his head. "That's just my stick for stirring the pot."

She dipped a sharpened hawk feather into blue dye and said, "A bird it is. Now this won't hurt a bit."

"Wait," he said with hand out. "Do you have alcohol?"

"Certainly. Grab a glass and pour from that wooden barrel on the table."

The scent of apples met his nostrils before the clear liquor flowed down his throat. Even before the alcohol took hold, he moved as if it had, shining like the moon and wobbling with crisscrossed steps on the wooden floor until he found the chair.

"A wee bit too much, me measure," Asser said, then laughed. "You'll be surprised."

"My powerful, homemade brew," she said. "Turns hideous back-woods peasants into princesses."

An hour later, Jeremiah woke and wormed against the cloth covering his back. "My *back*! I wanted a small mark on my arm!"

"Asser and I agreed," said Gwyn dryly. "A wolf suits you better."

"But don't worry," she assured him. "We also marked your arms. Congratulations. You're now a knight. I mean, at least you have the markings of a knight." She grinned at Asser and gathered her tools.

Jeremiah ran outside. A cross inked his left arm, and a shield with crossed swords inked his right. "Not bad," he said. "Like Alfred's. But no one will believe I was a knight. I need a story."

But the wolf mark! At least I can't see it.

"Tell the innkeeper you're a knight," said Gwyn.

"At The Grouse?" asked Asser. "He won't believe it."

"Yes, unless you two want to share me bed or the bed in the shed."

Asser laughed. "No, no, there's only one bed, and me not sharing you nor sharing a bed with Jeremiah."

"Fine. Ask for lodging there—he owes me."

"You're right, Gwyn. We'll go to the inn. The sheriff or king will comb the capital first before searching here. We'll need to make some more money before running again."

Spreading her arms, she invited Asser to hug and kiss her farewell.

"Thank you, Gwyn. Good seeing you again."

Jeremiah took a coin from his inheritance bag and offered it to Gwyn. "Will this cover it, madam?" he asked.

She folded her arms and told Asser, "Just see me before you run off again."

Leaving their horses near her shed, with her agreement to feed and water them, they walked a furlong—a furrow of a field—through forest. And then the pine forest floor turned to a well-traveled dirt path leading to a thatched country pub.

Averting plump-bodied, feather-legged chickens hunting worms in the lodging yard, they almost tripped, falling against topless, drunk women bursting out the tavern door.

Jeremiah's eyes widened at the unaccustomed sight and he followed.

"Believe me, Jeremiah. Been there. Done that. You don't want them. Once you ring that bell, or in me case, many times, it can't be unrung. It stays with you."

"Thank you, Dadde," said Jeremiah, his voice reedy.

"Well, here we are," said Asser.

Jeremiah's eyes rose. "Appropriate," he said.

Above the door, the pub's name welcomed travelers: *The Grouse*.

The door didn't stay open long, but the stench punched out at them. Still fresh from the mead-ball bath, Jeremiah took in the contrast immediately: urine in the courtyard mud, scattered refuse odors amplified by the spring sun, boot-patterned horse manure, dried vomit puddled in the infrequently changed floor straw, rotting food scraps, and skunky ale. His guilt-ridden stomachache worsened, and he dry heaved.

"Look, Jeremiah, horny herds sharing a meal with their escorts—a half-day's work consumed in minutes."

At first glance into the wooden interior filled with people the likes he'd never seen before, such as men massive as boulders, Jeremiah flashed back to childhood.

He recalled his figurines of giants and how they battled savages in role playing. Legends told of dark giants in the frontier lands of the kingdom, a race of men and women as big as oxen and noses as sharp as horns that could destroy their enemies with one punch.

Dim candlelight from circular chandeliers showed a range of browns and reds like his carpentry shop and long wooden tables and benches, stairs, and one bar. Mugs clanked each other and thudded on the planks; knots of customers quarreled and even punched one another. Some sat but others stood; some sang but others talked. Toddlers crawled on the floor next to drunk men lounging on harlots' laps. One played a stringed instrument.

Jeremiah had never seen this many diversely colored women.

"Many cannot afford a night's stay in the inn, so they sell themselves for money," said Asser. "The women"—he pointed— "they come off ships at the Witen Channel seeking transportation to more lucrative clients in Witenberg. Yet, as you can tell, some lords and Witen politicians travel here."

"Why?"

"Capital bath houses are too risky."

On the way through the courtyard from the tavern to the inn, Asser stopped at the outhouse. He opened the wooden door. "Odd," he said. A dozen men sat inside on chamber pots; six per row without partition, facing each other while defecating. Asser delayed in leaving, but Jeremiah pulled him away.

"Wait, wait," Asser said with a laugh. "Potty time—it's the colorful and comical potty talk. Much business is accomplished here." He slapped his knees, and Jeremiah sighed.

"Let's find a place at the inn," said Jeremiah in disgust.

One man hunched over punch-drunk and toppled as the door closed.

"There it is." Asser pointed to the inn.

When they approached the desk, the innkeeper began to take their names for a room but then stopped. "Hold on."

Two slender young women with stamps on their arms hustled past reception, trailed by their elderly, wrinkled woman handler.

"Bawd," the innkeeper said, waving his hand at the woman, "they need to pay for their rooms."

"Girls!" she called. "Stop. Show your license."

From her leather satchel, the bawd dug for the coin bag but pulled silk and satin dresses out instead and said, "When you pay your debts, you'll get one of these as a reward, instead of those drab, coarse tunics."

"I still need money, bawd," said the innkeeper.

Asser introduced himself to the girls. "Well, hello."

They ignored his advances. "Too short," one said.

"But he could pay," said the other hopefully.

Her smile had a trace of courteous mockery, and her eyes swept his body. "Too small. And lower class."

They brushed him away and headed to their rooms once the bawd paid.

"Lesson one about women," said Asser. "No matter how beautiful your face"—he smoothed his hands over his shaved chin—"or how charming you may be, or how intelligent, women will choose the most hideous, fearsome arsehole if he's tall. Women like tall men. But money helps, of course."

Jeremiah grunted, remembering the playful look Marianne threw to Harry on the stage.

"But I kicked the tall lord's arse," said Jeremiah.

"Who got your girl?"

A knot formed in Jeremiah's gut, and he managed, "Thanks. Thanks, Tiny Hands."

Asser turned to the innkeeper and reminded him of the promise to Gwyn. After negotiation, the innkeeper granted them both jobs and lodging in the tavern basement.

ORDERS

Rachel woke rested, full of energy, and alive. "Come on, girl," she said to Luta, "time for potty." Out of the castle and through the barren forest they wound on her vineyard trail. Thoughts of Jeremiah came to Rachel's mind as Luta circled and sniffed in the underbrush.

The queen had continued meeting with Padre and Charles over the years, but they kept agreeing Jeremiah wasn't yet ready to become king.

Should I have stopped the war? When will he be ready to take the throne?

The War of Unification had drained her mentally and emotionally; it had all gone as she feared. As the war surged and more young men returned injured or not at all, grief bubbled to the surface of her skin and tingles spidered throughout her body like the lines through cracking ice. She bore this as her people's queen.

"Come on, girl, go potty," said Rachel. After sniffing around, Luta lowered her massive frame to pee. "Good girl, let's head back inside." Luta tried to go past the maids and into the chamber to go to bed, but Rachel stopped her. The whisper of lace against her thighs reminded her of Richard. "Elena," she said, handing her the leash, "please watch Luta for a bit. I have business with the king."

She went into the chamber and quietly closed the door, then halted at the vanity mirror and noticed her reflection. Bags underneath her eyes had softened and smoothed after the war ended, and a familiar glow radiated from her warm cheeks. She puckered her lips and slid into bed, then crawled a finger along Richard's arm.

He turned and without opening his eyes, he said, "My Tulip," and gently combed his hand through her hair. After several heavy blinks, he gave a tired smile. Her hand went lower, and he said, "The crown and its responsibilities have almost withered me to nothing, Tulip. But I have some old fire left."

He tenderly kissed her forehead, and she added, "There's age in your eyes, honey, but the fire is still warm."

Beneath the sheets they disappeared.

"You're more confident these days," she said afterwards. "And acting like it, more assertive. Reminds me of the man I met years ago."

Knock, knock, and knock.

"Go away," barked Richard.

"Your Majesty, you have an important guest," said Vere.

"Go away!" shouted Richard, half sitting up in bed, then cuddling around his wife again.

"I'm sorry, Your Majesty, but I believe this is more important than what you're doing over the next minute."

"Ignore him," said Rachel and returned a kiss to the tip of his nose and upper lip. He can wait."

Knock, knock, knock.

"Your Majesty, you told me to interrupt you whenever there was news of the stone."

"Stone?" Like a trebuchet, his body levered upright in the bed.

"Stay with me," moaned Rachel. "That can wait."

"Come back, Vere, at half past the hour."

"Yes, Your Majesty, I'll return in a few moments."

After a few more moments of connecting tenderly, one thought popped repeatedly into Rachel's mind: should she confess? But Richard had been too stiff, too inflexible, too short with her, she thought. This was not the day. Maybe after she worked on his guilt . . .

Traditionalists had forgiven Richard for "diluting" bloodlines to marry Rachel because she was beautiful; however, they didn't forgive her son-barren womb. They tolerated a mixed-blood monarch, but they wanted a male heir and not the immature and flighty Isabella. Purists had plotted once they wed, but, over time, the intrigue had fizzled for most. But one hard-liner persisted in leading the resistance to this royal marriage.

"Richard, you devastated Isabella and me when you ventured on the quest to find the lost stone. I fantasized your return. Why not leave this? Hand over the crown. Let's move to the coast and enjoy our remaining days."

As these words leaked from her daydreams, her thoughts returned to the crown and training Jeremiah to take it. Relaxing days at the beach would have to wait.

Richard walked to the cloak room to dress and said with a tight voice, "I can't, Tulip. Too much responsibility, especially with the new territory. Too many people depend on me. My entire life has been building this kingdom. To what end? Leave it to one of my brothers? No."

"Ill-advised," she reminded him. She left the bed and stared out the window to the distant vineyards.

"Return to the old republic, the days when power was dispersed, and decisions were made at the lowest levels possible. The Crown has taken on too many responsibilities."

In his undergarments, he joined her at the window and placed his arms around her waist. After a long beat, he softened and said, "Sounds nice in theory, but in days of chaos and confusion and war, decisions should be made at the highest levels, from those with the most knowledge. We can't trust peasants."

"Be careful, Richard. I suspect the Church wants some of this power. Recall what I said: conversion of souls by the sword is no recipe for bringing the kingdom of God."

More knocks came to the door.

"Consider it, honey," she whispered, and kissed his neck as she hugged him around the waist. "You and I getting away, leaving behind these burdens."

"Your Majesty, it's time," said Vere through the door.

With slumping shoulders, she twisted away, played with her hair, and said, "Attend to your business."

His firm hands left her waist, and a pang of loneliness knifed across her chest. As he placed the crown on his head, a knot rose in her throat.

The door clicked shut, and she ran to place an ear upon it. The stone had been found, she learned, and it was with a man named Jeremiah. But Jeremiah had vanished, escaped from prison. The King's Special Guard Corps of knights was preparing to find him.

Her breath caught in her throat and burst out as a hiccup. The handle turned, and she bolted away for her dressing room. "Tulip," called Richard as he opened the door, "where are you?"

"In here, honey," she said and grabbed a washcloth.

"Meet me in the royal training grounds. I want you to meet the team who will find the stone."

After dressing, Rachel retrieved Luta, Elena, Klara, and younger maids, and they joined them on the fairgrounds. On the field a man with a head full of golden hair and muscles as toned as the fittest knight squared himself, raised his bow, and shot a crow perched on a tree branch. In between arrow pulls, he gulped something from a vial.

In the castle tower, spectators clapped, including Isabella and her four-year-old daughter Madelyn. The youngest maid, taking advantage of the familiarity the queen allowed, burst out, "Ooh, who is that knight, Your Highness?"

"He's Bella's former suitor," said Rachel dryly. "Lord Alfred, the carpenter's son. The best knight, and my husband's favorite."

"Why didn't they marry?" asked the maid, blushing at her words as Richard joined them. The archer was approaching them too, to receive honor of the king.

"Because the king convinced Isabella to marry Robert the Bearded. In return for bravery in battle, he rewarded Alfred with a noble woman near Château Gaillard in Normandy. But," she added as she crooked her mouth, "Richard will honor Alfred with finding the lost stone."

"Fantastic shot. Like father, like son," said Richard.

"I should've been your son-in-law," mumbled Alfred. Something caught the corner of his eye as he bowed. "Your Highness," he said to Rachel and glanced towards Lady Isabella.

"Listen, Son," Richard said with a firm grasp on Alfred's shoulder, "I have an important task for you, but the mission is confidential."

"Yes, Your Majesty."

"You know the stone has been missing for many years now, but we have a lead."

"Miraculous!" said Alfred loudly, with notes of sarcasm. Because he was on display for all at the tournament, he made a show of resuming target practice with the crisp snap of his wrist and a lightning release of the bow. "My lord, the trace has been cold for many years. Why, suddenly, do we think we know its location?"

"We believe your brother has it."

Alfred slowly and deliberately removed his sword from its scabbard to inspect its edge. As the sun reflected off the blade into Richard's eyes, Alfred reacted with nothingness—no remorse, no emotion—but a disciplined response.

"I'll do what I need to do to recover the stone," he said, his voice lifeless.

He looked to the tower again, Rachel noted, but Isabella was gone. "But the festival begins tomorrow," said Alfred. "Permit the next two days with my family."

The corner of the king's lips pulled slightly into a smile, and Richard said, "Of course. Enjoy your family. You'll find the stone in no time."

Alfred sheathed the sword sharply, making the distinctive sound of a perfectly matched sword and scabbard.

"Your brother assaulted one of my dungeon guards," added Richard. "He escaped with another criminal and stopped at your parents' house last night, but they say they don't know where he was going."

"Why do you think he has the stone? How would he have gotten it? We didn't keep it around when we were kids."

"After the guard regained consciousness, we talked to him. He said he saw something like a rock in the prison cell. We don't know for certain it's the stone, but it's worth a shot. We've had no other leads for a very long time. Therefore, I want you to pursue him."

"What about Jeremiah?" asked Alfred.

"I want the stone; do with him as you wish," Richard said indifferently.

"Where is he?"

"That's for you and your men to discover. But be careful. Those in possession of the stone retain special powers of strength and cunning."

"We'll see. I'll visit my parents first."

"No need," said Richard, "because they're here." He gestured to where Elfred and Sarah stood uncertainly by a tree at the side of the field.

Rachel covered her mouth. *The allure of the stone makes men mad,* she thought. Sarah the Strong appeared as white as the glaring sun, and Elfred carried something golden in his hand.

"Come with me, Elena," said Rachel. They walked to Sarah, and Rachel ordered her maid to get wine and bread.

With a sentinel leading him, Alfred came over to his father, who stood with open arms. "Son," said Elfred.

"Father," Alfred replied coldly and refused to hug. In a razor-sharp tone, he said, "Tell me where Jeremiah is. We don't have time for lies. He's a criminal and enemy of the kingdom. We believe he possesses the stone."

"The stone? That stupid stone? What about your brother? Don't you care about him?"

Rachel grieved at the distance between father and son. *No doubt the war did this. And the king.*

194

"Father, I don't have time for this. You know he has the stone. Tell me where he went."

"We don't know. He woke us in the dead of night, took his belongings, and left."

"He left no clues?"

"As I said, he didn't give time for a proper farewell. He asked for his inheritance and left."

"Did he have a stone?"

"Son, I don't know. It was dark."

"It seems it's in Jeremiah's department to become a thief. I bet he stole it. The guard he knocked out thought he saw some sort of stone in his cell."

Tilting his head, Elfred said, "I don't know what to say except we don't know. We're shocked from his actions this past week. If you find him, don't hurt him—" Elfred handed him the golden fabric and said, "Lord Harold found this at the mead ball."

Alfred received it, looked briefly, then promptly released it, letting it fall to the dirt and said, "What do you want? For me to give this to him? Apparently, those in possession of the stone are capable of unusual feats of strength or cunning. Though small, he's not the weak boy, the little brother I used to wrestle with as a child. He's always been smart, so he'll have an advantage."

Alfred paced beneath the tree a few moments until he seemed to decide something. "I know. I'll ask Marianne. He likely whispered something to her during the mead ball, trying everything in his power to persuade her to like him."

Elfred suddenly slapped him in the face and jammed a finger into his chest. "Son! Stop. You're brothers. You used to be inseparable. And you have a similar cloak."

Alfred's face twitched briefly, but his body stood rigid and cold. He inched forward and grabbed Elfred's wrist.

Rachel squeezed Sarah's trembling hand and promised, "Your son will be fine, Sarah. No one will hurt him." As she said this, her hand instinctively clenched firmer, not letting go, like the first time she held Isabella in her arms. But the emptiness, the uncertainty, the unknowing sank into her chest and stole her breaths as she remembered the many miscarriages. *All is well, all is well, all is well,* she told herself.

"Father, that was a long time ago. Jeremiah is different," said Alfred. He released Elfred's wrist and turned his back. "I have a duty to fulfill. I'll find the stone and return it to the Crown."

Now sweaty, Rachel's palms slipped from Sarah's hands, and Sarah covered her mouth to contain her cries. Rachel's chin sagged on her chest, and she said, "Elena, please take care of Sarah. I need to take a walk."

"Should I worry about you, my lady?"

"No, I'll be fine."

Rachel went past the maids and to her room and then looked out her window. There was no one below. She disrobed, then disguised in a long woolen tunic, and covered her head in a close-fitting cloth cap and wimple. Down the floors she sped. Out the door, she looked right, left, then right again.

Normally, she made this journey at dark, after trips to the winery. But time was critical. She came to a door that read *The King's Scriptorium.* She unlocked the door and walked inside.

On a bookshelf lay a note.

It was from Father William.

"About time," she muttered.

I come daily an hour before sunrise. Meet me, Your Highness.

<hr />

Later that night, she disguised herself in a brown cloak and was protected by two private sentinels as she slowly walked through the city to aid her thinking. As she neared the cathedral, she pulled her hood briefly, long enough to see the hems of a cloak swing into sight. A woman was leaving the bath house with a bag over her shoulder. She turned slightly, and in a pause, Rachel saw a spark flash in the woman's eyes.

Her face suddenly tightened into an injured look, and she suppressed her smile. She moved swiftly across the courtyard until out of sight.

For a moment, Rachel stopped, standing exposed with her hood pulled. That woman left her the same feeling of assurance she had when choosing Sarah as Jeremiah's adopted mother—an assurance backed with regal bearing and a smile with the dignity of a queen.

After considering several options, Rachel settled on one and went to Richard. She advised him to change the castle flag color from blue to purple to indicate an increase in castle defense protections because of the stone hunt. More importantly, this also signaled to Charles and Padre to meet her in the king's scriptorium tomorrow morning at sunrise.

PLAN

W illiam opened the outer door, then pushed in the correct combination of numbers to gain passage through the second door into the king's scriptorium. He bounced a little as he stepped onto the velvety carpet.

"Father William, you've changed," said Rachel, noticing his hat and longer hair.

With a sweeping flourish, William removed his wide-brimmed black hat and bowed at an angle to greet her. "Your Highness, your clues were very difficult, but"—he held the hat before him—"I remembered the archb-bishop."

"Yes, to ensure secrecy. Has anyone been following you?" She took his cold hand and blew out the single candle and beckoned him to the back of the library.

"I don't think so," he said. "I've been careful. Where are we going?"

"Through to another room. I want you to meet the others."

With a shoulder thrust, she pushed the vault door closed behind them. It locked into place and no crack would be visible in the library. "Airtight," said Rachel.

However, the air in the room felt heavy to William, sinking, almost visible, like incense residue raining past candlelight in fine particles.

"We can't be in here too long," she warned.

"Yes, Your Highness. Is there a clock? I have only half an hour."

"You won't need to return. You have an alibi."

"What?" asked William, incredulous.

"But first—introductions." She turned around to where two other men, swathed in brown cloaks, sat quietly. "This old chap is Lord Charles, as I'm sure you know. A gentleman of regard, he hails from one of the kingdom's founding families and insists on maintaining republican tradition despite the growing centralization of executive power over the years. He's affectionately known as Greybeard."

"Father William," said Charles. As he firmly clasped William's hand, a warm, peculiar odor seemed to hover in the air. The formal greeting made an audible creak in his lower back, and his long, thin legs nearly buckled as his noticeable nose neared the floor with the bow. "Or, should I call you Lord William, or Sir William? Your garments suggest nobility."

"Nice to see you again, Lord Charles," said William with a sheepish grin and a helpless gesture to his clothing.

"And this handsome fellow is cute as a cub—older in years but wise and firm as your favorite uncle. Meet Padre."

"You make me blush, my lady."

Padre hugged William, and his head rested briefly against William's chest.

"Thank you. I think?" said William.

"This is your new team," said Rachel with an arm wave.

"My team? An old man out to pasture, another priest—but an old one, and a queen?"

"I beg your pardon," said Charles and whacked him lightly across the knees with his cane. "Old age means wisdom—not irrelevance, *Bouncy*."

Rachel laughed. "But your legendary rocking on your toes has lessened, William. New shoes?"

"Yes, from the city," he said, pausing nervously. "Never mind— can we carry on? Time is ticking, and I need to get back to the abbey."

"William, I took care of it," Rachel said. "When Fuss sees your bed empty, he'll notify the abbot, and the abbot will tell him you're with the king."

"Fuss, the abbot . . . wait—how do you know them?"

"William," she said matter-of-factly, "I'm the queen. Like your Night Watchers, I have hands and ears in the shadows across this kingdom. And"—she looked towards the rest of the team—"we'll help you find Mati's murderer. In return, you'll help restore the kingdom."

Unrolling a scroll onto a small desk, Rachel continued, "We don't have much time before Richard wakes."

"And before we suffocate," added Charles.

"I assume I don't have a choice, Your Highness?"

"No," she said curtly.

"What's in this for you?" he asked.

Rachel tied her hair up quickly into a bun. "William, we're in the same fight. We want justice and restoration. Mati was our friend too. You can ask more questions later."

She placed thick, round candles on each corner of the scroll. "This is what Mati planned to make public."

"Wh-where'd you get this? From Ma-Mati?" managed William.

As she read the words *Love or Freedom*, an inner glow warmed around her like she had shed the brown cloak, shed her inner garments, and shed another layer, deeper—deeper still. Naked now, she stood exposed but bold before him, unafraid to speak truth and carry on her plan.

"The prophecies will be copied," she continued. "Mati's teachings will be distributed far and wide, and the power networks will fall."

As William skimmed the poems and the longer text, the longest instance of a pause struck him, and he remembered the letter from Rachel that he had delivered to Conti.

"The antidote to the pope's poison and the stone's power over men," she said as he continued reading. "Now, turn your attention to this list of suspects."

As she unrolled a small scroll, a voice could be heard beyond the wall—talking. Grunting.

"Not again," she muttered. An ear to the wall, she nodded.

"We need to go. William, these will be in this chest."

Blowing out candles, William said, "I thought you said this room was airtight?"

"Airtight—not soundproof," said Rachel calmly. "Richard must be awake. Quickly, through the door."

Rachel closed the door and turned the dial until it locked. She led the men up a spiral stone staircase, and just past what must be the ground floor, she halted. "Padre and Charles, exit here and walk through the woods—on my trail to the winery."

"Winery, Your Majesty?" asked William. "We must be careful."

"Don't worry, William," assured Rachel. "This is my winery—hidden behind the castle grounds, next to the river and forest."

William pictured the size of the castle complex and imagined more hidden doors and secret passageways. "I'll try not to, Your Majesty," said William.

"Padre," continued Rachel, "find Jeremiah. Protect the stone. Most importantly, train him to become king."

"Yes, my lady," said Padre.

"And William, come with me," she said.

The two of them climbed a long way up, until Rachel stumbled on the last step and fell through a door into a room filled with hanging clothes and drawers. "Stay here, William—and don't look."

"As you wish, Your Highness." He studied the fabrics hanging just behind him while she rustled around opening drawers and grunting as she changed.

Barking started choppy from beyond a far door and increased until scratching and whining replaced it. *Hope it's not a vicious one*, William thought, squeezing his eyes closed.

"Be right there, Luta," Rachel said as she flung fabrics around.

"Don't move," she warned William. "She'll think you're a toy."

She opened the door, and an enormous dog pounced onto the pile of garments, then wrestled through the clothes, until she found him and licked his face repeatedly.

"Meet Luta," Rachel said. "Stay here until I clear the room. Let's go, girl."

———

She returned maybe an hour later. "Come on, Father William. All's clear—return the same way you came and meet Chamberlain Vere tomorrow morning two hours after Prime."

Before he attempted to speak, Rachel added, "Yes—the abbot knows you'll be with the king."

He disentangled himself from all the garments, and she escorted him through the bed chamber to the spiral stone staircase.

"Richard's expecting you tomorrow. I've already convinced him you're trustworthy. Be natural and don't respond to his—his—tantrums. Go to the first-floor balcony and wait for Chamberlain Vere. He'll take you to meetings with Richard. Listen and take notes. Then meet me tomorrow afternoon after Nones in your old cathedral office. I want to show you something."

"Is that safe?"

"Yes," she said. "I'll have sentinels. Plus, the cathedral should be busy. I'll be dressed in a brown cloak as I was this morning. Now go."

JAMEELA

Two slashes knifed into the wall marked the number of days since heartbreak and prison break.

This day at The Grouse started without difference from the day before: Jeremiah fondled the stone, men drank, musicians played, barmaids wrote debts on a chalkboard, and harlots seduced customers while robbing them. Male procurers and female bawds took turns escorting foreigners into secret rooms.

"Welcome," said Jeremiah, speaking for himself and Asser beside him behind the bar. "What part of the kingdom?"

As two women with breasts overflowing their clothing plopped onto barstools, Jeremiah said, "Easy, easy. Those stools are made from the finest wood in these fine forests."

The women chuckled and revealed large gaps among their teeth.

"You don't remember us?" asked the blonde. "Misty and Scarlet."

"Me remember," said Asser. "Misty, you're the blonde. And, Scarlet, you're the redhead."

The corner of Jeremiah's mouth quirked up. "Sorry."

"The other night?" Scarlet reminded him. "Your outrageous marks?"

Jeremiah squirmed and grimaced.

"He doesn't remember us," said Misty. "Probably too drunk or too heartbroken over some woman named Marianne."

"I'm sorry, ladies. I don't remember."

"'Oh, Marianne. Why, why?'" mocked Asser. "You cried the next morning after your night with these ladies."

"What are you talking about?" asked Jeremiah indignantly.

"Your first, then your second time. How awkward they were?"

"I don't remember, Asser," Jeremiah said and put the stone in his wool shirt pocket, then hand-pumped the barrel. He lifted the tap and poured some contents of the pitcher into a mug and took a swig. The acquired taste coated his mouth and softened the bitterness he tasted there and the remorse from giving more than half his inheritance away in minutes. Heavy ale had eased the transactions with women and filled the empty pit he was left with as one of them rolled away from him—the fleeting sense of belonging rolling away with her. It was fun at first, but he desired deeper connection.

"What's the point?" he asked sulkily. He looked down the bar. He had vowed to design and build it sturdier. However, his blank stare lengthened, and he daydreamed nothing. His carpentry, even, was slipping away.

"We've come for the spring market festival," Misty said. "Best area in the kingdom to buy and sell our exotic birds." She looked towards the crate with two parrots she'd put up on the bar.

"Finest wood in these fine forests," said one parrot repeatedly.

Laughs mimicked laughs until they resounded throughout the tavern.

Imitating the same high-pitched, monotone parrot voice, Asser said, "Wilting wood Jeremiah weeps, wilting wood Jeremiah weeps."

A nearby patron fell on hands and knees in merriment, and the walls of The Grouse rattled with laughter.

Asser piped in again. "Much wisdom from those two cranky parrots. Are those all your birds?"

"No," said Misty. "We have more in crates outside."

"Where are you staying?"

"Why, wouldn't you like to know?" Scarlet said, opening her mouth in a taunt that showed enough gnarled teeth to make Asser cringe.

"That's why me asked. We have no room at this inn."

"Always vacant in this inn," said an older man in a slight drawl. "Ass can barely keep 'em in—one look at his mug and they be runnin' out."

The man slid the barstool closer and raised a giant hand sheathed in a glove, ready for a shake with the women. His words rumbled deeply: "Name is Maurice, but friends call me Mo."

"Friends?" asked Asser. "Me haven't seen 'em." Drying a glass, he added, "Unless you mean your bottom-of-the-barrel giant friends. Take another cider, Mo."

He was an imposing man with a broad torso, biceps like boulders, four-foot-wide shoulders, and a massive head. Fragments of wood clung to Mo's ashy beard and pine-stained overalls. He smelled of tang and pine. Jeremiah hadn't noticed his size until the women began to stare, for he'd become accustomed to the variety of people that frequented the place. But then he became aware of his face, including the massive mole on the tip of his nose.

He didn't resemble the giants in the legends—he was wide, but not as tall as Jeremiah imagined, and the stories told of battles against dark forces. Mo had darker skin, but his spirit seemed gentle.

Jeremiah looked around the room. Some people were larger than Mo and some were smaller.

Maybe giant *means something else,* he thought.

Dark chestnut skin contrasted thick, silver locks pulled tight to cascade down Mo's back. In the dim bar light, his eyes were ash-colored, but in the sun, Jeremiah had seen their deep black.

"Please, please," said Misty, "we have no time for older men. You couldn't satisfy us—you're not our type." She gulped the frothy beer. Before the aftertaste settled on the back of her throat, Misty burped and commented, "Great mouthfeel!"

Asser cackled, and like a snowball rolling downhill, Mo's laugh started in the gut and gained mass and depth.

"The burp or the beer?" asked Asser in between breaths.

Scarlet's throat pulsed like she was preparing to speak.

"Mo is a regular," continued Asser, "and women usually don't fall for his ill-begotten charms. He's a quiet man, and large—a giant, really—me massive sidekick. Keep drinking, laddy."

"Thanks, Ass."

"Anytime, Mo."

Scarlet burped, "B-E-E-R!"

Jeremiah wiped the counter as Asser laughed and pushed a pitcher to Scarlet.

A loud racket burst out nearby, and Jeremiah stopped and looked up. The woman appeared hazy, like he was looking through a fire. He wiped his eyes as his thoughts wandered through the past.

"Leave me alone," demanded the woman again. She lifted her drab tunic and kicked two rough-looking men with a strapped leather boot.

"What'll you do about it?" asked one man. "You're by yourself. Come on—come with us and we'll take care of you."

The larger man held her while the other tied a rope around her hands.

"Knaves," grumbled Mo noisily as he slammed his mug on the bar.

She kicked forward, her boot connecting with their knees, and the rope fell.

"Get off her," said Mo.

The larger man grabbed her wrists as she spun, and he pulled her into his chest.

"I said get off her!" thundered Mo. His sudden movement pushed the stool, and it thudded to the floor. Jeremiah looked up blearily again, then back down at the mug he was polishing.

As Mo rumbled past the tables, rattling mugs, the men released her and ran. Mo's massive boot pinned down the trailing hems of their cloaks sweeping the floor. The smaller one cast his cloak aside and weaseled through the door.

Mo's arm shot to the door and blocked the other man in.

"Giants," said the larger man through gritted teeth. He unbuckled his brooch, letting the cloak fall. He rolled up his sleeves and spat at the floor. "We don't want your kind here, smote."

"Me can help you, Mo," said Asser, his low voice echoing as the pub quieted.

Mo cocked his head, and his eyes became a shade more glazed. "You be runnin' and now you mouthin' to me?" asked Mo.

Jeremiah looked up again to see a black, thick substance ooze from the man's mouth and drip onto Mo's boot.

"She wouldn't even," droned Jeremiah. He removed the stone from his pocket, caressed it, and said, "She doesn't care that I'm gone."

Asser grabbed something underneath the bar and hurled it towards Mo. Jeremiah startled at the sound of the breaking glass.

"What's going on?" he asked, seeing a woman on the floor.

"Go for it, Mo!" shouted Asser.

"Not again," whined Jeremiah.

Mo huffed and pulled his thick glove more firmly onto his right hand.

The man reeled.

"Fine, I'll replace it. Again . . ." Jeremiah's voice trailed away.

Mo leaned in and shot a forceful hook into the wall.

The man cringed as the wood panel broke and smacked the back of his head.

"Stupid smote," the man said with an air of righteousness. As he crawled along the floor, Jeremiah cringed slightly, expecting a kick from Mo because the man used a derogatory word for outcasts.

Instead of kicking, Mo opened the door and threw him out. "Don't come here again."

"Parrot ladies," said Mo with a motion towards them, "take these drunkards home with you."

"Our pleasure. Let's go," they said to their parrots.

"You hurt, lady?" asked Mo of the woman sitting up against the wall.

A violin screech sounded from a troubadour, and the woman held her temple at the noise.

"What'd you say?" she asked.

"You hurt?"

"I'm fine, thank you. Who are you?" she asked, her voice relaxed. His hand enveloped hers and effortlessly lifted her.

"I'm Mo. Come, my lady."

Wiping in continuous circles, Jeremiah locked eyes on her. She followed Mo and bypassed the waddling ducks pecking barley on the straw floor. As she walked past procurers exchanging teenage girls for coins, she slumped in dejection.

"My lady," said Mo, "this is Asser. His wit is always fixin' to duel with court jesters in pun battles. His hole be blowin' the hottest air in here."

"Thanks, laddy. Pleasure meeting you," Asser said and kissed her hand. "Me is more of a gentleman than this brute."

"And this is Jeremiah," said Mo. "Good with his hands, he can craft anythin' out of wood, but woman talk spooks him."

She leaned slightly over the bar to show cleavage but promptly pulled back and put out a hand.

Jeremiah slid his hands off the bar and into his shirt pockets, gripping the stone with his left, and faintly said, "Hello."

Butterflies came alive within him.

"And not a man of many words either," she quipped and watched his hands, both stuffed in his pockets.

"And I'm Mo."

Asser interrupted him, "You've already said that. Me'll show you around. You met the drunks. Sorry. What's your name?"

"Jameela," she said.

"Jameela. Hmm, you're not from this part of the kingdom, are you?"

"No. I'm not."

"You're not much of a talker either, me measure. You and Jeremiah will get along fine. Welcome to this bar and this side of town."

"Thank you."

Jeremiah found her eyes, fixed upon them, and knew he would follow her wherever she went.

"Hello," he said.

She was different, but he didn't know the precise word.

Exotic?

With marked calligraphy on her hands, pierced nose, and a cautious smile, she moved gracefully and purposefully. Honeydew eyes with sparkles of greenish-blue softened her desert-sand skin, and her caramel-colored hair was chopped to the shoulder.

"Hello," Jeremiah said again.

"We've already established that. Will you offer me a drink?"

Narrowing his eyes, he sniffed. "You can have week-old mead on the house. It's made of agony, remorse, pain, and bitters."

"Don't listen to him," chided Asser. "He's still upset about losing the love of his life to an oafish lord because he couldn't keep his liquor. And this was weeks ago."

"No—days, Asser," corrected Jeremiah, coming to himself. "Well, your wife cheated on you with a peasant."

"You lost someone?" she asked flatly.

"It was just one date, but we had been friends our entire lives. She was perfect. Because of my actions, she left me and went to her ex-boyfriend."

"Move on," she said, and swiped her hand. "Obviously, it wasn't meant to be."

His head jerked back. "We just met and you're telling me to move on as if you know me."

"I don't know you, but I've met many men like you—immature and can't deal with rejections. It's time to get over yourself—and her."

Asser turned to Jeremiah and laughed. "Don't worry about it. Forget Marianne. Keep watch."

Jeremiah elbowed him and softly said, "Quiet, Asser. We can't let people know we escaped jail. We need a plan, our next move."

"Watch for summoners," he whispered. "Believe me, me know. Eventually they'll show. Rats like me will be our first clue. Or look for men dressed in clerical garb." Breaking their huddle, Asser said louder, "Me afraid she's right, Jeremiah. Get over yourself."

Jeremiah groaned and shoved the stone from his shirt pocket into his undergarment pouch. "Asser, pour her ale while I get more mead." With heavy footsteps, he plodded downstairs to retrieve a barrel of week-old mead. Drunk patrons wouldn't register how horrible the concoction had become, particularly at dirt-cheap prices—and neither would he. He hoped to remove all memories of Marianne.

As he tramped up the stairs, he saw Asser lean towards her. "Has anyone told you how beautiful you are, despite your despicable marks?"

"Has anyone told you how horribly disgusting you look? I bet those parrot ladies wouldn't be your mistress for a night."

"The ladies happen to love me," he said and winked.

"Yeah, when you're gone," snapped Jeremiah as he thumped the barrel down. "Jameela, what does your name mean?"

"Beautiful," she said. "And Asser, if you ever try to touch me, I'll kill you." She pointed to marks near her stomach, revealed by the tear the brute made to her drab tunic. "Each one represents a man I've killed."

Asser ducked away. "All right, all right. You're mad. But beautiful. Ripe enough for Jeremiah."

Placing the mead barrel on the tap, Jeremiah noted a figure with a hidden face, buried deep in a brown hood, approaching the bar. "May I help you?"

"A fine establishment you have here," he said. "Do you usually have women strewn over the floor with men touching them?"

"Not usually, but this is where peasants come to escape the drudgery."

He ordered an ale with a smile and sat. To Jeremiah, the man was strangely familiar, but he couldn't place him. Then the man raised a hand and asked, "Can I order flatbread?"

Asser tightened his face and said, "Flatbread? What kind of place do you think this is? Only ale, some liquor, and mead here, old man. There is some old rye bread wandering peasants left the other day." Asser warned Jeremiah in a whisper, "We may need to prepare our horses."

"Hold on," Jeremiah whispered back. "I think I know him."

The man sipped the cloudy ale, and foam lightened his beard.

"Good mouthfeel, right?" Asser asked and nodded.

"Excuse me?"

"Mouthfeel. The texture, the feeling of the ale resting on the back of your tongue."

The man sipped, bunched his forehead, and raised his eyes. "What is your name?" he asked.

"Master Ash of the Woods."

"Asser," corrected Jeremiah.

"Asser," the man said, "though I've lived most of my life in a small village not too far from here, I've traveled more than you, Son, including Rome, where they have the finest flatbread in the world."

"This isn't Rome, and we don't serve flatbread."

"Maybe you should. Maybe I need to quit the priesthood and open flatbread shops in these bloody old backwoods of the capital."

"You're a priest?" asked Asser with a raised tone. "What are you doing here?" To Jeremiah, Asser said, "Me'll be back."

"Father, you're definitely in the wrong place," added Jameela. "All sinners here."

"I came to teach that sinner the way—the way home."

He lowered his hood and smiled. Jeremiah recognized the blue-eyed parish priest who used to come over for family meals. Padre's loud belly laugh, grand smile, warm energy, and unconditional love hadn't changed. Without hesitation, Jeremiah skipped around the bar and hugged Padre.

"Good to see you," he said, but turned promptly back to the bar. "I can't go home. I assaulted a lord, escaped, and—" He stopped and felt the stone in his pouch.

Padre finished his sentence: "And you have the stone, which belongs to the Church and its people. The lies won't satisfy, Jeremiah."

MISSION

"**I** don't have that stone," Jeremiah said to Padre.

Asser reappeared and said quietly to Jeremiah, "The horses are ready."

"They're not necessary, Asser. I know this priest."

Asser looked up in surprise and Padre nodded at him with a smile.

"What do we do with the horses, then?"

"I don't know—leave them tied for now."

"What's been in your hand all night?" asked Jameela. "Not that stone, then?"

"Oh, this?" He removed the stone from his pouch and showed it to her, flashing it to the brown-cloaked man as well. "Nervous habit of mine to play with. Found it outside the bar."

"Fine, give it to me then," Jameela demanded and eyed the exit.

"No. It's not that important."

"If it's not that important, you can give it to me."

"Why do you keep looking towards the door?" asked Asser.

"Looking out for those men." She crossed one leg over another and leaned forward. "And I'm not mad, Asser. Came here to escape."

"A prickly one—me like." Wiping a pint, Asser said, "Hold on—escape? From whom?"

"I can ask you the same question." She rooted through her handbag tied to her waist sash until she found a small container. After twisting and opening, she dabbed, then spread cream with a finger over her lower lip, then upper lip, smacking them together, then licked and rubbed her nose ring. "Escaping from life," she said.

212

"Not sure if a dirty place like this"—Asser shook his finger—"is fit for the fairest of princesses, me lady." Asser shook his finger and added, "Me peg you for more of a fighter than a runner. But we do have room downstairs if you're looking for lodging."

Jeremiah squirmed as he had in Gwyn's chair and stuffed the stone into his shirt pocket and said, "Stop, Asser."

"Jeremiah," said Padre, "I know you have it." He nodded towards Jeremiah's pocket.

Jeremiah blew out his cheeks and said, "Fine, you can look." He pulled out the stone and held on to it but allowed them to touch it.

Jameela uncrossed her legs and fondled the stone. After humming a song, she said, "Such perfect symmetry and smoothness. This is no ordinary rock, Jeremiah."

"As if sanded by a master carpenter," said Padre. "Yes, he's been lying. We know. I suspected you had it for some time. How'd you get it?"

Jeremiah slackened in defeat. "Yes, it's the stone. I've had it for six years. I found it when Marianne and I wandered the grotto during the archbishop's funeral."

"Where'd you find it?" asked Padre.

"Buried in the corner of the treasury—when you were looking at the glass case and that priest approached us, something sparkling caught my eye."

Padre swirled his mug on the bar in a circle-eight pattern. After uncomfortable silence, he said in a disappointing tone, "You lied to me, Son."

Jeremiah took a deep, pained breath. "I always lied, Padre. I'm sorry, but the king . . . my brother . . . the war."

"When I told you and your family the archbishop had my rectory searched and Lord Harold's men interrogated me incessantly, you said nothing."

"I'm sorry, Padre. My family didn't know about the stone either. I hid it very well."

"It's not the king's, and it's not yours. It's a symbol of hope and points to a larger truth."

"Bollocks," interrupted Jameela. "If this is the stone from the legend, then other parts of the story are also true: murder and stolen land."

"Itneedbe get goin' on home," slurred a man slouching against the wall, his shaggy gray beard full of stale breadcrumbs. The words ran together, wheezing through stuffed immovable lips.

Jeremiah looked to Mo.

"Don' be lookin' at me," Mo said and showed his palms.

"What'd you say, Cyrus?" asked Jeremiah. "Repeat, but open your mouth."

"Stone go home."

"Home?"

"I'll translate," said Jameela. "He said the stone should be sent home."

"Me can speak gibberish too," said Asser.

"I've been around plenty of drunk men, Asser," said Jameela. "What he says is plain to me."

"Go home?" asked Jeremiah. "How would he know anything about that? Maybe this is a fake. Like Padre said, the stone symbolizes hope and doesn't supply special powers."

"I didn't say that, but I'm glad you've come around, Jeremiah. You've clung to it like—" Padre stopped and shook his head. "Never mind. It's more about the person who has the stone. People have fought over the stone, believing its possessor would be given great powers. And with those powers, the ability to conquer and control through fear."

"See," Jeremiah said, "It hasn't given me any powers—look where I am!"

Cyrus straightened and continued, "Legendsay stone Maghali DarkSea. Learn lessons and restore theLand."

"Jameela?" asked Jeremiah.

"If we return it home to Maghali by the Dark Sea and learn its lessons, the kingdom will be restored."

"Jeremiah," said Asser, "me and you have been seeking an escape. And this greasy old man with an untrimmed beard, who happens to be talking more this day that we've ever heard, has given you a way out. Me say we get out of this hell-hole."

"Wait a minute," said Jeremiah. "Why should we trust Cyrus? We barely know him. Maybe it's safer to hide."

"Me think you've already been found. Think," Asser said and elbowed him. "How did this fellow"—he gestured towards Padre— "find you? *Someone* must have told them. It's only a matter of time. Visitors to the bar have probably reported your description to a lord who knows a sheriff. We need to go soon."

Jeremiah paced behind the bar and poured himself an ale. The Grouse's door flung wide, and he jerked his hand. Men he saw in the outhouse, now fully clothed, spotted Asser and overstrode towards him.

One said, "Look, gents, there's the chap the girls rejected at the inn!" The men slapped hands and chuckled among themselves.

Asser grinned. "The hunched punch drunk. Me loved your jokes. What will it be? Ale, mead, liquor?" Before he answered, Asser tapped his lip with a finger and said, "Wait, me know—something better. One moment." Passing Jeremiah, Asser said, "See, me and you need to leave soon. Prostitutes talk, and they'll end up in the capital. Plus, the carpentry guild, your village—the king probably started with your immediate friends."

To Jeremiah, the men standing at the bar resembled his prison guards—fat, drunk, sloppy, and crude. *I'm not going back*, he thought.

Asser returned with a small batch of ale. He poured each man a pint and waved off payment. "Free of charge," Asser told them. Their mugs clanked, and he told Jeremiah in a stage whisper, "They'll be back on the pot in no time—months-old ale."

Mo laughed, but Padre shook his head and said, "Yes, that's how I heard of your whereabouts—someone confessed to me, a regular at your bar."

"Confessed, Padre. Isn't that confidential?" asked Asser.

"Funny—yes, Ass," said Padre. "Jeremiah, the abbot and archbishop are specifically looking for you. They want the stone."

"And me sure the king does too," Asser added.

Jaw clenched, Jeremiah darted his gaze around the room. He went out from behind the bar and knelt to question Cyrus. He pointed to the stone in his hand. "How do you know about the legend? Where's this mountain?"

Jameela walked up behind him and said, "I think I know."

"What?" Jeremiah spun in his crouch and stood to ask, "How would you know? You're now an expert on make-believe places?"

"The legend is popular in my culture. Few have visited, but many have heard."

"Padre, what do you think?" asked Jeremiah, crossing the tavern to Padre's side, hoping for common sense. "You came here to tell me—no, order me—to return the stone."

"No, I came to teach you the way home. Perhaps, if you returned it, the archbishop would protect you for its return. But it's not guaranteed. Since the"—he paused and stroked his beard—"since the archbishop's death, the Witenberg church has aligned with the king."

Jeremiah looked to his old friend Padre. Robed in gentleness, he poured out the familiar serenity in soft eyes even as he finished the ale and said, "There is a larger purpose, Son. We can't go back—we must return the stone."

Jeremiah rolled the stone in his palm and asked, "Everyone wants to do this?" He crossed his arms. "Where to begin? I mean, Asser couldn't get us past the next town—he's so directionally challenged he doesn't know any directions."

"Me'll follow Mo's nose as the north star. We'll have protection from beasts. If his size doesn't scare them, Mo's hands will crush all foes. Right, laddy?" Asser punched Mo on the shoulder.

They surveyed the mission-giver and expected the final order. Cyrus clapped, then smiled, showing overlapped, twisted teeth.

"Wadwill it be?" he asked.

They nodded in unison as a salute. "So where do we start?" asked Jeremiah.

Cyrus shrugged. "Noall answers, but clues willcome. He handed Jeremiah a cylindrical-shaped object wrapped with parchment. "A gift."

Jeremiah rubbed the package, unrolled it, and grinned. "A scytale! Where'd you get this?" Jeremiah had played with a puzzle like this as a child—and then he remembered—at Padre's house!

Padre imitated and said, "Like old times—but this time, it is a quest."

"Who cares?" said Asser. "We've already decided. We need to go."

Cyrus mumbled, and Jameela translated. "A gift from his father, and his father and his father, passed down over the generations."

S	L	A	Y	T	H
E	L	I	E	S	L
E	A	R	N	K	I
N	G	S	A	G	E
W	A	R	R	I	O
R	L	O	V	E	R

They tried different combinations. One read "Lover" first, another read "Slay," and another read "Lies." Jeremiah completed the cipher and announced its message: "'Slay the lies. Learn King, Sage, Warrior, Lover.'"

"That's it?" said Asser. He grabbed the old man by his whiskey-stained tunic. "Is this a joke?" Asser squeezed his lips together in fury. "Open your mouth and speak."

Cyrus laughed and slowed down each syllable. "No, Son. First reach the large church on the stone where pilgrims cross during low tide. It's called the Mont Church. There you'll find further instructions only a carpenter can solve—the riddle on the scytale."

They waited for Jeremiah's response. He looked at the riddle, looked at the team, and then looked around the room. "We have no choice. I have no choice. I'm not going back. Let's pack our belongings and head out in the morning."

Once the last straggler of regular customers exited The Grouse, Jeremiah shut the door and stored the bottles on shelves below the bar. He welcomed the team to rest where they were or come below and they'd find them a cot, but he blew out the candles, leaving the several members of the team in the dark, put the stone in his pouch, and began to head downstairs.

"Jeremiah, where you going?" asked Asser.

"I'm spent. We need to rest, Asser."

"That'll come." Asser dug around the bar and found a match. As he lit candles again, he said, "Let the glarious fun begin. Mo, go with Jeremiah into the cellar and grab the meats, cheeses, and breads. And me'll prepare the table."

"But we need to rest, Asser. And horses? Where will we get more?" Jeremiah clenched his jaw and tapped his thighs. "What will we do? What will we do?"

"Jeremiah," Asser said and shoved a mug into his hand. "Don't warry about it. Take this. A gift from a friend." He poured the clear liquor into mugs, then passed them around. "Mo, some cider for you. Let's toast."

"Warm-me-upper," said Padre. "Cheer up, Jeremiah. An adventure."

They raised their mugs and Asser started, "May the women be a-plenty."

Padre cleared his throat, and Jameela shook her head.

"Right, right, Father. May the days be many, the troubles few, and the blessings outnumber the shamrocks. And may we outrun any knights on our tails."

Keeping his mug raised, Padre said, "Hold on before you drink. May Abba bless us and keep us, make His face shine on us and be gracious to us, turn His face to us and give us peace."

"Aaaaa . . . men," said Asser. "Huzzah!"

They slugged their shots in full gulps. The bitterness slammed against the back of Jeremiah's throat, and his shoulders shook. "The shakes, Asser," he croaked. "Ugh—what's the awful drink?" He looked around the circle.

Padre scrunched his face and scraped at his tongue, but Jameela licked her lips.

"A special brew from Gwyn," said Asser, admiring the bottle. "We call it *Jeremiah* Mead." Asser waited for it, waited for it, then bellowed like a goat. "Whew! Who wants another?"

"I'm jus' sayin', Ass, but the look—" Mo's lower belly rumbled, forcing deep chuckles from the group. "I'm jus' sayin', I wish we had a painter to capture it."

"Will you go on, Big Mo, and get the food?" asked Asser. Jeremiah tried to follow, but Asser pulled at his collar. "Whoa, laddy, not so fast. Where are your mead manners? We didn't flip the mug over our head. One more shot."

They all groaned. After the shot, Padre moved tables to the center of the room, and Mo placed bread, cheeses, eggs, and a small bird, its neck wrung, on the table.

"Where'd you get that?" asked Jeremiah.

"I was fixin' to find your special ale collection, but this grouse was runnin' in between the barrels. So I got it."

"Don't put it on the table," said Jeremiah. "We need a fire."

Mo moved for the front door, but Jeremiah stopped him. "No, a fire downstairs, out our door. You can pluck it while the fire heats up."

Asser pulled a small stringed instrument and flute from a bar shelf. "A little ballad for me friends when me return."

"Where you going?" asked Jeremiah.

"To me lady," Asser said triumphantly, flipping an imaginary cape and dashing sideways across the bar. At the door, he proclaimed, "Me'll be back with rations and a glow."

Not long ago, Jeremiah thought, *I glowed.*

His dream had come true. A date with the prettiest girl, his friend and desire. The night had gone well until he saw her look of longing for Lord Oaf. A swig, a walk, then wrestling. His love for her spelled out in letters the oaf burned.

The fight happened in a flash. Harry crashed. The smirk of victory must have remained glued on Lord Harold's face long after he cuffed Jeremiah and dragged him to prison. But the look of contempt from Marianne got under his skin. Her body—she had trembled and was mired in anger.

Like the Jeremiah Mead jolting him, he chuckled bitterly to himself: *You never see a crash coming*, he consoled himself. He wobbled to the ground floor, past a row of barrels, and grabbed a blanket. Regret punched him in the stomach.

"Is the grouse ready?" he asked Mo as he walked outside.

"Still cookin'," said Mo. "Get an ale and stay for a bit."

Mo talked, but the words flew past Jeremiah. Orion's belt dazzled as it had days ago. Thoughts of Marianne disappeared, replaced by thoughts of the stranger.

Who is Jameela?

Once the bird was cooked, Jeremiah, a little sobered, climbed the stairs with Mo to offer it to the others.

The front door of the tavern burst open, and Asser fell through the door with Gwyn tumbling over the top of him. He had removed his tunic to show rainbow-stained undergarments.

"Witen me," said Jameela.

Jeremiah stared at her.

"What? Isn't that what you say?" asked Jameela.

"Why weren't you quiet coming in, Asser? You could've aroused suspicion from the inn."

"Jeremiah, we were quiet," Asser said and giggled. "A nightcap, dessert before dinner. Me payment, right, Gwyn?" He slapped her on the butt.

"My arses, Tiny Hands," she said in Asser's low voice. "No, your payment is food and song. Here, Jeremiah, rations for the journey." She dropped a bag onto the table and vials rolled out. "Tinctures, medicine, and healing oils from my cauldron." Her eyes bulged, and she attempted to remain rigid while Asser tickled her. "And this—this is sauce from my witch's closet."

"Thanks, Gwyn, but can we get on with it? We have lots of work to do."

"What did me say, Jeremiah of the Wood?"

"We only have two horses, Asser."

"And mine," said Padre.

"So, we're one horse short?"

"Don't warry, Woody. Let's feast," said Asser.

Jeremiah looked to Jameela. She shrugged and grabbed the grouse wishbone. "Pull," she said.

Jameela lowered her head, whispered something, and said, "Go!" The bigger piece broke her way, and she exclaimed, "Ha, my wish."

"And what'll that be, my lady?" asked Padre.

Jameela paused and looked around the room. "My second wish is for . . ."

"Your second wish?" asked Jeremiah. "No, that's not the rule."

"No, no," she rambled, "my first wish is for you to play me a song."

"I'm a carpenter. I don't know how to play."

"That's the rule, Woody," said Asser.

"Can we eat first?" Jeremiah pouted and stuffed cheese into his mouth.

"So, who'd win in a fight, Jeremiah?" asked Padre. "Dragon or a light-warrior?"

Jeremiah remembered burying his figurines. "It doesn't matter," he said and slumped over. "The dragon," he muttered and tore a piece of bread.

"Are you an idiot, Woody?" said Asser. "The light-warrior would win; he can blow fire."

"You mean the dragon blows fire."

"No, me sure as me mama's birthmark that it's the light-warrior."

"Do you know what you're talking about? What nonsense is that? Your mama's birthmark?"

"The light-warrior does blow fire—purifying fire," Asser said and purred to Gwyn.

"You're an idiot," said Jeremiah.

"Are you sure?" asked Padre.

"Asser, how do you pronounce *glorious*?"

"Glarious, Woody."

"And *worry*?"

"Warry. See, you carry the *a* and roll the *r*'s." The sound came harsh and grating like fingernails scratching a board. Asser stood and took another shot of Jeremiah Mead. His cheeks had become as red as the dragon's fire in Jeremiah's imagination. Asser picked on the strings and handed Jeremiah the flute.

"Oh, play me a song, you fine troubadour," said Jameela in a lighter tone. Jeremiah snatched the flute and blew straight through it.

"No, like this, Woody. With your fingers, up and down, and skipping around." Asser demonstrated.

"There, there, laddy, and to balance it out, me'll play something dark." Asser thumped the lower chords. "Dark and brooding and look mad around the room like someone had insulted your mama's birthmark."

"That is so stupid, Asser," said Jeremiah.

Asser lowered his voice but coughed. "Witen me," he said. "Can't do it. Now something from me mama. A one, a two, a three . . . ohhhhh . . ."

222

Tiny, tiny, oh, tiny, tiny, oh,
Fighting and swiping blows, loosed upon our foes.
Tiny, tiny, oh, tiny, tiny, oh,
Trolls brought the blight, but tiny hands came to fight.
Tiny, tiny, oh, tiny, tiny, oh,
Land of kindred nigh, the Sheas pine for love all night.
Tiny, tiny, oh, tiny, tiny, oh.

Asser sounded like a goat being strangled. His voice rose in pitch towards the climax with tighter bow-string pulls as he two-stepped around the table.

"Everyone stand!" invited Asser.

The others stood, but Jeremiah remained seated. "This is so stupid, Asser."

"Come on, Woody," Jameela said lightly, dragging him up to his feet.

"Hop on ya left, and hop on ya right. That's it," said Asser. "And clap your hands."

They clapped.

"To ya left, to ya right . . . that's it. To ya left, to ya right. Ohh . . ." As the team hopped, Asser pulled the bow string faster on the thinner strings. Mo beat his hands against the bar and drummed with his mouth as Asser sang.

My dear Assie . . .
Who can try, two little eyes
Off to the land of dreams you fly.

Close your eyes, soothe your sighs
Off to the land of dreams you fly.
My dear Assie . . .

Calm your whys, don't you cry

Off to the land of dreams you fly.
My dear Assie . . .

Jeremiah looked around and thought, *This is my new family.*

After a few rounds of spinning, most fell asleep on the floor; however, Jeremiah lumbered down and slept in the basement, the stone nestled tightly in his undergarment pouch.

◆———◆

The next morning, the team packed bags with provisions and clothes. Padre strapped his sandals and fastened his cloak with the brooch, then blessed the mission. Mo tightened his high boots and fitted on a hat. Asser changed from Gwyn's rainbow undergarments to his own black tunic. Jameela stayed in her strapped, leather boots and the olive tunic, but it fit her snugly so that Jeremiah stared. Jeremiah tied a tan cloak over his beige tunic with front pockets, and palmed the stone in his pocket for fortune. The team hugged Gwyn and she fared them welled.

With sunlight, the merry men looked around at one another. Mo stood taller and brawnier, and Jameela inched closer to inspect the mark on the tip of his nose and the dark freckles that dotted his chestnut skin.

"If you look any longer, Jameela," said Asser, "the mole will move to your own nose."

"For the hundredth time, Asser, it's not a mole—it's a scar," said Jeremiah. "How many times must he explain?"

"Come now, Jeremiah," said Mo. "We must be crossin' the channel," said Mo. "A day's journey to get there with the horses."

"And how do you suppose we cross?"

"I have friends in the fishing village near the port," Mo assured them. "They can arrange a ship for us."

Though Mo was a Grouse regular, Jeremiah barely knew him. Having worked multiple jobs throughout life and traveled frequently, Mo had recently settled in the capital. He was older, but his strength had not degraded. Of all stories he shared over drinks, he rarely described his family. But Jeremiah trusted him.

"This way," Mo said, pointing.

Due to Mo's massive size, they agreed he would ride alone on the king's largest horse. The two shortest people, Asser and Padre, shared Padre's, leaving one horse for Jameela and Jeremiah.

Asser offered Jameela a hand. She dismissed it and climbed onto the saddle to take the reins.

"Are you joining her?" Asser asked Jeremiah.

Jeremiah blushed, Asser laughed, and Padre sighed.

"Come on, Jeremiah," said Jameela. "Behind me, for now."

He jumped up, but in his nervousness, almost fell off the horse. He wrapped his arms around Jameela's waist to hold on. Startled, she scooted forward.

"Jeremiah, move back a bit. See this space around me? Mind the gap."

He released slowly from her waist and grasped the saddle with both hands.

Asser laughed and advised loud enough for Jameela to hear, "Ignore her. Women hate that. She'll crawl back to you."

"No, never," she crisply said.

The rest of the journey, Jeremiah attempted to look to the road, past the beauty in front of him, but he couldn't. He pictured touching her, but she rejected his directed energy. When the horse hit bumps in the road, he bumped closer to her. When he took the reins, he mostly obeyed the silence she imposed, but he quickly responded to conversation when she initiated.

They arrived at the coast at sunset, and fishermen were brushing fish guts into buckets. Women of varying shapes and sizes, with skirts lifted, roamed the central marketplace. Men with their breeches untied paced until they selected their prize and paid with coins.

Jameela snorted.

"Sell much today, Marcus?" Mo asked a fisherman, a large figure, climbing up from the water's edge.

They dismounted and tied their horses to wooden posts. Mo removed a glove and extended his hand to the man.

"If it isn't Mo," Marcus replied and returned a bone-crushing handshake. "How's the capital been treating you?"

"Fine," said Mo. "The timber business is makin' money."

"Ah, that's it, you must sell tree logs," said Jeremiah quietly. He noticed Mo's hands now, completely covered in callouses.

"I hate to cut the talkin' short," Mo continued, "but we're rushin' out."

Marcus tipped his cap and hiked up his fish-slicked overalls. Sidestepping flopping flounder, he said hello and looked over to the group, particularly Jameela. "Friends of yours?" he asked.

"Yes, but she's taken, and we're on a journey east," said Mo.

"Aye. Get on with it. What can I do for you? Want fish?"

"Maybe, but we need a ship. Crossin' the Witen Channel tomorrow."

"Can you pay?"

Throwing a bag of coins, Mo said, "Have I ever not paid?"

Eyes bugged out, Asser stared at the silver and said over his shoulder to Jeremiah, "Timber business must have been very good."

Marcus counted the coins and whistled. "Your ship will be ready in the morning. Take the usual route. One of my men will go with you."

PHILOSOPHY

"Are you all right, this lovely Tuesday morning? You are rather disheveled," Chamberlain Vere said to William.

"Yes, I'm perfectly fine."

"Without a notebook and pencil, unkempt in appearance, with hair all over you, yes, you seem ready to meet the king." Vere removed a small brush and roller from his coat pocket. Drawing in a dramatic breath and releasing it, Vere said, "What would you do without me, Father William? Maybe you need help investigating, after all."

William revised a frozen smirk into a smile of content as he was brushed and rolled.

"Been with a lady, I see?" said Vere.

"No, no," blurted William. "See my hair?" He pulled off his hat to show his longer locks. "I didn't sleep last night. Forgive me."

"Oh, I know," said Vere. "This is your first time seeing the king since you accused him of murder."

He blew out a long breath. "Do you have a notebook and pencil I could borrow? And a glass of water?"

"Certainly—and don't worry about him. But I do have something better for your nerves."

William followed Vere down the central staircase, underneath banners in the great hall and past statues of previous kings.

"Have you had a tour of the castle, Father William?"

"No. Where are we going? I assumed I was meeting the king somewhere more official?"

"Like you, King Richard didn't sleep well last night. There's a private kitchen and wine cellar on the ground floor."

Past racks of wine bottles, they descended two flights of brick stairs that opened into a large, circular stone room.

"When his tempers flare, he comes here to cool off—literally."

The cold instantly started William's teeth chattering as the luster on Vere's gold buttons frosted over. The lower they went, the colder it got. "Where are we?"

"One moment, Father William. I'll open the door." Light rays diffused and shot across the room, revealing a few blocks of ice. "We're in the wine cellar—the king likes his wine cold, Father William." Vere opened a chest and found the bottle. "There we are," he said and handed the bottle to William. "We'll pour this in the scriptorium and wait for the king."

Vere found a candle, lit it, then shut the door.

Compared to the royal couple's colorful bed chamber, this room was mostly brown and red, and William deduced this was the king's scriptorium and the door to his left led outside.

Does anyone else know the secret combination? he thought.

In the better light that came as Vere lit the candelabra, luxury was revealed: three golden lions, carpet covering a polished wood floor, a sumptuous fireplace, oak desk, mahogany table, leather chairs, and filled bookshelves. On the walls hung paintings of Richard's mother, wife, and daughter.

"Take this, Father William," said Vere, handing him a glass. "Aromatic, well balanced, fine, and round with character."

William sipped the ruby wine, trying not to stare at the vault door that he knew hid secrets. But the vault blended into the room, the painting of Rachel covering the door. "Clever," muttered William.

Richard paraded into the scriptorium in uniform: purple cloak with three lions, velvet belt with traces of gilding and enamel, and leather boots. He lowered the crown upon his head, grabbed the scabbard and belt, and went to stand by his desk.

Making sure I know his station, I suppose.

Vere sprang to attention and combed the remaining tufts of his brown hair to the sides of his bald head. "My lord," he said, "as you requested, a glass of red. And your former accuser."

Then, his neck spilling out from his too-tight black collar, Vere grunted and motioned to William to kneel.

William blushed. "Your Majesty, it was a long time ago." The hat went to his chest as he knelt on one leg. The silver rivets on Richard's belt—all that William could see from his posture—shimmered, as did the images of falcons on the tab and buckle.

Richard buckled on the wider belt and secured the sword and scabbard, as if he were ready to head out into the kingdom. "The stone has been found, and you confirmed this at the mead ball. Is that true?" asked Richard, as if he knew the answer.

William stood, about equal in height to the king, though they both towered over Vere. "Yes, I believe Jeremiah, the carpenter's son, has it."

"And why were you there at the ball? Investigating again?" asked Richard after a cold, high laugh. "Such a terrible mistake last time, right?"

"Certainly, a terrible mistake, one I won't make again, Your Majesty, but I want to help."

"My wife believes helping me find the stone will help you find Virdis' murderer."

William swallowed. "Yes. What do you have in mind?"

"You'll join Sir Alfred and his knights to get the stone."

"M-me, sir? I don't see how I'm qua-qualified," stammered William.

"Are you questioning me?"

"N-no, sire."

"Good. You'll meet him at the festival. He's investigating the whereabouts of his brother."

William rose to leave, but Richard stopped him. "Not yet. After my meetings. Please"—he lowered a hand—"sit, get comfortable. You can listen. Vere, bring in my first visitor. And start the fire—it's cold in here."

Vere opened the door, and Charles of Desford entered, his musty body odor tinged with pungent pine that seemed always to follow him like a cloud.

"Charles," Richard said coolly as Charles bowed, avoiding a glance to William.

"Have you met Father William?" asked Richard.

Charles firmed his grip on his cane and with his other hand shook William's. Making direct eye contact, he said, "No, no, not socially. Nice to meet you."

"So, what frivolous matter is the Witen discussing this week, Lord Charles?" asked Richard while sifting through reports placed on the desk by Vere. He held out a hand to invite Charles to sit.

Charles sat at the table and said, "We haven't met. It's been years, Your Majesty. Only you can call a winter session."

"Yes, but is it necessary? Can't we debate with freemen at the tavern like our founding fathers did? With a pint in hand?"

Charles stroked his beard. "No, not a good idea, Your Majesty. I don't like your decisions sober . . ."

Richard snickered. "No session is necessary. The kingdom is thriving."

"A matter of opinion. Not a reflection of facts."

"Charles, we've had this discussion before. You yearn for a time long ago, a time not relevant to today. Aren't your freemen still free?"

"Technically, Your Majesty, but technicalities often become the exception rather than the custom."

"Are the peasants able to leave their noblemen's property of their own free will?"

"Yes, but . . . ," said Charles. He paused and steadied his cane.

Richard removed a ring from his finger and tapped it against the desk. "It's always 'yes, but' with you, Charles. You babble idle nonsense each week, wasting my time. Listen, there was a time when people were truly free, not obligated to fulfill a degree of servility or compulsory employment."

Charles stroked his beard and replied, "Yes, during a time when the Crown didn't fully control land, and the Witen voted on taxes. Now, as king, you make these decisions."

Richard tapped the ring harder against the desk. "Enough history, Lord Charles. Why do you complain? Take it to the people. The people, Charles, these people you are fond of, they desired more assistance and more money. Those in your own tithing would agree with me."

Charles lifted his cane and moved it from the carpet to the wood floor, making a single knock as if in subdued protest. His voice controlled, Charles said, "Your Majesty, you have no idea what the other nine families in my tithing think."

Richard blew a long a breath and slid the ring across the desk.

Charles took his hand from the end of his beard and stopped the ring from falling off.

Richard stood and pulled the golden scepter with ruby orb from its base. He marched around the table and drummed the floor with the scepter. "My father, once your king, Charles, gave me that ring on the day he died."

Charles pulled the ring close to his eyes and read the cursive writing. A short laugh popped from his mouth.

Richard stopped drumming the scepter and asked, "Do you remember his last words to me, Charles?"

A glaze fogged Charles's eyes. Richard pointed the scepter towards Charles and said, "And you can stand, to honor your king, when he addresses you."

Knees cracked, and William almost stepped over to help, but Charles braced himself against the table to stand with the help of the cane.

"With frail bones, as the reaper destroyed my father's body," said Richard, his voice sullen, "draining his glow, leaving him a ghost, he told me to honor his death and be cautious of power."

Charles nodded while looking away. He handed Richard the ring and William watched the king go closer to the old man, as if he were stalking prey.

Richard raised his voice. "Don't lecture me about the king having too much power. The tithing is still the basic unit. And local councils and duchies still make decisions."

Charles flew his hand from his mouth to slap his fist upon his cane. "What decisions?" he asked fervently. "You're blind. The throne has too much power, and the balance between church and kingdom has skewed."

Richard laughed and returned to his seat at the table. "I'm leveling the system, Charles, creating the balance you pursue. The church has had too much power, wealth, and land."

"I understand many years of war made people weary of chaos, desiring order instead. But that is a false choice. Your father knew this; thus, you were chosen over your brothers—he thought you would understand."

"The Witen merely stamped and voted on what had already happened. I proved myself to Father over my brothers."

"King Henry and the Witen chose you to restore things."

Richard shook his head. "Times are different, Charles. My father couldn't see the big picture during his last years. He was right not to pursue restoration of our old ways. I'm sorry, my dear old friend, but restoration will not happen. Progress, on the other hand, will."

"The lords, the guilds, the military, and church don't need more money. You're not a new king in need of support anymore."

"Progress, Charles. Progress."

The king turned to fondle a brass figurine on the bookshelf and Charles risked a quick grin towards William, as if to confirm their plan was justified.

The sound of shoes on the stone floor corridor ended with two knocks. Three rings from the nearby chapel bells signaled the quarter hour.

"My king," said Charles, at the signal, "you should listen to your wife. She's as wise as Solomon. Farewell." Charles bowed and walked to the door.

"Leaving so soon, Charles?" ridiculed Richard. "Before tea? And it just got interesting."

"Lord Charles," said Vere, directing him away from the main door. "Through the cloak room. Follow me."

"Politicians," Richard complained as they left, "as arrogant as the Church. Right, Father William?"

William slightly nodded and grabbed a notebook and charcoal pencil Vere had placed on the table. "More wine please?" he asked.

Timed to coincide with the ending bell bong, someone pounded the door for a third time. William moved to pour another glass, but Vere asked, "Can you open the door? I'll be back shortly."

DECISION

William turned the knob. As he opened the door, he heard a cheerful man tell a maid, "And thank you for the shine, my lady." The maid walked down the corridor, and the man turned around.

"Ooh, a surprise," said the man in an elaborate silk Venetian suit. "You're not the honorable Chamberlain Aubrey de Vere, but you *are* a handsome fellow," the man said as he extended his hand.

William shook the buttery hand with polished nails and took in the full picture—black leggings and corset, and dueling swords at his side.

The man tipped his burgundy hat and announced, "I am George of Bath, the merchant guild master, and I have an appointment with the king."

William stared blankly into the man's ice-blue eyes that sparkled more for their outline of periwinkle blue against a chalked complexion.

"Come in, Master George, and meet William," said Richard.

George bowed and said in a velvety voice, "Always good to see you, my king, and to meet you, William, is it?" His leather shoes upturned at the toes like his curled lips, and they clicked, clapped, and clopped loudly against the wooden floor until deadened by his steps onto the carpet.

"Vere will return shortly; he was escorting your mate," said Richard.

"My mate, my king? And who is that?" asked George distractedly, looking over William. "A man of few words, but fantastic fashion, I say." George slid a finger along William's arm, causing a tickle to spiral down the priest's back. "After this meeting, you must tell me where you buy your clothes," he said and rolled his tongue.

"Of course you are mates with the wise Charles of Desford," mocked Richard.

"Young man," George said to William, "the king isn't serious. Charles is not my mate—he's my enemy." His eyes flashed, and he poured himself a cup of wine. "And who are you?"

William's jaw hung open as words were fighting to form, but his mind suppressed them. He clutched the notebook tightly in his grip. "A-a new addition to the king's court," said William, finally. "Name is Sir William."

George looked to William's hand holding a pencil. "His court? A new addition? Are you a scribe?"

William's thoughts pulsed to the accusation and subsequent firing years before, the long carriage ride with Conti to Rome, and the Papal Curia and its office that wielded significant influence: the Communicationis Secretariatus. *How do I answer?* The king was leaving him to it.

"Wait," said George suspiciously, "I know you—I've seen you before."

Only the abbey, the king, and chamberlain—Chamberlain Vere knew of William's prior identity in Witenberg. He didn't know how much Rachel wanted shared and whom he could trust.

George was presumably close with Richard.

Do I want Richard telling George?

He looked to the king, who was busy fiddling with a key and opening the desk drawer.

Vere returned to the chamber and George asked, "Chamberlain Vere, do you have a new assistant? I do like his outfit." George touched William's shoulder-length locks and ran his fingers down to the hat he held. "But I'm trying to remember where I've seen him. Oh, yes," he said and lifted his toes from the carpet.

William's body froze, but the pencil twirled between his fingers. Behind Richard was the painting of Rachel. "Your wife," said William.

"My wife?" asked Richard as he pulled the drawer and dug around.

"Y-yes, Your Majesty," stammered William, "s-such a wonderful portrait."

"Vere," asked Richard sternly, "what's going on?"

"William is just a little nervous around Master George, it seems."

"Whatever. Vere, stoke the fire."

After poking and blowing at it, Vere got the twigs lighted, and then the logs caught.

"And loosen up, William," added Richard. "Have more wine."

"Ah, yes," said George, "you are the chap with the flamboyant hat that I've seen walking past my bath house."

William's chest deflated, and his mind relaxed. "Yes, yes," he said calmly. "That was me—walking around the city helps me to think. I'm the king's new scribe, reporting to Chamberlain Vere, in charge of communications."

"Very well—please take notes of this important meeting," said George with an oily tone. Then he curtseyed, brandishing his hat, though it had already been removed for the king, revealing a white wig. "I represent the merchant guild's interests with the Witen and the king."

As George wandered through the room, admiring various tokens, he added, "I invested my inheritance and compounded it ten-fold in the infant banking industry."

William furiously wrote notes, then poured himself a glass of wine.

"Pottery?" George asked Richard. He glided his fingers around the edge of bowls, jars, and chalices. "For wine, Your Majesty?"

"No, I have plenty of those. Those beauties contained the scrolls which led me to Rachel."

"Oh, yes, I remember. You accompanied Virdis to the desert plateau and discovered the jars in a cave."

"Quite a find. And adventure too," said Richard proudly, his triumphant smile flickering in the firelight.

"And the stone, correct? The scrolls were the first clue? With Virdis?"

As the fire crackled, Richard found something in the drawer he'd been exploring. "Yes, George," he said breathlessly, as his open mouth closed to a thin-lipped smile.

"There it is," said Richard with satisfaction. He pulled out a large, dark feather and placed it on his desk beside an ink pot.

William sketched a quick drawing in his notebook with questions about the feather's size, use, and distinct color.

"What are you looking for, George?" asked Richard.

Thick carpet dampened the clopping of George's soles in the middle of the room, but not where he prowled at the edges on the hardwood behind Richard. Loud and louder, George stopped on the fourth step and lifted a clay jar from the shelf.

Richard snatched the jar from George and set it beside the military medals on his desk.

"I had forgotten you and Virdis were travel companions," said George as he stroked his thin, white mustache over his shining, ruby lips.

William's breath hitched as he stared at the mesmerizing George, who seemed fully aware of his effect—or the effect of his words—on the scribe.

The fire crackled, logs snapped, and flames exploded.

"Almost like blood brothers, you and Virdis? He was with you when you met Rachel and when you conquered others to steal the stone from the beast?"

A tendril of panic seized William's chest, causing him to huff. The logs crackled, then popped. Loud and louder, his chest heaved until he groaned and sipped at the wine.

"I'm sorry again, my king. It's just, it's just . . ."

"What? What is it George?"

George knelt beside him and with a hand on Richard's knee, he said, "I know how difficult this was for you, to lose a friend, but his death offers an opportunity."

"What are you talking about?" asked Richard gruffly.

"Yes, my king, you lost a friend."

"Yes, I know, George, but that was a long time ago."

"His death offers an opportunity."

"An opportunity?"

George stood and wandered the chamber again. Richard got up and followed nervously, pushing his shoulders back and his chest out as he walked towards the fire. "What opportunities?" asked Richard in exasperation.

"My lord, you should rest."

"Tell me, George."

"It's too soon."

"Tell me now, George. Stop fiddling." He moved into George's space, and William noticed how tall he was.

"The Church has been stealing from you and stealing from the Crown for far too long."

"Stealing? How so?" Richard asked and tightened his loose hands into fists.

"All their property and land. They control too much. Plus, shouldn't *you* make *all* ecclesiastical appointments?"

"I've been working on it, George."

"I'm afraid Virdis's reforms are still in place—your cousin hasn't fully repealed them."

"The archbishop is working on it, I said," said Richard strongly. "Virdis was a good man. We worked an agreement so that the Crown and Church shared land to increase crop yield. He ensured taxes were paid."

"But not their fair share, my lord. And he was also a Jew lover, a friend of those who charge too high a rate of interest. Maybe *their* taxes should be raised."

Richard turned from the fire, and a glow lightened half his face. "Why are you here, George?"

"I have ideas to replenish the treasury."

"Finally," drawled Richard, looking to Vere, "we come to the reason you're here. Go on. I'm listening."

With wide grin, George said, "Buying Rose Abbey's vineyard, my lord. Like we did with their bath house after Virdis died." He wrapped his arm around Richard's shoulder and waved his hand. "Their wine is better than ours, and we could save on costs by consolidating. Virdis was opposed, but he's been gone for many years."

Gone, William thought. The chill lingering from the ice-well flash froze his heart.

Richard tilted his head and paused.

"And I assume your merchants would benefit?"

"Why, yes, Your Majesty. But they'll repay you with their full support, and I'll convince them to send more dues to the treasury."

"Let me ask," said Richard.

George interjected, "But if you don't think it's a good idea . . ."

"Don't interrupt me, George."

"Yes, Your Majesty."

"Let me discuss this with the archbishop."

"It's settled," George said. "I'll start the paperwork." He clapped his hands, turned, and glided towards the door.

"George. Stop."

George twinkled with mischief as he turned. "Yes, my lord? Something the matter?"

"Where does the money come from? How do people have this money to spend?"

"Easy. Redistribute the additional income from increased kingdom levies on the upper class. Convince the Witen to pass the tax."

Richard stomped his boot. "I don't need the Witen. I'll decide the tax with the Exchequer. And I'm not worried about the rich. They'll fall in line."

"And you could do a few more things . . ."

Through a sigh, Richard said, "Go on, George."

George leaned closer. With glowing, direct eyes, he grasped Richard's hands and said, "Increase the coin supply."

"How is that done?"

"Two options. You could expand the realm again and plunder—no, steal—no, transfer—yes, transfer their gold and silver in exchange for us civilizing them."

"Who is *them*, George?"

"Constantinople . . . or near Constantinople. The last war didn't, let's say, *finish* the job."

Richard released his hands and paced. He poured wine and reclined at his desk. "I'll think about it."

"So be it, Your Majesty. But there is one more thing you could do with less bloodshed."

Richard straightened up and stacked papers.

"Dilute the coins. Melt gold and silver with other metals. The peasants won't know."

Eyebrows raised, Richard said, "That sounds more feasible in the short term, George. Any longer-term consequences?"

George smirked and thrust his chest out. "Your Majesty, I've been in the banking business most of my life. I think I know money."

"Yes, yes, of course, George. Low risk. I'll review with the Exchequer in the morning."

George knocked the desk twice with a knuckle. "Thank you, my lord."

"Your Majesty," said Vere.

George went to the door and asked, "Shall I report back next week?"

"What is it, Vere?" asked Richard.

"Your Majesty, it's time to depart for your council meeting."

"William, gather your notes," Richard said as he walked past him. "And come with me." With a hand on George's shoulder, Richard said, "I like the plan. Make an appointment with Vere."

Out of the scriptorium and up the stairs, they walked through the great hall. Under the chandelier and banners, they continued into a smaller hall with maps and a large round table.

"William, sit in the back row, against the wall," said Richard.

The Exchequer, military chief, archbishop, chief judge, and advisors entered and stood at attention. Richard strode into the room and clicked his heels together. Earl Marshall Stewart, the king's military chief, saluted. Richard stood tall with shoulders back and chin high and returned the salute. "Earl Marshall, go ahead," he said.

"No major problems to report, Your Majesty. Lords have been handling minor disturbances with their serfs. However, I'm sure you're tracking the pending case before the court next week."

Looking to the chief judge, Richard received assurance. "About the ungrateful lord in Normandy who thinks he and his serfs could sell wheat on my land without repercussions for the rest of the kingdom?"

"Yes, that case."

"Yes, I am . . . lords," said Richard and chuckled lightly. He shook his head. "The court will give him a fair verdict."

The earl continued. Unfurling a map onto the table, he summoned High Constable Smith. "My king, the commander over local constables and garrisons of major castles throughout the realm."

"Good day, my king, my lord," said Smith. "Our fringe outposts are different," said Smith. He stood at formal parade rest with feet shoulder width apart and chin up. He mechanically moved his hands from his back to point to the map.

"As the Earl Marshall said," added Smith, "this area near Clermont in the County of Auvergne has been experiencing minor uprisings. Officers have been knifed but not too seriously injured. The people there are angry about our new castles and posts."

Richard inspected the map and circled the area with his finger. "I won't allow our military to be attacked by those savages, those barbarians, those *Huns*. We'll stop them before they enter another territory and attack people there. Earl Marshall, I want a plan developed for deterrence operations."

"Yes, Your Majesty," said Stewart.

Arms straight, Richard locked his hands together into a fist. "Ungrateful people," he said. "They will learn."

"We'll prepare for the worst case," said Stewart.

Richard told the council to sit, then continued, "First, people clamored for a stronger king to defeat common enemies and secure peace. Next, serfs sold wheat on a lord's land. Don't they know the king provides security and resources? One serf couldn't sell his wheat in one duchy, even if the lord were to agree, without affecting others. The kingdom market would be affected. More importantly, serfs don't have property rights. All goods produced on lords' lands belongs to all the people."

The council nodded faithfully without commenting.

Richard reviewed his notes and asked, "Has anyone seen John the Short or Rohad the Round in recent months?"

"Who is Rohad?" William whispered to Vere.

"Richard's half-brother—he governs the newest duchy, from the last war."

William jotted a note.

"Only rumors, my king," said Smith. "John has sought allegiance from King Phillip in case you—"

Richard cut in, "In case I die? In battle? Many have tried."

"But the stone, my king."

Stewart turned red and sought to reprimand Smith, but Richard reclined into his chair and rested folded hands on his lap.

He smiled, and his glassy focus froze on red table grapes. He picked one and smoothed his thumb over its thick skin. The grape popped into his mouth and, as the firm texture broke, juices flowed over Richard's lips. "Gentlemen," said Richard joyfully, "we have great news. The man sitting behind you has confirmed the thief."

The men twisted their necks towards William.

"My newest scribe, William," said Richard, his eyes glittering. "He's leaving today to join Lord Alfred and team to find the stone. He'll write the report once he has returned. As for John the Short, he can try to steal my kingdom, but he will fail."

"What should we do?" asked Stewart.

"Tell your men to keep close watch on John the Short. Perhaps there are other lands he wishes to rule."

"Yes, Your Majesty," they said in unison and repositioned their chairs.

"Anything else? Around the room?"

Around the table, no one spoke but Archbishop Eames. "Have you forgotten the pope's request?"

Richard touched his crown and held it for moments. The same fitful look swept over his face as when George had recalled the memory of Virdis. Richard's gaze lengthened, and he popped several grapes into his mouth. "No, I haven't forgotten, but I must ask Rachel."

Fingering his collar, Archbishop Eames grimaced. "Yes, of course, my cousin, you must ask her again."

Richard opened his mouth but stopped short. Along his jawline up to earlobes, muscles rippled, but after a deep breath, they relaxed.

"Any saved arrows in your quiver, gentlemen?" After several curt nods, he said, "You're dismissed."

William stood and exited the hall with Vere. The chief footman greeted them with a slight bow.

"Master Vere," the footman said. He was dressed in a red coat with bronze buttons all the way down. "His Majesty has unexpected guests—from Duke Rohad. They are waiting in the foyer."

"Thank you," said Vere. "Father William, wait for me in the great hall. We will visit Lord Alfred after I see to this unexpected matter."

As William waited, he heard bells ringing at half past the hour and then on the hour, reminding him he only had three hours before the meeting with the queen. Vere motioned, and William walked to the foyer. As he exited the castle, he saw two men dressed in long tunics and fitted black bork hats being escorted by sentinels to the castle gate.

COURAGE

nother war, she thought. She had found his notes in the scriptorium—a letter from the pope, requesting assistance with a crusade. Soft persuasion hadn't changed Richard's mind, nor the softness of touch, nor her letter to Conti six years ago.

She had written to Cardinal Conti, now Pope Innocent III, arguing against the Crusades, warning they would have dire consequences for the Kingdom of Witen and her homeland. The systems of the world operated as disguised evil, and spirits of the air were agitating many to remold the Church and kingdom in poisonous ways. Moreover, she told him her intuition about the stone and its passionate hold over men.

Perhaps hard power, a tougher strategy, was required. "Force may be necessary," she told herself while walking alongside her two private sentinels. *Nonviolent, though,* as she recalled Mati's guidance.

Dressed in brown cloaks, the sentinels resembled Night Watchers. However, within their robes, swords hung from their belts, and knives lay flat across their sashes.

The pope's letter requested assistance and allegiance to secure land near Constantinople. "A re-supply base to convert Constantinople and Jerusalem to Roman Christendom, reuniting west and east. The King of Bulgaria has agreed. In return for part of his kingdom, near the Dark Sea, you will give him treasure and soldiers to protect his eastern flank from infidels. The Holy See has money and will support you. You could sell more titles, lands, and royal appointments to wealthy barons. There are likely plenty of restless young men seeking glory and booty."

The letter confirmed her darkest fears. Despite spouting separation of Church and kingdom, Richard would acquiesce to more power for *his* kingdom. And the pope knew this. He needed only the stone, Richard would say, and the separation he dreamed of would manifest.

Rachel wished that she and Richard were at the coast, sipping wine, eating sweets, and playing with dogs and grandchildren. *The allure of the stone*, she thought. But Jeremiah wasn't ready yet.

She recalled the vineyard meetings years ago. "God blessed the conception, my dear," Padre had assured with soft eyes. "A son came after all, not another daughter."

"Richard still doesn't know he has a son?" asked Charles.

"No, it's not the time yet," she replied, as she always did. "We'll wait to train him. I want him uncorrupted by the power centralized in the castle. He needs to live a normal childhood with regular people."

"Normal? He wasn't with peasants!" retorted Charles.

"Yes, you're right, you're right. We chose a prominent family in town to raise him, but it was for the best," she said.

The wine had helped erase the hideous memory that surfaced day after day. She justified it by the timing—that was a sign. King Henry had promised Prince Richard the crown if he recovered the stone, but Richard wanted a son to secure his line.

A foreigner as queen, she had chosen obedience to the kingdom, but the allure of power and the stone left her often alone while Richard fought his brothers and other enemies in France. Becoming friends with Mati had enabled her intimate knowledge of the stone's true power.

A trained son would restore the kingdom.

And avenge my father's death, she thought.

Since Richard's rescue, and her escape to Witenberg, she had wondered about the mysterious man named the Falconer in her culture, the Count in Bulgarian culture, and the Professor among the ruling class in Constantinople and Paris. No one knew his real name until Mati told her. No one knew his plan until Mati discovered it.

And Mati was dead.

He was killed before their planned meeting, before revealing everything. The symbol on the tree, she remembered, final instructions and a mark to the location.

"My son has the stone," she said abruptly. "Are they after him?"

Fear coursed through her veins. The others were silent.

"No more," she resolved aloud and pushed through the city in random patterns towards the cathedral. The sentinels followed her as she walked down alleys, bypassing women stroking cats and asking for help.

Sharp strike, sharp strike, sharp strike.
Ring up. Wait.
Long strike. Full circle.
Fourteen rings signify the hour.

Then a shorter strike—against a different bell, the sound higher in pitch.

She pulled back the brown hood briefly, long enough to catch Night Watchers scurrying atop the bell tower. The sentinels urged her forward, and she raised her hood as she pushed to the cathedral. Up the stairs, and through the front doors, they stopped at William's old office. "Stay outside for a moment," she told the sentinels. "Be on the lookout."

She surveyed the cathedral. An eerie stillness settled like a cloud bank with sounds carrying longer distances within it. Wind rushed through the church and whooshed inside her hood.

Open windows and doors, she thought. She inserted the brass key and turned.

Click.

Squeak.

William's office had been converted to a sacristy. Gold chalices and ciboria lined the shelves, vestments hung from racks, and altar linens were piled in a chest.

Curiosity had continued to poke her chest after the meeting with William. She followed her hunch. "Mati wasn't in his sarcophagus," William had told her. A large book with loose binding called her name. She pushed the chalices across the counter and opened the parish register.

Names upon names were written in sloppy cursive. "Baptisms, marriages, children . . . no," she read aloud and flipped through the pages. "There," she said, "burials."

A list of cemeteries and approved burial plots ran across the page. She moved her finger left and right until she found it: a plot of land off the trail towards the scriptorium.

My intuition was right!

"I'll show Father William," she said. "There must be something in there." As she closed the book, another book caught her eye. "Anointing of the sick," she read.

Inside were lists of names parishioners had asked for special prayer for. Common Witenberg names appeared, but one stuck out in larger ink: Dmitri of Falconer, boy, 10, deceased.

She hurriedly flipped through the parish register. Dmitri of Falconer appeared in the baptism section; parents' names were in the marriage section. Listed six years ago—before Mati's death. "Something isn't right," she said. "Could it be?"

She rummaged through the closets until she found a quill and ink. After tearing a piece from the register, she scribbled a note for William and placed it inside her pocket.

"Let's go," she told the sentinels. They followed her through the cathedral, through the grotto and treasury and into the crypt.

"He said it was through there." She pointed to the wooden board.

The sentinels removed the board and walked through the tunnel with hands placed atop their scabbards. Exiting into light, they saw the castle in the distance. "Look for something out of place, out of the ordinary," she told them.

Swords slashed through thick reeds; boots stomped on dirt, hoping to hit wood. On hands and knees, they scooped and shoveled soil. As she stood waiting, the bell tower warned from a distance. Two short bells, and the Night Watchers disappeared. "Half past the hour," she said. "Keep digging."

Down the trail, they cleared brush. "A proper burial for an archbishop would have a cross," she murmured. She lowered her hood and searched for crosses or a crucifix—wooden, metal, sticks—something. "Look for a cross," she told them.

Closer to the scriptorium, one sentinel stopped. "Your Highness, we found something." He had spotted it camouflaged in the forest. A looped cross made of reeds, resembling the crosses made from palms for Palm Sunday, stood upright, strung against two branches.

"Dig there," she said.

An urn. Similar to those found in the sacristy. Fired clay. She removed the lid. Inside were ashes and a note. She unrolled and read, *Here lies John of Sardegna, Archbishop of Witenberg, friend, martyr, heretic. Rest in eternal glory with your beloved.*

She placed the note into her pocket, then twisted the lid and buried the urn again. "We have it. We will return to the cathedral." As they approached the tunnel, she glanced towards the bell tower.

It was empty.

Her stomach sank. "Stay here and guard," she told one sentinel. To the other, "And you, come with me."

The slightest of voices reverberated around the tunnel, muffled by wind. The closer they got to the tower, the voices sounded more clearly, and the cracking popped more sharply. "Pull your sword," she said.

She stood in a fighting stance as the sentinel walked through the opening and peered.

Nothing.

Fading light from the exit showed nothing. "It's clear," he said.

The voices became louder and more distinct. *Three of them*, she thought, and held up three fingers for the sentinel.

"One older and two younger," the sentinel whispered.

With measured strides, they walked, light in step and smooth in motion. "Wait," she said, "stop here. Listen."

"My queen, we should leave—it's not safe."

"One moment," she mouthed with an index finger against her mouth.

"Where is the actual stone," came one voice, "the one that killed Goliath?"

"It was stolen!" one hoarsely exclaimed and coughed.

"Easy, easy."

Rachel heard pats on a back and cracks of ankles.

Through coughs, the hoarse voice continued. "The stone has survived several robbery attempts."

"Let's go, my lady," urged the sentinel.

"Wait," she whispered.

"The legend says only the pure in heart can use its powers."

"How did someone steal the stone from its casing?"

"Only a few know the code."

"With thousands of pilgrims visiting, I'm surprised more haven't tried to steal it, to profit from the relic."

"You said your name is Adam?" asked the hoarse voice. "Adam, most come to venerate the story—how God used a small man to defeat such a large enemy. It gives people hope their problems can be overcome too."

"But I'm still puzzled by your worship of David, both an adulterer and a murderer," Adam said icily, then grumbled noisily.

In sharper, clearer tone, the man responded, "We welcome you as visitors and you question our traditions, our hair, and, most importantly, our faith. Simply, God can use the most broken people and restore them to glorify Him. We're done here."

The sentinel pulled her arm. "Now, my queen."

Past sarcophagi and into the tunnel they sped. Ahead were sounds of swords clanking. Behind them, the voices stopped, but a loud, painful grunt came from that direction.

"Runnnn . . ." The sound reverberated around the tunnel.

The whiz and thunk of an arrow, and the sentinel fell.

"Stay here, my queen," the other sentinel said and handed her a knife.

Sword extended, the sentinel prepared for battle.

A short, stout man, robed in black, brandished a sword.

A Night Watcher, she thought.

He charged and clanked swords with the sentinel.

Rachel's muscles seized as thoughts rattled around her head.

Where do I go? Stay behind the sentinel or run through the church?

"Run!" shouted the sentinel.

With her peripheral vision, she saw a woman turn a corner and sprint with her ponytail swinging. Arrows flew overhead, and the sentinel ducked. The woman reloaded and shot again.

"Help!" yelled Rachel urgently and ran through the crypt into the treasury. Barely lifting her head, she paused. A tassel swung, and joints cracked. She made eye contact with someone.

It was Brother Francis, Rose Abbey chamberlain.

"Queen Rachel?" asked Francis. "Is that you? What are you doing here?" He inched closer.

She hesitated.

Run past them? Ask for help?

"We *need* to go, Francis. Before we're killed," she rushed out.

"The queen is here?" asked the shorter of the two men with him.

Francis and the two men followed her through the grotto and up the spiral stairs.

"Come on, Francis," she urged. She grabbed his hand, and his sandals flopped against the marble as his older, wobbly legs dragged heavily.

"To the door," said Francis breathlessly.

"But the gift. And the king," reminded one of his companions.

"Later, Adam," thundered the other.

She tried each door, but they wouldn't budge. "Quick. In here," Rachel said as the grotto door burst open. She quietly closed the door and said, "Sit beneath the vestments."

The two men sat, and one carefully set a box onto the floor. Expecting the lighter skin of the locals, Rachel lowered her hood and discerned their differences. They were more like her: desert skin and dark, wide eyes. One was slender with a long face, thin nose and thick, lighter hair and a beard; the other was compact, dense with massive chest and wide shoulders, round face, protruding nose, and a mustache to make up for his bald head.

"What is your name?" Rachel asked the shorter one.

"Adam, Your Majesty."

"Adam, where are you from?"

"Constantinople," he said flatly.

"Me too," she said. "A long time ago, but my family is there. Listen, I want your help. Do you have a weapon in that box?"

"No, it's a gift to the king from our duke," said Adam.

"Adam, we must deliver the package to him before our meeting," the slender one said and jerked his head. "Our orders."

"I'll give the gift to him," said Rachel. "Can you help find a way out?"

Outside the door, a man in the narthex said, "They couldn't have escaped, my lady. We locked the doors."

"Cracky," barked the woman. "Check the chapels. I'll go upstairs."

"A Night Watcher?" Francis asked incredulously. "Brother Cracky. I don't understand." He stood, and his elbow hit a chalice.

It slid and rapped against another chalice, first on the slide and next on the topple.

"Did you hear that?" asked the woman.

"Please?" asked Cracky.

The chalice slid from the ledge.

With hushed breath, Rachel extended her arm and caught the cup. After an exhale, she mouthed, "Sit down, Francis."

"No, Smoky," said Cracky. "I'll meet you at the altar."

"Who's after you?" Adam asked Rachel as the sound of steps came closer to the sacristy.

"I don't know," she said, her thoughts probing heart and mind. "Francis, is there another way out?" she asked.

"We tried the front, and the roof leads to the narthex. Maybe the rumors are true," Francis said excitedly. "But we don't have time for a treasure hunt."

"What?" snapped Rachel.

"A secret chamber under the treasury, my lady," said Francis. "But just a rumor about Archbishop Virdis."

Of course, she recalled. The marker was somewhere in the cathedral.

"The only way is to force our way out, then," she decided. "Look for something to open the front door."

As they searched the sacristy, her attention focused on the package. *Maybe a clue*, she thought. She took the package and opened it to reveal two folded tapestries.

"What are you doing?" asked Adam.

Rachel ignored him as her body heat rose, and her heart beat like a hummingbird's wings. Rachel unfurled the tapestries, recoiled, and gasped: "Oh no!"

She dove a hand to her abdomen to apply pressure to the exploding pain.

Through shallow breaths, she said, "Oh no, oh no, no. Rohad knows."

Eyes lazily rolled back in her head, and she dropped to the floor in a swoon. Through rapid blinks, she saw Francis stooped over her, examining her body.

"The queen!" he yelped. "Help! Help! Somebody help!" The sound of steps in the cathedral pounded closer, and she wriggled on the floor to find the knife that had fallen.

"Adam, I'll get the package," said the slender man. "You grab the candlesticks. We'll force our way out." With long, heavy candlesticks in hand, Adam kicked the sacristy door open and ran to the cathedral entrance. He rammed the front door.

"Smoky!" yelled Cracky. "Those men."

"Allies, Cracky," Smoky said calmly. "Look for the queen."

Francis knelt and helped Rachel stand. "Our chance, Your Highness. We must go."

As she stood, a loose floorboard rattled against the wall. It lifted slightly and showed a small opening.

"Wait, Francis," she said weakly. She searched quickly and found the quill and ink bottle near the parish register. After drawing an image on the wall, she opened the board and hid the urn note and torn piece of register paper. "Now," she said.

After several blows, the front door opened, and Adam and the slender man escaped.

Francis snatched a shorter candlestick and followed Rachel through the sacristy door.

"There's nowhere to go, Your Highness!" screeched the woman's voice by the front door. "We've been watching you sneak around with Father William."

Francis turned around and swung the candlestick. "You won't get past me, witch," he blustered.

"Smoky, you want me to handle him?" asked Cracky. Neck cracking, joints popping, he marched forward.

"Please, go ahead," Smoky said. "I'll get the queen."

"Run, my queen!" said Francis. The candlestick blocked several sword thrusts, but he succumbed to the fourth blow.

Rachel ran and pushed over chairs into the aisle, hoping to get to the grotto and make it out.

"Face me, you coward!" shrilled Smoky.

Cracky lumbered behind Rachel, and Smoky sprinted to the

grotto door, blocking Rachel's escape. In front of the altar, Rachel thought, *Go down fighting.*

She clenched the knife and declared, "I am Queen of Witen, Lady of Constantinople, wife, mother, sister, and daughter of God. You don't frighten me."

Smoky wielded a sword behind dark-set eyes and a blond ponytail.

"Anna, you don't have to do this," said Rachel. "I know about your son, Dmitri. You can start a new life."

Her son. Rachel remembered that morning: a pink horizon, a doorstep, and Jeremiah swaddled in a blanket.

"Did Virdis tell you?" Anna asked, then laughed coldly. "Or, rather, *Mati*? Isn't that what you called him?" Anna paused and continued in sharper tone. "I don't care about you, how much you know. Your death will help our mission. Your husband will start a war to avenge your death."

A surge of fear swelled in her heart—she knew Anna was right. Her son and his team must carry on.

Anna rushed and dealt several blows with her sword. Rachel blocked several swipes with her knife as they struggled around the altar, Anna cursing revenge and spouting justice for her son's death.

Once Rachel heard why Anna's son killed himself six years ago, her heart stormed in fits of anger and sorrow, then expanded, pushing her ribs until she gasped for air. She froze, and Cracky blocked any possible path of escape. Anna struck Rachel in the side. Suddenly, her thoughts took on a nostalgic and fleeting tone as the world rushed away.

They fled, and Rachel staggered into the sacristy as images flashed of her wedding, Isabella's birth, and the note she left with the baby:

Elfred and Sarah, please love my little Miah and teach him
to love the Lord. He is named after a noble man, my father,
Jeremiah.

With love,
Rachel

PARROT CLUE

For the trip, Vere wore his customary rich, full-bodied uniform: wine-colored cloak and a pressed white coat with gold buttons covering a silk tunic, embroidered with violet lions.

"You changed, Vere. And no boots for the journey?" William asked, seeing the same floral design from Anna's shop on the insteps of Vere's slippers.

"I prefer low-cut, Father William."

"With thick heels?" joked William. "To make you taller?"

"Yes, that's it," he said with dignity. Chin up, Vere raised his leathery voice and emphasized, "A *cleric*. With *knights*."

"You didn't have to come," said William.

"Yes, but the king ordered me." Vere's deadpan face relaxed, and his throat deflated inside the stiff collar.

"How do you stay so calm? Being around the king and the court would make me nervous."

"There's a stiffness in my blood, Father William, from generations of being chamberlains. My father was one, his father one, and so on."

William noticed the ruby stains on Vere's lips and teeth and unconsciously licked his own lips.

"Very observant, Father William. There's more wine in my bag. Want some?"

"No thanks." He patted his own bag, knowing he did not yet have enough supplies for the journey.

"We won't be long; you can purchase food in the city if you're hungry. Lord Alfred should be with his family in the market."

As they crossed the bridge, the cathedral bell tower came into focus, and William thought of the investigation and suspicious men at the castle.

"Who were the men from Duke Rohad?" asked William.

"Guests from his court," said Vere, "to present King Richard with a gift. I instructed them to return in an hour when he was available."

"And the sentinels?" William asked nervously.

"Are you worried, Father William? Protection is standard protocol when guests visit."

"Yes, of course. Why would they visit?"

William stopped his flow of thoughts to study a tall man who walked beside a woman and child. "Is that him?"

"Yes, the king's favorite," said Vere with a dreary sigh. "I'll be waiting on this bench as you carry on."

How should I approach him? William wondered. *"Nothing eccentric,"* he reminded himself. William flung his satchel across his shoulders and casually approached a booth. Alfred lowered his hood, then leaned over and kissed the woman, who must be his wife.

"Yuck," the little girl walking beside them said.

Alfred grasped his wife's hand and extended his middle finger.

She looked towards her as she jumped a little and blurted, "Oh!"

"Hold *my* hand, Dadde," said the girl as the woman smacked his shoulder and said, "You know I don't like you doing that."

"Dadde, *my* hand," cried the girl.

"Yes, I know, Rèse," he said. "It's my way of saying sorry."

The corner of her lips depressed, she held onto his arm. "I readied your pack. When you say farewell to Maren tonight, she'll sleep if you tell her the story."

"Thank you, Rèse," he said and grasped her hand. "It won't be long. I promise."

"That's what you always say," she dragged out. "Don't hurt him when you find him."

"I'm after the stone," he said and reached for Maren's hand, but she had run ahead to a booth near William. "Maren, come back!" shouted Alfred.

"Can I fancy you in a wonderful parrot, little girl?" asked a merchant.

William moved closer to Maren and pretended to shop.

"Dadde, can I have the talking bird?" pleaded Maren.

"No, honey."

"Remember the dinner, Alfred?" asked Thèrèse. "And the days after? His name couldn't be spoken."

"Smote," said Maren. Her lips tightened and arms crossed. "Uncle Miah is a smote—he called me a princess."

"Maren," scolded Reese, "we don't say that word."

"But Dadde said it. And I want a bird."

"No," said Alfred in disgust, "we don't need a bird flying around the house. How about a pretty doll? Can we add one to your collection?"

Maren threw herself to the ground, kicking and flailing her arms. "Two dolls!" she demanded.

"You can have one, Maren," said Rèse.

"Two, Mummy. I want two."

"No, Maren, you can have one. Your mum said one."

Pants became cries, and she hit a loose cobblestone with her fist.

"I'm over it, Thèrèse," said Alfred in sharper tone. "Get up, Maren."

Thèrèse dug in a pocket for some coins, but Alfred waved her off. "I've got it. Maren, do you want a doll or not?"

"No, if I can't have two."

"Fine. None, then. No dessert tonight if you don't get up."

Though Alfred had attempted to conceal his insignia with a sash, one crusty peasant recognized the lion patch sewn into Alfred's tunic.

"A special knight," mocked the short, greasy man. "Out for a stroll with your lady? Where is the king? Not flicking his snot for you, you crotch sniffer?"

Some around them laughed.

Shoppers in surrounding booths spotted the knight, and crowds began to gather around them.

William took a step back and leaned against a wall.

"Nothing to see here," said Alfred.

"Not even your family listens to you. Did the war castrate you, Lord Alfred?" mocked the peasant.

Rising to his full height, Alfred loomed over the peasant and grabbed the scruff of his neck. "Don't test me, you maggot-infested scum bucket. Leave me and my family alone."

Alfred released him, and the peasant stumbled. After steadying himself, he formed a fist. The crowd hushed and made way for a woman with an entourage who yelled, "Halt!"

With sentinels and ladies-in-waiting, Lady Isabella glided through the opening in the crowd. Standing alone in the square, the peasant shrank away. "Well done, Lord Alfred," she said.

Thèrèse bowed. "Princess Isabella, thank you for the help."

Alfred's lips barely curled, just enough to say, "Lady Isabella."

"Making my way back to the castle," said Isabella. She briefly glanced towards Thèrèse but focused on Alfred. Her cheeks rose and held her smile. After a tense moment, she gave a knowing and profoundly accepting look, as if confessing to Alfred.

"I'm sorry," said Isabella.

Alfred's head immediately lowered to the right and shook.

"The king tells me you're after the—" Isabella said but stopped.

Alfred raised his brows and looked towards his daughter.

"I'm sorry, you're right," said Isabella.

After a few bell strikes, lengthening the nervous discharge of energy, Isabella asked, "So, how have you been?"

"Fine," he muttered. Then he bent a little to his daughter and said, "Maren, where are your manners?"

Maren scrambled to her feet and stood. "A real princess," she said weakly and hid behind Alfred's leg.

"It's fine, honey," Alfred said, his body posture relaxing. "You can meet her. This is Princess Isabella."

Maren slowly peeked at her.

"It's permitted, Mar. Go say hello," Thèrése said and nudged her.

Maren bowed and said, "You're very pretty. Like my dolls."

"You have good taste," Isabella said and bent to Maren's view. "Like your dadde. Maybe someday you'll be a princess."

Alfred bit a lip.

"It was a pleasure meeting you, Lady Maren," said Isabella.

"Can you buy me a doll?" asked Maren.

Isabella stood and turned to Thèrése, saying, "Yes, if your mummy doesn't mind."

"She has a stout heart, strong in perseverance like her father," said Thèrése.

"You mean his stubbornness?" asked Isabella.

The women laughed.

"Well, we must be moving on," Alfred said and took Thérèse's hand.

"I understand. But let me buy a doll for your daughter."

Thèrése nodded, and they walked to the booth.

"Father William?" Isabella asked in a tone of surprise. "Are you Father William? Is that you?"

He cowered, slinking until his back bumped the wall.

"You know this man?" asked Alfred.

"I've heard of him," said Isabella. "But I haven't met him. My father told me a slender man with a black hat was joining you on your quest."

"Joining me? Why?"

"Yes, yes, Lord Alfred." William stumbled and braced himself against a bird cage. Removing his hat and bowing to Isabella, he said, "I've been appointed by the king to help you."

Alfred's eyes flashed. "Who are you? What are you? The king appointed a merchant, a tailor?"

"He's a priest," said Isabella.

"A priest," Alfred said irritably. "Even better. Why would the king send a priest?"

"His stubbornness," Thérèse said to Isabella as if his words were proof. "Maybe he can help, dear."

"I don't need help."

"It's true, Alfred," said Isabella. "He found the stone in your brother's possession. William is also a scribe, and the king wants a detailed report when you return."

"If you found it," Alfred said accusingly to William, "why didn't you take it? Being a priest, you know how important it is to the kingdom and to the king."

William shuffled his feet and fiddled with his eyebrows. He ran a hand beneath his coat and tunic and grabbed his chest. It was a nervous habit, one he should quit, he thought, but squeezing focused his mind.

Think.

"Nice seeing you again, Princess Isabella," Alfred said and grabbed Thérèse's hand. "Let's go, Rèse."

"I saw Jeremiah at the mead ball," blurted out William. "Was I going to take it then? From his pocket?"

"His pocket?" asked Alfred.

William pulled the scarf tightly around his neck.

I'm not telling him how, he thought.

"Goodbye, William. I must leave," said Alfred.

William leafed idly through some items in the booth. Beside him, parrots talked, chattering something about wood.

Witen me, he thought.

"Duty and your honor, Lord Alfred. I must go with you," said William. "It is an order from the king."

Alfred stopped and about-faced. "What do you know about duty? About honor?"

"Alfred," Thérèse said, her voice trailing and impatient. "Let's go home and eat and tuck your daughter into bed."

William looked to Isabella for support, but she was busy with the dolls at the booth. She paid and gave one to Maren. William's fingers fidgeted with breadcrumbs on the table, knocking some into the bird's cage.

What do I do? The king had given him an order to join Alfred. *What if Alfred refuses? Should I ask Vere for help?*

He bowed his head and prayed.

After picking at the breadcrumbs, the parrots sidled up to the side of the cage to chatter at him. "Wilting wood Jeremiah weeps, wilting wood Jeremiah weeps." William put a finger through the bars and contemplated the mysterious line while giving the parrot a head scratch. It twisted its neck and closed its eyes to enjoy, and the other parrot crowded in for its turn.

Alfred turned around with a look of shock and hurried to the booth, where William pulled back from the cage at Alfred's expression, bypassing William. "Excuse me, ma'am. Your parrots repeated the name 'Jeremiah.' Is that about a person?"

William pulled at his scarf, loosening it from his neck. He looked to where Vere was sitting on a bench, sipping wine.

"How much you have?" asked the redhead. "This'll cost you."

Alfred jammed a hand into his pocket and threw them a coin.

"More will do," they said.

Hand on table, he leaned forward and said, "Now tell me, or I'll have this booth turned over."

Counting her unexpected money, the redhead responded, "Why yes, we met a sullen gentleman named Jeremiah at The Grouse."

Alfred scratched his chin. "At The Grouse?" he asked with raised tone. "Thank you. I know where that is." He gestured in the direction of The Grouse as if visualizing the way. He retreated but spun around again, "Wait, what did he—"

"Short, curly brown hair, a few marks, dark complexion, full of misery," said the redhead. "And he kept playing with his balls."

The blonde laughed. "I think it was only one—a stone."

"You're a magician—that's what you are," Alfred told William.

Closer in, Alfred said softly, "God or magic—whatever you bring—I guess we'll need it. Meet me at the royal training grounds in an hour for preparations. We leave tomorrow morning. I suggest you plan to arrive early."

Sharp strike, sharp strike, sharp strike.
Ring up. Wait.
Long strike. Full circle.
Fifteen rings signify the hour.

"Thank you, Lord Alfred," said William in a rush. "Thank you, Lady Isabella and Lady Thérèse. I must be off." Late for the meeting with Rachel, he rocked into a jog, then a run, leaving Vere behind.

"Where are you going?" asked Vere.

"To prepare for a quest!" William said breathlessly. He carried the satchel in his hand and ran.

Across the square, he noticed the front door was ajar. As memories came from the initial investigation, when he discovered the latch had been cut, a sense of dread rushed to him, extinguishing the flame of excitement he carried just moments ago.

He ran.

A candlestick holder was preventing the door from closing completely.

Fragmented colored lights from the rear rose window danced on the chairs. A breeze blew in, and tree branches swayed. "Hello, hello," he called.

No one responded.

Red stains dotted the marble floor and trailed from the narthex to the altar.

"Rachel!" he yelled. "Where are you?"

His mind went to the worst case, and sweat sprang out. His body temperature cooled, and his heart pulsed faster.

The door to his old office was open.

A woman with a brown cloak lay on the floor against the back wall. *Oh no.*

Velvet sloshed back and forth in his bloodstream to warm an icy heart.

He collapsed to the floor beside her.

She was pale, blank, and still—love drained away with her life.

"Rachel, Rachel, no, no, no," he said. He cradled her and put his ear to her mouth; she wasn't breathing.

As he eased her onto the floor, he saw the circle. And a line down the middle. The same symbol as was on the Levan tree, Mati's tree.

Coldness blasted to his core, and his skin and lips tingled. His breaths shortened again, his limbs wobbled, but he firmed himself to escape.

On the bridge, bells rang; he pulled at his hair and covered his ears. He bolted to the castle gate and briefed the sentinels. Through the castle, they escorted him, running with him, yelling with him for the king.

"What's the matter?" asked Vere, who must have returned to the castle as William had left the square.

"The queen," William said, his voice filled with fear. "Where is King Richard? I must tell him."

"Tell him what, William?"

"King Richard! Princess Isabella!" shouted William.

"Tell him what, William?" Vere asked nervously.

Atop the central staircase, Isabella shielded Madelyn. "What's wrong?" she asked Isabella. "Weren't you just with Alfred?"

Richard marched into the hall. "What's the meaning of this, Priest? I sent you to Alfred."

"Yes, yes, sire, but . . . ," he fumbled.

"But what?"

Trembling, he managed, "The queen."

"William! What? Tell me!" barked Richard and took him by the shoulders.

Eyes cracked red, William bit a lip and said, "Rachel is dead."

Richard pulled William into his face, eyes wide with rage. "Another absurd accusation, you fool. Leave my sight and find the stone!"

"But Dadde, look at him. Why would he lie?"

"Come with me," Richard said. "Show me, Priest," said Richard. "Isabella, stay here."

✦———✦

Time passed.

With fists raised, Richard roared over her body, the sound echoing against the limestone walls.

"As God is my witness, whoever did this will pay!"

Sharp strike, sharp strike, sharp strike.

Ring up. Wait.

Long strike. Full circle.

Fifteen rings signify the hour.

Two short strikes signify the half-hour.

William covered his ears and ran, struggling to follow Richard carrying Rachel's body back to the castle and into his bed chamber. Hair standing out where he'd raked his fingers through it, Richard swallowed excessively with blank looks. He grimaced and almost collapsed his chest, and his lips quivered. "I'm sorry, sorry, Bella."

After initial speechlessness, Isabella ran and touched her mother's face. Her mouth fidgeted, and she repeated, "What? What? That can't be! That can't be! No!" She rocked slightly back and forth, then bolted and crisscrossed across the room, searching for something. Clothes flew into the air, and a creamy white veil landed next to Richard's feet.

"Luta!" she yelled. "Where are you? Dadde, where is Luta?"

Body stiffened, face frozen, Richard couldn't speak. Shaking, he lowered Rachel to the floor and seized a veil strewn with embroidered flowers to spread over her.

264

Hand to mouth, Isabella stuttered, "A gift from Mum—from Mama."

Her chest caved, and she collapsed to the floor.

She scampered to a corner.

Richard handed the veil to her, and Isabella brought it beside her mother, taking a corner of the veil to her own cheek.

"Light and soft," she said.

Madelyn had been silent against the wall and now scooted beside Isabella. "What's wrong, Mummy? What's Nana doing?"

With tears, Isabella hugged her and said, "Maddie, your nana is sleeping, that's all."

"I like the veil, Mummy," she said. "Can I have one?"

Isabella whimpered and wiped a tear. She hugged, then released her daughter and said, "Yes, honey, one moment."

She got up and rummaged, tossing clothes until she went to the dressing room for her mother's cloak and wrapped it around the girl's long brown curls and olive skin, a rich contrast to the deep crimson of the cloak.

"Maddie, Maddie," she struggled, "you look more, you look more and more like Nana every day. Beautiful. Beautiful." After a soft kiss on top of Maddie's head, Isabella broke down—whimpers turned to sobs. Madelyn followed.

"Luta!" Isabella called with a shrieking voice. "Luta! Where are you?"

The sound of clicking raced down the corridor, and a large head appeared at the doorway. Luta pushed through the bedchamber door and skittered to Isabella.

Luta slobbered Rachel with kisses first, then Isabella and Madelyn. She joined the women with their wails. Richard knelt to join them, but his legs froze and would not bend. He swallowed and swallowed, then ripped at his hair.

Breaths stopped or tore raggedly out of one or another of them. Glassy stares froze.

Attempted family embrace froze.

William froze; he didn't know what to do, but he understood. "I'll find the stone—and Rachel's murderer," he vowed to them all.

He skipped every other step in his hurry, and just outside the door, he stopped. The bells struck. The sound carried across the river and tingled down his spine.

Sharp strike, sharp strike, sharp strike.
Ring up. Wait.
Long strike. Full circle.
Sixteen rings signify the hour.

Oh, the bells, the bells, the bells!

PURSUIT

The ringing circled William's eardrums in tight spirals. From high to low, his emotions seesawed as his legs propelled him forward.

Alfred had accepted him on the team. Perhaps Richard was smarter than William thought, agreeing to William's cover as a scribe. Perhaps he was cunning. Perhaps Rachel had married intentionally.

He stopped.

The ringing settled in his chest and unloaded like a wheelbarrow being dumped. Anger simmered, mixed with an overwhelming sense of duty. He didn't need to tell Alfred Rachel had died, that he knew of it; he would find out soon enough. He wouldn't blow his cover and risk not solving the cases.

Ahead, Lord Alfred and knights were ditching heavy armor. He pushed through the stables gate.

"Reporting on time," William said and saluted as he saw Richard do, hand cupped like a *C* with a quick push of the wrist.

"On time is late, Father William," Alfred said while wrapping cloth under his thumb and around his wrist. "You hold the salute at a sharp angle." Alfred dropped his salute and pointed. "Beside the stables, there's an extra byrnie. It may be a bit big in your chest, but you'll manage."

The team laughed, and William rocked slightly. Walking to the stables was like navigating through a cathedral; the men's legs were thick like pillars, their chests wide as altars. *They all have the same*

CORNERSTONE | THE KING

shape, he thought. Beside them, William looked like a flimsy pine in a forest of redwoods.

Knights were placing helmets into their shelves and removing neck chains.

"We won't need the helmets, Oths," Alfred said firmly. "But you can keep the hat, William."

"It's a good look, Bouncy," a knight joked and slapped a towel against William's butt. He flinched and covered his mouth.

"Forget Danny Boy," said Alfred. "You gotta keep it somewhat light around here despite the gravity of our work."

"Gravity?" asked Daniel. "The damsel in distress fits in my palm—a magic stone." The square-jawed knight pulled the mail over his head. William counted a four-to-one pattern of closed, tightly woven steel mesh rings on the waist-length shirt.

"And this will protect us?" asked William. "Will I need weapons?"

"No, we'll take care of you. And we'll be lighter without the heavy armor. Plus," Alfred said while walking towards a wall-mounted sword rack, "we'll find Jeremiah and the stone soon."

Expecting a scraping, the familiar sound when the knights sheathed their swords, William heard nothing. The swords went quietly into their tooled leather pouches with a *shh*. Images, tails maybe, were etched into the leather.

"What is that?" asked William.

"The scabbard?"

"Um, yes, Alfred. No, what's *on* the scabbard?"

"The symbol of our pride. Look up."

Beside the sword rack was a chart showing fifteen men's faces, with Alfred on top. "These have recently become hereditary, a decree from King Richard, but our unit was able to design its own," Alfred said, fingering the coat of arms. A red cross centered the white shield, and down to the right was a large blue *O*. Blue herald lions supported the shield.

"What does the *O* mean?"

"Othniels, or Oths. Lions of God."

"But the top, the crown and crest, I think? What is that?"

"Baby-face over there thought we were the otters. It became a joke, so we crossed an otter with a lion and a dragon for more ferocity. Thus, the dragon tails etched onto our swords."

Alfred buckled his scabbard and sheathed the sword. Bypassing white surcoats hung on pins, Alfred donned a black one bearing the same symbols on its long sleeves. "Look around for your size," he said. "They may be big, but we won't be out long."

Alfred helped William with the byrnie and surcoat. The mail weighted heavy against William's chest, and the sleeves extended beyond his hands.

"A real knight," said Daniel. "Do you need help on your horsey too?" Laughing, the knights mounted smaller, lighter horses, and Alfred asked, "Do you know how to ride a horse, William?"

"No, and I think those are more my speed?" William said, pointing to taller, majestic, heftier horses. *Probably not so fast*, he thought.

"King Richard recommended those as a show of force, but we're not monsters hidden behind metal. We're after a boy and a stone. These," he said and saddled William's horse, "these are swifter, stealthier, but unarmored horses—better for reconnaissance, scouting, and search and recovery."

"Do I need to practice first?"

"You can try now, if you like, but you'll be fine. Boomer is our oldest horse, so he'll go slower. Comb his mane and tell him he's a good boy."

"Good boy, good boy," William said and stuck his boot into the stirrup. His long leg bent awkwardly, and his foot pushed through the stirrup.

"Charles—isn't that your name? Come here," called Alfred to a boy who could be a younger version of William, with a slender frame and thin nose. "Stay near William to help with his horse when he needs it."

"Yes, Lord Alfred, but please call me Charlie, my lord." The boy was reassuring to William by his mere presence—he saw a younger version of himself: baby-faced, wide-eyed, and eager to travel.

"Thank you, Charles," said Alfred.

"Charlie, my lord. Call me Charlie, sir."

"Very well. Charlie," said Alfred. "You were trained to be a scout, correct? And you recently graduated from the academy?"

"Yes, my lord. With top honors. A wonderful day for me and my family. Honor, duty, kingdom," he said and stood tall.

"Did the commandant speak of wolves wanting to kill us?"

"Yes, so we must protect the sheep; otherwise, the sheep will be no more, or subservient to another man's rule."

"Impressive, Charlie," Alfred said with a beaming smile. "Duty, honor, kingdom."

"Yes, sir. We protect the kingdom, our ideals, and our values."

Alfred pulled a cross from around his neck and showed it to Charlie. "This was a gift on my graduation day. Our protection," he assured him.

"I've heard, my lord. No injuries in all your battles?"

"Correct. Like you, at eighteen years old, I entered service after graduation and fought right away."

Under his breath, Alfred mumbled something about his mind and a stupid relic but then loudly said, "We'll complete the mission. Charlie, unroll the maps and lead us to The Grouse." Then he climbed onto his own horse and a horn blew from the castle, directing all their attention to the ramparts for a message.

"Yes, sir," said Charlie.

Alfred climbed onto his horse.

Before leaving, a horn blew again.

The rampant-lion flag atop the castle lowered to half-staff, and the castle buzzed with people milling about—the gates slammed shut and sentinels manned their posts with torches ablaze.

"What's going on, Lord Alfred?" asked Charlie.

"Something is wrong," said Alfred. He kicked his horse and rode towards the castle.

William's stomach bound into knots, and his breath blew meaty with the sudden tang of panic he smelled in his own sweat.

A minute or two later, Alfred rode back and waved for the attention of them all.

"We must hurry, Oths," Alfred said on return. "The queen has died, and the king demands the stone—we must ride tonight. I'm sorry, but you have only an hour with your families. Say farewell and get your packs."

The team departed, and as Alfred double-checked his pack, he pulled out a golden cloak. He shook his head, mumbled something, then shoved it back into his pack. He stopped William. "We won't be long, I'm confident. Pack for a few days, including the equipment we've just given you. Get food and water bags from that chest over there. A creek runs behind the training grounds for your water."

———

When they reassembled an hour later, with a twirl of his finger, Alfred said, "Time to stone hunt, Oths."

"And Alfred's measly, ill-bred brother," mocked one knight.

The knight laughed, but Daniel promptly rebuked him. Alfred ordered, "Stop. Alive, Oths. You won't hurt him. Is that clear?"

They nodded, and Alfred said, "Our mission is the stone. Let's go while we still have some light."

They left the royal stables and connected to a wider trail that led southeast. Following the river for a few miles, they stopped once it merged into the Witen Channel. Charlie dismounted and asked locals near the shipyard the whereabouts of The Grouse. "Sir," said Charlie, "The Grouse is three miles southeast of here."

"Thank you, knight. Daniel, stay here with the men and protect our flank," said Alfred. "William, come with me."

They followed a narrower trail to a thatched country pub. As they entered, the stale scent of old beer and unwashed bodies turned William's stomach. Candles showed an empty pub.

Alfred swept the ale-soaked straw floor with his sword and strode to an old man slumped against a wall. Alfred tapped him, then tapped him again, and he grumbled.

"Lift your head," ordered Alfred. He pulled from his bag a rough portrait of Jeremiah and showed the man. "I am Lord Alfred, commander of the King's Special Guard Corps. Have you've seen this man?" He highlighted Jeremiah's long, dark curls, dusky skin, and his striking light eyes.

The man slowly roused himself to respond and rubbed his eyes. In low, groggy voice, he mumbled, "Melord, thatis a rough sketch. Eyes and earspicturedraw in me mind. Lotsindese parts with darkhair-n-skin." He gestured to the bar.

Alfred smacked him. "Slow down and speak up. Have you seen a man named Jeremiah?"

The man palmed his reddened cheek and grinned. "Yes, of course! I'm a regular. He's new—always complaining about his women troubles. About a wench named Marianne."

"Yes, he's the one. Is he here?"

"I haven't seen him today, but I was asleep 'til ye ruffled me."

Alfred lifted the sword and poked the man's chest.

"I'm in no mood, peasant. Where is he?"

Holding his head, he said, "I don't know, my lord. He wanders about to clean midmorning before the supper crowd comes." Wiping crumbs from his trousers, he said, "Have a go at the inn or my village."

The sword poked again, and Alfred leaned into him. "More specific, or this goes deeper."

The man's smile widened, and his drunken breaths blew Alfred back a step.

"Would they go west, Sir Alfred? Or east? Or gather supplies first? Not much in The Grouse. My village is a few leagues north. Wouldn't know, sir-knight."

Alfred lifted his sword, disgusted, and he and William walked outside to join the team. "Come on, Oths," Alfred said. "Jeremiah and the stone are close."

William mounted and gave a slight kick with his heel, but the horse didn't budge. Chewing on grass, contentedly, the horse seemed to be saying it was about time he'd had a break. William leaned over and combed the mane with his fingers. "Good, good boy."

Boomer chewed more slowly. "No, Boomer," said William, "go." He kicked him harder and repeated, "Good boy, good boy." His ears pinned back, and Boomer took off from a walk to trot to canter in seconds, to catch up with the others.

"Good boy!"

As Boomer sped along the trail, William saw something moving among the sycamores and spruces.

CATTLE DRIVE

After crossing the Witen Channel, the ship sailed. Marcus's man navigated through a river and dropped the passengers and their horses at a village near a water mill. He farewelled, and Mo secured the horses.

"Let's camp here for the night," said Asser. Jeremiah and others tailed Asser as he approached a man with a floppy leather hat and bushy mustache sitting on the porch steps watching cattle chew grass.

"Good afternoon," shouted Asser. The man with a floppy, leather hat and bushy mustache didn't respond but stared and tore a chunk of bread with his teeth. "Me name is Asser, and these are me merry men and woman. We're on a grand quest."

The man stood up and left. The cows briefly looked up, with grass dangling from their mouths, but didn't move; they remained plopped on the beige turf and carried on minding their business. Asser ran and swung the gate open at a farmyard and went in.

"Asser, come on," said Jeremiah, and Jameela called out, "No, Tiny Hands!" The dried grass crunched as he walked. Asser crossed the manure-covered barnyard behind the man and tapped him on the shoulder as he prepared to milk a cow in the barn. "Excuse me, sir."

Calves fed, and one mooed from the hard pull of its udders from Mo-sized hands. Asser covered his nose with one hand and extended for a handshake with the other. Dung lay as butterscotch pools on the floor.

"Leave me alone and get off my property," ordered the man. He grabbed a rake and hurled hay at Asser, but Asser moved closer.

"Leave," the man said.

"Me not leaving. We need help."

The rake hammered into the floor.

"Why didn't you start with that? Wasting my time with non-sense." He stomped off towards the house with a gruff look and a wave to include both Asser and Jeremiah, who had tentatively followed him into the enclosure.

Asser and Jeremiah followed him to the house, and a woman with blond pigtails stood outside the door. Asser and Jeremiah tipped their hats to her.

"Where should we stay the night?" asked Asser. "We're traveling to the church on the rock."

"My help will cost you," the man said.

"Cost us? We don't have anything."

"Then, you must be getting on," the man said and pulled Asser by the hood, but Mo had been watching and sped and slammed the gate open.

"Easy, Giant!" the man shouted and let go of Asser.

"Stop, Mo," said Jeremiah. "We'll move on."

"You can help them, Bailey," said the woman. "Guide them to the springs. That would be a wonderful place to rest."

"Ashlyn, you have no business—"

Asser walked over to her and clasped her hands with both of his. "Thank you very much, me lady. Could you please tell us where these springs are?"

"Fine, Asser," said Bailey. "I'll tell you if you and your mates help me move these cattle to the other pasture."

"Throw in food, and you have a deal."

Ashlyn shook Asser's hand. Bailey opened his mouth to argue, but the look from Ashlyn stopped him.

My chance, Jeremiah thought. He smiled at Jameela and climbed into the stirrups. The horse snorted, and Jeremiah pulled the reins and waited until it put its head down.

"First time?" Jameela asked and giggled.

"Moved cattle?" he asked and released the reins.

"No, ride a horse," she said with hands on her hips. "Yes, move cattle. That's what we're talking about."

After a few more pulls of the reins and encouragement from Jeremiah, the horse relaxed and trotted a lap around the yard.

Asser, Mo, and Bailey went to their horses.

Padre stood with Jameela at the fence.

"Aye," Bailey said, "I'll be in the front. Our aim is to move these hundred cows from here to there." He pointed to a pasture across a small creek. "You"—he pointed to Asser—"I heard the woman call you Tiny Hands. You seem confident in the saddle. At least, you talk the talk, but we'll see."

Blushing with anger, Asser pulled himself up as if to deliver the acid words on his tongue, but he resisted. Jameela shook her head in disapproval.

Bailey pointed to Jeremiah. "Your name?"

"Jeremiah."

He moved his horse closer and pulled up Jeremiah's sleeves one at a time to reveal the cross and shield marks. Bailey lifted an eyebrow, cocked his head, and did a double take. "A knight? You?"

Jeremiah shrugged and grinned. Bailey looked up and down his scrawny body and wrapped his hand around Jeremiah's entire bicep. "No, you'll be called Sarge."

Jameela said to Padre, "What does that mean?"

"A knight of lesser rank."

She snorted around the hand that could not quell her exploding laughter. "I'm sorry, Jeremiah."

She covered her mouth, but it filled with air, cheeks ballooning, until erupting as a flow of laughs.

The cords in his neck tightened but soon softened when he heard her sneeze in a fit of three and saw the faint wrinkles around her nose crunch. *Charming*, he thought.

"Sarge and Giant, you stay in the rear. Ensure that no cow leaves the group. If one becomes lost, you must pursue it. A few may stray, but it's your job to guide them back to the group."

"Understood," said Jeremiah.

"Aye," said Bailey. To the new cowherds, he said, "Let's see how you move 'em along!"

Asser howled, and Bailey whistled. Not one cow lifted a hoof until one received a wallop. Some moved, then more stood until the group huddled. Like a snowball rolling downhill, the herd gathered steam and sped. They zigged and zagged as Bailey took control.

"Tiny Hands, go to the side and move those cows back to the front," instructed Bailey. Jeremiah and Mo rode in the back to block deserters. From the forest, a stray shepherd dog appeared and chased black crows sipping from a rainwater collection pond. The startled flock took off and flew for trees across the pasture. A few cows separated from the herd.

"Fixin' to corralin', Jeremiah," said Mo. "Follow me."

Deep from his diaphragm, Mo bellowed.

Most of the cows stopped at the startling sound, but one tripped along, heedless.

"Mo, stay with them. I'm going after this one," said Jeremiah.

The renegade stuck along the creek, which cut through the woods on the edge of the village. Within the forest darkness, Jeremiah detected two men on horseback; however, he galloped ahead to steer the cow from the channel creek and back to the herd.

Once they got all the herd to its new pasture and returned to the farm, Jameela said, "Great job, Sarge."

Jeremiah sparkled with pleasure but didn't know how to respond. He lifted a hand to clap hers, but she withdrew and gave him a questioning look.

Alert posture slumped. Deflated, Jeremiah felt his smile freeze, then droop.

Stupid! She doesn't like you.

She looked him up and down, and he felt his face go hot.

"Thank you, men." Bailey tipped his hat as he joined them. "Especially Sarge. Each cow has moved to the next pasture. Good work, there."

In the house, Ashlyn distributed to them oiled bread, jam, oil, and dried venison.

"Follow the creek as it snakes around the woods," Bailey said. "Eventually, it'll open into a clearing. Good spot for camping, secluded with close access to the river for water and bathing. And there is a hot spring adjacent to the river. The wife and I visit there occasionally," he said with a grin. "There isn't a direct path"—he pointed near the water mill—"so you'll need to retrace your steps to travel along the main road to the church."

Jameela gracefully leapt onto the horse and scooted back to allow Jeremiah to take his turn with the reins. Once he was in the saddle, she grabbed his waist but pulled back a little to make distance between them and said, "Great job, Sarge. Great job."

Jeremiah frowned at what that might mean. She inched away, yet his posture remained strong. His smile froze.

"Tally ho!" he commanded the horse. Its ears perked up, but the horse didn't move.

She laughed.

"Tally ho!" he repeated. He snapped at the reins, and the horse pushed off. They trotted along the trail until finding the clearing where the farmer had directed them to stay. While they established camp and built a fire, Asser disappeared into the woods.

The fire smoked from wet wood and crackled from burning pine needles. Mo left to search for drier timber. Once he built a better fire, he sat as Asser reappeared and asked, "Who wants to check out the hot spring?"

"It's restin' time," said Mo. "Have fun."

"I need to rest these old bones too," said Padre.

"Missing out, laddies," said Asser. "Aye, old men, enjoy each other's company."

To Jeremiah and Jameela, Asser asked, "Lovebirds, are you ready?"

Asser led them on foot. The trail narrowed as the descent steepened. To the right were thick ferns. To their left was a rock with ancient paintings. When the trail ended, the clearing opened, and the river welcomed them. An older couple soaked in the springs.

Jameela tiptoed into a shallow area of the river and began undoing the sash around her waist.

"What are you doing, Jameela?" called Jeremiah. "Come back. There are others up there."

"I'm fine, but don't look, Jeremiah."

"I'm not," he assured her, but he couldn't help peeping through his fingers.

Poets may say "bountiful bosom and plentiful posterior," but Jeremiah thought in simpler terms. He watched her undress and almost swooned when the light from the fading sun showed her white undergarments.

Time slowed.

Asser had already stripped completely naked and was chatting with the couple there. "Sorry to interrupt," he said, climbing into the spring and lounging against the surface, "but we're on a quest." His back wriggled. "Ooh, me loving this smooth, slimy surface."

"How'd you hear about this place?" asked Asser.

"Oh, my wife and I have been coming here for years. Not many people know about it except for residents in the village. And many of those people swear by the water's healing powers and ability to increase conception odds."

Asser submerged into the water. Sinking, he said, "Fornication in the spring, huh?"

"Not tonight," said the woman dryly. "What's your name?"

Letter by letter, Asser spelled his name.

"And your friends?" she asked. "They're bathing in the river first."

Jeremiah reluctantly removed most of his clothes and stripped to his underwear. He hung his cloak, tunic, and hose on a tree.

"Too afraid to show all?" Jameela asked and waded through the water. She snatched his clothes off the branch.

"Put those back," he said.

"What will you do?" she said lightly.

"Put those back," he repeated with a slight edge to his voice.

"No fun," she replied and flung them around the branch again.

He ignored her and navigated gingerly into the river. Shivering, he said, "Cold."

"Cold?" she teased and splashed water on him. "This feels great."

"Really mature of you," he said and wiped his face.

"Lighten up."

"Sorry, but the last time I bathed was the day of the mead ball—with Marianne. It's a bad memory."

"Jeremiah," she said sternly, "get over it. I can't hear about your woman issues. So she likes a lord. Who doesn't? Wealth, prestige, power, good looks. She made her choice."

"You're not helping."

"The sooner you let go, the better off you'll be. Join me in the spring." She climbed up out of the river and set off in the direction of the hot spring.

What's wrong with me? A beautiful woman flirts with me, but I keep thinking of Marianne.

He followed her and could not suppress a sigh of pleasure as he slipped into the warm spring. "Much better," said Jeremiah.

"Asser was telling me," the strange woman said, "that you're a knight? No offense, but how'd you pass physical training?"

Jameela touched his arm and said, "He's stronger than you think."

Witen. I left the stone in my bag. A coil of panic slinked back and forth across his back. Cold and numb, his fingers tingled.

Mo and Padre wouldn't filch it.

"Yes," he confirmed, "mind over body, I guess."

The woman stood, saw something, and pointed down river.

"See something?" asked Jeremiah.

"No, just guiding Asser here," she said. "The church you seek is due west. If you follow the river that direction, you'll reach the best crossing during low tide."

She reclined again and rejoined the conversation, and they all chatted about the capital—they claimed to be from there—until the husband stood to leave.

"This has been fun. And it could have been more fun," he said, admiring his wife so that they all chuckled. "But it was pleasant, none-theless, since we met you. Good luck with your journey."

Once they were gone, Jameela said, "How'd they get here?"

"They've been coming here for years. A secret getaway," said Asser.

Jeremiah got out of the spring and went back for his clothing and dressed. "And the channel too," he said to Asser, who'd left Jameela to enjoy the spring on her own and joined him at the riverside. Asser was testing the chilly water with his toe.

"But their horses?" Jeremiah asked. "Where? How'd they get here from the capital?" *How could they cross the channel so easily?*

"Don't worry, Woody. They probably have friends in the village. We have a day at least on any knights chasing us."

"We should get moving," Jeremiah said.

"Me'll meet you at camp. Me's curious what's along this river-bank," Asser said as he pulled on his own tunic, then disappeared behind the vegetation.

"Asser sure is unique," said Jameela, who'd reappeared and was pulling on her dress again.

"That's only half of it."

They climbed the hill towards the campsite, but they hadn't gone far when they heard shouting, tree twigs snapping, and Asser panting. His pale face showed his panic, as deer in the torchlight look. He shouted, "Run! Run!"

Jeremiah grabbed Jameela's hand and climbed as fast as they could. At the top, they turned and saw some men with hair and coloring like Jameela's.

Jameela looked at Jeremiah with panic, and they sprinted.

They moved from jog to sprint and returned back to camp to find Padre and Mo poking the fire with sticks.

"What's goin' on?" asked Mo. "Why you runnin'?"

Out of breath, Jeremiah huffed. He released Jameela's damp hand, and both of them slumped to their knees. "Where's Asser?" he asked when he caught his breath.

Asser emerged from the trail, limping.

"Asser! You made it!" shouted Jeremiah.

"You're bleeding!" cried Jameela. One arrow had grazed his right arm, and another had landed in his right thigh.

"Mo, pull it out immediately," ordered Padre.

Mo yanked out the arrow, and Asser screamed and then calmed down. "Thank you," he said. "Hurry," he managed through the pain. "Someone's after us."

They quickly packed their belongings, and Jeremiah put the stone in his tunic pocket. Mo smothered the fire with dirt, and smoke billowed upwards into the twilight.

"Mo, you idiot!" Asser said sharply.

"But the fire could reveal us more easily even than the smoke," Mo explained.

"Sorry, sorry, the pain," Asser replied. "You're right."

Jeremiah circled the firepit and said, "Now they know where we are. We should find a doctor before the wound gets worse."

"No," Asser said, "let's go."

"Or I can bless it and ask for the Lord's healing," said Padre.

"Father, that's a serious wound," said Mo. "The bleedin' keeps runnin'."

"Have faith, Mo. I saw these earlier . . ." He plucked some berries from a nearby bush. He squished them together in his hands with spit. "The oil from Gwyn, Jeremiah. Give it to me."

When he'd added oil to the mixture in his hands and instructed Asser to sit and expose the wound, he said, "Asser, this will hurt somewhat." He rubbed Asser's thigh with the ointment and prayed.

Asser's deep groan bleated up and down, deeper and deeper, wavering like goats talking to each other, revealing his agony. Padre wrapped a cloth tightly around the leg, and they breathed a collective sigh of relief.

Then arrows whizzed by and struck a nearby tree.

"We must move now," said Jeremiah. "Now!"

"Can you run?" he asked Asser.

"Me'll try. Just gotta get to the horse." Mo put an arm around his waist to help him limp along. Padre scurried to ready both horses for them.

With hands held fast, Jeremiah and Jameela ran to their horse. Jeremiah grabbed her waist and hoisted her with ease into the saddle, then he jumped up too, and took the reins.

Padre scurried.

Asser tried to run.

"Let's go, Asser!" yelled Jeremiah.

Asser tried to run again, but he fell. He hopped with clenched teeth. Padre reversed to help, but Mo waved him off and threw Asser onto his back. After plopping Asser and Padre onto a horse, Mo mounted his own.

Ahead lay a forest trail. As if enveloped by dense fog, light vanished from the twilight, and the path disappeared. They looked over their shoulders, looked then at each other, and looked at their sweaty palms.

"We don't have a choice but to follow wherever this trail goes," said Jeremiah. They kicked and went to a gallop; horse hooves clipped and clopped. Spring pollen shot like blinding rain. Breaths accelerated quick and quicker as more arrows zipped through dim light and lodged into brush and bark all around them.

Horizon moonlight broke through the clearing ahead.

Jeremiah halted abruptly, and the convoy followed. The trail had ended. Beneath them, a twenty-foot fall into a gushing river offered escape. Distant hooves were closing in rapidly, and the crack of branches snapped to clear their pursuers' path. To Jeremiah, the rush reminded him of repeated and rapid backsaw cuts with a straight blade and sharp teeth. He dismounted and surveyed the drop. "I don't think we have a choice but to jump."

WARRANT

The search through Cyrus's village was a waste. Vague answers from villagers led Alfred to conclude Jeremiah had gone east.

Threats of pillaging against a few fishermen pointed the trail to Marcus, who confessed more and more of the detailed route with the returned sea captain as additional coins were given to encourage his memory.

After crossing the Witen Channel, Alfred and his men went past the water mill and knocked on the door of each house. "As the king's representatives," Alfred told William, "we don't need permission or cause."

Doors were locked against them, so Alfred ordered his men to open them, whatever was required.

"With honor, my lord," they said.

Their blades hacked at enough wood until the splintering allowed a punch and passage through each door. Screaming at each house alerted the neighbors. In the large farmhouse, the woman yelled for the man and covered her wailing toddler with her skirts. "What right do you have barging in?" she demanded.

"Ma'am, relax," said Alfred. "This is a search ordered by the king." He showed the written credentials. "I'm Lord Alfred. We've come for some fugitives." He went on to describe them, and the woman nodded.

The sketch sufficed. "My lord, they've already passed."

"Which way?"

"They mentioned the river and a church. There's only one main trail route heading west."

"Cover our rear," Alfred told William, "and alert us of trouble."

From the village, past the water mill, along the river, the Oths galloped ahead into forest. William drew the sword and studied the ground as Boomer trotted. "Pieces of paper," he said. He dismounted and drew his sword for protection while he inspected them. "Eastern markings." He squeezed his lips to whistle, but the sound whimpered out breathy. After several attempts, with a finger and thumb, he hit the note, and Alfred threw up an arm.

Doubling back, Alfred asked, "Already, William? What is it?"

"I found something." Shards of birch paper scattered along the path, torn and trampled upon.

"Oths," called Alfred, "dismount and tie your horses. Draw your swords."

"Do you know the language?"

"No, sir, but it's Eastern—a different alphabet. Something I saw around the archb— . . . b . . . bishop." He pieced them together on the ground, then dug more pieces buried in horse prints. "English!" he exclaimed.

"Queen, brother, vengeful death."

Images resurfaced and drenched his heart with the air stalled in his lungs, as his airways tightened from an invisible hand that choked him.

Brother? Revenge? Whose brother? William wondered.

"Lord Alfred, this message needs to be delivered to the king," he said.

"Why? He wants the stone."

"B . . . b-because," stammered William, "this . . . this could mean something for Queen Rachel's death and his death—the archb-bishop's murder."

"Six years ago?"

"The murders must be connected to the missing stone—something larger is at stake."

Alfred dropped the pieces into William's hand. "You keep this, but we'll find Jeremiah soon. On the map, the river flows into falls. So they couldn't have gone far." With a finger twirl, Alfred pointed to the trail. The soldiers scattered and took their different positions with heads pivoting, looking for danger.

WATERFALL

"**W**ait, wait!" cried Jameela, sliding off the horse. "There must be another way. Why don't we find another trail or hide in the woods? Or try talking to them?"

Yusuf, she thought. *Freedom. Stone.*

Arrows zipped by Jeremiah's head and lodged into trees. Another arrow sliced bark that crumbled and fell off onto her shoulder and then onto the trail. Her foot slipped on pebbles and pine needles, but Jeremiah caught her arm, and then he dismounted.

"Are you woody?" asked Jeremiah. "They've been chasing us, shooting arrows—trying to kill us, for Witen's sake!"

The rest got off their horses, but Asser didn't land the dismount; he wobbled properly on his wounded leg, and he yelled, "Bloody curses!"

Bloody curses.

+———+

"Mama, I'm bleeding," nine-year-old Jameela had said. Sliding on a stone, she had toppled on a mountain trail, and blood spilled from her nose. "I don't want to go to the top."

"This is penance for what you saw in Constantinople," her mama had said. "The ceremony will clean you—the waters will purify."

+———+

Jameela paced and walked towards the darkness. "I'm trying to think through all options," she told Jeremiah.

288

"Where are you going?" asked Jeremiah.

Home, she thought. "I'm thinking."

"We only have one option," said Padre. "Jumping."

The steps pounded loud and louder behind them, and branches snapped crisp and crisper. A man shouted, and another arrow zoomed past Jeremiah and landed into the river. More men shouted as they ran through the woods.

"How many are there?" asked Asser.

The team released the horses and pushed them until they galloped into the forest. The team inched closer to the ledge, ready to jump. "We must jump now," demanded Jeremiah. "Jameela!"

Combing a hand through her hair, she balked. Her mama's lullaby had slipped through her lips like a gentle stream that day. But the river had raged in the twilight.

She shook her head, then crisscrossed back into the woods, making a circle eight with her paces in and around trees. She moved farther into the darkness. Crouching low against a tree in thick underbrush, she saw the team pace and Adam and Yusuf dismount their horses.

"Adam, hurry," said Yusuf. "We can't stay."

"I dropped the letter," said Adam.

"The letter?" grumbled Yusuf. "You didn't give it to the wizard?"

"No," snapped Adam. "I forgot—remember? We didn't have time. The wizard had to go."

Yusuf groaned. "Forget the letter. The king's men, Adam. We must go. The river leads to the Mont Church. We'll find them there."

"What will Rohad say?"

"He doesn't need to know, Adam; the tapestry will work."

"Yusuf, through the trees—that's one of them."

A man with a distinct strange hat tumbled over roots and vines and into a ditch.

Jameela gasped.

They stood over the man with swords and daggers dangling from their cloth belts.

"I smell them," said Adam and beat a fist against his chest. "Western vermin. Look, he's there, close to a boy. Tie the horses, Yusuf. I'll prepare the bow."

"Adam, we came for the stone and the money."

Adam's snarls came muffled, and he pulled back the bow.

Jameela's legs suddenly weighed very heavy, and her spirit dragged at her too. As her world closed in, she couldn't move. She had to decide.

Love or freedom?

"No, Brother, I came for the stone and revenge. You came for her. You still love her."

That word shot like an arrow to her heart, crackling the heaviness into tinier fragments. As Adam pulled the bow and released, she stood and ran towards the river.

A boy grunted, and a man roared. The boy scouting the river fell with an arrow to his neck.

"Shoot!" yelled a man, and a barrage of arrows flew.

She burst from the darkness into the clearing.

"Jameela! Let's go!" shouted Jeremiah.

She came to herself, then froze, turned, and slumped. With a half grin, she mumbled, "Jeremiah, I see you."

He snatched her hand and pulled her to the ledge.

"Oh, how cute," said Asser with a glance at them. "Screw it." Asser hurled his torch into the river and jumped off the ledge. Mo and Padre followed.

"Let's go," said Jeremiah. He strapped his bag over his shoulder, clenched the stone with one hand deep in his tunic pocket, then clasped Jameela's hand with the other.

With her fingers interlocked with his, Jameela felt pangs of anxiety shoot from her hand to her heart. A familiar voice called her name: "Love or freedom," Yusuf sang.

"On the count of three, Jameela," said Jeremiah. He swung her arm.

"Wait," she said, "I'm not ready." She pulled her hand away.

Asser and Mo and Padre had jumped.

Splash—down, then up, gasp! Down, then up, gasp! Asser ducked and thrashed. He found tree branches and held on by the twigs and leaves. Legs motored furiously to stay afloat.

Kerplunk—down, steadily down, Mo had dived into darkness. Up, he rocketed from the bottom. The current propelled them fast and faster. Mo extended his wandering albatross arms to balance, then waved, waved, and flew through the water past Asser and protruding tree branches on either side. Mo slammed into some floating logs and wrapped his arms around one.

Splash—down, then up, gasp! Down, then up, gasp! Padre clutched to a large rock. His hands slipped, but the rock remained close.

Peak, then pop! A head catapulted.

Above them all a tear formed in Jameela's eye, and Yusuf's song carried closer to her.

"What are you waiting for?" yelled Jeremiah. He touched her fingers, but she moved aside. "I can't do this," she cried. Blood drained down from her legs, and she became numb.

The stone is in his hand, she thought. She snooped over the ledge. There she saw Yusuf and heard a man scream, "Get down!"

Jeremiah locked onto Jameela's wrist. "One, two, three!" he rushed. They leapt at the same time. Falling, Jameela heard Yusuf calling her name.

Splash—splash—down, down, up, up, gasp, gasp! Fast—bodies bobbed and hearts throbbed. Fast—breaths shortened, knots tightened within. Faster—warmth spread through her upper body and face; fear sheared through her and blotches of heat warmed her cheeks.

"Jer—" Down, then up. "Jerem—" Down, then up.

Hands loosened, but she firmed her grip onto Jeremiah. The current slowed, and she saw the other members of the team thrashing in dimming twilight.

Short arms and legs chugged; Asser struggled to stay afloat.

"Asser!" shouted Mo. "Reach for it. Hurry! Before the rocks ahead." Mo pushed a log towards him, and Asser paddled closer. Their fingers touched but slipped as the log rolled. Down—they descended a level of the rapids; the current dipped, then flattened.

"Rocks ahead!" shouted Asser.

Mo pulled him in, and they held on in the center. Down—they dipped, they dipped, bobbed and bobbed. Mo propelled with a free arm and kicked his legs to maneuver around the boulders.

"Hold on tight, Asser."

Down—they dipped, they dipped, then thud! The lumber struck like thunder, thunder, and they rotated a quarter turn. They lowered a level into a whirlpool. Waves spun and powered the water wheel; they squealed and twirled until Mo extended his legs to push off a rock.

The flow slowed, and they floated.

Padre pulled his torso onto a log; he blinked quickly to clear his vision. Left, then right, left, then right, he churned and turned in the water, wrapping his arms and legs around the log; he steered around one boulder, then two, then more until shore appeared. He rode the wave down; the current flapped and angled around the funnel trap to guide him to calmer waters.

Jameela's mouth fell, teeth chattering as freezing water splashed over the rock she clung to. Her fingers slid.

Padre freed a hand and waved to Asser and Mo. They glided into a shallow area, and Padre slithered from the log. He swam to shore and stood.

Her hands loosened their grip as the current accelerated. "Jameela, look!" yelled Jeremiah. She panted and rocks rolled over her—boulders grew, water smacked, and waves swelled; currents pulled at her—frenzy attacked her, though nothing showed above the surface.

"Hold on!" shouted Jeremiah.

"Jeremiah, Jeremiah, where are you?" she cried.

Fingers slipped, fingers slipped, and mind tripped.

◆———◆

"Mama! Where are you? Papa! Where are you?" Jameela had cried. Her brother had found a sword and left their house to fight. Her papa found a sword and left their house to fight. "Don't go!" her mama shouted. "Don't go." She collapsed to her knees and sobbed. She wrapped Jameela in swaddling blankets. The door pounded loud behind him; the door pounded louder behind *him*. "Don't go, Mama! Don't go."

Her mama whispered, "Stay here. Curl underneath the blankets and hide." Her mother rose.

"Don't go, Mama! Don't go."

Mama kissed her forehead, but Jameela hung onto her hand and the lullaby. Fingers had slipped, slipped, and slipped—the last time.

◆———◆

"Jeremiah, where are you?" Fingers slid, slid, and slid until no more. Heat flashed once more; she thrashed like before. She sank, sank, and sank. Her mind lightened and spun around. Small—bubbles echoed Jeremiah's name. Small—eyes narrowed but searched.

Where is he?

Smaller—bubbles lessened with shorter breaths. Time slowed; she floated away, but Jeremiah stayed. He pulled, he pulled, he pulled, but he couldn't loosen her from the entanglements. Weeds snared at her; moans rippled from her. She envisioned the nightmare, but the trap didn't cripple her completely. He yanked, yanked, yanked, then kicked. He flew to her and grabbed a leg.

He pulled her in—up! Gasp! Down—he turned to avoid the boulder. Down—steadily down, they dipped and dipped to the lower level. Her mind spun, and their bodies spun. Into the whirlpool, further they sank; each orbit shrank and shrank.

Love or freedom, love or freedom whirled in her head with Yusuf's voice, her mama's song, and Jeremiah's rescue.

"Mo, look!" she heard.

Frozen eyelashes cracked; through splashes, air sprayed with water, she saw an enormous man lifting a log. Someone else captured her leg. With an arm, the man held her. Once she was secured, Mo straightened the log.

She felt the tugging and kicking, the bouncing in his arms and the cold air whipping against the tiny metal nose ring, of all things. She was lowered, and soft sand cushioned her aching back.

Someone knelt beside her and lifted her head in his arms. He blew warm breaths. "Jameela! Are you hurt? Jameela! Are you hurt? Say something."

Coldness stiffened her, but she thawed once her eyes opened fully. She lifted her head and coughed water. She palmed his cheek and smiled. "Hello, Jeremiah. I see you."

Mo released the log, and with heavy, frosty breaths they watched it carry on, topple, and disappear out of sight.

Down—steadily down it fell, down the waterfall into the dark, dark night. Down—steadily down her eyelids closed, down to sealed shut, to slumber in the dark, dark night.

CHARLIE

Blood stained the cross Charlie wore on a thong around his neck. Near him on the ground were a letter to him, signed "with love from Mum and Dadde," and a wooden boy stick figure.

William compared the shards of paper with the different alphabet in his left hand to the love note. *For a stupid stone?*

Charlie had recently graduated, and it must have been the proudest day in his life. Parents would have been beaming, clapping, hollering, wrapping their boy in hugs and kisses, he assumed.

It would have been like the day William graduated from cathedral and from law school—though his parents were absent—it was the other students' parents he saw. Fire blazed in his belly and swept across his chest.

He yanked away the cross from Charlie's neck and considered tossing it into the river. *For this?* He shook his head in disbelief. *The stone must mean more.*

"Come on, William," said Alfred. "We'll grieve later, but we must carry on. Collect his belongings. We'll give them to his next of kin when we return."

Alfred ordered Charlie be thrown onto the back of the free horse's back. "Oths, return to the main trail. We'll ride far enough away for a while and set up camp for the night. Daniel, you're first watch."

SHANTY

When Jameela woke, Jeremiah was kneeling close and beamed, then bent over and lifted her from the ground and hugged her.

No, no, can't get too close. She rolled away from the connection and onto her hands and knees, then stood, wobbly and dripping.

"Is anyone hurt?" asked Jeremiah. He checked his body for cuts and checked his pockets. He still had the stone, clenched in one hand; however, most of their food and packed clothes had washed away. He placed the stone inside his tunic pocket.

"Whoa—that was the best ride of me life!" exclaimed Asser. "And way to go, Padre. Riding that log. What were you calling him?"

Though initially speechless, Padre grinned, and his joyful expression showed a thousand words. "Raphael," he said, "the name of my son if I'd had one."

Mo broke tree limbs and rubbed sticks together until enough friction ignited the tinder he had found in the woods.

"Whoa, Mo," said Jeremiah when he spotted it. "No fires."

"Jeremiah," said Jameela anxiously, "we must warm up, and dry ourselves, or we'll get sick."

Jeremiah tugged at tufts of hair.

"It looked like a half day ride," said Mo.

"Don't worry, Woody," said Asser. "Remember the farmer? He said there was a main trail to the Mont Church, but it cut through the village."

"Unless they took the river too," quipped Jeremiah. "Fine, but a small fire and in the woods. We should find shelter."

They moved to the woods, and Mo started a fire.

"Why were they chasing us?" asked Jeremiah.

"Me have an idea. Two escaped convicts? Knights after us?"

"That may explain some of it," said Mo. "But there were others chasin' us too."

"The king doesn't want his people to see him lose control," said Padre. "I bet he's become a laughing stock, the first time two people escaped prison. And Jeremiah, you were a high-profile prisoner."

Jameela pointed to where the stone rested in Jeremiah's pocket and said, "You idiots! They want the stone."

Her words appeared jumbled to Jeremiah; though she spoke clearly, Jeremiah mumbled a bit, unconsciously, as his eyes scanned her body.

"What is it? Is something wrong with me?" she asked. She rubbed her face and arms, noticing the red blotches on her arm.

"No, no," he said as he turned away to retrieve the stone from his pocket. "Making sure you're fine."

"Yes, I'm fine, thank you." She followed the stone as he rolled it around his palm, then looked up and he caught her gaze.

He stopped and looked.

Her voice rose. "Quit staring. Has the stone warped your mind?"

"No," asserted Jeremiah. "We're on a quest to return it to its original location and restore the kingdom."

Wiping her brow, she said, "Knights are after us, but others are chasing us too. The first series of arrows came from those men."

"We must move quickly, then."

"Where do we go now, our leader?" Asser bowed slowly enough to accentuate his mockery.

"There." Jeremiah pointed to the large church on the rock, visible in the clearing with enough moonlight. "The river must lead directly to it. We'll hide there."

"Those chasing us will think the same," said Jameela. "They'll suspect we're on this river trail. We must take another route."

Padre pulled out their remaining vial of oil for the torches.

"One torch," said Jeremiah. "We can't have too much light."

Padre lit the torch as Mo hummed. Then they extinguished the fire and walked deeper into the woods. Mo broke from humming and belted out a song from his diaphragm.

> **And we'll guide the ship straight along**
> **Guide the ship straight along**
> **Guide the ship straight along . . .**
> **And we'll keep calm and carry on.**
>
> **And a rough storm won't do us any harm**
> **A rough storm won't do us any harm**
> **A rough storm won't do us any harm.**

With a big gesture of his arm and with raised eyebrows, he guided them into the chorus with him:

> **Ohh . . . And we'll guide the ship straight along**
> **Guide the ship straight along**
> **Guide the ship straight along . . .**
> **And we'll keep calm and carry on.**

Then on to the next verse he went.

> **And a rough landing won't do us any harm**
> **A rough landing won't do us any harm**
> **A rough landing won't do us any harm.**

They followed his cue and picked up with the chorus again, then he added yet another verse.

> Oh, no enemy's arrows will do us any harm
> No enemy's arrows will do us any harm
> No enemy's arrows will do us any harm.

Getting the hang of it, after the next chorus, Padre created his own verse.

> Oh, week's-old ale won't do us any harm
> Week's-old ale won't do us any harm
> Week's-old ale won't do us any harm.

All were laughing now, so Asser took courage to try yet another new verse, stumbling over the quick syllables:

> Oh, fat, old, ugly women won't do us any harm . . .

Jameela halted—not in disbelief this came from Asser—but at his terrible singing voice. It was uncontrolled and hard, with hoarse screeching up and down the scale. She shrugged and joined in, singing in an off-note tune.

> Fat, old, ugly women won't do us any harm!
> Fat, old, ugly women won't do us any harm!

When they concluded the chorus, Asser smiled and said, "Even Padre sang me verse! Padre, me've met many priests, but you've been the best."

Padre shook his head. "Son, even fat, old, ugly women need love too." The team paused. When Padre rested his hands on his belly and grinned ear to ear, laughter erupted among them again.

Jameela felt a warmth she hadn't felt since childhood, when she had been in bed and listening to Mama's soothing voice lull her to sleep. The warmth coated her throat like the sweets Grandpapa snuck into her room after dark.

But there was that look from Jeremiah—the misleading look of love—no, lust, she assumed. She had caught him admiring her hair, smiling and fixing his gaze on her mouth and lips. She had done the same with him—her gaze imitated his; she went to his mouth, his full lips. *What am I doing?*

His full lips. She blushed. The lightness that had ballooned in her chest dissipated in a poof. *Stop it! The mission. Freedom!*

They turned their heads. As they came out of a clearing, the full moon hung over them, shining towards the Mont Church. "Where are we going?" asked Jameela.

Continuing to hum, Padre pressed ahead and said, "This way."

Jeremiah spoke in a calm sort of way, his words drawn-out and hushed. "Padre, you've been here before?"

"Many moons ago, yes."

They walked more than a furlong. Moonlight disappeared for a little while, and soon the grand pine-tree canopy blocked the remaining moonlight just as they saw spruce all around them. But spring spruce painted the picture.

"We're coming upon a holy sanctuary," said Padre. "Try to be quiet for a bit as we walk through this area. Smell the cedar, the pine—look around in the dimness, and pivot your head. Touch the trees. We'll be at her house soon."

Asser and Jeremiah raised eyebrows and said together, "Her house?"

SPIRIT

Jeremiah slowed to absorb the beauty. Like among the overhanging pine branches in the early morning, his dreaming suspended as he gazed upon the mystery—not the forest—but her. Bluebonnets sprung along the path.

He studied her gait and gestures. What would she be thinking about? She wasn't like women he knew from the village, and she was very unlike Marianne. She looked around with her head in the forest cathedral, closed her eyes, and inhaled deeply.

Jeremiah impulsively grabbed her left hand and held it. She didn't disengage immediately. *An opportunity!* His heart beat wildly, and his breath quickened. He bit his lip.

Go!

Eyes closed, he lowered his head and reached with his lips extended. He missed her mouth, but his foot caught in a tree root, and as he fell, he grabbed onto what he could—Jameela.

She came back to the present from prayer with her mouth falling open. He wrapped around her, drove her as they fell to the pine-needle-cushioned ground and landed with him on top. The soft pine floor cushioned the blow and absorbed the impact.

After a brief silence, she pushed against him and squealed, "Jeremiah!"

"Are you hurt?" he asked, blushing.

He smiled sheepishly and picked a tiny blue flower beside them and presented it to her.

Asser turned to ask, "What's wrong? Oh." He smiled, then laughed. "About time," he said.

Padre sighed. "Get up. There it is."

Jeremiah helped her up and then dusted off and joined the others.

A small cabin welcomed them with front porch candles. They followed the oblong-shaped, creek-smoothed stones until they had crossed to the other side.

Padre breezed across the stones as if he could walk on water—or, as if he'd been there many times before. The forest sanctuary seemed to have this holding as its nerve center: peaceful and calming energy as emanated from the cabin and its clearing as they approached it. They climbed the stairs and admired the wrap-around porch.

"It's wonderful," said Padre with a contented sigh. "Wanted a front porch around the entire house to welcome any peaceful spirit."

Padre knocked on the front door, and a woman about Padre's age opened it.

"John!" She enveloped him in a hug.

"Great to see you, Aliyah. It's been awhile."

"How'd you know I'd be here?"

"I just felt it."

"Aliyah, meet my friends from the village."

No one escaped the warm rapture Aliyah offered.

"Come in, travelers. Any friend of John's is a friend of mine."

During the hug, Jeremiah sensed the subtle aroma of pine needles and smoke. It was a calming combination. For a woman her age, she looked young. Despite having silver hair, she seemed younger than the color suggested, and her curly locks fell long, with fullness of life. She wore a blue shawl over her cream-colored tunic. Jeremiah asked about their connections.

"Yes, I've known her since childhood," said Padre to Jeremiah, as Aliyah helped the others to get seated.

"Why are you here?" she asked Padre as she gestured to the table and offered them bread and fruit. "Please sit and rest."

Asser jumped in, "Me don't mean to be rude, but will anyone else find this place? We have at least two groups chasing us."

"We're safe, Son," she answered. "No one will harm you—or me. I'll make sure of it."

Asser nodded, grabbed an apple from a bowl, and chomped down on it.

"What is your name?" Aliyah asked, holding a hand out to Jameela.

Jameela didn't make eye contact, and she responded to questions delicately and timidly as she watched the door.

"No one will hurt you here," said Aliyah.

Head back and eyes widened, Jameela feigned relief.

"Did you hear that?" asked Asser. "Are there people outside?"

"Only the trees rustling. It's getting windy and misty." Aliyah went to the front window. Closing the curtains, she bowed her head and whispered a prayer. "We're safe," she said. "Only the forest dancing."

After they'd all eaten bread and cheese and drunk some cider, Jameela said, "I'm sorry, but I'm tired. Do you have a place I could lie down, please?"

"I have beds for all," Aliyah responded, and showed first Jameela and then the others where they could sleep.

Jeremiah lagged Jameela and went into a room with Mo and Asser and took the bed closest to the wall of Jameela's room. *In case she needs me.* He pulled back the curtain; through the window, outside, fog collapsed into a gray mass that formed something that was long and cylindrical. Air blew, *like breaths*, he thought, but once the mist vanished, he saw logs across the creek. He closed his eyes with weariness, but he heard a knock at the door of the next room.

+———+

Jameela sat on the floor, huddled with a blanket over her shoulders.

"Knock, knock," said Aliyah in a comforting low tone. "Jameela, are you asleep yet? May I come in?"

"Sure. I'm awake."

Aliyah had changed into a thin blue dress. "I thought I heard whimpers," said Aliyah. "I brought some warm cider. Can't sleep?"

"No."

"Can you come to the kitchen then?"

Yawning and dragging her feet, Jameela replied, "I guess." She sat at the table with Aliyah, sipped cider, then asked, "What's the matter?"

"You've been distant," Aliyah said warmly. "Why'd you join this journey?"

Jameela hesitated, then answered. "I left Witenberg. My life there had become routine, and I needed a change. My family wasn't there, I had no friends, and when I stumbled into The Grouse that night, met them, and heard about the quest, I agreed to join."

Aliyah was silent in response, then said, "Yes, finish that up—it will help digest the food from earlier tonight."

Thinking, Aliyah rapped fingers against the table. "Do you want tea?"

"No, thanks."

"Here, I'll take the cup." Aliyah then asked in a lower, confidential tone, "Anything else?"

"No," Jameela said, "I just desperately needed an escape."

Aliyah moved to the window and stared. After too many heart-beats, she said with a note of finality, as if she'd given up questioning, "Fine, then." Then she added, "You have a beautiful name. Does it mean anything?"

"Yes, it means 'beautiful' in Arabic."

"Arabic? Are you from the East?"

"From the East, yes, but I've been on the move for about six years—since the war began."

"Parents? Siblings?"

"All dead," she said. "Listen, Aliyah, I appreciate you asking about me, but I don't want to talk anymore."

"Right. Of course," she said. "May I show you something?"

She shrugged. "Sure."

"First, we need wood for a fire." There was the sound of creaking of a bed, then Aliyah said, "Come outside with me. Here, I'll give you my shawl."

As Aliyah grabbed a bag from her bedroom, a door creaked, and they were gone down the hall.

+————+

Padre entered the kitchen as they exited the house.

Mo and Asser were fast asleep, but Jeremiah's stomach roared. His senses were on high alert, and he could at least explain he was up for more food. He crept out to the kitchen and met Padre, who said he was still starving and went right to the bread box and pulled a knife from a block with practiced ease.

Without betraying his interest, Jeremiah peeked through the curtain and watched Aliyah, carrying a bag, walk Jameela towards a tent he hadn't seen before.

"Can't sleep?" Padre asked Jeremiah.

"No. I—I can't."

"What's troubling you, really?"

"Nothing. Reflecting over the last few months, I guess. They've been woody."

"Yes, you're right."

"My heart was troubled, and it still is—at least restless, like I'm searching on a winding road."

"You've been searching for things that won't satisfy."

"I've been preoccupied with other things."

"I know. Chasing drink and women."

"It was fun at first," trailed Jeremiah, "then it got tiresome and unfulfilling."

"Marianne devastated you?" Padre went straight for the gut.

Jeremiah smiled—the kind that admitted the priest was right.

"I think so. I'm not the most attractive person. I was always jealous of my brother. Most women didn't say hello, let alone think of me for a date. Then she said yes! At last! Our friendship would turn into something more—what my heart longed for. Then, I messed up. I prepared to read the poem I wrote and publicly declare my love for her. But Lord Harold—"

"And you messed up regarding your parents too," Padre reminded him.

"My parents?"

"Yes, you also abandoned your parents and a promising career. Took your inheritance and spent it on women and drink. You left your father and mother in the middle of the night without much of a goodbye. They were devastated. They still are."

Jeremiah breathed heavily and tried to explain, but no words came. Thoughts attacked him. In his mind, Harry's lips kissed Marianne, and then he pulled away to look at Jeremiah triumphantly. Harry's eyebrows angled more deeply, and he mouthed the word "bastard" to Jeremiah. *I'm a bastard. Rejected.*

He couldn't stand being in the kitchen any longer. He fled down the hall to the back door. Standing on the porch, he waited for the mist to clear so he could better see. He saw the Mont Church in the distance, through a passage in the woods, but in his immediate view, a small mountain rose between them and the Mont Church.

Padre joined him outside.

"Has this been here?" Jeremiah pointed to the mountain.

"Jeremiah, have you been initiated?"

"I'm thinking no, since I don't know what you mean."

"Aye, then follow me." After filling wineskins with water, they passed the women in the tent and made their way towards the mountain.

"Are you sure you can climb that mountain?" Jeremiah asked. "We're already weary from the journey."

"Yes, Jeremiah. I've made the hike before, though not in many years."

"Aye, old man," Jeremiah joked and patted him on the back.

"Good thing we took water from the house."

"Good thing it's early morning and cooler too."

Jeremiah lightly pushed Padre. "Bet you can't beat me to the top."

He ran ahead, and Padre jogged. "You're right," he called out. When Jeremiah slowed, Padre caught the edge of Jeremiah's tunic and pulled at him. "But I'm a better wrestler," he teased.

Huffing, Padre stopped and slowed his breath. The mountain range rose a few cathedrals in elevation, and the trail was impossibly steep.

The air blew crisply, and pine coursed through their noses, coating the inside of their mouths. "I have to pee, Jeremiah," Padre said and walked to a nearby bush. Jeremiah did the same. As it flowed, he heard Padre exhaling deeply with eyes closed, dimples showing, and mouth open. "Truly a holy moment, Jeremiah."

Jeremiah laughed but tightened and trickled after hearing the sound of howls.

"Don't be afraid," said Padre, "There isn't food here for them—only trees and stone. And it's too high a climb." They returned to the trail, and soon sweat flowed uncontrollably as the hike intensified. About halfway up, the angle steepened, and, pouring sweat and gasping for breath, they lowered to their hands and knees.

"Need rest, Padre?"

"Yes, yes—I need a break," he replied. "Let's sit here for a bit."

They found a sturdy log.

Jeremiah spotted some mountain wildflowers and, plucking them, he thought, *for Jameela.* He placed the flowers inside his tunic pocket beside the stone.

After they'd had enough water, Jeremiah asked with a grin, "So, you and Aliyah?"

"What do you mean?"

"You know what I mean. I didn't think priests could marry."

"There wasn't a rule when the Church began. Not until recently, when the Church expanded and controlled lots of land, did our glorious leaders enact this rule. It was more to end property disputes and inheritance issues."

"Then why honor the vow of chastity if you own no land?"

"I pledged when I entered the order many years ago. Have I struggled at times? Yes, in my mind, but I haven't acted on it."

"But why the vow?"

"We are called to devote our mind, body, and soul completely to loving Christ and glorifying Him to as many people as possible. Practically speaking, the Church sees a married man divided among serving the faithful, the land, and his family."

"Couldn't it be a choice? An option?"

"Perhaps. And some could manage that balance. But I suspect many would carry on and choose the calling of brotherhood and sisterhood of religious life. Some aren't called to be married."

"But I've known very godly married men and immoral priests."

"True, true, and your father is one of those godly men—Elfred is a role model in the community and an excellent father."

Jeremiah understood and groaned. "I get it. I messed up. Hopefully, he'll forgive me one day." He was quiet for a few moments, then added, "You could be married to Aliyah and still serve the faithful, couldn't you? Maybe even better, since you know the challenges with marriage?"

"Perhaps, but not in the current Church. Though unmarried, that doesn't mean I didn't—rather, don't—still love her."

"Physically?"

"A long time ago, before I took my vows. But sex is only one component of it."

Jeremiah stopped him. "Important component."

"Yes, it's important, but it's only part of intimacy and the overall relationship. One can be intimate and not sexual with another person."

"Tell that to anyone at the bar or brothel, and they'll mock you."

"Yes, but those people are fools. And the money they give to the brothel owners only fuels the trading of women for sex."

Jeremiah sighed from the depths of his spirit and said, "You're right. . . . Come on, let's climb to the top." He helped Padre stand. The steep angle soon leveled off and flattened.

"Why didn't you pursue marriage with Aliyah?" Jeremiah continued.

"We both realized my heart and soul loved Christ more. Plus, I knew my purpose was to help as many people as possible know and love Christ."

"We've still maintained our friendship through the years as she got married and raised children. I've been thankful for the friendship. Best one in my life. And, Jeremiah—"

"Yes?"

"You weren't ready for a serious relationship with Marianne."

"What do you mean? How do you know?"

"I've watched you grow. You haven't dealt with yourself yet. Before entering any serious long-term relationship, you should remove all masks and be content with yourself mentally, physically, emotionally, and—most importantly—spiritually. You wouldn't have been a restful place for any wife to find refuge in, nor would you have been ready to handle the challenges with relational strife. You're still too selfish."

Padre continued, "Have you noticed how restful and natural the relationship is between me and Aliyah? We don't project." He bent to find a rock and stick. "See this lever? This fulcrum?"

"Yes, of course."

Padre tilted the lever and balanced it.

"Aliyah and I have mostly been balanced. We don't battle each other. Too often, couples compete for control."

"But I'm sure you've both grown into that balance? You've preached many times we're broken people in need of Jesus."

"Yes, we're both still broken, but we don't fight for energy. We let go, lift each other, and give positive energy."

"Yes," said Jeremiah, "she is not your traditional Christian woman, but I feel the love."

"The woman you're meant to discover and marry will come to you, if it's God's will. Once you find her, you'll know, but you still must nurture the relationship and pursue her, even in marriage."

"You pursued Aliyah as a friend? What about her husband?"

"Her late husband knew the friendship we had. I didn't pursue a sexual relationship with her. Of course not, but I did pursue friendship. In any type of relationship," he explained, "pursuit is not an exact science but more of an art. A man should study his wife, court his wife, ask good questions, engage her heart and mind, and be an expert in her hobbies. You must be the master artisan of a masterpiece God gave you. Women want a strong man—strong in every way—with a tender, merciful heart that is healthy, attractive, emotionally and spiritually strong."

"I hope to find the woman meant for me someday. I don't know if it'll happen. I could have been married years ago already," Jeremiah complained. Shoulders lowered, and he drew circles in the dirt.

"It'll happen when you're ready for her. God is shaping her, too."

Jeremiah snapped the twig. "I became jaded with all the rejections."

"I understand. But rejections are signs for redirection. I didn't say this was easy. If it were easy, you wouldn't be as grateful when you finally meet her. Rejection is potent—and powerful—but try not to become oversensitive. Your future wife will reject you within marriage too. If you respond with rejecting her, it will create a downward spiral. Hesitate to become self-centered, but continue to be selfless and serve her."

They climbed the final steps to the top, and Jeremiah said, "Wow, that was quick."

Padre found a seat to rest, but Jeremiah continued to explore the terrain and the view. The flat clearing presented several paths among moss-covered rocks, and stones of various shapes and sizes dotted the clearing. One path guided him through a narrow pine-cone- scattered trail that ended at a cliff's edge. "Whoa," said Jeremiah.

Clutching the trunk of a tree with both arms, he leaned over the ledge to see through a gap in the stone, a window to the great expanse below. A flowering tree growing in the gap broke the pine-tree monotony.

Jeremiah carefully navigated among the hanging rocks on all fours. *My mum would kill me if she knew I was doing this alone—at this time of day.* Gingerly squatting, he scooped a handful of cold water from a notch nature had carved into a depression in the white stone. Leaning against sturdy but jagged quartz rock, he dangled his legs off the cliff. He gazed outwards and down.

On one side of the prospect, there were rolling hills with numerous mountain peaks, one of which kissed the rippled cloud blanket. On the other side, it was clear through a great expanse to the valley below.

The rising sun showed the Mont Church clearly alone in the distance, seemingly an island just offshore. Fortunately, the wind was still, so he felt steadier. In fact, he realized, there wasn't much sound: no birds, no squirrels, and no swaying trees. There was only his breath and heartbeat, occasionally skipping a beat. But there was still the intermittent howling.

Jeremiah returned to the clearing and joined Padre at the fire he had built. After several minutes of watching flames flicker, Jeremiah asked, "Why did you bring me here?"

"You haven't dealt with your brokenness," Padre answered. "You've always covered it up with work and now with drink and women. Your brother became initiated through the military, but you haven't experienced the liminal space."

Jeremiah rolled his eyes but went along with it.

"Close your eyes and try to release any infiltrating, interrupting thoughts. Smell the pine. Feel your body. Feel your breath. Sit in silence."

Jeremiah reached into his tunic pocket for the stone and palmed it while he sat upright.

Padre opened in prayer. "Abba, you're a good Father. You give us what we need. Thank You for Your many gifts and blessings over the years. Thank You for Your Son, His life, death, and resurrection. Holy Spirit, descend on us now. Teach us to not be afraid, how to go from death into life. Help us let go. Guide us on the journey and help us to find our purpose."

Inadequacy, rejection, and his abandonment by his parents choked his mind. Why did they leave him? Who was his real father? And real mother? He couldn't let go. He clenched the stone and gripped tighter and tighter as his eyelids fluttered; his mind fought the surrender. "I was abandoned!" he cried. "Rejected." Almost an octave lower, Jeremiah roared with a booming bass voice, "I'm not broken!"

Accusations and angry words babbled through his mind, and his body quaked.

Padre raised his voice to say, "Jeremiah, let go. Know you are loved by the Father and will always be loved. Life is hard, but turn to Him. Rest in His hug, His embrace and love. Sense the multitude of stars around you."

"Father?" scoffed Jeremiah. "The father who left me, dropped me off at a doorstep? And ran?"

Padre shuddered.

Jeremiah saw the brief weakness and glossiness in Padre's filmy eyes. A sense of power, dull, and cold rawness overtook him, and the stone chilled his palms. In a lower, almost unearthly tone, Jeremiah asked, his voice grating and icy, "Who is my real father? Do you know, Padre?"

With both arms, Padre grabbed Jeremiah. "On a dark night, one star in the sky can give us hope that the universe isn't an empty abyss, an endless void. And you and I are called and created to let our light shine in our space, in our unique place where we've been planted, to be signs of hope, even if no one sees us."

The shaking settled into more gentle bobs of his head as beads of sweat cooled his body.

Padre continued, "As humans, we never see most stars. Only God does. And God names *each one*. And you and I are called and created to let our light shine in our space, in our unique place where we've been assigned, to be signs of hope, even if no one sees us. And maybe that should be enough, to be loved and created by God, and given a mission to brighten and give light to the particular place and time where we've been planted. Maybe it will be a place where only God sees, or a situation about which only God knows or appreciates."

"It's true you're not that important," he went on, "but your name is written in Heaven. Your life is not about you; it's not your own. Awaken and discover your true self. You are a child of God."

As Jeremiah calmed slightly, listening to these words, he hardened again as the armor of trust he had placed in Padre since childhood weakened. Voices rose within him, accusing Padre of not answering the question, of running through a rehearsed monologue on God, of ignoring Jeremiah's real pain, glossing over the problem of a God that allows immense suffering.

"You're not in control," Padre said. "Surrender to the divine flow. But this isn't about becoming passive, capitulating, or not thinking. Surrender to this love and be open to what He's calling you to do. Finally, you'll die, but your life in Him is for eternity."

Padre stopped. Leaves rustled, and wood crackled. Jeremiah was emotionally exhausted. His eyelid flapping halted, and his body reclined, instantly falling asleep with the stone in his hand.

INITIATION

After collecting firewood, Aliyah led Jameela to a small domed tent that stood a little below their height. It was constructed of saplings and branches from the surrounding forest, topped with various animal hides.

"Stop here, please, and help me," said Aliyah, as they reached the clearing just before the entrance.

They collected the logs and placed them in the fire pit, ringed with smooth stones, a few feet from the tent's entrance in the clearing.

"What are we doing?"

As she asked, Aliyah hammered a log into the ground next to a small earthen platform and crowned the log with a wolf skull. From the bag, she pulled a white dress, sandals, a bundle of white sage leaves, two ceramic bowls, a pipe, and what looked like some other plants or medicines, cedarwood incense, and henna. One by one she placed these items on a small raised earthen platform at the base of the post.

"Your spirit is troubled," said Aliyah. "It needs to be purified."

"I'm sorry, but I didn't agree to this," opposed Jameela, crossing her arms in front of her. "Whatever *this* is." She reversed to turn back towards the house but stood still.

"Mama, I don't want to go," Jameela had shouted that day. Holding her bleeding nose, she had descended the mountain.

"Jam," her Grandmama Anahita said with outstretched hands, "come back. We've all gone through this." Her brother, mama, papa, and grandparents stood behind her on the trail, and Jameela had to turn back to look at them all.

"The living springs at the shrine will heal you," said Anahita. With mouth open, showing no teeth, she smiled her charming toothless smile and contorted her face into a wrinkled ball. At first Jameela shook her head, but Anahita's shuffle dance caused her to laugh.

"That's my Jam," said Anahita, when Jameela slugged back uphill into her arms. "If my old legs can climb, so can you. Let me heal you, child." She had kissed Jam's forehead.

✦———✦

Aliyah placed a soft hand on her shoulder and said, "Let me bless you for the remainder of your journey. There's nothing to fear."

Jameela turned to watch as Aliyah knelt and furiously rubbed sticks together, blowing on the tinder until it sparked and caught. Then the kindling, then the logs ignited and smoked. "Jameela, hand me the sage bundle and a bowl."

As if she knew I wouldn't go anywhere, Jameela thought with irritation.

Aliyah unwound the purple string at the tip of the bundle and held it over the fire. With the other hand, she shoveled black soil into the bowl.

"Spirit, descend on us," prayed Aliyah. "Defeat the Evil One and purge the darkness."

✦———✦

The family had stopped at a hanging bridge, its wooden planks swaying gently with the wind. A long distance beneath them, a river rushed, fed by water falling from the cliffs of the stone mountain.

"The shrine is directly across here," said Anahita. "We'll bless the water and pray for light."

Jameela took three steps forward but, below, the swinging bridge caught the dizzying corner of her eyes; a gust blew, and she crouched and clawed her way back to the cliff.

315

"Hold my hand, Jam, and close your eyes. It's not far."

Lips trembled, hands held tight, but she made it across.

"Open now, Jam, and let go of my hand. The living waters at the well are around the bend."

Jam had made it.

+———+

Aliyah blew out the fire and laid the sage into the bowl when embers smoked. Then she circled Jameela twice, and the pungency of the smoke lingered on her skin. Aliyah returned the bowl to the platform—*really an altar*, Jameela realized.

"Now the pipe, Jameela."

Jameela handed her a wooden pipe, with hawk feathers tied around the center.

Aliyah lit it and puffed, held the smoke, then let it out in little exhalations of wispy rings that rose and dissipated. "Here, take this."

Jameela accepted, feeling the coarse smoke fill her being, suppressing a cough.

"Is there anything you want to humbly offer Mother Earth? Lift up in prayer?"

Jameela gave in to the gentle persuasion and whispered a prayer and contemplated the rising sun. She inhaled and blew experimental smoke rings of her own.

"Finished?"

"Yes," she said mildly after another deep draw, suddenly floating away from the stubborn objections that had rooted her to the ground before.

"Good, let's move to the tent."

Jameela followed Aliyah along the trail from the fire pit to the flap. She lifted the flap and crawled into the tent.

"Sit upright, cross-legged with your back against the wall. I'll be back with the heated stones. First, though, I recommend removing your clothes and putting on this white dress—because you'll get

316

sweaty. Remove your boots and put on these sandals."

Aliyah returned as Jameela settled herself cross-legged in the white dress, and from the bowl, she slid seven red-hot stones into a small pit inside the tent. She placed a water jug, beads, and what looked like cones of incense beside her.

"Jameela, you're free to leave at any point if this becomes too intense and you can't endure any more of it."

Jameela conceded; she shrugged. Aliyah closed the flap, and they sat in darkness. The heat swelled the space, prickling on Jameela's brow and arms first.

Aliyah waited a few minutes in silence, then opened with prayer.

"Mother Earth, thank you for bringing me one of your lost daughters. Thank you for the many blessings you have given us. Teach us to be grateful."

"Father Sky, place the Holy Spirit upon us now. Bless these stones and the purification to come. Lead Jameela to where you need her to be."

Aliyah poured water onto the stones. Steam slowly filled the tent, and some escaped through the small hole in the top.

"Jameela, I'll guide you through four prayers, each asking for something different. At the end of each round, I'll open the flap if you want to leave." She handed the beads to Jameela.

"In the first round, we recognize the spirit world and its Creator. We honor all those people and things we've been grateful for over the years."

Jameela struggled to start because this was the first time she had concentrated on gratitude. "Um, thank you for my papa . . . and . . . mama . . . and brother." She stumbled: men gleefully slaughtering her parents. Why? Papa and Mama ordering her to hide. Her brother Haider defending her, protecting her.

She paused and sat in silence for several minutes, then offered thanks for her health. The next half hour seemed to last a lifetime—the stillness was suffocating her.

317

"First round over," Aliyah said and opened the flap, allowing steam to escape. "You are able to continue," she declared with a nod.

"During the second round, we ask for courage, endurance, and strength. We summon the Holy Spirit to liberate anything or anyone holding us hostage."

Jameela prayed aloud but indifferently, her thoughts rambling. Sensing this, Aliyah gradually asked pointed questions.

"Jameela, is there someone in your life you need to forgive? Are there attachments in your life you need to let go? Is there someone in your life you need to love?"

Jameela breathed harder, her throat constricted, inhaling shallower as if through a mask. She could not utter the words, nor even feel the thing to utter, but she could still sit with that uncertainty.

The second round ended, and Aliyah lifted the flap and nodded again. "In the third round, we seek wisdom to follow the road to peace." With her fingers, Aliyah sprinkled droplets onto the stones and into Jameela's face, startling her. More steam filled the tent, and the spots of cool water clung refreshingly to her face and then trickled down, joining rivulets of sweat that had soaked the bodice of her dress.

"Jameela, we are like these drops of water—small, insignificant, yet coming from the same well, the life spring. Come to the well." Jameela whiplashed when the water hit her face, and some landed on her lips.

"Taste the infinite, Jameela," Aliyah said, raising her voice. "We are but dots that drip and drop, and disappear in ever-expanding ponds. But, fortunately, grace overflows from the master artist above, inviting us to play in sprays of light shows and melt into an everlasting bond."

+ —— +

"Drink, Jam, drink from the well. Don't be afraid," Anahita had said. She rested the bowl against Jameela's lips. Having pressed and pounded pomegranate and haoma twigs from nearby bushes, Papa then mixed them with well water and strained it to a clear, tinted liquid.

Anahita continued, "Dust to dust, ash to ash, Jam. Taste the earth. Your body is a temple, not to be abused, for it houses the Source. The Holy Spirit dwells within you."

Twigs burned in a fire, and Papa chanted offerings.

She choked, coughed, and finally vomited the drink. "I can't do this, Anahita. I'm sorry." She had fled the gathering and, despite her fear, run across the bridge and down the mountain.

+———+

At this point, the combination of anxiety, steam, and sweat with the power of the pipe combined to force Jameela to let go and offer her spirit in prayer.

Memories flooded in. Her parents and brother were killed. She escaped from the raiders, screaming. Her village was on fire. Running for safety, she hid in a nearby ditch and waited for them to leave. Once they departed, she was left as her family's only survivor. It was strange though, for men arrived immediately to grab her, as if they were waiting for that opportunity.

Or was it immediately? Possibly longer. The chaos sped up time.

Her body absorbed the past emotions from the time of her loss: the loneliness, the anger, the desire for vengeance against those who had done this—and those emotions filled her at the entry into slavery.

The trance numbed her. She didn't feel her body writhing, aching, or stretching, nor her spirit yearning to escape those men. This was no impulse acquisition—it was an opportunity well planned out. Though young, she was a pretty girl and would fetch quite the money for her owners. But at least those who bought her were from her own tribe. Better to know the devil you're familiar with. Easier to be angry at those who looked different than you.

Jameela blurted random words as these memories came, and

Aliyah tried to decipher the meaning as she poured the remaining water onto the stones. Jameela stood, her face buried in steam, and held out her arms to whirl around in the sodden white dress, and offered her body and chants to the Holy Spirit.

Aliyah matched the chanting with her own raised voice. "Help us lust for wonder to humble our hearts anew and know it's You. Overwhelm our senses in fantastic spaces with diverse faces to know it's true, that to accept the feast with eternal community and stay to swim and see, we will ride in infinite waves of light and love and perfect energy."

Jameela whirled in tighter circles, her arms clamped to her sides, trying to let go. Pain shot like lightning and knifed across her empty stomach lining. Grabbing her abdomen, she screamed loud and louder, "I'm sorry! I'm sorry!"

Finally she quieted and stilled, and Aliyah waited in silence as Jameela relaxed enough to sit down again, and then to lie on her side, at peace. Her entire body was fully pliable, as bendable as a soft pine twig.

Before standing to leave, Aliyah rested the tip of the incense stick against a stone until it lit. She blew out the flame and the stick. It smoked, and the scent of cedarwood filled the tent.

JOINING

An hour later, the fire expired. His eyes blinking rapidly, Jeremiah's dazed, confused, and cold body tossed and turned for warmth. The stone felt slippery in his hand, so he dropped it into his tunic pocket. His pulse and breathing accelerated as his subconscious communicated.

Padre wasn't there. Vision blurred, he repeatedly rubbed his face and body to warm himself. He wandered around the fire pit, then turned towards the woods and away from the rocky surface.

There was sudden movement on the trail.

Jeremiah froze. Before him was an enormous wolf, another—*The female?*—behind it with pups.

Vapors puffed out from the bushy gray snout when the beast growled.

I can make it! he thought. But the wolf blocked his way. Jeremiah ran back to the clearing but stopped at the gap, trapped.

The wolf taunted: *Jump, go ahead—it's over, better for you.*

Jeremiah leapt across the gap onto protruding rocks he might be able to grasp.

But the wolf lunged and caught his coat. Jeremiah attempted to wriggle free, but the coat seemed glued to his frozen body. The wolf wildly chewed the coat, lashed at Jeremiah, and cut with his claws and sank his teeth into the fabric. Then he pulled back and howled.

The howl frightened the mama she-wolf and her pups, and they scurried into the woods.

Man and beast wrestled and rolled until the pair came close to the cliff's edge. Jeremiah almost broke free.

From a dead tree jutting from the rock, a falcon dove from his perch, with claws extended for Jeremiah. A goshawk saw and swooped in as well to stop the falcon. The aerial fight ended with a bloodied falcon plummeting to the valley floor.

Arms and legs loosened from the death grip the wolf had on him. Using his last ounce of strength, with hind legs, Jeremiah powerfully heaved the wolf into the air. He flew and thudded down near the fire pit.

Wriggling like a dog when wet, the wolf righted itself, stared at him, and said with a low growl, "Well done, Jeremiah." He turned to find his mate and pups. After a snuggle, they scampered into the woods.

+———+

She tiptoed from the tent but realized the night was still young—and cold. Visualization of breath hastened the return to the comfort zone of slumber and dreams. She tried to sleep but couldn't; she squirmed in pain and ecstasy.

+———+

Sweating profusely, and his heart hammering in his chest at the vision, with a glassy-eyed stare, Jeremiah searched for Padre and a cave—a shelter to protect him until more light. Then he would risk the downhill with sunlight down the mountain.

Uttering gibberish, he sleepwalked until he found a large cut in the rock near the forest edge, beyond the rocky ledge. He crawled in and covered himself with pine needles and oak leaves. His weary body jerked and wrestled at first as he relived the fight with the wolf, but then less and less, until he fell into a deep sleep, thinking of his bride, who awaited him.

+———+

Jameela writhed with rapid eye movement. Her groom explored the area and fortunately found a trail. Still sore, he limped down the path and came upon a tent outside the house.

He was almost there.

Out of curiosity, he looked into her tent. There she was. She dreamed peacefully, curled into a child's pose as if she had fallen asleep after praying and remained in that position. Her white dress had dried, and she radiated, even in darkness, the essence of an angel.

The air was musty and earthy from the sage, but it was balanced with otherworldliness with incense. He carefully knelt and softly crawled to lie beside her.

He gently combed the short hair from her forehead and placed a tender kiss directly between her eyes. His lips tasted her sweet sweat.

She yawned, stretched, and slowly opened her eyes.

"I see you," she whispered.

"I see you too, my queen."

She moved closer and rested her head on his lap. "Hold me, please."

He obliged.

"Jameela?"

"Don't talk," she said. "Just hold me."

He lay down beside her, facing her, and was enveloped in her scent. "Jameela?"

"Don't talk," she said. "Just hold me."

He felt his body absorb her pain and somehow healed her wounds. And she his.

Some time passed.

She pushed herself up to sitting, her back to him, and he sat up too. He rose.

Cross-legged, they sat erect.

She turned her head back to him and bit her lip and caressed her leg, welcoming him.

He closed the gap and scooted forward.

He touched her back and arms and went higher but stopped, as if asking for permission. She accepted, so he ran his hands to her shoulders and neck, then stroked them more deeply, taking possession.

He turned her around to face him and brushed her hair to the side so her soft honeydew irises showed. His gleam twinkled; he gazed down and up and down and up again from her eyes to her lips and back.

Energy jolted throughout their hyper-aware bodies, and their stomachs fluttered. Quiet lingered for too long. The silence spoke without words; then it shouted: succumb! Soon thereafter, they both surrendered.

Breathing intensified, and the beam of energy penetrated their lovers' souls. In the distance, a mama she-wolf called her family.

"Your eyes are like doves," he said and placed a warm kiss on her cheek. Then a kiss on the other cheek. His heart pounded.

He moved to kiss her soft lips. Crackling sensations fired within him, and within her too, and she trembled at his touch.

The passion paused—they opened their eyes for a moment, enough for each to behold the inferno blazing.

"May I?" he asked his lover.

"Yes," she whispered.

He shoved her boots to the tent's side, removed her sandals first and then disrobed all his own clothing. She stared at him, and her pulse quickened; she yearned; she invited. With finesse, her groom slid her dress off one shoulder and then the other, until her beauty was exposed and the white garment lay around her hips.

Eyes wide and body excited, he fixed on this most beautiful gift from God. Her neck was jeweled in Eastern ornaments. He admired and removed, brushing by her bosom as he lifted the beads and chains over her head.

It tickled; she giggled. His eyes searched her body from top to bottom, drawing the dress down her legs and away, to ensure nothing hid from him. He grasped each limb, each part in turn, and her skin glistened and glowed at his touch.

He reached to his pile of clothing and brought out the flowers he had plucked on his way up the mountain, stripping the petals one by one from their clusters and sprinkling them upon her. Bluebonnets slid underneath her nose. He showered her breasts with a cluster of the henna beside her pallet and rested in its aroma and her softness. Musty earth vanished, and her flower gave forth its fragrance.

"Calm," she said to guide him.

"Show me," he said.

"Be calm," she repeated. "Slow."

No longer coarse but smooth like silk, finer than his most polished wooden work, her tawny skin invited his tasting. His mouth followed her hands with spaced kisses on each remembrance mark as she explained them—one for her mama, one for her papa, and one for her brother—down the trail to the secret recesses of her cliff, then roamed and browsed the lilies until tasting its sweet fruit.

"Arise, my beautiful one. Come!" she instructed.

He obeyed, and far away the mama wolf howled.

"I love you, Jameela."

A portal opened to another world for a moment, temporarily, and energy rushed through as a deluge. Heaven fell, and their heated dove song crooned between them until morning broke.

Two souls became one.

WRESTLING

Disoriented, she yawned, stretched, and knelt to open the tent flap. A misty shower rinsed her face, and drops sprinkled the white dress that already clung to her skin. The scent of pine penetrated the garment and soaked her body, replacing the sage and incense.

After the shower, she closed the tent flap, lay flat, and pulled and wriggled until the wet dress came off and her tunic went back on. She opened the tent flap and went outside and looked for a puddle. Her hair was a mess—matted in knots and angled in multiple directions. She raked her fingers through it to establish some order.

Into the kitchen she wandered, balled-up dress in hand, to rummage through jars and pots on the table for Aliyah's special tea—a high to cure the high. She was delighted to find the tea, but a honey pot conjured the spell. She recalled the lesson: "Today we practice manipulation," said the teacher, "how to manipulate men into doing what you want."

She shivered and shook the memory as she sat at the table with the pot. As she dipped a spoon into the honey, Jeremiah burst through the kitchen door.

Honey pot—"Honey pot," she murmured as he slid into the seat beside hers.

Jameela jumped from her seat—the ceramic pot slid from her hand to the floor and shattered upon contact; honey oozed onto the floor.

She turned and said, "Jeremiah! What are you doing?"

Wide-eyed and wild-haired, Jeremiah hummed a song. "Saying

hello, beautiful," he said. He nestled beside her, purred, and played with her hair.

"What are you *doing*?" she yelled. Blushing, she swatted at his head. He carried on and kissed her cheek.

"Stop! Are you high or just woody?" She snatched the crumpled white dress on the table before he noticed; she tossed it to the floor to cover the shards and honey.

I can't tell him.

"Sorry, sorry," he babbled. "Am I all right? Are you all right? It looks like you've been through a rough night. Were you wrestling?"

Was I dreaming? she wondered.

"Did I? I only remember the tent. And lots of pain."

"Oh? Pain?" asked Jeremiah. "Wait." He touched the base of his neck and frowned. A rag lay near the sink; he went to it and wetted a cloth from the pitcher of water. Attempting to clean her cuts from their journey, he pulled back when she flinched.

"Did you fall?" he asked. "Are you hurt?"

"I don't know."

"Your clothes are damp. Who were you with?"

"Aliyah."

"Anyone else?"

"Have you seen Aliyah this morning?" countered Jameela.

"No—I've been out searching for Padre too. I was with him earlier this morning, but then he disappeared."

Padre and Aliyah floated into the room from outside, with laughing.

With the rag in his raised hand, Jeremiah demanded, "Where have you been? You left me for dead! And why are you smiling?"

"Because it's a beautiful morning, Jeremiah," Padre said. "What a wonderful and relaxing stroll to the river. We picked these for breakfast." He dumped on the table a bunch of grapes from his knotted-up tunic hem.

Aliyah grabbed bread and a knife and commenced slicing.

Walking into the kitchen, yawning and stretching, Asser and Mo joined them at the table. "Right in time for breakfast," said Mo.

Aliyah broke bread and handed pieces of bread around as Padre washed grapes.

"You both look like garbage," said Asser to the two young people. "A battle? Were you wrestling again?"

Jameela blushed; Jeremiah looked at her, but she turned away.

"I don't want to talk about it," said Jeremiah. "And they don't look very cleaned up, either," he said, looking at Padre and Aliyah feeding grapes to each other. "We'd better get going. We were being chased, remember?"

After breakfast, they quickly packed their belongings and fare-welled. Aliyah applied homemade ointment to Asser's leg and wrapped a fresh bandage around it.

"Looks like it's healing quickly," Aliyah said, glancing to Padre, who went to her for an embrace and squeezed her hand, then slowly released it.

"Wow, such a long hug, Padre," said Asser.

Padre exhaled sharply. "When you get older, Asser, you appreciate true friendship and companionship more than physical connection."

"Me wasn't thinking of sex."

"Sure you weren't," Padre said as he rolled his eyes. "Come on, let's go."

＊———＊

Jameela flew lightly across the creek ahead of them all. Jeremiah searched for wolves in the woods to either side of their path, but the only paw he felt was Mo's rough-as-rocks fingers and leathery glove gripping a shoulder.

"Rough mornin', Jeremiah?"

"I don't want to talk about it, Mo."

Padre sped ahead of them to the solitary Jameela and asked her a question, but he pulled back the gentle hand on her shoulder as she turned and spat an answer at him.

"I feel like that piece of horse manure you barely missed stepping on."

"You haven't fully healed, Jameela."

"Your friend manipulated me into an ugly memory, a place I wanted to forget."

"She was trying to help."

"Helping is not bringing it up again."

Then Jameela fled from Padre and stormed past Jeremiah to the creek. "Jameela!" shouted Jeremiah. "Let's go."

She kept walking fast away from them, but Jeremiah called out, following her with longer strides, "Do you *want* to be caught?"

"Leave her be," said Padre. "She'll find us."

"Why'd you leave me alone on the mountain?" Jeremiah asked him bluntly.

"Jeremiah . . . ," Padre's voice lagged his slackened mouth.

"No, I demand an answer. I could've been killed."

"You weren't even harmed."

"That's not the point. I could've been killed, and you could've been killed. You never leave a man behind."

In crisp flatness, Padre said, "You weren't a man, Jeremiah."

Jeremiah turned away from him and saw in the distance Jameela. She continued walking, seeing the creek ahead, its current sloshing with higher water. She sat on a log and removed her boots. She sneaked a look his way and then turned back and waited for Jeremiah to follow her.

"A man doesn't walk away from his fears!" shouted Padre. "He confronts them. He wrestles with them. Most importantly, he asks for help. Fools try all alternatives except the one option which satisfies. Why are you so afraid?"

When Jeremiah reached her and quietly sat beside her, she dangled her feet over the rushing current and dipped them occasionally into the cold water.

Having dried her tears, she curled her lips and said, "Hey, Jeremiah. I knew you'd come for me."

"Listen, Jameela—about yesterday and the kiss . . ."

"Stop," she said. "Let's not speak of it."

Silence.

They listened to the sparrow mating symphony. Their wings flapped and fluttered; they danced in and out and around them, but Jeremiah skipped a rock that scattered them.

Jameela spotted Jeremiah fondling the stone and placing it back in his tunic pocket. He plucked a tiny flower growing out of the log they sat on and twirled it in his fingers. She watched the spinning petals and pinched her bottom lip.

I can't do this.

+———+

"Find a man who cherishes you, Jam, for more than your body," her mama had said once they left the mountain. "Remember, your body is a temple. Mind, body, and spirit are one."

Cross-legged in the grass in a field of sunflowers, Jameela said, "Mama, I don't want to talk about it."

Her mama placed a kiss on the top of her head, then said, "My Jam." Mama grabbed Jam's chin, and with a warm, direct smile, she had said, "Find a man who radiates when he looks at you. You'll know he's the one if you feel he sees your soul."

+———+

"I'm sorry, Jameela," said Jeremiah, interrupting her memory. He slid the flower into her hair atop her left ear as pine trees whispered with the breeze. Her hand thawed when he softly found her fingers and held them. She lifted their twined hands and held his open in her own—she noticed the three lines in his palms that formed triangles. And she reached for his other hand and confirmed the pattern there as well.

Bringing her hand to his lips for a kiss, he said, "I was too forward. Forgive me. Please forgive me." He gripped her fingers, smiled, and released them.

330

Like a hot tea on a cold day, warmth fanned throughout her body and melted her frozen veins. She lifted her eyes to make contact with his; his almond eyes sparkled—she grinned with a heavy exhale. "Thank you," she faintly said. "But I prefer the right ear."

Jeremiah tenderly pulled the flower from her left ear, and with both hands, set it over her right, as if it—or she—were a fragile piece of art.

Her heart cracked, and she buried her head into her hands.

"What are you doing here by yourself?" he asked quietly. "You know people have been chasing us the last few days. You shouldn't be alone."

"I don't want to talk about it."

Sighs and silence.

More sighs.

"Come on, let's go," he said. "We need to catch up with the others." He stood and extended his hand.

"I want to sit here a while longer."

He sat and dug for the stone but didn't remove it from his pocket.

Birds returned to mate. Jealous and lonesome, with uptight stiff posture and a tail cocked, a crow landed on a branch before he strutted by the couple and cooed, cawed, and clicked. Jeremiah waved it away, scooted closer to Jameela, and moved a hand. But he retracted and looked beyond the creek.

"Tell me more about you," he said.

"Not now, Jeremiah." *Doesn't he know when to be quiet?*

She returned to her form of prayer—meditation. She blocked out her thoughts and focused on the sounds: gurgling water, singing birds, and swaying tree branches. She imagined the sprouting trees and emerging flower buds beginning to bloom. And the aroma they would have—spring was her favorite season. She dreamed of freedom when she smelled spring.

"So, you had a rough morning too," he said.

She startled. "How do you know?"

"I can tell by looking at you," he said.

CORNERSTONE | THE KING

"You seem to do that frequently."

"Like now?"

"Hard to hide, Rosy Cheeks."

He placed his arm next to hers. "Rosy cheeks I have, true, like father, but my skin is—no. More like yours."

They both laughed.

"But I like when you look at me," she confessed.

He smiled. He also confessed, "You know, it's taken me time to get over Marianne."

She stopped him. With folded arms, she sternly said, "Listen, Jeremiah. I don't want to hear her name again. Understand?"

She shot up and stormed off with her mouth open, thinking, *Stupid, idiot!* Down the trail she raced, away from their traveling companions, then stopped at Aliyah's porch and thought. She returned to him a little shamefacedly.

He had stood waiting and brightened but stumbled over his words. "I-I had a rough morning too."

She contorted her face and mumbled, "Jeremiah, tell me now before I give you my heart."

Clearing an ear, he said, "I'm sorry. What'd you say?"

She turned her head away, then snapped back and looked levelly into his eyes.

Witen it. Freedom later.

With both arms, she pulled him into a long embrace, capturing his arm between them. The stone in his hand warmed and shined, casting a glow on both their faces. She melted into the kiss he offered. It felt right, but then he stopped briefly to look at her, then return.

They kissed as crickets vibrated their wings, birds danced and flapped their wings, and frogs inflated and deflated their air sacs to serenade the couple. The sounds sung in harmony and resonated in the form of ripples across the creek.

Jeremiah pulled away, wiping at his lips with the back of his hand. "I'm sor-sorry. I need to go."

He walked alongside the creek, absently fondling the stone.

Jameela blew out ragged breaths, and her gut fell to her feet.

Did I do something wrong?

Jeremiah returned, beckoned her to sit on the log again, and held her hand. "I'm sorry," he said. "My heart."

Can't get too close, she remembered. *Freedom.*

"Jeremiah."

"Yes? What is it?"

She let go of his hand. "We should rejoin the group."

"Why? I like being next to you."

"Yes, I know. I know, but we should go. Those chasing us— remember?"

"Now you want to go?"

She bent and picked up two rocks. One went into the water and the other into her pocket. She stood and refused to respond.

"What's wrong?" he asked.

"We don't have time to talk about my entire history right now, Jeremiah. Let's say I'm very profitable."

"What do you mean?"

She pulled him into a run. On the lookout for horses, wolves, and men, she swiveled her head until meeting the team.

"You look better," said Asser to Jameela as the couple caught up with them, noticing color had returned.

"I needed time to think," she said.

Though he didn't speak, Padre's face expressed disbelief, skepticism, and concern simultaneously.

After a couple of hours of walking, watching, and listening carefully for pursuers, they came around a bend in the woods, and the forest opened to a clearing and a tidal body of water. Forest darkness transformed to full day with clear blue sky and sun sparkles on the water, blinding them.

"There it is." Padre pointed to the huge church atop the rock. Asser went into ankle-deep water. "Shall we cross?"

"I need rest first," said Padre.

"We should go now and rest once we are across," countered Jeremiah. "Better to hide in the town before others find us."

Asser clapped and said, "Correct answer, leader. Let's go."

"I'll carry you part of the way, Padre," said Mo. "Then Asser can."

Padre laughed. "I'll walk at that point."

They all looked around to be sure of their safety, looked at the Mont Church, and looked back at the woods. There were no sounds of hunters.

Mo squatted, and Padre climbed onto his broad back, wrapping his legs around the giant's hips.

Into the basin they went, squishing their way through reeds and mud and wading until sinking into the wet sand on the other side.

MONT CHURCH

Church bells rang to indicate half past eleven. Two guards manned the arched entrance to the town, but they allowed passage once Padre explained they were pilgrims looking to make offerings at the church.

The town immediately rose up from the sea, the primary cobblestone street winding up and around buildings, carts, cows, chickens, goats, and villagers. Animals ruled the road and ignored the incessant bartering between merchants and tourists. One vendor shooed away a bull that was head-deep in his cart full of fruit.

Salty sea air coupled with roasted chicken combined to create an aroma that awakened strong desire to satisfy a hunger which hadn't been fed since Aliyah's house. They purchased chicken legs and continued the climb in haste.

"Why are we here again?" asked Mo in between bites of chicken.

"Remember, me and Jeremiah are fugitives?"

"It's been a minute, Asser," said Mo.

"A few days and you're already tired?" teased his friend.

"No, I'm jus' sayin' it's been a long minute since we left. Why this church?"

Jeremiah dug into his pocket.

"Still clingin' to that rock?" asked Mo.

"Yeah," said Asser, "you've been attached to that rock more than that Marianne woman."

"Shut up, Asser."

"Not again," said Jameela with a weary sigh.

"Oh, she's nothing, really—just the reason why he was in prison."

"I know, I know, Asser," she said. "She must have been special."

"Can we not talk about it?" Jeremiah whispered, leaning in to Asser.

"Why this church again?" asked Mo.

"The Moses statue," said Padre.

"We're here because legends point to the stone's original location," said Jeremiah. "At least that's what Cyrus said."

"Exactly," said Padre. "There it is."

Remnants of the main fort wall remained, but it blocked the bottom half of the Mont Church. The visible top half was unimpressive; however, the views outward to the river, the tidal basin, and beyond were breathtaking. "Reminds me of the river at home," Jeremiah said to Jameela. "I'm not sure if I can ever return."

"Same for me," she replied.

"Where is your home?"

"Far away," she said, her voice barely audible. "Forgive me for—for earlier at the river. I was still recovering from the night with Aliyah."

"What happened?"

"She attempted to cleanse me of past sins. And to let go of sins committed against me."

"Sins? What do you know about sin?"

"Isn't that what Padre calls it? I've never known the kind of life you've had, Jeremiah. You think your life has been rough? Because of a girl?"

He grew angry and looked daggers at her. "Jameela, you know nothing about me."

"I know you act tough, you escaped from prison, but inside you're a scared boy who misses his family."

He glared past her to the water and cliff below, then pushed off from the wall, and with the spin of his feet, pebbles kicked up into the air. He trembled in fury. "You're no angel, Jameela," he snapped.

She held his glance, coldly and with full attention. After a moment, she said sadly, "You're right, Jeremiah."

She left for the church, trailing the others.

"Come on, Jameela," Jeremiah said in a flat drone. "I'm sorry."

He quickly brushed by her and got close.

"I'm sorry," he repeated.

She leaned against the wall, and then pressed herself against him. "You're right, Jeremiah. I'm no angel."

He softened as he made two horizontal cuts across her face.

"Something wrong?" she asked.

"No, I'm sorry," he said and extended his arms. "That's all that needs to be said." They held, and their ears touched during the hug. She held tightly while she searched.

After they released their hug, she sneezed in a fit of three.

"I love when you do that," said Jeremiah.

"Thanks," she said wearily, and they both laughed at the absurdity of the compliment.

"Let's go!" yelled Asser from ahead of them.

Beyond the blackened and shell-pocked fort wall lay an interior courtyard where large patio cobblestones had turned to fine pinkish pebbles that formed in a perimeter band. Within that circle was a ring of rimmed bushes that dotted the inside edges. The center had luscious green grass—and Jameela stopped there in a kind of trance.

Jeremiah stood by her and waited, then asked, "You look far away—a memory?"

"Y-yes!" she said, surprised. "We had this kind of soft grass in my childhood backyard, a warm carpet where my family would spend hours imagining funny cloud shapes. Fountains burbled there, just like they do here . . ." She looked up, smiling shyly.

Jameela stepped up on a bench to peer through the window arrow slit to the sea below. Jeremiah snapped a twig from a bush and pretended to sword play with her.

"So now this carpenter can fight?" she scorned. "Not now, Jeremiah."

She snapped the stick from his grasp and softly jabbed him. "Not good at fighting, my lord. And I have the advantage of you from up here."

"Come now," rebuked Padre, stepping across the lawn and bringing them both to attention and waving them over to where Asser and Mo were standing, waiting.

Asser studied the wispy strips attached as slender noses and elephant ears to puffy, dark clouds rolling in. "Looks like the evil trolls from me mama's bedtime stories," he said.

"How'd the song go again, laddy?" asked Mo in a deep, grating voice.

"The giant made a funny. Ha, ha."

"No," said Mo as he hit Asser in the back, "please no bleatin' and no singin'."

The church door opened to a wide interior and a stairwell to their right. Massive stone columns supporting the central arched structure permitted a wide space with a decorated tile floor.

Now at noon, a short priest dressed in a white robe pulled a knotted rope extending from a small circular opening in the roof at one end with rhythmic, sweeping strokes. By the twelfth pull, Jeremiah and the newcomers had made their way up the aisle and arrived at a statue of Moses in his normally depicted artistic pose, holding the tablets of the Ten Commandments in his right arm, with a long beard, stoic gaze, and curious horns on his head.

"Why the horns?" Jeremiah asked Padre.

"From Exodus. When Moses descended Mount Sinai, he held two tablets, and he didn't know his face had changed from his conversation with the Lord."

"To me," Jeremiah said, thinking of his many figurines he'd carved and admired over the years, "the artist wanted to show beams of light stemming out from his head. The smaller horns too."

"Exactly. A few think the translation is wrong. The Hebrew word *karan* often means 'horn,' but their interpretation is 'shining' or 'emitting rays.'"

Asser had just joined them, and jumping backwards, startled, he said, "Ugly statue. The horns make him look devilish. Is this why we're here?"

"I don't know," said Padre. "This statue is fairly common across the kingdom."

The hooded bell ringer finished his work and offered them a tour, but Padre waved him off with thanks. The square tile pattern varied in blues, blacks, pinks, and whites, and colors contrasting with the white stone columns and clear windows. Next to the small, bare altar stood a vase of violet flowers and a large candelabra.

Jameela discovered a cozy alcove of pink stone at one of the windows, scaled the steps to it, and sat with her crossed legs extended across the ledge. Head turned to the view through the wavy colored glass, and she dreamed; the dreams floated and glided through the window and coursed through the funneled, brilliant light.

Some dreams escaped to the one who granted wishes, she believed. The angled light whitened the stone above her head, but the steps, the arched roof, and the opposite wall were dark.

Jeremiah, forgive me.

"Asser! What are you doing?" exclaimed Padre, interrupting her reverie. She swung herself off the ledge and went to join them for whatever the ruckus was about.

Asser had been snooping around and stumbled upon something strange in the ambry. He held out his hand to show that a little door was open.

"This is the tabernacle," Jeremiah explained, "where they keep the holy Eucharist. It is the bread used in our holiest rite, never to be eaten outside the service. That's why Padre is so upset." The tabernacle door housing holy Eucharist was ajar.

"Me didn't take the wafers," Asser assured Padre. "But me see a small niche on the side which seems out of place. Inside was this."

Asser handed Padre a key with an emblem of Moses on it and said, "Me think we need to find a statue resembling this." He pointed to an emblem on the key, and Padre showed it around.

They searched but found nothing on the main level; down the entrance stairwell, they went to explore the lower level full of the aroma of freshly baked bread and friars in brown robes and tonsured heads hunched over, sipping bowls of warm soup. The tiled, powder-blue arched roof and vast dining hall dwarfed the dozen brothers packed tightly around a wooden table.

"This looks like something Alfred described," said Jeremiah. "A soldier's mess hall."

"They're certainly eating like soldiers," said Asser.

They ate their meal of bread, water, and soup with military efficiency: no talking, and they all dipped, chewed, and sipped in repetition until all the crumbs and drops disappeared. One lifted his eyes to peek at the odd mix of people trespassing in the hall, but he shook his head and lowered it again to his meal.

Words bubbled to her mouth, but Jameela remained quiet.

They continued walking around the table, through the kitchen, and past a door leading to their living quarters and to another stairwell. The door opened to a courtyard that was similar in appearance and layout to the first but facing the sun differently on the other end.

Upward they looked, to the back of the church.

Birds sang loudly, louder than whistles, and someone, two people, in the distance were coming closer and yelling.

"Freedom!" heard Jameela.

Mo spotted a wooden gate partially hidden by overgrown trees and brush near a corner. He opened the gate, and the others followed him around the spiral stone stairs.

Soon they touched the large stone wall towering over them. At the bottom was a wooden door. Before Asser tried the key, Mo broke the handle.

A large, irregularly shaped stone wall allowed for only narrow passage through its doorway. A small wooden plaque read: *Foundation*.

"Foundation wall," said Jeremiah.

"To the entire church?" asked Asser.

"Must be," said Jeremiah.

"Cornerstone," confirmed Padre.

Past the stone passageway was more stone before them.

A dead end?

All of them were dejected. Asser whined, Jameela and Padre stayed silent, and Mo pounded the stone.

"Mo," Jeremiah said sharply, "stop. There's a hole in the wall." He palmed the stone in his pocket, drew it out, and said, "My stone is warm—maybe the key will fit?"

It fit perfectly. Padre twisted it.

Jameela's eyes widened, and she gaped.

But nothing happened.

Padre twisted clockwise, counterclockwise, one time, several times—but nothing happened.

"All this way," complained Asser. "All this way—and the stone is a fraud, a fake. Me knew it."

Mo grabbed the stone and shoved it into the wall, scraping some of its edges.

"Mo!" shouted Jeremiah. "Stop!"

While fidgeting and biting her nails, Jameela thought carefully. She rubbed her hands against the smooth wall. Whistles and shouts of "Freedom! Freedom!" intensified outside, the sharp sounds banging and recoiling, trapped in the stone tunnel. Jameela covered her ears.

"Yes," she said. "Jeremiah, there must be another way, another entrance, a clue of some sort to guide us."

Jeremiah touched the wall. "Yes! Thank you, Jameela. Slay the lies," he said. "Padre, remember the scytale?"

"Yes, but it washed away in the river."

"There was a riddle on the back, but I forget the exact words. Do you remember?"

Padre roamed his beard with his fingers and said, "A picture of a circle, I think?"

"Yes! And a square around it. And the number three in the center. Cyrus mentioned that only a carpenter could solve the riddle."

Jeremiah crouched and found a rock to scratch a circle with a square onto the wall.

"The approximate constant," recited Padre. "This dessert is a fraction of infinite beauty. Irrationality transcends left, right, left."

Taste the infinite, Jameela remembered.

Can I do this?

Jeremiah drew another circle and square. Tapping his mouth, he also sketched a triangle. "A triangle!" he proclaimed. "Dadde . . . thank you."

"Dadde?" asked Asser. "What does your father—"

Jeremiah stopped him with a hand raised. "I know the answer. The riddle is a combination—a lock: three numbers, a fraction . . . pi!"

Jeremiah put the stone back into the hole and turned it counterclockwise two rotations, clockwise two rotations, then counterclockwise seven rotations. On the final spin, Jeremiah released, and his hands formed a steeple while the team waited expectantly.

Yes! Exclaimed Jameela in her mind. Leaning forward, she took Jeremiah's hand and squeezed.

Click.

Dust blew out from the seams as the wall became a door. It started to open but stuck fast. Mo pulled, and dust billowed as stone chips fell. They waved to dissipate the pulverized stone. Asser leapt and hugged Mo, then Padre and Jeremiah.

During the celebration, Jameela stretched out a finger to speak but promptly startled and jerked forward when Asser slapped her butt. After she squealed, she jerked forward and relaxed into a smile. She then avoided a kiss from Jeremiah but accepted his arms.

He wrapped them around her and said, "Thank you, Jameela, for encouraging me." She bit her lip as she caught his tone of pleasure blurring the drawl of syllables.

After Mo, Asser, and Padre entered through the door, she extended a hand towards the wall to the niche where the stone rested.

"It's another church in here," Padre announced from within. "The original church here?" asked Padre.

Jameela touched the wall and turned her head to see the stone there; Jeremiah tried to release himself from the hug, but she held on tighter.

Almost! A wave of joy sprung from within her, and she held it and savored the feeling, as if trying to hold a sunrise within the small space of the passageway before the wave that would inevitably crash down upon them.

Her fingers slipped and the stone fell out of the wall, but she caught it before it went beyond her reach. She held Jeremiah for a moment longer and pushed a rock from the creek into his tunic pocket.

"Keep this safe," she murmured.

"This must be it," called Padre excitedly.

Jameela released Jeremiah, and he rushed into the inner church, forgetting about the stone momentarily.

The ceilings hung lower within the secret door, and the stone walls were lighter and more varied in color than in the building they'd just explored. Embroidered white linen covered a small altar, and ancient incense lingered in the stagnant air.

Padre walked to the stone statue of Moses sitting with his wife, Zipporah, and his father-in-law, Jethro. "This is a much different picture of Moses than the typical representations of a lawgiver and warrior," said Padre. "Here he is a family man, looking lovingly into his wife's eyes and being respectful of his father-in-law."

To the right of the sculpture was a wooden box in the shape of an hourglass. Padre removed the key from his pocket, inserted it into the box, and turned it. Two small scrolls fell out as the door opened.

"Can you read it, Padre?" asked Jeremiah.

"No, I can't," he said with a glance at each, "but Aliyah can."

After rolling the scrolls and placing them into the sash around his waist pocket, Padre locked the hourglass-shaped box and handed

Asser the key. "Please return it, Asser," said Padre, "to where you found it—when we get back up there."

Mo shut the door, and they walked back through the tunnel. Once they passed the stone wall and started up the stairs, Jeremiah turned back. "One moment," he called. "I need to check on something."

"Come on, Jeremiah," Jameela said in a biting, nervous tone, grabbing at his hand. "I told you to keep the stone safe," she said in a sultry voice as intended to convey shyness but confessing fearful urgency instead. "We can get the stone later; let's celebrate."

She grabbed his arm and she pulled him into her chest. As they kissed, heat swept her face as coolness spread across her chest to her heart. She guided his hand down to his pocket and felt him relax at the touch of the stone.

Then she let him carry on with the kiss and take her hand to lead, following her through the upper church and into the courtyard.

As they emerged into the bright sunlight, Jameela shaded her eyes against what she saw: Adam and Yusuf rested in the grass like patient pythons waiting to ambush their prey.

"Jameela," said Yusuf. He removed his hat and held it against his chest gallantly.

Jameela's heart plummeted to her feet, and she felt herself go pale; her creamed-coffee skin whitened. "Come home," said Yusuf with an extended hand, "for freedom."

Asser groaned, "They've found us!"

Jeremiah's mouth fell open, but no words came, and he clutched at her hand.

A gurgle bubbled from her gut near to her heart. Blood drained, and a pang of anxiety tingled down her arm into her interlocked fingers. She released Jeremiah's hand.

"Jameela," pleaded Jeremiah, "don't go. This is your family now."

"I wish it were that simple," she mechanically replied.

Her dream in the tent came flooding to her now, the time where she and Jeremiah had connected. It was like the real thing. And then:

her theatrical dismissal of Jeremiah in the kitchen the next morning, after fending him off. But she would never confess the dream to him.

If only the feelings she had developed could mean more. She hadn't expected she would fall for him. That wasn't part of the mission.

Find Jeremiah, get the stone, and then meet Adam and Yusuf.

Wincing, she stumbled forward with her belly in knots and then turned back and said, "I'm sorry, Jeremiah."

She abandoned the group she had intimately come to know. *It was only days*, she told herself, that she had known these people. With leaden arms and legs, she flung away the guilt and paraded the prize with a forced smile, her shoulders back and her arm extended, hand closed.

For freedom.

"Do you have the stone?" asked Adam.

"Yes, here," she said and handed it to him. She had hoped to feel the same warmth Jeremiah had described, but she felt nothing—only cold stone.

"Good girl. You'll be handsomely paid."

With an eye on her recent companions, Yusuf hugged her, kissed her cheek, and took her hand.

"What in the king's name, Jameela?" asked Asser.

"You deserve better, my child," said Padre.

Mo moved to stop her, but Padre scolded. "Let her go, Mo."

Jeremiah couldn't move, his body paralyzed, his feet sinking with his heart, as if stuck in quicksand.

Muscles in her head twitched; she rushed a hand to massage the spot and block her view of him. But the itch had to be scratched.

He fell for me, she thought.

She locked onto his almond eyes, softened herself, and mouthed, "Take care, Jeremiah."

And I for him.

BROTHERLY LOVE

The Oths buried Charlie before crossing at low tide. Exhausted from wading through marshy reeds, the horses rested on the hardened sand. The knights craned their necks to gawk at the engineering marvel.

Brick walls and steep, rocky cliffs protecting the city and church forced them to enter through the main gate. In some areas, the walls naturally extended from the marshy land the town was built upon. From a distance, pilgrims struggled to differentiate between the natural and the man-made.

One primary tightly packed cobblestone road wrapped around the foundation and rose steeply to the summit. They searched for a place to rest and eat. A startled wife washing clothes in a wooden barrel accepted them after only light resistance.

"Thank you, ma'am," said Alfred. "Hello, children."

"You're welcome, my lord"—she bowed—"but, please, no reeds in the house." Alfred raised eyebrows and showed the king's seal. She shrugged and said, "Rules are rules."

She forced them outside to pull off the reeds pasted to their wet boots. "Remove your boots too."

"Like Mum," he said and reentered. Around the kitchen table, the woman served bread and soup. Her brunette daughter stood beside Alfred and touched his arm. "My dadde is bigger than you."

The woman blushed and hastily reached for the ladle. "I'm sorry, my lord. Here, have more soup."

The girl stared at Alfred with wide eyes.

"Emma, respect these knights. They're from the king."

Alfred smiled. "It's fine, ma'am. She reminds me of my daughter." The knights finished eating, and Alfred pulled from his bag a portrait of Jeremiah. "Have you seen this man? I'm looking for him—my brother."

"Hmm, different from you, but no, I don't know, my lord," she said. "I haven't seen him, but," she said and wiped the girl's mouth, "if they're like most, they're probably visiting the Mont Church."

"Thank you. May we leave our horses and bags here? We won't be gone long."

"Yes," she said, "and return before dinner or you won't get any."

They squished into their wet boots outside, and Alfred told the kids, "Be good to your mum and dadde." He flashed a wink to Emma as he exited. "Your dadde is bigger than me," he said.

She giggled and waved goodbye.

"Father William, that's why I fight," Alfred said and untied his horse.

"Young and naïve, I joined our forces for power and glory, a romantic seeking kingdom glory and defending our way of life. My father didn't understand, I thought. We used force to protect our values. He wanted talk. But deterrence, Father William. The stout-hearted deter the strong-headed, and we protect the weak."

"A noble intention, Lord Alfred," said William.

"But as I've been chasing this stupid stone, I remember all the men I've killed. And my men who have died. Why did they die? For duty, honor, kingdom? For a God none of us knew? But all I want, Father William, is to be home with my wife and daughter."

Daniel tilted his head and said, "Around there—another road."

"Let's take it," said Alfred. "William, guard the rear. When we have the stone and are on our way going home, we'll continue our talk."

"Of course, Lord Alfred." William tied Boomer and watched them run ahead. Around the curves, they flew with swords out; however, Alfred's fist immediately rose, and they halted.

Villagers ran past them in fear. In an alley, William stopped while the Oths scaled ledges and hopped over rocks, up a level, and another level.

William slowly climbed behind them. Backs to a low stone wall, the Oths readied their bows.

"Those men we saw chasing Jeremiah," Alfred said softly, "are up there." He reminded the Oths Jeremiah may be close and to capture him alive. He raised his fingers and said, "One, two . . ."

They popped and turned.

William heard screams and yelps. A woman, definitely. And a goat?

He low-crawled along the pebbles and peered over the wall with his hat tipped down. Two men and a woman took position behind boulders. The men had fitted black bork hats with a metallic emblem in the middle. *The men at the castle.*

Jeremiah appeared in the courtyard. *The same boy from the mead ball*, William thought. *Br-brothers.* Alfred stared at Jeremiah, but Jeremiah averted and then lowered his gaze. He appeared lost momentarily and then dove with three others behind large stones and thick bushes in the courtyard.

Alfred's accusation came immediately. "You killed my knight, you cowards. Come out and face us. We've come to bring you to justice."

A stout man grunted, "Lord Alfred."

Alfred would not answer him but roared and led the charge with his sword high and shield out. His knights followed. A taller man pulled the woman's hand and told her to run. He stood on a bench, shot arrows, and retreated. Two struck a knight's neck, and he fell.

"Adam!" yelled the man, "There are too many. Fight another day."

Alfred ran faster. "Kill the runner!" he ordered Daniel.

A man and woman scurried past William to the main road.

Adam touched the dead knight's quiver, but it was empty. "Ugh!" he growled, and flung the bow away. Arrows flew from another knight but missed him. "Witen," Adam said, then threw a dagger and ran. "Jameela, Yusuf, run!"

Alfred ducked, threw his shield, and removed his shirt mail. "Find the others," Alfred ordered a knight. "And William, William? What did I? Someone go back and close the gate!"

William panicked and watched it all unfold from the wall. The knights carried on downhill for Yusuf, chasing, stopping, and shooting. Homes appeared along the road, and villagers screamed and hid. Yusuf returned fire and yelled, "Run faster, Jameela! Get the stone out of here! I'll fend them off."

Stone? William thought.

Jameela ran through the gate and was soon disappearing like a dot from William's vantage. Yusuf tore through narrow corridors of the town. In and out, he found alternate routes; jumping and dropping, he descended to the lower levels until finding the primary path again. Two knights tried to follow but lost him. Once at the gate, Yusuf killed the gate guards with wicked slashes from his dagger.

"Witen," said William with a low whistle. Shaking, he closed his eyes and prayed. "What do I do?" *Jeremiah or Alfred?* He rocked on his toes, then ran into the courtyard. He didn't see anyone, but it was empty.

Below, on the street, sunlight reflected off a man's bald dome; Alfred pushed and forced the slower-footed Adam to a dead end. Stone houses with thatched roofs lay to their left, and a stone wall to their right protected them from the tidal basin plunge. Alfred punched and drew his sword; Adam kicked and pulled too. They clanked for several blows without damage.

Adam shoved Alfred, dropped his sword, and leapt for the straw roof. Though he was short, his wide shoulders and considerable upper body strength propelled him to a climb. He jumped onto the next house, and onto the next house until he could clear the wall. He sprang for the vines running along the stone and hung on. Rappelling down, the basin disappeared, and he then released to fall onto a lower level path. Alfred sheathed his sword and followed, jumping house to house.

"What do I do?" asked William, but no one was there to advise him. He twisted and turned on the pebbles. He considered the church and looked around and finally said, "No," as he saw rocks. His back curled, and he scraped up one after another and hurled them below towards Adam.

The dead knight sprawled in front of him. From his bloody hands, William removed the bow and took arrows from the quiver. He leaned against the wall and aimed. The bow wobbled, and the arrows landed short of Adam. "Need to get closer," he said to himself.

Lurching forward, he ran one level down. One arrow remained. He steadied himself but shot it too high, and it deadened into a building. "Witen!" screamed William.

Alfred shot too, but his arrows thudded against stone buildings. Racing faster, Adam tripped on loose cobblestones and rolled. Alfred halted before the man. He unsheathed his sword and thinly sliced Adam's thigh where the muscle was the thickest. Standing over him, Alfred exclaimed victory: "This is for killing my men."

He lifted the sword to finish the man, but Adam cried, "Please, my lord, my wife and daughter."

Alfred froze. He shook and sheathed his sword.

"What's he doing?" asked William nervously.

Alfred formed a loop of rope to tie the man, but the hesitation bought Adam time. Adam recovered, grabbed a dagger from his belt, and repeatedly jabbed Alfred in the chest.

Alfred moaned. Adam loomed over him, took his sword, and finished the task with a sword thrust through the middle.

As he ripped part of Alfred's tunic and tied it around his thigh, Adam yelled a spirited tirade on revenge against the king's invasion. He then forgot the dagger and sword and ran. He pulled the rope at the city entrance, and the rusted, lattice gate slammed onto the stone. Jameela, Adam, and Yusuf mounted their horses and fled.

William skipped over the steps to Alfred. While grasping for air, Alfred confessed. "I'm so sorry, William. That man . . . that man," he struggled. "Why didn't I?" He coughed blood. "A similar man, six years ago, begging for mercy because of his family. But I killed him."

"Alfred," William said jerkily and scrambled to remove his surcoat. He stuffed a sleeve into Alfred's wound.

"William," moaned Alfred. "It's too late. Let it be."

William sobbed. "But your family, the stone."

"Forget the stone," his voice came harsh and shallow. "Justice, William. Tell my family I love them. And Miah. I'm so sorry, Miah."

As Alfred breathed his last, William said, "Rest in peace, Brother. You're forgiven."

William looked out towards the tide. The murderers had escaped. He searched for Jeremiah, but he wasn't there. He hopped on Alfred's horse and kicked and kicked him up to a trot to find Daniel and the Oths.

"Tell King Richard the stone was stolen," Daniel told William. "And Alfred is dead."

"What about the Oths? And finding Jeremiah?"

"We're staying here until we find him—and properly bury Alfred."

⊕ESPAIR

When the bell tower struck the next hour, Asser pulled branches apart to peek out from the bushes among the large stone blocks. He emerged and started to climb out.

"Asser," warned Jeremiah, "we don't know who's out there."

"Don't worry, Jeremiah. Me'll look."

Asser gingerly left the courtyard and walked to the fort wall. "It's clear," he said.

A strange silence lingered like a low fog drifting until finally dissipating when enough sunlight penetrated. There were no people, no birds, and no sounds.

Jeremiah spread his arms through the bush and saw a body Asser was approaching.

Asser moved towards the man. "It's a royal, me measure," Asser said. "Jameela was right—the king was after us too."

Jeremiah walked to the knight. His hand ran over the white shield, with blue *O* and blue lions. Thoughts of childhood rattled his mind: Martin and Alfred, singing their songs of glory with roars like lions.

He looked past the scabbard symbol as if answering his own unspoken question. His countenance fell as he remembered seeing a knight from the corner of his eye when he dove behind the stones and bushes in the courtyard.

That man was Alfred. He flew out into the courtyard and down the street. The others followed.

An aimless jog turned into a run. "Alfred!" he yelled. The others followed as the rudderless weight in Jeremiah's chest pulled him downhill in slants and around bends. He ran faster and faster. He yelled again, but this time louder. "Alfred! Where are you?"

The sloping road flattened, and he ran past bodies strewn in the market corridor. The city gate was shut. He stopped and looked around him, and there it was—a body emerged into view.

His already-dry throat swelled and thickened as nausea overwhelmed him. His hands trembled in fear at the possibility.

"Oh no, no, no, no, no," mumbled Jeremiah.

It was Alfred.

Jeremiah ran to fall to his knees by the body, with chest and belly wounds and a dagger lying beside it, and lifted his face to Heaven to scream, but no sound exited. His heart had stopped, and the tightness in his chest squeezed out any audible sounds. Only gibberish escaped. And then came gurgles of vomit, and then heaving. He held his nose, but the odors bubbling from his mouth escaped. He covered his mouth, but he couldn't stop. He heaved. Vomit blended with the blood on the cobbles.

In the cracks of the cobblestone were pebbles. He scooped a handful, and as he flung them towards building windows, he yelled. When the rocks missed and thudded against brick exterior, he bellowed a deeper, primal scream.

The iron pungency mixed with sickening sweetness reminded him of the incense his mum used to purify the kitchen after Alfred slaughtered pigs. He gagged again. The heavy stench lingered like rotten eggs and cabbage, clinging to his nostril hairs.

Why is he here? Why is he dead? Did he die because of me? These questions eclipsed his questions about Jameela and her sudden betrayal. *Why did Jameela leave? Didn't she hate them?*

Four dimensions blurred—blinded by sweat and sunlight, deaf from the roaring in his ears, and mute with a throat that would not obey his heart, Jeremiah's mind didn't know where he was. Sweat poured into his eyes, and the sunlight blinded him. He wanted to rise and run, and keep running, running from his brother's death, running from every woman's rejection, running from those who cared for him—his parents, his friends, and his brother, including this one. Full circle. Now his brother was gone.

How would Dadde react, or Mum? Once he thought about his father's reaction, he lost it. He retched again. Alfred was to carry on the family name. Who would care for his wife and daughter?

Jeremiah's natural inclination—his history— was to run rather than fight. Fine. Customers didn't buy his products? Forget them. Women rejected him? Forget them. Friends weren't being good friends? Forget them. Always moving on from rejection had its advantages, Jeremiah thought, but endurance in relationships is what his heart desired.

Should he fight or flee? He spotted a dagger in Alfred's chest. His hands trembled, but he managed to remove the dagger. Hunched over Alfred on knees, he grabbed it with both hands and turned it to rest the tip against his gut. He considered. . . .

Sunlight reflected off the dagger and directed into Asser's eyes as he thudded into the market.

Curled body. Hands extended. Sob, sob, final grunt. Slow-motion recoil.

"Oh, bloody curses," Asser said and sprinted, then dove for Jeremiah, knocking the dagger away from him. He tackled him until the dagger released, thudded, and skipped down the hill. They wrestled and rolled. Jeremiah punched him; Asser punched harder.

"Snap out of it, Brother!" Asser cried. He's dead. We have a mission."

Mo was silent. Padre, when he joined them, gasping raggedly after his own lagging trip down the steep street, expressed more sympathy, offering the usual pastoral words for such an occasion.

Asser found a water jug and dumped it on Jeremiah, who still writhed and groaned on the ground.

Gasping and dripping, Jeremiah was shaken out of the trance. Where he saw and smelled nightmare, the others found Alfred's real body. He had multiple wounds to the chest, and Padre composed his limbs into a posture of peace, covering his face with the neckcloth that had protected his skin from his helmet.

Jeremiah, calm now, looked about at his friends, at the curious townspeople, then palmed Asser's sun-burnt cheeks. He discerned compassion from Padre, confusion from Mo, annoyance from Asser, and curiosity from the townspeople.

He stretched his neck. A hawk, caught in a wind tunnel, glided in a circular pattern with an easy and smooth purpose, imperceptibly adjusting his wings to correct his course.

He decided. He would fight.

"Thank you, Asser. I needed that scuffle." He looked around at the others. "Thank you all."

"We're going to Aliyah's house to translate these scrolls," he explained, taking charge. "Then we're going to find Jameela. But first, I want to bathe." He started to stagger to his feet, every muscle and joint aflame and leaden.

"Jeremiah," cautioned Padre, "I think you need rest, emotionally and physically. Let's bury your brother first."

They stayed in town that night and ate with the knights and the family that had fed Alfred his last meal. Padre thanked the woman for Alfred's bag.

With little inheritance money left, Jeremiah, Asser, and Mo sought employment from a village pub. "Just like not-so-old times," Asser joked. They lodged in a local monastery on the town's edge, in its housing for free, courtesy of Padre's office—or rather, his willingness to ask the Mont Church for mercy and accommodations.

With permission from Daniel and the Oths, they earned enough money within three days to bury Alfred in the Mont Church cemetery. Jeremiah kept the sword but left buried the dagger with Alfred.

After the burial, Jeremiah asked his new brothers to leave him alone to pray. When was the last time he had prayed? The conversation was awkward at first but came easier the longer he stilled himself in silence and admired the spring flowers in the cemetery, showing their finest colors and aromas.

He wandered to the edge of the cliff ledge as the journey and his childhood memories twisted through his mind like a ribbon on a breeze. Saddened by his neglect of his family, he wiped tears, closed his eyes, and managed to articulate smoothly, "I am very sorry, Alfred, Mum, and Dadde—and even Grandpa. Please forgive me. I love you."

Confession came in choppy sentences when he later went into the church to write the letter.

Dear Mum and Dadde,

It's been a long time since we've spoken. I hope this finds you healthy and happy. However, with much sadness, I must tell you I buried my only brother—your son—today. He died, defending me from enemies who would have taken my physical life, and my emotional life as well, for they also took the woman I loved.

I'm very sorry for my actions before I left—I was completely selfish. My selfishness and cowardice prevented me from running after Alfred to defend him in battle. I hope to see you someday. Please forgive me. Please ask Lady Thèrèse and Maren to forgive me too.

Love,
Miah

He sealed the letter and handed it to Daniel.

"The Oths will seek justice for his death," assured Daniel.

"Thank you, Daniel," said Jeremiah. "What will you tell the king about the stone?"

"Do you know where they were going?"

"No," Jeremiah said with a tone of anger and annoyance in his voice. "I can't believe Jameela would—" He stopped.

"We'll tell the king it was stolen from you. And we lost the thieves. And that your team was lost—all of you killed."

"Thank you, Daniel."

"It's our code, Jeremiah. Queen Rachel would have wanted it this way. When you return to Witenberg, seek me in the royal stables. You can help us plan a mission for the stone—I'm sure the king will want it."

MOTIVE

Having the king's seal granted William immediate access to ships crossing the Witen Channel to Witenberg. As soon as he hurried the crew to unload Alfred's horse, he mounted and sped from the port to the castle.

"I have urgent news," William told the gate sentinel as he dismounted and wound the reins around a post. "I must see the king."

"No visitors," said the sentinel coldly, his eyes vacant behind a sheet of metal.

"You don't understand," explained William in a rush. "I was on Lord Alfred's mission." He showed him the king's seal.

"One moment," said the sentinel, and he walked into the guard shed.

The iron gates rolled back, and William ran into the castle. He went straight to Richard's chamber. Maids were cleaning the room.

"Where is the king?" asked William.

"Not here, my lord. One moment. Klara," called the maid as she walked to the balcony, "where is His Majesty?"

"Somewhere with Isabella, I believe," said Klara.

William ran to Vere's chamber. "Vere isn't here either?" he asked Vere's aide.

"No—try the bath house, my lord," said the aide, gesturing through the window to the bridge near the cathedral.

Across the bridge near the cathedral, he came to the bath house. Arriving there out of breath, he spotted him.

"Vere," William said to the man in the dressing room. "Is that you?" A man about Vere's size disrobed and wrapped a towel around him. The man neatly folded his uniform and put it on a wooden shelf. Then he looked over his shoulder.

"William?" Vere asked quietly, then waved him over. "What are you doing here?"

"I have vital information to tell you."

"Not here," urged Vere. "Wait until we're somewhere safer."

William came closer.

"I thought you were in Normandy," said Vere.

"I was."

"Lower, Father William."

"Why?"

"I came to spy on Richard's brother." From his bag, Vere unpacked a jar of cream and handed it to him. "There's another towel beside my clothes on the shelf. Apply this onto your face and join me."

William removed the stopper from the jar.

"No, disrobe first," said Vere. "I'll be upstairs. Through the door and up the stairs there." He indicated a door.

William took the cream and towel.

"No rocking," said Vere. "And no hat."

Vere tightened his towel and left.

William pulled off his boots and quickly dropped his trousers and undergarments. He stripped, wrapping the towel around himself and storing the rest of his clothes. Across his face he spread the cream that smelled of lemon and sugar.

Heel to toe, he slowly walked from stone floor up stone stairs to wet tile and joined Vere on a bench overlooking the heated pools below. Colorful wall frescoes depicted images of voluptuous women in various stages of undress.

Similarly attired, unaware of the two men in the gallery over their heads, George of Bath and John the Short sipped wine from mugs. "What about the blonde?" George asked and slapped John on the shoulder as a slender, light-haired woman wearing a short linen white dress with a gathered neckline passed. "Your wife doesn't know your taste for whores?"

"No, and keep that quiet, George. I prefer brunettes."

George chuckled. "She doesn't know? I should hire you to manage my money."

"I can't fool her all the time. Why'd you call me here, George?"

"For the women, my lord," said George. William remembered eyes twinkling as the man crinkled his face in an ingratiating smile.

"Yes, yes, but I came for business today. You have money. You can finance a revolt against my brother."

"I knew it," Vere whispered to William.

"Knew what?" As the steam rose, the lemon sugar burned, and William smudged the unevenly applied cream from his cheeks to his hands.

"Shh," said Vere.

George threw the mug, and a servant ran to pick it up. He removed his towel and hopped his flabby body into the pool. "It's better in here, John."

"Business, George. The money?"

"You're no fun—just like Richard. Yes, the Count," he said and sank lower into the water. "The Count said he would help fund the plan."

"But there hasn't been enough chaos to remove Richard—we need the system to collapse, George, so I can step in."

"John, money flooded in after the invasion, and more will tip it over."

The blonde returned and approached John, staring at him while she undressed. He shooed her and said slowly enough for her to understand, "Later, my lady. Business now."

Air pushed through her lips, and she stayed until she was paid with coins. "Richard needs to be gone now," said John.

Water splashed from a kick, and George pulled with his hands until he hoisted himself onto the ledge of the pool. He wiped his face with a towel and said, "John, go to France with your court. Act like you're seeking alliance with Phillip—Richard hates that."

John fiddled with the coins. "Yes, yes. Good idea, George."

"Richard feels Normandy is his home. After all, his mighty castle, Château Gaillard, is there. He never stops talking about it."

"Almost drained the bloody treasury," whined John, "and killed so many during construction."

"Correct, my lord—or soon-to-be king? It's almost finished. Richard will follow you to spy on you, and he'll inspect his fortress while there."

"But I need him farther away. I assume he'd seek revenge for Rachel, but he's been either too drunk to start war, or something else has changed."

George scooted beside John on the bench. "Perhaps you can curry favor with the archbishop? After all, Richard has been so distraught in remembrance of Rachel's desires for no more war that he wouldn't dare go on another Crusade."

"George, if we convince the Witen, the archbishop, and the pope to approve, Richard will be gone for a long time."

"Brilliant idea, John." George whistled, and a servant appeared with a fresh towel. "Thank you, my lady," said George.

John stewed for a moment, shaking his head.

Before George exited for the lavatory, he flashed a smile and called after him, "Find me after you return from France."

William pushed off the bench, but Vere flung an arm out to hold him. "Wait until they're gone."

"What will we do?" asked William.

"Does anyone else know you've returned?"

"A few sentinels."

"Good. The court doesn't know you're back. Get dressed, gear up, and go to Normandy. The king is meeting the pope at Château Gaillard."

"Why?"

"About the court's recommendation for another war."

"What do I tell him?"

"Tell him about their plans," said Vere, holding his hand out to demonstrate the scene of the conspiracy below.

William wiped his face and rubbed it onto the towel. "Can I tell you the urgent news now?"

"No, dress and meet me in my castle chamber when you are presentable. But wait until I've left." Vere swiftly rose and padded down the steps.

<hr>

In Vere's residence William told him about the stone, Alfred's death, and his suspects for Rachel's murder.

"It's all muddled, William. But each seems to be battling for power."

"And the stone," added William. "During the meeting, Richard mentioned his half-brother. Perhaps he wants it too."

"Perhaps," said Vere. "Rohad lost to Richard."

"What do you mean?"

"Though he was the oldest, King Henry and the Witen passed Rohad over in favor of Richard."

"Why?"

"Richard got the stone for King Henry."

"So Rohad wants the throne."

"Or revenge for Richard being chosen over him."

William handed the letter to Vere. "I can't decipher the code, but the three words point to that possible motive."

Vere read the translated Arabic and grimaced. "Are you sure this came from Adam and Yusuf? You know Richard. This could start a war."

"I'm not certain, but he should see it."

"Very well. Heed this advice though," warned Vere. "Gauge the meeting with the pope before delivering the news."

During a few days of rest with Vere, William updated his line chart to include Adam, Yusuf, George of Bath, John the Short, Rohad, and a man named the "Count." He took Alfred's horse on a ship back across the Witen Channel and followed a map to the Les Andelys castle. Envisioned and designed by Richard, the beautiful structure lay at a strategic spot alongside the River Seine in upper Normandy.

"No wonder he loved this place," William murmured at the sight of it.

No castle expert, but William marveled at the numerous fortifications, moats, and an inner bailey with rounded walls to absorb impact from siege weapons. He showed the sentinels the king's seal and walked through the gate.

Through the castle, sentinels led William to the pope's study. William knocked on the antechamber door. "Pierre," William said and extended a hand to the man serving as a receptionist. "So good to see you again." He loomed over the shorter, balding, round-bellied barber.

"Father William, what a pleasant surprise," Pierre said in a Parisian accent. "You've come to visit the Holy Father?"

"Yes, before his meeting with King Richard."

"I'm sorry, but the king is with him right now."

"Can you tell the king I have news?"

"News? Nothing else?"

"He'll know. Tell him it's about Luta."

"Very well. Wait here."

After a few moments, Pierre opened the antechamber door and quietly walked into a great hall beyond. The air held the familiar nutty and sweet fragrance of cardamom, nutmeg, cloves, and sugar— steeped in wine overnight.

From where he'd chosen a low stool, William could see Pope Innocent nibbling on pomegranate slices and green grapes. William heard him ask Richard, "You seem distraught. What troubles you?"

"Haven't you heard? My wife died." Richard trailed and resigned to mope outside on the portico.

"Father William," called Pierre, choosing his moment. "You may enter."

"I'm sorry, Richard," said the pope. "I know how much she meant to you. I think something else troubles you, though."

William stepped forward into the hall with the glued birch paper in his hand. "Father William, nice to see you again," called Innocent across the room.

William knelt and kissed Innocent's right hand covered in a white glove. "Your Holiness," he said with a slight coloring of anger and annoyance in the tone of his voice. "Yes, you as well."

"Father William," said Richard, his voice hopeful. "You have news?"

Hands on his belt and standing at the open doors to the balcony, Richard appeared to have lost weight; his tunic didn't balloon as much as before, and the crown sank lower on his head. He turned away, as if too overcome to deal with affairs of state, and surveyed symmetrical rows of vines beyond the castle. Further out, square green pasture plots distinguished the work of peasants from that of merchants on the cobbled street of the town.

"Yes, I have news, but I don't mean to interrupt."

"Then take some wine," said Innocent. "Barber, get our guest a glass. What's the news?"

Richard turned back quickly, and his eyes bulged in warning, as he tapped the lion medallion on his coat. William considered telling about Alfred and his list of potential suspects, but he wanted to observe the pope. Innocent squinted as if calculating a chess move. "It's nothing urgent, Your Holiness," said William. "An update on kingdom matters. I heard the king was close."

Innocent glided his hands through his thick brown hair and stroked his shaved chin. His gray eyes underneath thin eyebrows appeared older and tired. The distress from feigning unnatural charm and negotiating with too many moody cardinals and pompous princes over the years had coarsened his baby face more so than would have any sunlight he wished he had received, William thought.

"The court recommended war against Rohad a few days ago," said Richard, "and the archbishop blessed it. I issued a warning order to the military to mobilize."

"Only a warning order, Richard?" asked Innocent.

"My wife would've argued for more evidence to support war—that we shouldn't go to war for vengeance."

"The archbishop was correct to bless a war," the pope told him. "The stakes are much greater—a Crusade for people's souls, Richard, conversion to the one Church. We don't need to stop it."

Richard jerked backward and babbled nonsense.

Innocent held up a hand to calm the king. "Was it proven how she died?" he asked.

"No, not exactly, but she was murdered—that I know."

After a few steps forward, Innocent joined Richard at the railing. "I hate to say this, but maybe God wanted this? Rachel's death a sacrifice so God can be worshipped across the kingdom? Your brother has failed to keep order and failed to fully implement my conversion policies. Perhaps we need the Crusade."

Richard couldn't muster a word. He wandered to the balcony for a chalice.

"Do you really need wine right now?" sneered Innocent with a hard smile. He pulled out a white handkerchief. "Do you need this?"

Witen off, you virgin, mouthed Richard.

"I don't want much bloodshed," Innocent said firmly. "We need an overwhelming show of force to quickly vanquish the enemy. Deterrence is the goal—minimize the bloodshed. Remember, Richard, we fight for the kingdom of God. We fight to convert souls for eternal rest with Him."

"So, there's nothing we can do, then?" asked Richard.

"No, Richard, my son. This just war will happen. The Bulgarian king has already approved a war near his border."

Richard raised his forehead and lifted his eyebrows. "Oh."

"End it as soon as possible," Innocent said with the finality of a rehearsed actor. He then blessed the weary king and prayed for a quick victory.

"William, before you depart," said Innocent, "did you receive my thank-you note?"

William tugged his scarf, trying to remember. *I would have remembered getting a note from the Holy See*, he thought. "No, Your Holiness, I didn't receive it."

Underneath a Bible, Innocent pulled a piece of parchment. "It must be with the abbot then. I sent a courier. No matter. In haste, you left Rome six years ago, and I forgot to formally thank you for your assistance with the manuscript—which has become very popular," he said proudly. Innocent wrote a note and sealed it with a purple inked symbol. "Give this to the abbot."

William grinned, then said, "Thank you, Holy Father." He kissed the pope's hand, stuffed the note into his coat pocket, and fared him well.

Richard then went out to the reception hall, waving William after him. Just outside the pope's hearing, Richard said, "I need more to drink. Father William, follow me to the ice well."

So he has one here too?

William joined Richard on the ground floor after they'd both descended several floors beneath the reception hall. When the priest was standing eye to eye with the king, who had gulped down a whole glass of wine as the priest followed, Richard asked, "Do you have news of the stone?" For a brief moment, color had returned to Richard's face, but it soon drained in the cold dryness of the ice well.

"We're on the trail," William said and tucked in his upper lip. "The Oths will soon have it."

"Good news then! Huzzah!" Richard refilled his glass, then raised a glass for William and emptied the bottle into it. "I must tell the court. And we have a war to prepare."

William took two long sips while he composed himself, and he squirmed with indecision as the wine flushed his cheeks. He ran his hands across his face, then loosened the scarf around his neck. "I'm sorry, Your Majesty, b-b-but," stammered William, "I can't lie."

"Lie? What are you talking about?"

"The stone. They stole it."

Though he had lost considerable weight, Richard's presence and voice filled the room as he fixed his eye on William and boomed, "Who has it?"

William's mind spun. *Stoke the fire*, he thought. "Innocent is playing you."

Richard came closer. "William, tell me who stole the stone."

"Why go to war with an entire people to avenge her death when you could assassinate the murderers?" As the word rolled off his tongue, twinges of pain shredded across his stomach.

Richard laughed. "You've come a long way, Bouncy. You want to kill the murderers?"

"Adam and Yusuf stole the stone. And there are two more things, Your Majesty—"

"Wait—Adam and Yusuf . . ."

"The men from Rohad dressed in long tunics and fitted black bork hats."

"Those heathens who met with me?"

"What meeting?" asked William.

"A brief meeting. They brought me a gift and a duchy update."

"What gift?"

"A tapestry with a map of the kingdom—what do you care? And what's been in your hands?" He snatched the letter from William. "Swiggly lines? I can't read this rubbish." He paused, then said, "Upstairs to my study."

In brighter light, Richard grabbed a charcoal pencil and a piece of paper from his desk. He examined the letter more closely.

"I know," said Richard, "Witen columnar substitution."

GAEHUEEKL OTNGSRTBM ETEIROLIE VEUKTTPHV
IGQESCOEO HOENEUESD MHTMPPAEP

He read the keyword: ALKINDY and said, "Seven letters." With his pencil, he wrote the correct number for each letter according to alphabetical order. Then he jumbled the words into columns by the corresponding order.

GIVE HOMAGE TO THE QUEEN. THE KING MUST RESPECT OUR PEOPLE. TAKE HIS BELOVED.

"Adam and Yusuf," he concluded. As his voice reverberated around the room, he swept through the study as if the floor were an enemy to be stomped upon.

He howled with arms thrown and shouted, "This is how you repay me, Brother? I give you part of my kingdom and you take my wife?" He pounded his fists on the desk as if it was a drum, then flung the door open and yelled for the sentinels.

"Your Majesty," pleaded William, "consider the pope. He shouldn't know where the stone is."

Sentinels ran into the study and stood at attention.

"Prepare my carriage," Richard told them. "We're returning to Witenberg."

After informing Richard about Alfred's death, William proposed a nimbler solution—for Daniel and the Oths to capture Adam and Yusuf and return them to Witenberg for trial.

Richard forcefully dismissed it.

He called the council the day after his return.

"Earl Marshall Stewart," said Richard, "prepare to use overwhelming force. And do it quickly—I want to leave tomorrow."

After the council meeting, Richard requested William to his chamber. "You're coming with me," said Richard.

"Are you sure, Your Majesty? I'm not a fighter."

Richard sloshed ale with fitful swigs. The aging, sad dog Luta came to him, and waited obediently, drooling. Between gulps, Richard tore partridge flesh from the bone.

"My only true companion these days," he said and gave pieces of meat to her. "Sit with me, William."

William sat on the cold stone of the hearth. After she cleaned the bone, Luta plopped her massive body onto Richard's lap, and he talked to her like she understood. He complained about his day. When she sighed, he snapped out of it. "You're not Rachel," he muttered, and shoved her gently off his lap. She trotted away to fetch a rope to chew on.

"Yes, yes," he agreed. "William, you're correct when you say you're not a fighter. But you are the *investigator*." He spoke the word with confidence, as if he were painting in bold strokes. "You promised me you'd find the stone and my wife's murderers."

"B- . . . but," stuttered William, "you called for war."

Richard stood and searched for another jug. He found it buried among the clutter of his shipwrecked room—clothes intertwined with shredded papers atop the feather mattress. He accused Luta of tearing the documents, but then he mumbled that he was guilty of it himself. Gulping more ale, he finished the bottle. He tossed it, and it disappeared into the snow-covered clothes mountain.

Luta dropped a rope on his lap, backtracked and growled in noisy medium pitch with her tail wagging. He refused to play. "My wife! My son!" he wailed with head raised to the ceiling. He howled, and the gentle giant howled too.

Luta pushed the rope towards him again. Richard tugged it from her mouth and threw it as far as he could. She clawed underneath the tapestry until it ripped, but she retrieved it. She avoided the collapsing curtain and placed the rope on his lap again.

"Stop!" he shouted, yet she repeated the nudge with her snout.

"Leave me alone!" he ordered, yet she continued with high-pitched whines. He freed the rope and, with a mighty blow, smacked her in the face. She whimpered and cowered in fear. Tail between her legs, she scampered away. He fell onto his back and blubbered gibberish, as if William were not watching it all. She returned, determined, pointed her head to a clothes pile and rummaged with the rope in her mouth.

"Wh-what is it, girl?" stammered Richard. He wrapped his arms around her and hugged her as an apology. She dismissed him and sniffed until she seemed to recognize something—Rachel's scent, perhaps. She pulled at a woman's scarf. Beneath the scarf lay several letters from Rachel.

Richard snatched them up and clutched them to his face, eyes closed, breathing deeply.

If he didn't care I was here before—now he's simply forgotten me, William thought.

Hand shaking, Richard fumbled with the letters and blindly backed up to the bed to sit, but as he lowered himself to sit on the bed, his legs wobbled and head spun. He bounced off the bed and crashed onto the floor, striking his head on the stone.

Luta barked; William rushed to the floor and propped Richard's head on a pillow.

"Help!" shouted William. "Help!" He hurried to the door and yelled.

Vere ran in. "Call the doctor, Vere," said William. "The king fell."

As the doctor tended to Richard, William told Vere the story. "Where did Luta find the letters?" asked Vere.

"I don't know. It happened suddenly; the curtains fell, and Luta brought out a scarf. The letters were under it all." William pulled apart the curtains on the floor.

Buried underneath were papers, clothes, mugs, and empty wine bottles.

Clothes, he thought and remembered Rachel's closet.

"Excuse me, Vere," he said. Through the bedchamber into Rachel's closet, he found her vanity drawers opened, as if she'd just left the room, leaving the mess for a maid to deal with. But Richard had forbidden anyone in since the queen's death, they'd told him. He quietly pulled out each drawer. Through undergarments and other delicate fabrics, he ran his fingers over the surface of the drawer bottom—an etched circle. Then a line down the middle.

His thoughts flashed to the Levan tree. And a drawing. A drawing? *Yes*, he remembered, in the sacristy, where he had found her after the attack.

"Everything well, William?" asked Vere.

"Yes, basic investigative work." As he covered the secret compartment with clothing, he spotted another letter on the floor, its seal showing—a Church seal with a bishop's staff. The words *To William from Matia* shocked him.

Tension drew down the corners of his mouth, and a stutter bubbled out. He took a deep breath. *The-the archbishop*, he thought. *A letter to me?* His heart beat high with joy as he put the letter in his coat pocket.

"William," called Vere. "The king is awake. He asks for you."

William closed the drawer, mentally checked off how to be sure he'd restored the way the room looked before he entered, and went to Richard. Luta was licking Richard's head. "How are you feeling, Your Majesty?"

"How do you think, William? My head throbs, and my heart hurts. I'm drunk. My wife and son are dead." Richard struggled to untangle himself from the bed to stand, but Vere steadied him.

"We set sail tomorrow, William," said Richard. "Go prepare."

ARTFUL VENGEANCE

Rachel's death flung William into higher stakes, as a private investigator hired by the king for a mission that he couldn't share. The court believed he was a scribe, and the Night Watchers hadn't seen him for weeks. Yet, how could he pack for the voyage and bypass the Night Watchers to avoid questions? How could he ask the abbot for the pope's note? Or search the cathedral?

William hadn't the time to grieve Mati's death, nor Rachel's nor Alfred's; the world was spinning, speeding faster to some conclusion someone else was orchestrating. There was a puppeteer pulling the strings in a grand drama. And William was a player in this mystery play.

Six years. Six long years in Rome. Helping the cardinal write a manuscript on human misery had numbed his pain—a cruel antidote to the poisoning of a parched heart. But he had circled back to the beginning—he'd gotten nowhere, nothing advanced, and had no further clues to solving his friend's murder than when he'd first started. Now the queen and the kingdom's most celebrated knight were dead—murdered. Whom could he trust?

He rode to the abbey, quickly tied the horse, and entered through the ground floor. He told himself most of the brothers would be in the fields or in the winery.

After hastily packing and checking the Night Watcher schedule, he mounted the horse. He sped away as the voices of Stinky Feet and Fuss shouted behind him from the winery.

"May I see Chamberlain Vere?" William asked a sentinel once he arrived at the castle gates. The guards granted passage, and William knocked on Vere's chamber door.

"I need to sleep here tonight," William said and unloaded his bags.

"I assumed so, William," said Vere dryly, "now that you're the king's private investigator."

Vere took William to the guest room. "You know where the food is. I'll see you in the morning."

"Thank you, but the occasion calls for a glass of wine. I know my way . . ."

Under his arm, William carried his notebook. Whistling, he hurried to the ice well, grabbed a bottle of red, and entered the scriptorium. He salivated and licked his lips with zeal as he imagined what might be in the letter from Mati. His wiry, lanky frame came alive, and his heart beat hard in his chest and in his ears.

He sat at the table and looked where he could see Rachel's portrait. Though he held Mati's letter in his hand and dearly wanted to linger over it, connecting the dots to solve the murders became more important. His mind desired justice, but his heart pulsated for vengeance. In quicker beats, urges charged him to speed the investigation before someone else died.

Six years ago, in the grotto, the same feelings had come—buried emotions rising to the surface, pushing through blockages and spilling over the dam. Anger, sadness, loneliness, envy . . . and lust. Lust for a man, yes, but now lust for a passion, a passion to find the truth.

Guilt reminded him he was a priest and had taken vows. Jesus was nonviolent; he absorbed the pain. But warring thoughts bombarded his own human mind and heart—he wanted the murderers dead. Like a hero in the tales, he wanted to avenge this injustice.

He forgot about Rachel momentarily, got a glass, and poured wine. After taking a drink, he opened his notebook to the last page, where he had stored the letter he found in Mati's desk six years ago. While in Rome, he often pondered what Mati meant by the "one matter" and starting a revolution. Mati had discussed reforms to the Church but hadn't shared details.

Curious. It was carefully torn. The letter had an edge treated in a way he had only ever seen one person handle a document—folded and dampened, and then carefully torn straight along a ruler. Only one other person he knew was that meticulous—the pope. Mati was more spirited, creative—theatrical. He glanced back to his notes.

Before opening the letter he found on Rachel's floor, he rubbed his fingers over the top half and its smooth texture. He recalled the pope always wrote on the finest parchment. He dug deeper in his memory to six years before, when he'd been on his knees with dragon's milk incense bathing him in the grotto, when he'd read Mati's letter that condemned his eccentricity. Yes, it had been a letter like this one.

Wait.

He stopped.

This was parchment.

Mati's letters—the ones he'd written in the years before the letter that condemned him—were on coarser material.

"It's the same parchment!" he shouted. He leapt from his seat. He inspected the writing style, not just the hand; the words read monotone *and* stayed within the lines. Mati's writing had flair and color.

That wasn't Mati's writing; it came from the pope!

So now he had three letters supposedly from Mati, but the letter condemning his eccentricity he had torn to pieces and thrown away.

He attacked the letter he found on Rachel's floor, ripping the seal with a fingernail, and combined it with the letter from his notebook. The parchment texture matched, as if a single letter had been cut in two.

William trembled, and if he had to speak, it would have been in a stutter. But William prevented that agitation by calming his mind with lovely memories of Mati.

Why would Rachel keep this from me?

"My beloved Father William," he read aloud. He placed the first letter he had read previously on a table.

"My dear brother in Christ, you have been most gracious and

attentive to me. For fun, play with this homophonic cipher: use key phrase 'Ogdoad, Live the Eighth! Baptismal Crosses.'"

"Ogarc ca acomc o mioahrceab!"

"Thank you for the debate. Keep our conversations private. The king and cardinal cannot know yet that the plan is from me."

Before reading the last line, he remembered the solution to the puzzle: "About to start a revolution."

He stopped—the last line—the part before the letter was torn. "I'm sorry, but I need to address one matter, my friend."

Weak knees trembled, and his cheeks burned. This part was new. He read on to the missing section.

I have noticed over the months your affection for me. I am sorry, but my love for you is agape, storge, and philia—not eros love. You have become like a brother, but that is the fullness of our love. I hope this changes nothing between us, as I value your friendship. Can you help me? I need you.

Agape, Mati

William felt the color drain from his face, and he arched his back to gaze at the dark ceiling.

I thought he loved me! His heart plunged to Hell.

He straightened his back and hurled the wine glass off the table in a fury, then slid his back down against the wall until he sat, legs splayed out, undone. Eyes watered, and tears followed the fall. Tears began to course down his face.

Time stopped.

Constricted lungs made it hard to breathe. He rolled up to his hands and knees, but this time he refused to sob. He instinctively swept together the mess and organized the broken glass into a pile.

I'm as meticulous as the pope . . . the pope!

He rubbed his eyes and dried his tears. He read the letter again:

"I need you . . . love . . . a brother . . ."

My brother.

Complacent in the fifth circle of Hell while assisting the pope, he had bargained and finally accepted his anger at Mati. Now he confirmed the truth—Mati had not written any letter—the pope had written both—but why—why did Conti, Pope Innocent III, write the letters—why did he stop answering questions when puzzle pieces connected him to Mati's murder?

Plummeting to the last and ninth circle, he plotted his treachery and vengeance. Taking Mati's long-ago advice, he rummaged for blank canvas, then scribbled and sketched a rough draft of his manifesto.

The pope will fall.

He stayed awake in Vere's chamber and waited until the castle tower struck three. Then he went to the scriptorium and navigated through the darkened tunnel and into the crypt.

He stopped suddenly at a sound far away.

His sense of hearing radiated outward.

A clear tone rang from a bell, then faded.

He waited until the sound deadened.

Pius is reading now, he thought.

He struck a brimstone match against the tinderbox and lit a candle, then eased the grotto door open.

He slid his boots silently across the marble until stopping before the sacristy door. He turned both ways to listen for anyone who might be there, then opened the door and inspected the room. Down and up, left to right, he moved the candle, peering towards the back wall. Low down he saw the symbol—a circle with a line down the middle—the same symbol as was on the Levan tree, Mati's tree. It must be a clue, he thought.

After running his fingers across the symbol, looking for a hole or another clue, he stood and looked up. With a step forward, a floorboard creaked. His neck cringed, and he quickly backed up.

Something white peaked above the floorboard he'd just loosened.

He moved the candle closer and knelt. There were two notes. He read the first:

William, I found Mati's urn. Meet with the team. Discuss the pope. The Count is likely Dmitri of Falconer's father. More information: the code to my jewelry box.

He laughed when he read the code and her signature. "Naturally," he muttered.

The peace he often felt when alone in the silence of an empty church eluded him this day. Instead, a stillness settled like mist and alerted him to the foreboding calm he'd felt before his mother verbally berated him for the sin of wanting too much of her affection when his father was absent. That spirit of agitation pushed him forward.

Through the chapel, up the spiral stairs, and past the gargoyles, he stopped on a terrace to soak in the sweeping panoramic views.

All was quite lovely, he thought.

Love is what he wanted, what he desired, and what he yearned for. *Love or freedom*, he remembered.

The bookmark.

Witen! he thought.

He crouched on the terrace and kept a low profile until Pius struck the bell for the fourth time. Pius pulled his hood over his earmuffs and left, giving William a few moments until the shift change.

He watched a Night Watcher, someone he didn't recognize, greet Pius at Rose Abbey. He sped to the bells and examined them by candle-light. Pius had the bookmark, but what was that? A card? A picture of Innocent? He tugged at the card made of cut parchment until he was able to yank it out of a tight joint in the mechanism holding the bell.

He ran down the steps to the square. Another card was stuck beneath a cobblestone, halfway out, as if someone had tried to pull it but quit. He saw a symbol, a different one than on the sacristy wall—maybe a cross—or a circle—or a flower?

He also saw the torso—a picture of a king, but it wasn't Richard. "What is *this*?" he said aloud. "A card game?"

"You there!" yelled a Night Watcher. "Stop!"

William flew to the cathedral and into the grotto. He sprinted through the tunnel and then caught his breath in the scriptorium. He secured the card in his notebook and retreated to his room to gather his pack and satchel.

When he awoke from a short nap, Vere was knocking, telling him to meet Richard in the king's bedchamber, and to bring his things.

Richard looked healthier as he spoke to an assistant, like he had slept through the night. Maybe it was the old uniform or the glow of facing battle again. William excused himself to Vere, as the king did not yet look ready for him, and went to Rachel's closet for one last investigative check.

From the secret box, he pulled trinkets, letters sealed in purple ink, and a journal bound with string. He stuffed these into his satchel and met Richard where he waited for William to walk with him to the harbor.

Forgoing metal armor and a helmet, Richard wore only knee-length mail and a cloth brigandine, edged with a rich leather for shape, and garment fastened all about with small oblong steel plates riveted to the fabric. He clenched his sword with Rachel's name emblazoned across the leather grip.

Beside Richard was Daniel and the Oths.

Daniel's jaw was rigid with anger, and deep lines showed on his furrowed brow. When he turned and looked towards William, one by one, the lines unfurled, slowly, gently, and relaxed. His glance held a solemn command, then he nodded, as if to communicate justice for Alfred's death was forthcoming.

William wondered about Jeremiah and if Daniel had told Richard about him.

The shipyard buzzed with workers preparing vessels, sailors hoisting sails, and soldiers sharpening swords. Several climbed the masthead and set the main topsail, as high as the cathedral bell tower, to set the main topsail. "Eighteen point five yards precisely," Richard said, beaming.

As Earl Marshall Stewart and the fleet's commanders saluted Richard, William dropped his bag and stared in awe. The colossal ship shone in clear, bright colors, and its upper works were gleaming in deep, regal red color.

William craned his neck upward to the crest of the ship, seeing hundreds of ornate, emotive sculptures colored in many carved figures of indigo blue. "What are those by the boy?" William asked Richard.

"The boy sculpture?"

"No, the beasts beside him."

"Griffins," said Richard excitedly. "Maybe you'll see one when we arrive."

"And those?" William pointed to other carved beasts.

"There are other myths too, William—the savage and the troll, for example . . ."

Brothers from Rose Abbey laid their hands on each mast and sprinkled them with holy water. When they finished, Archbishop Eames raised a pendant and swung it three times and released it to fly into the water.

"William, the christening," Richard said and grabbed the bottle of wine the captain offered. After speaking a few words of dedication, he shattered the bottle with vigor against the bow. The sails filled with wind as sailors hoisted the final one.

"Ready, William?" asked Richard.

A chill swept across his cheekbones, and his rocking returned, at first just a wobble, then irregular bounces where he stood. A man in a brown robe, wearing a hat, waved farewell from across the shipyard.

"Yes," said William nervously. "Let's go."

"You'll be fine," assured Richard. "Seagoing is a healthful business."

As the soldiers and sailors stood in formation, William turned his gaze from calm waters to the dragon figurehead to a magnificent sculpture upon the prow—a woman robed in royal purple who held a white stone.

"Rachel," muttered William. He turned towards the shipyard, to see Vere was barreling down the street towards them.

"Your Majesty!" he called, "I'm sorry, but you must see this! You must disembark and see . . ."

William accompanied Richard to the Witenberg square buzzing with commotion. A tapestry hung from the bell tower.

In the weaving, richly filled with dark green meadows sprinkled with flowers, Rohad stood behind a nude Rachel with his pants down and a crown on his head.

An indifferent Night Watcher pulled the rope. Suddenly the bell tolled from the tower.

Sharp strike, sharp strike, sharp strike.
Ring up. Wait.
Long strike. Full circle.
Seven rings signify the hour.

"Fitting," said William. "Mati's and Rachel's number."

PART III

ONE WEEK LATER
LATE FEBRUARY 1198

WARRIORS

For Jeremiah, life was meaningless as the days dragged on, and whining intensified until his shock faded away.

With pub money, he bought an axe, a bow, and arrows. He reasoned he would be busy with the same kinds of activities Alf had always done: chopping wood, shooting arrows, and strengthening sword skills. Improving from zero to slightly above zero wouldn't be difficult.

He slugged up the hill towards the monastery, where he kept to himself out of fear his anger would affect others. In the courtyard, feathered scarecrows received the brunt of his rage, but his strikes weren't disciplined or precise, so the scarecrows lasted longer than they should have.

As he shot an arrow once, a foot slipped, and his face fell into the cobblestone. The arrow buzzed by the dummies and thudded against the glass. "I can't even break a window," he said wearily. "Even with a sharpened tip."

The faces on the targets morphed for him from Adam to Yusuf to Jameela. Those faces were full of anger, mocking, and sympathy—*no, pity, manipulated pity,* he thought as he lay there, miserable.

I fell for her? Why am I thinking about her?

Intent on pursuing Jameela, Jeremiah pushed down the pain he felt for Alf, preventing despair. But why pursue her? She had probably forgotten him. He should move on, but it was hard. A breeze cooled his forehead and his cheek but not his aching heart, and he climbed wearily to his feet.

The longing pulled and stretched him thin. Drinking had helped him bargain with God over the loss, but his friends held him accountable to moderation. Weapons secured, he mumbled the shanty chorus and went to his room.

When not working at the pub, Jeremiah joined Padre at the Mont Church to practice prayer. The spot of Alf's death and Jameela's betrayal became holy sites for him. The area to avoid? His own betrayal, the bush where he cowered from fear, the spot which provided temporary safety but prolonged his suffering in his remembrance of it. To help heal him, Padre had encouraged Jeremiah to burn the bush and plant a perennial.

Before this afternoon's service, Jeremiah rummaged through a bag of clothes gifted by the monastery. He found a long-sleeve white placket shirt with front pockets. He stopped and shoved it back in the bag and threw it into a corner, and it landed beside another bag.

Alf's.

Tied shut and stuffed into a corner, he had refused to open Alf's bag that waited for him ever since Padre had handed it to him. However, curiosity now courted Jeremiah; he reached, fetched the two bags, and then dumped them onto the floor.

He found his golden-colored cloak—with the key hole and key—from the night with Marianne. He pushed aside and separated the pile of clothes. He tossed aside some undergarments, but four items remained—three handkerchiefs and a woodcut.

He put a hand to his mouth; the woodcut showed a young Miah, Alf, Mum, and Dadde. Each handkerchief showed the same family symbol, the blue lion, but two held two swords, for a warrior.

The same symbol on Alf's cloak, Jeremiah remembered.

But what's that?

He pulled closer. On the other handkerchief was the outline of a small hand, as if a palm had been drawn on the fabric.

He pressed his five fingers into the image.

"Love you, Dadde, Maren," was embroidered into the cloth.

Remorse bubbled to the surface again, but he swallowed; this too he would try to bury.

A petite nun he'd seen display her fiery energy wherever she went in the monastery passed his room with Padre.

"Jeremiah," said Padre, "the abbot asked me to help celebrate Masses, so my friend will be praying with you too. Don't worry— you're in good hands. This is Louise, a picture of strength, grace, and beauty."

Padre hugged Louise, then left.

About Asser's height, she had a quick gait and a sharp tongue. *Maybe that's why she winks at Asser*, Jeremiah thought.

Her beady eyes examined him as if with a magnifying glass. "Are you open to healing?" she asked.

Jeremiah slumped and didn't respond.

She grabbed a small ruler in her pocket and sat beside him where he moped on the bed. She whacked him on the thigh and shocked him upright until he straightened.

"That hurt, Sister," whined Jeremiah, feeling like a little child again.

"Oh, stop it. No, it didn't. What's troubling you?"

Jeremiah didn't speak, so she whacked him again until he started talking. She listened to the short, though taxing, monologue on life's unfairness, then cut him off to admire the brilliant colors of azure blue and gold on the cloak on the ground and the handkerchiefs in his hands.

"You're ill at ease because you didn't get what you want? Enough of that," she said. She stood and looked out the window to watch where a goshawk was circling the monastery grounds.

"You've been training like your brother," she said. Tapping on the glass, with a smile, pointing down to his practice area, her eyes flickered, as she added, "But you're not quite to his skill level yet, I understand."

"Helps me deal with the pain." He tossed the handkerchiefs to the floor, rose from the bed, and found Alf's sword. Gripping it made him feel stronger, like a warrior, like his brother. He practiced thrusting.

"A carpenter is now a warrior?"

"My brother, Alf, died protecting me, and I retreated from fear. But I would've been killed instantly otherwise. So I practice; never again will I cower. I will fight."

"Fighting for revenge? With those arms?" The smile radiated mockery; she laughed and snatched the sword from him.

"Sister, give that back," he said, his voice toneless.

With smooth step and proper footwork, she danced and thrusted into the air with intense focus.

His mouth fell open. "Sister, that was amazing. But your arms are weaker than mine."

"Thinner, yes, but not weaker." She pointed to her head. "Mentally, I'm stronger than you, Jeremiah."

Jeremiah sat again on the bed and listened as she told her history—a wife and mother, then a widow ten years before, after bandits killed her family. To assist with the grief, she learned self-defense. Later, she harnessed her anger to fight for the faith and train others.

"Your brother trained physically, yes, but more importantly, he trained mentally. Padre told me he led the knights of the King's Special Guard Corps; his was a profession of arms."

"He was a warrior who fought for a war of division—not unification."

"I agree with you—it was an ill-advised war—but I imagine your brother fought for ideals, not for the king's power. Ultimately, he took orders from the king."

Jeremiah snorted. "And what of you? Are you a warrior?"

"Yes, Jeremiah," she said and turned resolutely with her back straight and chin up. Her voice came as sharp as her heel clicks. "I practice daily with the sword and hourly with the heart. If you live by the sword, you'll die by the sword, but the sword will defend until the Word transforms injustice."

"Loaded word, Sister. One man's injustice is another man's justice."

She handed him the sword and said, "It's a complex subject. You're right, but it depends whether you follow subjective or objective morality."

"What do you mean?"

"Do you determine right and wrong based on your feelings or thoughts? This changes on any given day as the wind blows. Objective, on the other hand—"

Jeremiah broke her off abruptly. "Let me guess. Jesus is the fixed reference point? And his morality never changes."

"Exactly," she said. "You've been listening to Padre. I suggest you study the prophets he recommended. A warrior takes initiative and fights for what matters most: the noble and eternal things. Warriors have purpose. What is your purpose, Jeremiah?"

He looked to his empty palm for the stone, then tugged his tunic at his longing heart. He knew his eyes betrayed him. His empty gaze revealed the desire.

She lightly tapped him on the thigh with the ruler. "Pursue that purpose, Jeremiah. Women like warriors, but don't push it too far. And don't surrender or easily surrender and become passive. Cowards are worse."

Jeremiah nodded and continued, "My father and I often argued with Alf; Alf fought in defense of the faith, extending Christendom by uniting Church and kingdom."

"Perhaps misguided," she said. "Forceful conversion through conquest is never as beautiful as voluntary submission through repentance and grace. But what of his heart?"

"I don't know." He clutched the sword with both hands.

"And what of your heart? Still stone cold? Too stiff-necked? I know his death was a shock, but you haven't forgiven him."

Jeremiah stood with a hard smile and audible nasal breaths. "Thank you for the wisdom, Sister."

Sighing, she said, "Very well." Scooping to take up the cloak and handkerchiefs, she asked, "Jeremiah, do you want these?"

"I have no use for them, Sister. Take it all. I'm heading outside to practice."

"See you at the planting."

"Wait," he said with one step towards the door. "Leave this." He took the handkerchief with the handprint.

·———·

The service healed and acted as the final burial for Alf. Jeremiah tried to let go and forgive, so he accepted it all on the surface; he would learn to live with the agony. The bush burned longer than planned due to a cold, light rain shower, but Jeremiah shivered through the catharsis cross-legged on the ground, with arms wrapped under a cloak, until the last twig turned to ash.

After prayer, he planted a pine-tree seedling. Others departed, but Louise remained with a hand on his shoulder. "It will grow, Jeremiah, if we water. But we may need to replant later in the spring."

A hawk dove and perched on a scarecrow.

"Jeremiah," said Louise, "want to learn how to hunt?"

"Hunt?" he asked. "With what?"

"With her," she said, pointing to the hawk.

"You're serious, Sister? With a hawk?" he asked in raised tone.

"Yes."

A thin-lipped smile moved the curve of his mouth. "Thank you for the joke. I needed that."

"I'm not joking, Jeremiah. The sport is called falconry—your brother likely learned it in his training."

"Thank you, Sister"—his voice broke in a righteous tone, remembering an argument with Alf—"but I'm not interested."

"You know where to find me," she responded, "when you're ready."

The rain showers passed, and he spent the rest of the day wandering the town like a pilgrim, to the summit, through the winding streets, and in the market.

The following day he left the monastery to buy bread and beer. Vendor to vendor he wandered, learning these essentials had risen threefold in cost. He handed over the coins, and during the transfer, he realized how soft and bendable these newer coins had become.

The destitute pounded on the fort wall, crying for food; near the monastery, beggars slummed for crumbles. Some were granted access. Jeremiah walked to the hall and sat beside a man with peasant's clothes but the cloak of someone wealthier. Yet he sipped soup hunched over like the other beggars.

"You were once a lord with knights?" asked Jeremiah.

"Yes."

"Why are you here?"

He sipped again.

"Where are your peasants? Where are your vassals?"

"Transferred."

"What was your crop?"

"Wheat."

The conversation was like pulling teeth and missing the wrong finger placement on a violin.

The lord hugged his wife and tousled the head of one of his children and told part of his story.

"They told me I went beyond the bounds. At first, the peasants and I grew grain on the king's land to feed the animals—more than the capital treasury allotment. I refused to pay the tax penalty."

"What happened?" asked Jeremiah.

"The peasants were already suffering, I told the king. The coins were becoming worthless."

"But the court didn't agree?"

"No, they said I was selfish. I could've sold grain into the market."

"But you didn't."

"It didn't matter. That wasn't my land, they told me. The peasants belonged to the king. Think of the others in the kingdom, they repeated. The market price would be affected."

"What happened to your land?"

"There was burning, then seizure, then transferring. I was left with nothing." He lowered his head.

"Precedent, they said when the court had ruled from thereafter. The king could regulate any commerce. Guilds would be affected. No longer were they private associations—they would report to the treasury."

Jeremiah thought of his parents and Elfred's criticisms of the king. "My father would sympathize with you."

"Thank you," the lord said and returned to eating.

The beginning of Lent, purple light brightened the darkness inside the hall and guided Jeremiah upstairs to the church, where Padre waited. Jeremiah questioned, and Padre taught him Scripture.

They studied the prophets Isaiah and Jeremiah. A King was coming, one that would bring universal justice. Maybe Jeremiah should redirect his longing to Him. Fitting, he also learned about Moses, whose statues enticed Jeremiah to study his life: Moses had led his people from slavery, then to freedom; from centralized rule to more decentralized governance. Moses had integrity and strong conviction, and he made courageous moral choices, with a servant's spirit and righteous leadership.

Trust and follow Yahweh. That was the message.

"I enjoy teaching, Jeremiah," Padre said. "But Sister Louise will be better for you. With the increase in beggars, the abbot asked me to help with the sacraments full-time during Lent. Please ask Louise to train you," said Padre. "And take this."

"Your cloak and brooch?" he asked reverently.

"Yes, you can have it. Use it when you pray."

"What about money? Working in the pub?"

"Don't worry about it—we'll have enough for the journey."

Jeremiah went to the nun's room and stood outside the open door in the corridor.

"I accept," she said, trying to hide a grin once she heard Padre's proposal for them. "Meet me at midnight in the crypt—with this." She held out a linen net.

"Sister, but don't we need to sleep? And it's Lent—doesn't seem right."

"Jeremiah, this is your first lesson: trust me."

"Yes, Sister." He slung the net over his shoulder.

Halfway down the nave and double stairway, he saw the warm glow given off by the candles in the crypt. The lights were placed high on bare stone columns, lifting his vision beyond the arch to the stone coffin and behind it, where Louise was kneeling in prayer behind a marble altar.

He dropped the net at her feet. "I'm here, Sister Louise," he said with a false forced smile.

Turning, she said, "Lower your hood, Jeremiah, and join me."

He knelt beside her.

"Do nothing but stare at the cross—no thinking. Pay attention to your breath."

He shuffled on his knees and grumbled. Several uncomfortable minutes in, she hummed in measured rhythmic sets of three. The crucified body on the crucifix before them communicated death; his mind wandered and went to other worst-case scenarios, replaying recent events.

More time passed, and her humming grew louder. A tingle shot from his head to his left arm and leg; he shook his restless feet, then stood.

"Come back, Jeremiah; remain fixed on the cross."

Humming turned to words, but the beat remained.

"Abba, You are good, good, good," she sang.

Rather than slowing down, time sped up; rather than slow melody, the lyrics tore through. "You are good, good, good."

The stillness suffocated him; thoughts blew like a trumpet in his head. "You are good, good, good."

He was not good—Alf gone, Jameela gone, the stone . . .

"Take my hand, Jeremiah."

He slowed his breathing as she sang the Lord's Prayer. "The hour has come; we are finished; it is finished."

He raised his hood and gripped the net, feeling its rough texture in his hands.

"The courtyard at sunrise, Jeremiah. Bring the net." Her voice was precise and earnest, as she added, "What do you desire? Love or freedom?"

Those words again!

He feigned attention, very sleepy as he dragged his feet from the crypt to his room.

The next morning, he reluctantly shuffled under arches and into the courtyard colored of pink and white stone. The net hung heavy around his neck, and cold nipped his nose. Overhead, goshawks in juvenile plumage circled.

"They look repaired," he said through chattering teeth.

"Good morning, Jeremiah," Louise said cheerfully.

"How are you not tired?"

"I slept well. Do you like my practice dummies?"

"Yours?" he asked and followed her jogging around the courtyard.

"Yes," she said and ran another lap. "The jugs have water, when you need it."

"Why are we here?"

"You've become lazy."

"Understandable, right?"

"No," she said and stopped. "Release the net and lower your head."

He loudly exhaled and said, "Fine."

After a morning exercise in gratitude, she handed him a wooden sword. "To warm up, we'll do simple exercises. Focus on my hand and bounce lightly."

Footwork slow and arm heavy, he received many pokes in his chest, enough to bruise later. Again, he whined, "Sister, why are we here? What are we doing?"

A hawk dove in and landed on the roof.

"You've become lazy, Jeremiah—your heart, mind, and body. We'll train, and you'll become disciplined."

"Why?"

Warmed by the jogging and sparring exercise, they weaved in and around scarecrows with their wooden swords thudding against wood, up and down, up and down, the swords seesawing.

Losing breath, he stopped.

"Break time," she said. "Take water."

He plopped to the ground in a heap.

After a short break, Louise put on thick gloves. "Now with your hands, Jeremiah."

"Your deepest desire, Jeremiah," Louise said in between calls to punch her left, then right, then left hand. "What is it? You need to be prepared for the long journey. Each day will be the same: prayer, physical activity, Mass, breakfast, physical activity, dinner, prayer, studying Scripture, supper, prayer, and midnight vespers in the crypt."

They sparred around the courtyard, Jeremiah distracted by the hawk, overwhelmed by this program, and the bird stared beyond him to a small bag that was wriggling, moving, opening—a mouse escaped and scurried across the pavement.

"Oh," blurted Louise. "Too soon. Jeremiah, ready the net."

He ran towards the mouse and asked, "What do I do?"

The hawk dove with its talons and captured the mouse.

"Throw the net, Jeremiah," she ordered. "Now!"

The net caught the end of a wing, but the hawk ascended and soared out of sight, squawking as if to mock the meager attempt.

"Second lesson," she said as she rose, "is failing forward. Come on, back to the sword."

They moved onto dummies, and she focused on his footwork. "You will make mistakes, Jeremiah, but keep them small, move on, and apply the lessons learned."

His lungs burned, and he rested on his knees.

"Better," she said. "Time to eat."

They walked to the large hall. A bald brother in a brown robe dipped a ladle into soup and poured it into bowls. She accepted the bread for herself but refused a slice for Jeremiah.

"No bread. For the next forty days, only soup and water for you. And no seeing your friends."

"What happens on the last day?"

She smiled. "Talking, a feast, and a ceremony, assuming you pass."

They maneuvered around a long table to the corner and sat on a bench away from the others. "No talking. You'll eat quickly too; I'll tell you when we leave." After slurps and commotion, brothers stacked bowls, then left the hall in rapid fashion.

"Time to go," she said and disappeared into the kitchen. Returning with a bag filled, it suddenly twitched.

"Another mouse?"

"Very good, yes. Take it."

Out in the courtyard, Sister Louise placed gloves, straps, and a hood on top of a metal cage she'd carried out there. "Normally, it takes a long time to trap one of them, but maybe we'll get lucky."

Outside, she lowered the cage in the courtyard. She set the cage down on the mud-and-straw practice ground and ordered, "Release the mouse inside the cage."

He emptied the bag into the cage, and the mouse scurried to each corner of the cage, seeking a way out. "You'll be tired and hungry in the future, Jeremiah. And your mind will go to darker places. Now, ready the net . . ."

Ahead of them, the hawk glided, watching. It maneuvered to slow her descent, then she perched on a scarecrow.

"The net and hood, Jeremiah." She put the glove onto her left hand and backed away from the cage, motioning to him to do the same. "Get ready."

"Darkness?" he questioned.

"Yes, the first week of the exercises, we focus on sin. You need to discern evil with all your senses so it becomes second nature to your perception. It will then be easier to fight, and to overcome."

The hawk swooped in, talons extended, and its wings flapped furiously when it became entangled with the bars atop. Stuck on the cage, the bird tried to grab the mouse inside, but the creature flattened in the corner.

"Throw the net, Jeremiah!" Louise called, and he hurled the net over the hawk and cage together. Wings flared but slowed as Louise came close and cleared the talons stuck from the wire.

"Good girl, good girl," she said, wrapping her arm carefully around the hawk, its head bent down by the compressing net, pacifying it for a moment and moved her to her glove. Then Louise told Jeremiah, "Put on the other glove, and then I'll hand her to you."

Her? How can she tell? he wondered. Cold bones came alive, and his heart fluttered as he put on the glove, eyeing those fierce talons. "Wow!" he said. Louise pulled back part of the net, the bird still safely contained with her arm against her body, placed the small hood over the bird's head, put a chain around one of its ankles, then removed the rest of the net and transferred the suddenly quiet bird and its confining chain to her gloved arm.

"What's next?" he asked.

"Manning—she needs to get accustomed to humans. You'll feed her the mouse now, and you'll feed her at the same time each day after weighing her. We need to be sure she stays healthy, so we need to feed her the right amount."

Without thinking, he hummed in cycles of three.

"Give the mouse to her. Be calm."

He put his ungloved hand in the cage and closed it over the mouse, then hung it by its tail from his gloved fingers, the creature squirming and fighting. Slowly, he lowered the mouse. He held it before Louise and she nodded at his positioning.

"Steady," she said, and removed the hawk's hood.

Snatch! The hawk's razor-sharp beak snapped the neck of the

mouse, and down her throat it went. "Very good, Jeremiah!" exclaimed Louise. "Now stroke her feathers."

"Good girl, good girl," he said.

"Think about a name, Jeremiah, for her."

"Don't need to because I already have one."

"Oh?"

"Yes—Louise Rûaḥ."

She tried to hide it, but her lips curled. She smiled enough that her teeth showed.

"Very well. Good choice—she won't disappoint you. Did Padre suggest that?"

With an arm around her shoulder, Jeremiah smiled and said, "He taught the Hebrew word for spirit and breath." Pausing, he lowered his head, then lifted it. "But I chose Louise, the name of my teacher."

Her rosy cheeks became a little rosier with her merry smile.

"How long does manning take?" he asked.

She petted Rûaḥ and said, "During the first two weeks, we'll spend much of the day with her, then our time will shorten. You need to stay disciplined with her feeding and hunting."

A chattering sound, something like a bird, screeched from a tree overhanging the wall into the courtyard. Rûaḥ snapped her beak and completely turned, her head stilled and focused on the sound. The alarm call beat accelerated from a squirrel, and Jeremiah pictured a longer, bushier tail dangling from her mouth.

"The rest of this week we'll hunt," continued Louise. "After lunch, you'll help move my perch and box to your room."

"You already had one?" he asked.

"Yes," she said, the suggestion of a smile hiding her pride. "I'm a falconer, Jeremiah."

"The legends are true," he said with the perceived answer in the tone of wonder betrayed by his voice. He imagined sculpting a figurine, a woman clad in a purple cloak, with a sword in her right hand and a falcon on her left. "A master falconer," he stated. "Who taught you?"

"One of the best," she answered promptly. "Now go. Lunch, then you'll build the outdoor perch, perhaps improve upon it with your carpentry skills."

+ —— +

The construction continued past supper, but Jeremiah enjoyed the feel of each cut, the heft of the hammer, and the precision of each nail immensely. Once he had taken the hawk into his room and gotten her settled, he shut the latch and said, "Good night, Rûaħ."

He walked downstairs.

A golden glow again brightened the crypt, and the room was hazy. Flames flickered around a ring of stones, and the room smelled of rotten eggs. Jeremiah coughed and waved his hand in front of his nose. "Sister, what's that awful smell?"

"Hell," she said. "Kneel and close your eyes."

The crucifix had been removed, and Louise pushed the stone coffin slab aside, and he focused on the skull and bowl of yellow powder below.

"Come close," she ordered. "Tonight, we discern evil. You can't defeat what you don't know."

Hunger roared in Jeremiah after his skimpy meals, and crimson washes appeared against the darkness in his view, like on a summer afternoon. "Stick out your tongue and taste the sponge."

Sour, tart—vinegar, he tasted. He coughed, then licked his lips while scrunching his face.

"People don't like discussing sin," she started, "because often those preaching, those judging, are hypocrites. But we're all sinners."

She moved from his right to behind him, to left and back and forth, and in soft and loud tones, softer and louder, she taught.

"Satan works in riches, in honor, and, most dangerously, in pride. Like a snowball, it builds and builds until an avalanche flattens you."

I wish I were outside, he thought and wiped beads of sweat from his forehead.

"Fear, a lie, a worry—it builds and builds. He'll tell you it's not bad, that it's only a small matter. With one hand he shows you pretty things, but with the other hand he knifes your back. The poison slowly permeates until all your veins are ice and your heart ice-cold towards others. 'You're most important,' he says. 'God will take what you love and leave you wanting.'"

Alf and Jameela.

The fire crackled as she placed another log upon it, and the stench intensified with another scoop of yellow powder.

"When you fight and ask the Advocate to help, Satan grows stronger and digs in, deceiving you, telling you to stay attached. You think you've beaten your sin, but it roars back with vengeance, with seven more demons."

Images of The Grouse and fornication streamed in his memory—temporary bliss followed by vomiting. Like empty gopher holes always ready to lame man or horse unwittingly crossing a field, so were the unexpected holes across his heart.

Raising her voice, she said, "Let go and surrender to Christ."

His heart accelerated, and his eyes opened and zoomed to the enlarged sockets in the skull. He imagined cockroach legs moving back and forth like a pendulum, from inside the skull and out and back in. He grabbed his neck—and felt only raised hair there, he confirmed—then he exhaled deeply.

"Sin is separation from God, like missing the mark with your arrow. One act leads to another and to another, rationalization trumping reason, until you feel no remorse, until you're alone, harassed until full of anxiety. Jeremiah, Hell is torment because God is absent—love is absent. And the most treacherous thing? The most evil, devilish scheme? We choose this."

She scooped a fistful of holy water from the crypt font and poured it onto the powder and fire. "Take my hand, Jeremiah, but keep your eyes closed."

From the crypt she guided him around columns. "Satan leads

us to chain ourselves, attach ourselves to sin, and he confuses us in mazes. We become restless because we always want more—another toy, the prettiest jewel, satisfaction."

The spirit of agitation clenched his hand and quickened his breath.

"We substitute these objects for our hearts' true desire—the love from Abba."

This is all Padre's fault, belted voices in his head. "What about your suffering, Sister?" Jeremiah snarled, bracing himself and planting his feet. "You train me, but you couldn't protect your own family."

She yanked his arm to propel him forward, as if he were a stubborn dog. "I grieved for a long time, Jeremiah. I became angry and yelled at the Lord in fury. How could He do this? I was *good* and obeyed His commandments."

A measured, lower tone went through each syllable of his voice. "Because you weren't good *enough*, Louise."

In longer strides, she pulled Jeremiah along with her as she paced the room.

His gut churned, and his mind clouded in a vision. Gwyn's saucing broom popped into his focus. She stirred a yellow mixture. Thick as sludge, it clung to the broom, and the acrid smell of sulphur and vinegar gushed over him. He pushed Gwyn aside, and she fell . . .

Padre and Louise each touched one of his shoulders, but he flinched and shook them off. Their faces looked like blobs to him, smeared over by his misery . . .

Thoughts drummed through him. *Hit them!* screamed the voices.

"Kneel and open your arms," ordered Louise.

Rusty like weathered iron, his knees locked, and he stayed as he was. His vision broke, and he returned to the present moment.

"Now!" she yelled.

He groaned, and his knees came unhinged with her push. He opened his eyes to see that a statue of Mary with open arms stared at him.

"The love of a woman, the love of a mother, Jeremiah. Like a warm blanket, the Spirit comforts us, consoles us, and provides wisdom. Accept the love. Choose love."

Bits of powder clung to his nostrils and escaped with a sneeze. Beneath the ribbed and vaulted ceiling, his eyes adjusted to colorful frescoes above him.

"Satan is a false lover and hides behind empty promises, vanishing in our time of need," Louise went on. "In our darkest hour, in our moment of deepest pain and isolation, Christ descends and enters our Hell to pull us from the brink—if we let Him—if we ask."

Now cold, Jeremiah's lips trembled, and he ground his teeth.

"We must constantly guard, and examine ourselves, and, most importantly, pray. Like we train any muscle, we must strengthen our soul through prayer."

A bowl of holy water sat on the floor next to the Mary statue. Louise took it up and dumped it over his head as she spoke. "Grace overflows like the water. By the end of the spiritual exercises, you will know love and joy."

Cold as ice, the water soaked his hair, and he shivered.

"The hour has ended, Jeremiah. Let's get you warm. Stand and join me in prayer."

COOKIE

William woke to the sound of men singing. He dressed in his room, in a cabin shared with military officers and Daniel and the Oths.

William wobbled onto the deck. Water foamed at the stern, and wind filled the sails. Over a hundred mariners and soldiers, he guessed, ran in place to the barked commands of their superiors.

Some looked as young as fifteen and dutifully responded to peer pressure when jeered at to climb the topsail mast and shout glory to the kingdom. Richard stood beside the ship's captain on the quarter deck and cheered on the newest recruits.

The formation broke, and the ship became a hive of activity with maintenance and battle drills. William watched, ate heavily salted meat, and sipped at a liter of beer while idly pretending to write in his notebook. Then, a bell rang, and sounds from the lower deck rumbled.

"Duty change," said a frail man who took a seat next to William. As he lowered, something creaked and cracked as he moved. "Not sure what's louder," said the man, "my ankles or these new spars."

"Spars?" asked William.

"Those stout poles for the masts." The man pulled a bag from his pocket and offered some to William. "Dried peas?"

"Sure," William said, noticing ash smudged on the man's misshaped, blackened nose. Beneath his hat were sunken deep eyes.

"Name is Sebastian, but everyone calls me Cookie," he said.

William popped a pea into his mouth. "Thank you, Sebastian. I presume you're the cook?"

"Yes, sir—been on and off ships for years. And been in many fights, as you can see." He held out his broken knuckles for inspection.

"Cookie," William said distractedly as he closed his notebook and stood, "I must go."

"I didn't get your name," said Cookie.

William lifted his hat and looked towards Richard coming his way. "Scribby," said William hurriedly. "I'm a scribe."

"Nice meeting you, Scribby. I'll see you around. There aren't many like us on board."

"What do you mean?"

"A cook, a scribe, a barber, and a few knights. That's it. The rest are military."

"I know," said William, his voice tired.

A week at sea, and William hadn't slept more than a few hours a night. Thankfully, he had three liters of ale daily to forget the recurring tossing, turning, and smells that churned his stomach.

Fish stench seeped into each man, his breath and his clothing and his flesh, like armor as the stink wafted from basket to basket over men sleeping seven abreast in their quarters.

✦———✦

"Thanks for the peas, Cookie," William said, as he did every morning after his early "watch" and visit with the cook, then went to Richard's cabin and waited for him in a spacious room with real beds, furniture, and tableware. The king always got a late start.

"Having a bit better time of it than the seamen?" asked Richard heartily as he sat at the table. He dismissed the sentinel assigned to him and poured ale into a mug. "What's the score again?" Richard asked and opened the backgammon set.

"Three to nil, Your Majesty," William said, as with bored amusement. "You must have magic dice."

"Not magic, Father William," joked Richard, "but I do have skill and strategy."

"Your Majesty," William asked nervously, "we're not calling me 'Father,' remember? Helps me with my cover."

"Yes, I remember," Richard said as he rolled and removed two checkers.

"No one knows I'm investigating?"

"No, *Bouncy*," said Richard irritably. "How many times have I told you?"

"I'm sorry—I'm on edge from all the sleepless nights."

"William," Richard paused and eased his shoulders, "if I've moved on from Rachel's death, so can you."

A muffled laugh traveled to the back of his throat. The first day on ship, Richard had challenged soldiers to sword practice. Facing the king, many feigned combat and took minor blows. His pride inflated as his confidence grew, and anger at Rohad grew into a determined vengeance. Soldiers set up games around the ship with images of Rohad behind various animals as target practice for arrows, pissing, and spit.

"She would want this," said Richard.

"A war?" asked William skeptically.

"No, not war, *Bouncy*. An overwhelming show of force. Plus justice. That's why she convinced me to summon you. She told me you'd help uncover the plot."

"The plot?" William asked and twirled hair that flowed down his neck. "I don't understand." *Why has it taken so long for him to speak of all this?*

"I'm not stupid. Your friend's murder and my wife's. They must be connected."

"Oh," said William, trying to make his voice sounding surprised.

"Plus, at the Les Andelys castle, despite my despair, I saw the way you looked at the pope with a feeble sneer of your lips and the way you spoke to him with a coating of mockery."

Thoughts raged inside his head. He felt uncomfortable. Did Rachel tell Richard something? Did he find something? William opened his notebook and nervously scribbled some lines.

"You despise him like I do." The words rolled off Richard's tongue like velvet carpet spread for formal ceremonies. "And you're a bit afraid of him—and God," he said crisply with color.

"What about the stone?" William asked, wondering when Daniel had presumably told Richard about Jeremiah. "And Jeremiah?"

"Divine justice, William. Daniel confirmed what you told me— that Adam and Yusuf stole the stone from Jeremiah. He also said Jeremiah and his team were killed."

"Are you after the stone?"

"I'm after justice, William—Adam, Yusuf, Rohad—and the stone. The Oths will find the stone."

A knock came to the door. "Time for breakfast," said Richard. "I'd like you to join me today, so I ordered it for you as well. Come in, Cookie."

"Porridge, gentlemen?" asked Cookie.

"Yes and please. Thank you. Do you have sugar? I'm in the mood."

"Of course, Your Majesty." Cookie untied a bag and poured lumps into their bowls. As Cookie stirred, William noticed unusual attention paid to his satchel.

"That's enough, Cookie," said William. "Thank you."

"Of course, sir," he said respectfully. "Will there be anything else?"

"No, but thank you," said Richard kindly. "We'll look forward to your dinner."

Cookie bowed, and his hat shifted when the ship rocked. Pieces of something brown clung to his dark hair, and as the ship settled, Cookie brushed himself off and grabbed the tray. "Good day," he said.

After the door closed, William crunched on sugar and ate the ale-cooked porridge. "He looks strangely familiar," said William.

"Who? Cookie? Haven't you seen him each morning? Is something the matter with you?"

"I'm fine—but something feels off."

"You may have him confused with the barber; they're brothers."

William looked at his satchel and kicked it farther underneath the table. "You're right. To be honest, Your Majesty, I'm surprised how happy you seem."

Richard bore off the last checker and exclaimed, "I win again."

"I know . . . ," trailed William.

"Why don't you join the seamen later and piss on Rohad? It'll help get your mind off her and refocus with some fun."

"Good idea," said William with notes of sarcasm.

"Same time tomorrow?" Richard asked as he stood, the silver rivets on his belt shimmering from light flooding through the open door. "Backgammon is a good way to pass the time."

William agreed.

"Good. Maybe I'll tell the story of these," Richard said, pointing to the falcons on his belt tab.

Once Richard left, William reflected on the last week and how strange he had felt when Richard requested daily meetings. At first to talk, then talking over eating, now talking over games, with eating. He pulled everything from his bag and set it on the table.

The revenge plan zapped in fitful spasms in his mind, like storms at sea. Then it quieted, and it looked like a maddening mess on paper. He pinched the bridge of his nose and wiped matter from his eyes.

After placing his satchel in a cupboard beside the table, he left the king's cabin and wandered the ship. The sea air blew gently across his face, and he remembered Mati—his smiles, his laughs, and his hugs.

And Richard's words. How he despised the pope.

He's right, William thought.

His heights and depths paralleled Richard's ups and downs. Perhaps others on the ship shared a similar bond, as war often cements men together, but William shared internal battles with Richard.

"There must be something more to the tapestry," he posited. "And something about George and John the Short." He sighed and fanned himself with his hat.

Did it matter? That mutiny brewed at home? Richard couldn't do anything about it at sea. It was best to keep him calm and prevent war, he thought, to bring Adam and Yusuf to justice and replace Rohad as duke.

Pissing on Rohad with seamen didn't satisfy a hunger for justice. Through the lower and upper decks, he came to the main deck and walked towards the king's cabin. A man with a hat turned the knob and entered. He went to the door, and Cookie was pouring ale into a mug.

"Cookie, what are you doing?" asked William.

"Please?" asked Cookie.

"What are you doing?"

"Freshening up," he said coolly. "Cleaning and preparing the king's snack. Would you like one?"

William scratched his patchy chin stubble, and he focused on Cookie's face. "Didn't you have a beard?" asked William.

"Yes, Scribby, I did, but my brother—he said it'd be better if it was shaved off. More sanitary with food."

"Yes, I see that, of course," babbled William. "Thank you for the ale."

"My pleasure. I'm at your service," Cookie said and slinked away.

"Eccentric man," said William. He looked around the cabin; the king's clothes had been folded and the table had been wiped. He knelt and examined the cupboard and his satchel. "Am I mad?" he asked. All was in its place—no papers had been removed.

ORDER OF THE KEY

E ach day had the same routine. In addition to sword practice and sparring, Louise added archery to the day's physical
activities. She coached Jeremiah until he had a smooth and
fluid release of the bowstring, one that produced consistent,
repeatable shots.

By the end of the first week, Jeremiah yearned for more sleep and
more food, but bonding with the hawk satisfied his loneliness and
being separated from the team.

After the morning's lesson about Christ the King, Louise packed
soup in containers for their dinner and supper. She hooded Rûah and
said, "Put on the blindfold, Jeremiah. We're going to the water."

Louise guided him from the monastery but released his arm in the
city. Sounds of the market surrounded him.

"Be still, Jeremiah. Feel the ground, feel the pavement cobbles,
and feel Rûah on your arm. Listen to the city. I'm right here if you
need me."

"Jeremiah, Jeremiah, what's that on your arm?" called Asser's
hoarse voice from the pub.

Jeremiah opened his mouth to respond, but Louise touched his
arm. "No communication with your friends for the month."

"Fine! Don't answer me! When will you return?" shouted Asser.

Jeremiah heard Asser run and yell from somewhere higher.

The smell of roasted chicken wafted through the air, and his stomach gurgled. Arms out, he searched for the food and flattened into a
wall. The hawk screeched.

"Sorry, Rûah!" he said.

The air warmed as they wound down the streets until his boots suddenly dove into sand and water.

"Open," she said.

He pulled up his blindfold and then Rûah's hood, causing her wings to flare.

"She's eager to fly, Jeremiah. Take this yellow lure and rope."

He hesitated.

"Don't be afraid. She'll return; she has bonded with you. Release her."

He undid the jess, and Rûah climbed high into the sky.

For hours he waited, sitting cross-legged on the beach, pouting and twirling the lure, hoping she'd return. After his second container of soup, he wandered the beach.

"Jeremiah, look!" exclaimed Louise. Rûah was perched on the church courtyard wall. With vision locked on something, she dove.

"Jeremiah, twirl the lure. Run back!"

He sprinted and swung furiously as he called her name. Talons retracted as she descended. She snapped the lure and the mouse Louise threw into the air.

"Brilliant!" he said. "Wait a minute," he added with a sharp bite in his voice. "You had a mouse. She didn't come for me. She came for the mouse."

Louise clapped. "Bravo, bravo!"

But Jeremiah frowned.

"Oh, don't be so sour," she said. "Fix your face. She came for you! Yes, for the mouse too, but she also saw the lure. Every day, take her out, and let her fly and hunt. She'll return to you without a mouse when she's full. The food is out for her necessity."

His boots were still soaked, so his footsteps squished when he walked, and she laughed at the squeaks.

"Let's go home, Sister."

Louise explained as they walked how he should design the mew building—the permanent shelter for the hawk. "We need lots of wood, Jeremiah."

While he chopped wood for the mew, Louise watched and held the bird on her arm, speaking softly to her. Louise taught logic, and when Jeremiah asked questions about the subject, she readily answered. She questioned, and he answered. Questions led to more questions.

The second week taught illumination and Jesus's life. The third and fourth weeks covered union and the Passion of Christ—His suffering, death, and Resurrection.

On day thirty-nine, after attempting to lead Jeremiah down the rabbit hole into the abyss of useless argument and reductio ad absurdum, he wagged a finger at her. "Nice try, Sister, but I saw it coming. Let's play another game—proof by contradiction and law of non-contradiction."

"On one condition," she said. "We will do it during chess."

He shook hands on it, and she smiled.

After the match, her eyes glittered radiantly. "Well done, Jeremiah." From her pocket, she pulled a large brass key. "I think you're ready."

"Ready for what?"

"Tomorrow is the last day—you can sleep in, talk during the feast, and see your friends. And we will have your ceremony."

"On Good Friday? Is this another trick? No, I want midnight and sunrise, Sister Louise."

"Very well, Jeremiah. Follow me—I want to show you something by the beach."

They found their way to the shore and there, tucked in a cove, waves splashing nearby, lay a nest. "A puzzle, Sister?" he asked.

"Look closer—and kneel."

One crack, then several cracks came. A head popped out with big black eyes, like the hood over Rûaħ. Curled in a ball, the baby bird's head dwarfed its body. Several more eggs then hatched.

"We need to keep them warm. I think their parents are gone."

"How do you know?"

"During your afternoon sessions alone, I've been coming here to pray. I haven't seen the mother in a few days—that's the reason for the bigger mew—to give them a home."

"Ah," he said, rocking back and forth, "very clever. But what are they? Dragons?"

"Those, my friend," she said factually, trying to hide her excitement, "are the fastest animals in the world."

"What?" he exclaimed.

"Yes, they dive like lightning bolts and have vision to see prey from half a league away." The finely drawn lines at the corners of her mouth rose into permanent hints of her wise grin.

Carefully, he cradled the nest and asked, "What are they?"

"Peregrine falcons. As with the hawk, we'll train them, but this time we'll feed them from birth and teach them to fly and hunt."

Lightning bolts flashed across his mind, and he felt focused energy shoot down his legs in columnated beams. "Think of their names too," added Louise. "Their bond with you will be closer than the one between you and Rûaḥ."

As they returned to the monastery, Jeremiah imagined light-warriors and their allies spread across a battlefield, clad in white robes with peregrine falcons on their arms, ready to charge into enemy territory to defeat the dragons.

"Go rest, Jeremiah," Louise told him. "I'll see you at dinner."

Because these were his last training activities, the air carried a subdued tone like the muted glow of the sky after a thunderstorm. He slept soundly that night but still popped out of bed before sunrise to seize the day.

Light flooded into the church at noon and reflected off Alfred's sword in Jeremiah's hand. Having bathed, he sparkled in a tailored white robe and shined boots. He clicked his heels against the stone floor until his walk down the aisle, flanked by the nuns in their cream-colored habits and the friends he hadn't seen in weeks, ending at the altar. Confidence radiated from his upright posture, steady march, and tunneled, glowing gaze.

He knelt, and Padre, also dressed in a white robe, sprinkled him with holy water. He lightly dubbed his left shoulder with Alfred's sword and his right shoulder with a key.

Padre then handed the sword to Louise, and she repeated the dubbing and said, "Jeremiah, you are the inaugural member, the first Knight of the Order of the Key. Bravo! Remember the lessons—keep them close to your heart and pass them on to others."

From a bag, she pulled a cloak she had fashioned herself, cutting and sewing elements of Jeremiah's cloak with Alfred's handkerchiefs. The brothers were one, sage and warrior together, the key unlocking proper use of the sword and the sword defending the key. The lion in the insignia held a sword in his right paw and a key in his left paw.

Cowardice and grudges resurfaced to lock on Jeremiah's heart, but brotherly love fought the Evil One and he regained his composure. Around his neck, she draped the cloak. She clapped and hollered; the order of nuns in cream habit followed other nuns. Before he left, Louise whispered, "Let go, Jeremiah. Let go of the past. Pursue her. Pursue love."

After the ceremony, some nuns tuned their violins, and others served dinner. Roasted lamb and chicken tasted like Heaven on his lips after those weeks of soup without bread, and the presence of his friends brought additional fullness. One beer flowed smoothly into him, and it soon awakened senses he hadn't felt in a month. Hugs were long with his friends.

As Jeremiah sat, Louise poured more ale from a pitcher and transferred it to another mug. Puzzled, he accepted the new glass and drummed his fingers against the table in beats of three, watching his teachers without knowing why.

"Do you think he learned the lessons to his core?" Padre asked Louise while moving his frosted mug in a circle eight.

"Ah, the pattern. Round two," Louise said, and poured her ale into another mug. "I see your figure eight and add to it."

"Very good," understood Padre. "Yes, round two—with time and understanding."

"I don't know," she answered. "I'm afraid he hasn't fully submitted."

"We shall see. Often, we need to be born again, sometimes multiple times, in life. For now, we celebrate."

"Care to dance, Padre?" asked Louise.

A loose smile hung from Jeremiah's mouth. *Two beers and I'm drunk,* he thought. He looked at the table again—Louise and Padre were gone. They had started dancing: two quick, one slow, two quick, one slow, they two-stepped to the vibrancy of strings.

"A perfect metaphor," Jeremiah overhead Padre say. He rolled his eyes but laughed as bubbles sprung up to a burp.

Like old times, he thought.

Marianne and mead.

Jameela and Jeremiah's Mead.

"Witen me," he said sloppily. "What's with me? Women and mead?"

⊕ESERT

fter Easter, the team packed for Aliyah's house. The nuns blessed them, and Louise gifted them all hats—a forest-green flat cap for Asser, a wide-brimmed leather hat for Mo, a gray beret for Padre, and a gray flat cap for Jeremiah. Jeremiah also received a book with warrior lessons inscribed within. "Your birds will be safe with me until you return," Louise said. "Fight for your pack," she instructed one last time. He packed the gifts with his remaining clothes into a bag and bundled his arrows into quivers.

In the courtyard, Louise presented them with four horses, tents, and wine skins. "Gifts from the diocese."

"And me earnings from the pub, Woody," Asser said as he tightened the cap over his head. "You're welcome."

"*Our* earnings," said Padre.

The team loaded the horses with packed bags hung across their backs. They tightened the leather straps and bade farewell to Sister Louise and the monastery.

Jeremiah pressed the team across the path before the tide covered it, and then through the woods, and they retraced their earlier journey.

"I knew you'd return," Aliyah said on her porch swing as the team dismounted and tied their horses. "But where's Jameela?"

"She left," said Jeremiah tonelessly. "Can you help us?"

"Of course, if it's the right kind of help. What do you seek?"

Jeremiah handed her the scrolls.

She took them but glanced at Padre.

"Jeremiah has finally found a purpose," said Padre.

She returned to the swing and skimmed both scrolls and a map rolled inside one scroll.

"How do you know Hebrew?" asked Asser.

"Hebrew has been passed down through my generations. I'm a mix of many peoples, some native to this land, some Scandinavian, and some Hebrew."

Jeremiah hadn't met those types of people before but had heard descriptions of them. Though aged, Aliyah had skin that glowed, and its tan hue contrasted with her lighter blue eyes.

"I don't think it's proven," she continued, "but oral history has told stories of a Jewish tribe migrating many moons ago from Judah to these lands via Scandinavia. Scholars speculate this tribe followed Ezekiel's prophecy: the Kingdom of Israel settled in the northwest isles of the sea after the Exodus."

"Merely metaphor," said Padre.

"Possibly," she said, her voice hopeful, "but it would explain why Hebrew was passed down through my ancestors."

"From what me know of Christianity," said Asser, "it seems you don't practice it."

"Are you asking if I follow religion or Christ?"

Asser paused and asked with hands on his hips, "Who is Jesus?"

"Asser, that's a question you'll need to answer yourself one day," she said, the response rolling off her tongue gently. "As for me, Jesus is love and justice. And please sit," she continued. "This translation may take a while. I'll return with paper, feather, and ink."

After spending hours translating, while the team members wandered around or rested up against a tree or washed a trail-dusted face from a rain barrel, she reviewed the text. When she came outside, they returned to her porch and sat.

"Quite boring," she said and yawned. "The best part was the spiritual practices and commentary on loving one's neighbor. The governance principles put my hand to sleep." She flopped her wrist and stood. "I need a break."

"Governance?" asked Asser, suppressing annoyance. "We were nearly killed for that?"

"Quiet, Asser," rebuked Jeremiah. "Aliyah, can you read, please?"

"I need a break," she reminded him, and gave the scrolls and birch papers with the translations to Padre.

"Can you brew tea for us?" asked Padre. "Would that be an imposition?"

"And food," uttered Mo.

"Yes," she said. "I know you need refreshment, and preparing those things will be a good diversion from the scribing." She went inside.

"The part about loving your neighbor," Asser said, his smile broadening. "Would that be Aliyah's favorite?"

"Likely," said Padre. "She's been thriving on her own for many years."

"How does she love her neighbors, then?" challenged Asser. "She has none."

"She used to live in the capital. She became fed up with the Church and the king and moved. People regularly visit her for guidance, community, healing, and love—as we have. Here is a sanctuary for retreat."

"You're one of those people?" Asser asked with one arm around Padre's shoulder. "Coming for healing and"— he drew out and made smooching sounds—"for love?"

"Enough, Asser," said Padre.

"Yes, for love," Aliyah said lightly from inside as she blew a kiss to Padre, then brought a tray with teapot and cups onto the porch.

Padre smirked so broadly that his soft eyes reduced to slits. "Enough, Asser," he said in between coughs of embarrassment. "I'll read now."

"And I'll return with food soon," said Aliyah.

Once Padre finished reading the manuscripts aloud, Asser said to Padre, "Hogwash! Those principles don't apply to us. People need kings—there's too much corruption. Witness the Church and its abuses. Who checks its power? People don't like King Richard because he's gone mad. People prefer being led and having decisions made for them. It's biblical. Right, Padre?"

"Certainly, there are kings in the Bible. But God is more concerned about your heart and your loving the King of Kings. Everything else is secondary. The importance of money? Jesus found money in a fish's mouth. Does a fish need money? No. Money is a tool. Glorify God with whatever you have."

"From what you read," said Jeremiah, "I think it makes sense. Who would argue with most decisions being made at the lowest level possible? How can one person make decisions which affect the entire kingdom?"

With a hand out towards Padre, Mo asked, "Where's the food?"

"She'll be back soon," said Padre.

"And here I am," she said and placed a plate of dried fruit and bread on the porch.

Jeremiah continued, "Should each duchy send a representative to a meeting to discuss the king and his government? According to the scrolls, we had an ancient constitution written from Moses at Mount Sinai, amended as practiced from his experience as ruler."

"I don't think," Mo said in between bites, "many people know about this."

"Of course not," said Asser. "Freedom? Most are thankful to live past thirty. Work the land, give over what is owed to the lord, the king, and the Church. Ensures a seat in Heaven. Simple but short life. Enjoy where me can."

"I'm talkin' about the ruling class, the lords, the merchants and artisans," said Mo. "I bet they don't know about this."

"Probably not," agreed Asser. "They became wealthy under a king."

"I bet my father knows," said Jeremiah firmly. "He spoke against the centralization of power at his guild meetings." He paused, then brightened. "I understand the hourglass shape."

Padre passed the papers to Jeremiah. Pointing to the hourglass, Jeremiah said, "You missed these parts, Padre." He read aloud, "The top half of the hourglass represents how Moses tried governing, making decisions and solving problems for three million people."

Jeremiah continued reading, getting louder with his summary to drown out Asser's arguments.

"Flip the triangle, the bottom of the hourglass, and that's how Moses governed after learning the balance between rulers' law and no law, tyranny and anarchy, from his father-in-law. He emphasized strong local self-government which solved most problems. If one couldn't solve a problem, then they were to take it to the next level. Moses divided the people, consisting of around six hundred thousand families, into groups of ten families each."

Jeremiah stopped as a thought dawned over him. "Like the tithing," he said. He continued reading, "Each of these groups containing ten families elected its leader. If a leader in charge of ten families could not solve a problem, he could take it to the leaders in charge of the fifty families of which he was a part. And so on, the higher it went, decisions only reaching Moses if necessary. Delegates met at various intervals when problems became too difficult to solve at the lower level."

"Like the Witen," said Padre.

Jeremiah stopped.

None had heard this lost history.

Jeremiah read the parts Padre glossed over: principles of private property, sound money, and preservation of life and liberty with the justice system.

Once he finished, Jeremiah kept the map, folded the papers, and gave them back to Padre.

Padre handed Aliyah the scrolls and asked, "Can you secure the originals?"

"Bloody lovely," griped Asser. "Me could've summoned criminals to court with this. They would've begged to stop the torture."

Aliyah laughed and took the scrolls. "Yes, of course."

"Come on," Jeremiah said and stood. "Let's prepare to go find Jameela."

"What does this have to do with her?" asked Asser.

"The map shows the Danuvius Flumen leading to the Pontus and the Princeps Unus. We'll learn more there."

"Translate," said Asser.

"The Danube River, the Sea, and the High One—the high mountain," said Padre.

"Oral tradition has passed down to my family their local names," said Aliyah. "The river is known as the Turla, and the sea as the Dark Sea. The mountain is known by some as Mont Visok and by others as Mont Elyon. Most call it Maghali."

"According to legend," added Padre, "the place of the convention is near the Dark Sea."

"That will lead us to Jameela's location," said Jeremiah confidently.

"Perhaps," said Aliyah. "She looked Near Eastern. And the origin of that rock you were holding so tightly seems—from my study of these things—to have come from a large mountain by a tremendous sea, the sea that the Bible describes as having been flooded. Travel southeast by the route sketched on the map. You'll journey through mostly farmland until you see a great large river, known across the kingdom as the Danuvius but locally known as the Turla. Follow this river to the mountain by the Dark Sea. You may find her there."

Jeremiah reviewed the map. "And this?" he pointed to a desert and tributaries from the Turla River. "Is this a shortcut?"

"Yes, but it's also a desert and treacherous."

"Great," he said, his voice quick and impulsive. "We'll take this trail."

Jeremiah started for the trail, but the team remained sitting.

"Jeremiah," said Padre, "we should rest for weeks, build our strength, and gather our provisions."

For a moment, Jeremiah's mind went blank with shock at the suggestion of weeks. His internal drive was pushing him forward, but he took a deep breath and remembered guidance from Louise.

"You're right," he said and returned to the house.

+———+

On many days, Jeremiah woke early with an intense desire to get moving and find Jameela. He helped to clean the house, cook the meals, and maintain the horses, but he often declined nightly gatherings on the front porch and climbed the mountain.

After several weeks of rest, the travelers dressed and readied to travel. Padre, Asser, and Mo donned their tunics and hats, but Jeremiah opted instead for hose and a long-sleeve white placket shirt.

They gathered their bags, untied their horses, and farewelled to Aliyah. Jeremiah marched them southeast through months of farmland, and into increasingly barren stretches of terrain. Water sources became dusty riverbeds, and their waterskins coughed air.

If determination were a color, his face showed it: he resembled his saddle, tanned from the sun, worn by all weathers and pressing to their destination. His lips crusted, and his tongue tingled. He rested his eyes and imagined water.

She reappeared in his mind—splashing, playing, jumping, sinking—no, he sank, and Yusuf rescued her and kissed her. Asser was laughing, Mo humming, Padre teaching, and Jeremiah's heart shriveling at the betrayal.

Why is Padre here in this dream?

Stop! Jeremiah thought. *Why am I thinking this way?*

Waves of heat rolled across the trail; the brown hills merged into one, and his hands fell from the horn of the saddle as his heart leapt, and his vision focused. Blinking awake, he saw that it wasn't Maghali but just flat desert for miles.

The bow and quiver thumped against his back, and searing sunlight flashed into his eyes. Unwanted thoughts intruded and poked his mind.

You could hurt Padre with the sword, worried a voice.

Why would you do that? You're a good person, comforted another voice.

But you could. It could fall. You're tired and angry.

The distress furrowed his brow, and restless sleep dozing as they rode deepened his delusion. Jeremiah recycled and reused the same dream from the mountain to connect with Jameela, to relive their ecstasy.

When he laid his head down to sleep, his mind awakened and replayed the scenes from their journey. Remembering Sister Louise, he tried to fight the growing darkness, the building anxiety, but he was too weak.

Padre deserves it! screeched voices.

But he's a holy man.

Jeremiah, it's just a thought. Ignore it.

But he couldn't. Thoughts of pushing, thrusting at, and hurting those who had caused him pain attacked him.

Any moment now! came the voice.

It could happen. Look at the sword. It's at your side.

Far away. No need to worry, said the other voice.

But very close! confused the spirit.

Cowardice was a major theme in his mind. If only he had done this, or did that, then maybe Alf would be alive. If only he were a better brother and better uncle, then maybe this guilt wouldn't suffocate him. If only he knew his real parents.

Transactions in The Grouse overlapped—he relived moments with the women who connected briefly with him, then suffered in his brokenness the next morning. Marianne reappeared. Excited to be with a nice man, she left once anger overtook him. These memories blurred because his sexual fantasies about Jameela dominated his consciousness.

But each dream ended in nightmare. When they became intimate, she betrayed him—she stole something—either the stone or his physical heart. Then it ended. He woke and tried to erase the hand-holding, the hugs, the flirting, and the kiss by the creek.

She used me! Why am I pursuing her?

She's the past.

Because you're not capable of being loved.

A bastard—these words brought into his vision Harry's bushy eyebrows moving like a mouth and then angling to form the tip of a spear, on fire, about to pierce Jeremiah's heart.

He dug for the stone but found an empty shirt pocket instead.

Jeremiah leaned too far forward on the horse, with his head on the pommel; his body swayed in slow motion as one arrow slipped from the quiver but hung out without falling. He roused himself a bit, straightened up, and pushed the arrow back into the quiver. The lack of sleep started to take a toll.

One morning, Jeremiah slid from the horse, and a familiar pain shot across his right armpit from shoulder to breast. But nothing showed. Soon a red rash and blisters had made a broad stripe across his torso. He'd known flare-ups of this sort over the years, often worse when his thoughts plagued him.

See, those people have caused you pain! Ditch them; you don't need them.

Spiny plants warned with thorns; two trees provided spotty shade. But these plants provided their only water, and water was beyond taste unless they tore the green, horned flesh.

Slowly, though, the distant horizon resolved, and Jeremiah lifted his gaze to red rock formations and small mountains.

Jeremiah wanted to gallop ahead of the group again after a brief stop. The nuns' gift horse neighed and nickered in a low-pitched guttural sound, as if to complain about the prodding, but then obeyed.

"Slow down, Quick Feet!" shouted Asser, his own horse's legs entangled with rolling sagebrush. Jeremiah rode hard for an hour, the wind intensifying and blowing more sagebrush ahead of them, the curious balls bouncing off sand and rocks, occasionally getting caught in a cleft of something.

Jeremiah thrashed when the red rash burned, and the stinging, tingling pain traveled along the nerve pathways under his skin. He wormed because he itched, but he hesitated to scratch at the itch for fear of popping the fluid-filled blisters. He was unable to suppress an occasional yelp at the pain of the flared-up rash, and no one had questioned the occasional shrieks when the flares fired, but now, the bumps covered his chest and crept up his neck.

Asser kicked his horse to catch up to Jeremiah, then tugged at his shirt.

"That hurts, Asser!" barked Jeremiah. "Don't touch me."

"Moody, moody. You know, none of us have slept well. Do you need help?"

"No, I don't need help," snarled Jeremiah.

"What are those bumps over your neck, then? Are you some sort of leper?" Asser pulled at Jeremiah's shirt again, gasped, then formed his fingers into a cross.

"What's goin' on with you?" asked Mo, trotting up. "I'm noticin' that ever since she left, training aside, you've been like a man possessed."

"It's called love," said Asser. "And those are love bumps."

"I'm after the stone, you fool," he corrected them.

"You're woody—either mad in love or mad in the mind. This desert heat has been playing with your mind—and me mind too. Can we just slow down—take it easy?"

"There's shade ahead, Asser," Jeremiah pointed.

You may hurt them—don't linger! cautioned the voice.

You wouldn't—they're brothers.

But you could.

"We'll have more shade soon," said Padre, from behind them.

What does he know?

Will you just shut up?

Ahhh! Jeremiah howled in his head and bowed it for some relief.

"How do you know, Padre?" asked Asser.

"I can feel it in my shoulder; when it severely aches, a storm will come soon."

"We should slow down," said Asser. "It's at least a few weeks' journey to Maghali, from Padre's reckoning."

"Yeah, you're right," said Jeremiah.

Better, just a thought, reminded the wise mind.

"What's the point anyway? She's probably moved on," said Jeremiah, his voice bitter.

There you go again.

"Ah, see, you're more concerned with her than with the stone." Asser smiled. "Padre, tell him me is right."

"You're both right. He's in love with two things. One is an object."

They came over a rocky cliff to spy below them a kind of oasis with found reddish logs. They dropped their bags and tied the horses to let them drink from the trickling creek after they'd filled their own skins, then dropped their bags and reclined under the shade of leathery tree leaves. "You don't believe in the power of the stone?" asked Jeremiah.

"Legend states David found the perfectly shaped stone, carved from many years of pressure, in a creek nearby his home," said Padre. "He found it as a child and kept it because of its brilliance. It must have been God-sent because the same stone killed Goliath."

"How do you know it's the same stone? Silly belief in a stone," Asser argued and fanned himself with his cap.

"So what, Asser," retorted Jeremiah, "if a relic brings people to the Church and God?"

"Yes. But hope in a rock? Me thinks that's silly."

"Stop taking the other side," said Jeremiah forcefully.

"The Church and king are using people."

"Didn't you just excuse the corrupt system? Witen me," Jeremiah said and threw up his arms. "The Church *paid* you, Tiny Hands."

Mo and Padre watched the few birds perched in the tree branches; both took long drags of breaths as the dry wind blew. "The desert heat isn't terrible with a cool breeze," said Padre.

"You're all mad," Asser said and crossed his fingers again.

"I'm rested," said Padre. "Shall we continue?"

"Wait a minute," said Jeremiah. "You've been too quiet. No comment about the stone?"

"You already know my thoughts about it."

"Me don't," Asser reminded him. "And why does your face look feverish, Jeremiah?"

"Fine, fine." Padre paused and thought. "I visited a church in Rome once, to see a relic of John the Baptist."

"His head?" asked Asser grimly.

"Yes."

"Knew it," Asser said and pecked his head like a chicken.

Padre's expression looked blankly. "Anyway, after seeing his head behind a glass case in the cathedral, a priest motioned to me, asking if I wanted to see another relic."

"'Another?' I asked? 'In this church?'"

"'Yes,' the priest said as he giggled and shuffled his feet towards the stairs. 'Downstairs,' he said. 'We're blessed to have another one.'"

"I didn't know what to expect, but when I came to another glass case with a smaller head, the man cheerfully declared, 'John's head as a child.'" Padre looked around at the others as it dawned on them, then delivered his final note: "I stopped but said nothing except 'thank you.'"

Jeremiah laughed with notes of scorn. "Very funny, Padre. But that didn't answer my question."

Padre rested his hands on his belly. "Jeremiah, I've never been interested in superstitions, magic, fairy tales, or legends. If a relic is what it's said to be, then I'm thankful it's in our cathedral. I'd rather break bread with someone, drink good ale or wine and, amidst good company, share stories about Jesus. Objects from legends cause too much conflict. Fools place trust in things like stones."

"You're wise, old man," said Mo.

"Wise, but ignorant," countered Jeremiah, "and not practical about the real world too. The real world will take advantage of you and reject you."

"The wise man knows what he doesn't know," explained Padre. "He balances between knowing and not knowing and when to seek and when to faithfully wait."

"You're wise, old man," repeated Mo in a tone of support.

Padre continued, "But I do believe in mystery, miracle, and the power of dreams—another way God communicates." He looked at Jeremiah. "Like your wolf dream on the mountain near Aliyah's house."

"I don't want to talk about it."

"Wow, you dreamed about a wolf?" Asser asked and scooted close to Jeremiah's back. "Did he resemble your mark?"

"Piss off, Asser," hissed Jeremiah. "Get off me."

"Moody one today. A figurative wolf, Padre? Or was it real?"

"Figuratively, Asser," said Padre. "Jeremiah, in the dream you defeated the wolf and were supposed to wrestle free of your demons and give them to God. Does a wise man stay alone on a mountain, or does he seek help?"

Jeremiah leapt from his seat and stood with the sun at his back, casting shade on the priest. He shouted, "I didn't want to stay up there! You left me. Remember?"

Jeremiah threw up his arms and grunted. The voices returned: worry, false comfort, fleeting wise mind, worry, more worry, terror, and evil. Walking in circles away from his companions, he palmed his warm forehead and massaged the back of his head to soothe the aching.

He squinted; the rays brightened and intensified, so he sought shade under another tree. But his bottom missed the red logs as he sat, and he stumbled and fell to the sand. Padre stood and walked over to offer a hand, but Jeremiah smacked it away.

"Leave me alone!" screeched Jeremiah. With his fingernails, he dug into his head and arched his back when the next flares of pain ignited. He repeated, but more quietly, "I didn't want to stay up there!

You left me. Remember?"

"No, that's not how it went. I showed you a place where you could let go of past attachments—I did not put you in danger. I stayed for a while, but you argued with me. You told me to leave, thinking you could find your own way. Then I thought, it was best for you to learn the lesson."

"What lesson?" dropped Jeremiah's voice, until it was cold as the crypt-water bath.

"This life is not about you, Son," said Padre. "Since your brother's death and now since Jameela's betrayal, I saw hope. You sought knowledge and wisdom during Lent with Sister Louise, but you've taken a step back. You're still too stiff-necked. You're not ready."

"Ready for what?"

Padre walked away.

"Ready for what?" shouted Jeremiah.

Hit him! He deserves it!

Under his breath, Padre muttered something, wiped his brow, and said, "Maybe this entire plan to make him a man has failed."

"What'd you say? I could barely hear you." He ran to Padre and forcefully turned him around. He stood there in a rage with fists clenched. "What'd you say?"

"Jeremiah, please." Padre lowered his head and prayed.

Jeremiah lifted Padre's head with a thumb to his forehead. "Tell me."

The priest placed both hands on Jeremiah's shoulders, and with tired eyes, he pierced Jeremiah's soul in a low but declarative voice: "You're not a man yet, Jeremiah. Let her go. Let all of it go. Fear not."

The demons inside Jeremiah boiled; he shook, and his face reddened to deep crimson. Like pulling the string of a bow, he pulled his right arm as far back as possible and released, walloping Padre across the head.

Padre crashed to the ground. The sand cushioned the blow, but his neck whiplashed at a sickening angle.

Clouds rolled in suddenly, and heat lightning flashed across the sky. "What have you done?" screamed Asser.

"Padre!" bellowed Mo, then he scooped Padre into his lap.

The horses lifted on hind legs and whinnied with panic. Asser ran to calm them, then came back as Mo placed a hand over Padre's heart. The priest's closed eyes struggled to open.

"What have you done?" blared Asser again.

Jeremiah's ears pounded; his vision fuzzy and tunneled, he panted, hyperventilated, and jerked backwards. Rushed breathing dried his throat so he searched to stumble away for water.

Both Mo and Asser roared after him, and they pushed him away. "Leave!" they roared.

The birds exploded from the leathery tree, landed, and scurried to seek shelter in brush and overgrowth in the scant vegetation.

From his lap, Mo helped the now-conscious Padre to sit up and then to stand.

Jeremiah stood at a distance, watching.

"I'll be fine, thank you—a bit dizzy," Padre said and stumbled but steadied himself against Mo.

Asser looked accusingly towards Jeremiah, but twirling sand blinded him and prevented passage in growing whirlwinds. "Leave him," said Padre, holding up a hand.

Asser avoided the spiny plants and answered, "You're right, Padre. He needs to feel the thorns."

Padre prayed aloud, so he could hear, for Jeremiah's deliverance. "Lord, obliterate the caverns in his soul."

Jeremiah's thoughts froze, but his body ordered him to fly.

Water came in on top of the flying sand, then drops that went from sprinkles to blinding sheets in moments. It happened suddenly and lasted briefly. They huddled, held hands, and clung their bodies around the red, short thorny tree. They stuck their tongues out in the hopes of catching drops, and the horses, pulling at their ropes, did the same.

Jeremiah remained standing—alone—then twirled in the blinding sandstorm and spotted the sage rolling in the distance. He went from a stumbling, slow jog to a run, then a sprint, following in his mind's eye the rolling sagebrush of the desert, but it eluded his outstretched arms.

He thought of Alf and the fighting games they had played with their figurines when they were kids: light-warriors versus dragons.

"No—dolls, Miah," Alf had teased and hit his figurine again. Alf marked the board with another mark, which was the end of the line. "Two marks left, and your energy is gone, Miah. Dead. And I win again," Alf had said.

Dead, Miah hoped.

BAPTISM

Jeremiah ran faster with a fierce tailwind propelling the outcast towards the sage. The sky closed in, with fingers slowly curling and forming a claw—a sinister version of the games he saw Alf playing with Maren, when his hand had lowered to tickle her and she giggled and laughed in anticipation.

But this hand choked him, shortening his breaths as the clouds rolled in faster than any he'd ever seen. The sky became a dome, and he was trapped.

Steadily fast—he shielded his eyes from the blowing sand with his hands.

Steadily faster—smaller sages flew past and harassed him.

Steadily faster—dust and dirt swirled, twirled, twirling and whirling.

Foggy and groggy, confused in his flight, Jeremiah was tangled up with the sage, and he found himself curled and rolled like a scroll; they unwound against the base of the red rock plateau.

He left the sage, followed the flow, and climbed high and higher on the mesa's dark side to enter the show. Light faded as the sun disappeared behind storm clouds, and he tripped in the confusing dark; the dimness, shadows, and sprinkles tripped his footing, but he recovered and sped up again to checkmate fate.

He found the fortress built upon cliffs that had been leveled to flat. Through the gate, he buzzed past the barracks, the armory, and into open space.

Whip, whip, wings of crows flew and pecked his face.

Bang, bang, pots flung and smacked his face.

Ping, ping, pebbles flew and pelted his face.

Confusion ran him in circles.

Drip, drip, his mind pounded to the beat.

Drip, drip, the drops grew to sheets.

Drip, drip, dirt coated, then covered his body complete.

He tripped, and his bearing turned. New rage catapulted him forward to the stone wall of the palace. He hesitated, then climbed and stood at the top. Beneath him, the cathedral-height fall tempted his despair. Light disappeared; the panorama blackened. Three points in the distance united, and the single speck dissolved into dust tornados. Past sins of lust plagued his body, soul, and mind.

He felt polluted.

He felt gross.

He felt empty.

You're a bastard, he heard, as much outside him as in his own mind. *Your parents abandoned you. No one loves you.* With increased strength and fury, he tore his placket shirt in two, and the wind scraped at his skin, rupturing his blisters.

Sand shifted into the wind, and, like a million arrows, flew to each sore to hasten the crusting effect. Lightning jagged down, and nearby stones turned to dust. Jeremiah's pain exploded beyond his bearing, but thunder, thunder eclipsed this release.

The sky fell.

End it, voices invited in an odd, lifeless, and uncritical tone, urging him to concede defeat and let go of the pain. The voices were simple, open, and riding on the edge of an order, but nagging and pushing him to decide on his own.

Jeremiah decided; he would surrender. He whispered goodbye to his friends and family and extended a leg over the abyss.

Suddenly, a strong wind burst against him and threw him backwards onto the mud floor.

"What are you doing?" asked Alf as he loomed ghostly over Jeremiah.

"Alf? Is that you?" Black dots moved in a figure eight, but he imagined his brother.

"Get up," Alf commanded. "Now."

"But, but . . ."

"Get up!" barked Alf.

"But . . . but," he stammered, "I thought you were dead."

Alf radiated in white, without blemish in his glorified body in the drenching rain. Jeremiah reached to touch him, but the mist collapsed and reformed.

"That's not how this works," said Alf.

"What do you mean?"

"You haven't submitted."

Emotion overwhelmed like the flood storm around him. Jeremiah fell to his knees and blubbered. "I'm so sorry, Alf. I'm so sorry for abandoning you, for hating you, for ignoring your family. And you died protecting me."

The vapor turned solid, and the wings of the vision disappeared. Alf extended a hand, and Jeremiah connected to it with his own.

"Look, Miah," Alf said and showed the dagger and sword cuts across his chest and stomach. "I have scars, but they've healed."

Jeremiah rubbed the callouses on Alf's hand and touched his wounds. With a firm grasp, his brother pulled Miah in and buried him into a hug. Something else—something bony or, like a stick—was in Alf's hand.

A figurine.

A light-warrior—restored.

"We're at full energy, brother. To fight another day." As fast as the storm had unleashed, the sun reemerged and dried the ground of the fort floor.

Alf smiled. "I forgive you."

Jeremiah hugged him again and said, "I love you."

"I love you too. I must go. Tell Mum, Dadde, Thèrèse, and Maren I'm in good hands. Take care of them."

"Yes—yes, sir," he said with sniffles.

"And Miah," he finished, "return the stone. Rescue Jameela, fight for her cause, and restore the kingdom. Let teachers guide you."

With that, he waved and vanished.

Jeremiah looked around, wiping his hands on his leggings, and ran down the mountain shirtless, in reckless regard for his safety.

"Hello, old friend," he said to the sage that stopped rolling before him. It rooted in the ground, and its stems stood up slowly like a reverse claw relaxing and reaching upward. Purple buds burst on the anthers, and wind carried its seed and intoxicating minty aromas.

The scorching sun had returned, and the sun's rays penetrated deep, blinding and blistering Jeremiah. The sand shimmered as if it held a refreshing pool, but the closer he got, the pool disappeared into the mirage it was. He locked his eyes onto the leathery leaves and plunged towards them.

The team had broken the huddle and were packing. The horses first notified. "Look what the storm brought in," said Asser. "And he's half naked."

Jeremiah collapsed to his knees and begged for mercy. Once Padre forgave them, Mo and Asser grudgingly accepted his apology too. "Teach me," he said to Padre. "Teach me to pray. Teach me to listen."

Cleansed by his mud bath and the following rain, Jeremiah's skin glowed and his spirit shone through. Lightened, vibrating, his soul sang.

They all paused in their preparations and reclined underneath the trees, and Jeremiah shared his testimony. Then all of them, refreshed by his renewal, pushed on in their journey.

After several hours of travel the following day, their eyes were almost unable to take in the variation in color. Flat land gradually rose to small hills and rocky formations with pockets of shrubbery and trees—some poplar and some jujube and some palm. The sweet fruit quenched their thirst like ambrosia.

An oasis awaited them too. The horses secured, they climbed rocks to where the sound of falling water drew them in closer. Over the rocks and down the valley, a wide and deep pool invited them. Their vision opened fully, and their smiles widened until their cheeks hurt.

One ran, one jumped, one dove, and one tiptoed, but they all immersed in the refreshing bath to soothe their aching bones and tired muscles. They horsed around, dunking and throwing each other in the air to celebrate Jeremiah's return.

He asked Padre if he could renew his baptismal vows.

"Have you let go?" asked Padre.

Kneeling in a shallow area, with tears and cupped, opened hands, he beseeched, "Father, forgive me." Remembering Sister Louise, he prayed:

You are good, good, good.

Winter worn, cold with cool breeze, mid-morn;
Alone, many miles from home;
A road-less-traveled showing;
Rûah growing, Spirit flowing,
Slow-walking, no talking,
Bending and ascending with Louise.

When I lose sight of the Way,
When I wander away,
Call me to return and pray.
Remind me, remind me of the
Order of the Key,
And that—
Life is not about me.

You are good, good, good.

"Know that you are loved, my son," said Padre. "It is finished. With a servant's spirit, honor and glorify God's love. Go rescue

Abba's lost children. Enter the mess, redeem, and make all beautiful."

Padre blessed him with the sign of the Cross and dipped him into the warm waters. He prayed for the Holy Spirit to descend.

As on eagle's wings, Jeremiah rose and inhaled with closed eyes. Purpose emanated with his exhale.

Asser shrugged, turned to Mo, then clapped and hollered.

"Come here, me brother, for a smooch," Asser said and kissed Jeremiah's cheek.

"You shinin' fine, my brother," Mo said and sank him into a bear hug. After hours of soaking and playing, they climbed out to be on their way.

"Let's not fill up with water here," Padre reminded them. "The smaller pool, where no one bathed, is better for drinking."

"Good point," they said.

They filled their wineskins with enough water for them and their four-legged companions. Padre unfastened his cloak and draped it over Jeremiah's shoulders. Like armor, it felt sturdy and protective. He rubbed his fingers over the thistle brooch, around the silver ring, and down the pin. Its three decorative panels of purple crystals shimmered.

As they began to ride, they sang songs of liberation and baptism. Mo hummed in bass, then clapped loud and louder in rhythmic sweeps. Asser and Padre joined him on the chorus.

> **Went down to the land of giants,**
> **Where Miah fell to knees,**
> **Where looked the devil in Hell,**
> **Then rose to his feet.**
>
> **I say, roll, Miah, roll. Roll, Miah, roll.**
> **Your soul arise, oh, my Lord! Roll, Miah, roll.**
>
> **Some say he was a coward,**
> **Some say he was a sage,**

But I say he was a fighter
Because the Devil came uncaged.

I say, roll, Miah, roll. Roll, Miah, roll.
Your soul arise, oh, my Lord! Roll, Miah, roll.

Rise to your feet.
I say, rise to your feet!
Wind those arms, hurl that stone,
And kill the beast!

I say, roll, Miah, roll. Roll, Miah, roll.
Your soul arise, oh, my Lord! Roll, Miah, roll.

Asser and Padre joined.
Jeremiah sniffled, then tears fell, and he joined in the chorus.
The chorus rang out loud and louder.

I say, roll, Miah, roll. Roll, Miah, roll.
Your soul arise, oh, my Lord! Roll, Miah, roll.

PEACE

unlight broke through the circular window. Jameela roused from an early afternoon nap, stretched, and walked from her domed bedchamber through smaller conical-shaped rooms onto her front porch. A cool breeze blew in from the sea with the songs of birds.

"Home," she said and looked towards the water. Freedom granted, she had found a home, met neighbors, and settled into her new life. She hadn't explored beyond the village, a community tucked in between forests to the west and north, the Dark Sea to the east, and a tributary off the Turla River to the south. Maghali dominated the region's culture and identity, and generations of people told stories based on its mysteries. Though many miles to the south, its massive size distorted the distance.

A river path twisted throughout the village with the river that emptied into the sea. There were no gates nor walls in the village, but concentric circles of homes, and parks between them. Fishermen were hauling the day's catch onto shore.

The fresh scent of thyme from the rectangular brick beds a few steps away deepened her calm and inspired her to brew tea. She picked herbs and carried them into the kitchen. Children's books lay on the table beside a pot. "My favorite part of the day," she said and put the herbs into a bag.

An hour later, she set up a tent on the beach with neighbors, then walked through the village with a heavy bag, past a stage, a large tent, and an octagon gazebo. Laughter came from under a log archway and with a sign that read *Story Circle*. She opened the latch of a cupboard there and changed out the books for others from her bag. Under pine trees, on cut logs waited children, some talking, some fingering in the dirt, and some playing with toys.

Jameela pulled a book from her bag and showed them the first page, illustrated of a man with a crown.

"Why did you pick that book?" asked a neighbor girl.

"I like it, Simone," said Jameela.

"But why this book?"

"Because it's important."

"Why?"

"It's important to me."

"But why? Because of him?" Simone asked and pointed to the man with a crown. The girl's mother, a taller, dark-skinned woman with close-cropped black hair, said behind her hand, "Jameela, say 'yeah' and move on."

"Thanks, Bhakita." Jameela turned to the second page and firmly said, "Yes, because of him."

Simone left the log and ran to her. She took Jameela's hand and said, "Let me show you something."

"After story time. Go on," Jameela said, sweeping her hands, "back to your mama. We read first, but"—hands on knees, leaning forward, she drew them in—"then we'll watch a show."

"This is a story of a prince rescuing a princess and a princess rescuing a prince." She continued reading about love and loss and dragons but skipping over the more violent parts of the story.

"The groom then kissed his bride," Jameela read the last line, "and they lived happily ever after."

She closed the book, and the children clapped.

Jameela beckoned them all, and the children followed her to the beach, their mothers behind. They all sat cross-legged on the sand in a large tent of fabric so dense it was very dark inside. The children filed in, but their mothers stayed outside, speaking in whispers with

Jameela as they arranged the surprise.

As the women took their places, Jameela knew the light poured through a tiny hole and projected images onto a wall.

"The book!" exclaimed a child within.

"Very good, Riona," said Jameela, recognizing her voice.

As the mothers acted out a fairy tale outside the tent, Jameela watched with feelings of gratitude and sadness.

A few weeks at her new home, she didn't know what to do with her unbridled spirit. She had hesitated when choosing to leave Jeremiah and the team. What did they know of her reasons? Jeremiah knew parts but not the whole. She had been reluctant to share most details with him. So why, now, does she think about him?

Regret? . . . No, cannot entertain that idea.

Boredom?

That must be it.

She mentally dusted her hands off against her legs. She needed to find meaningful work or a hobby beyond this story thing. Painting and telling stories to village children had become her life. Their laughter and smiles helped to erase the pain, but it wasn't enough.

Each man from her past melted into an indistinct impression that morphed into a blob as she occasionally recalled gyrating through the motions of her dance and other transactions without feeling. The exchange in the back room lasted for a few minutes, maybe more, for silver that went towards her debt.

Jeremiah was the first man to see her as a person and not an object. In fact, he was embarrassed when she caught him staring at her. But she could tell his attention was genuine—love, not lust.

Well, must move on.

After the ending song, Jameela clapped and moved towards the entrance of the tent. One child pushed through the flap, then another, and another, and soon they were running circles on the beach.

"I hoped that would put them to sleep," Bhakita told Jameela as she lifted her mask.

Simone called for Jameela, "Chase me, Aunt Jameela."

"Not right now. I'm tired."

"Come on," pleaded the five-year-old. "I bet you can't catch me." She ran towards a field of flowers away from the beach. "I guess you'd better catch her," said Bhakita, her voice tired.

The tiny child was lost among the vibrant, red poppies. Jameela called half-heartedly, "Where are you? Where are you?"

———

"Jam, Jam, where are you?" Jameela's mama had called. Sitting cross-legged in an aisle of dirt, tall sunflowers on either side had dwarfed Jameela, who stayed quiet until she was found.

"There you are," said Masha. "Let's go."

"Wait, Mama. Look at the flowers move with the sunlight," five-year-old Jameela had said.

"My ray of sunshine, Jam. Yes, they're beautiful."

Through the sunflowers, Jameela had trailed her mama back home. Her older brother, Haider, with a head full of curly, brown hair, played with a long, wooden stick near their house.

"Zoom, zoom!" he said and danced around the yard. "Watch out, Jam!" he shouted.

She walked past him and asked, "Your sword?"

"My light sword of lightning," he said proudly.

Jameela's grandparents sat around at the kitchen table, where her papa, Abbas, played chess with a fellow scientist from the university.

"I don't think we should move yet," Kristoff had said.

———

"Why aren't you moving, Aunt Jameela?" asked Simone.

Jameela snapped into the present and looked blankly across the field of flowers towards Maghali.

"I knew I'd find you," said Jameela.

"You didn't find me. I came out from hiding."

"Come on, let's go home," Jameela answered wearily.

"Carry me." Simone pouted and lay on the ground.

"Aren't you old enough to walk? I just chased you and you were running well."

"But I want you to carry me, Aunt Jameela."

Relenting, Jameela picked her up and put her on her back, the child's legs around her waist to help hold on. Simone kicked her legs during the walk, agitating Jameela's old wound. Once the girl released her death grip around Jameela's shoulders, she slid down and waved goodbye.

At home, Jameela dabbed a finger into a healing cream and massaged the horizontal scar below her navel in a circular motion. It had reduced in size, so it was now smaller than her marks, but it was still too long, and too hideous, and too painful to bear looking at. She felt ugly.

She flipped through the vibrant-colored dresses in her wardrobe; after tossing several onto her bed, she chose purple and slid it on after stepping out of her everyday dress. She walked to the water bowl and stared at her reflection. Heat had flushed to her neck and head. She picked loose threads from her dress; between her fingers and thumb, she curled them into balls and flicked them into the water.

"I can't wear this," she said in a defeated voice. "It's too revealing." She fidgeted and examined herself once more.

After an afternoon nap and early supper, she pulled the dress off and donned the same outfit she had worn during the journey with Jeremiah: leather-strapped boots with an olive-green tunic.

"I need a drink," she mumbled.

With a mug of wine and a bag of art materials in hand, easel under her arm, she strolled to the dock. She set up the easel, surveyed the surroundings, and considered painting a solitary fishing vessel at the edge of this vast sea. The boat was pointing outward, with a story unknown but with limitless possibilities. She sipped wine and thought of him, then hummed the shanty song.

Two small golden birds flew past her, up and down like a wave, and landed on something in the distance. A flower, maybe, she thought, but the birds blended together, and she turned back to the sea.

Pleasant memories and wine warmed her soul, but her smile vanished quickly. She looked into her mug, sloshed the wine, and gulped to finish it.

She was still longing for Jeremiah occasionally, her feelings subsiding somewhat with time. But not today. She sang the shanty song and drew an outline of the dream.

She stopped; suddenly, the longing shot through her like an arrow.

She furiously rubbed out the image and sketched two lovers with legs dangling over a creek. The woman and man were physically together, but each thinking of separate dreams. The woman looked at a child and a house, and the man looked at her and at the mountain. With simple facial expressions, both were lost in dreams and wonder.

The birds returned and chirped in beats of three, ducking and losing altitude as a larger bird with black wings as long as oars soared over them. Jameela shuddered. The itch of sand pebbles clung to her legs. *The dirt will never leave.*

Above her right hip, a dull pain sharpened to a sting. She pinched her hand there, then ran it through her hair. The golden birds flew past again and landed on something yellow down the beach, just past a dune, under a large ring that marked the end of her village.

She followed the birds to the ring.

"I recommend you return before sunset, madam," said a sentinel guarding the entrance to the ring.

Another sentinel dressed in the same beige striped linen shirt with band collar, white leggings, and strapped boots walked down the path and came to the ring.

"Hakon, we leave at sundown to patrol," said the newer sentinel.

"May I go a little further?" asked Jameela.

"Where?" asked Hakon.

"To follow the golden birds to that yellow I see in the field."

"The flowers?" asked Hakon. "You may go, but don't be long."

She thanked them, left her belongings, and followed the birds under the ring into another field of what looked like poppies she hadn't seen before.

The chirps continued, but she couldn't see the birds.

"Where are you?" she asked.

A path dipped down the dune, and thick vegetation soon dwarfed her, the lower leaves touching her legs. No knee-high poppies here. Instead, round buds had claw-like leaves folded over shades of yellow.

"Sunflowers," she said and laughed with notes of relief.

Beyond the trail, a sea of red danced with the wind. Hints of a glow and shadows of rings faded with the setting sun. A large bird colored like the field left its camouflaged home and flew up and towards the mountain. She was sure it would fly beyond.

I'll return, she thought, when they've flowered.

Returning to the ring, she noticed the sentinels had donned something around their chests that had a shimmering appearance of golden hues. It looked composed of golden threads woven in tight patterns of small shapes connected in a grid.

Maybe a cross, or a circle, or a flower?

"Thank you," she told the sentinels.

"You're welcome, madam," said Hakon. "Have a good night."

Their white leggings appeared thicker around the thighs and knees, and swords of dazzling white hung from their belts.

My brother's light sword of lightning, she thought.

They put on close-fitting caps that covered the tops, backs, and sides of their heads, then left the ring and walked into the night.

SAVAGES

They passed through dry, mountainous terrain for weeks, Jeremiah in a tunic and Padre's cloak draped over his shoulders.

Since his renewal of baptismal vows, Jeremiah had felt refreshed, renewed, and determined. Lighter in spirit, he slept better, but the high of the first days had dropped to a deep restlessness. Peace eluded him.

He thought about her. Asser singing—he sang and thought of her. Padre folding his hands—he looked at his palms and thought of her. Mo snorting—he wrinkled his nose and thought of her—the way her nose scrunched with lines of indifference, annoyance, or disgust, angling when he said something, did something, or did nothing at all. Was that why he rushed them all forward? To find her? To rescue her?

From what? he wondered. *She left me.*

Remembering Elfred's counsel from long ago, he should forgive, but it was hard. Forgive and forget? He couldn't forget. But maybe he could give her a second chance, and his determination would win her.

But your anger, said the voices. *You had Marianne. You will lose Jameela too.*

A diet of berries had left him thin as a thread. They were wandering along together one day, weary and hungry and at first thought the animal in front of him was a mirage. He stopped. A chicken! He was right, but upon closer glance, it was hideous: red body, black beak, eyes, and feathers.

"How did you survive wrestling with a wolf?" asked Asser, just to start a conversation to ease the boredom.

"Was it real?" asked Mo, taking up the topic.

"Profound question," said Padre.

"This again? Yes, it was real," joked Jeremiah. He pointed to his back and playfully punched Asser. "The damn thing nearly threw me off the mountain. It was a haze and happened instantly. I don't remember much but the dazzling green eyes."

"Would Padre leave you alone on a mountain with wolves?" asked Mo. "Why would they go there?"

"For the view," snickered Asser.

"Don't wolves travel in packs?"

"Very funny, Mo."

"Look, there's the red devil," Jeremiah said, and hopped off his horse to chase the chicken at full speed.

"Idiot!" shouted Asser. "You needs to encircle it—in slower, deliberate strides."

Jeremiah flew and dove for the rooster but missed. Three times he flopped. After the third fall, the others joined him and slowly encircled the bird, as Asser had explained. Slowly, slowly, they moved, then Jeremiah pounced. "Got him!"

Ears as red as the rooster and sweating, lips pressed tight, Jeremiah stood tall to watch the others' reaction. *Vindication*, he thought.

———

It was good enough to eat but terribly chewy. "It's rough because of its distressed muscles at the end," said Mo. "Should've stewed it . . . a *long* time."

"Or snuck up on it as me advised," said Asser with a definitive nod.

Oh well, Jeremiah thought. Next time, he would kill quickly. He would be more efficient.

They packed and started on the journey again. Blue, clear skies became gray and overcast, hidden behind tall pine trees. Their moods briskly improved as water became plentiful beside the trail.

After being in the desert for so long, they found the green popped—night to day—the contrast was startling. When they left the woods, they came to a narrow pass, a pinch in the river that flowed towards them, broad and meandering in the valley beyond, that seemed to have streamed down in different tributaries until widening through-out increasingly higher mountains and higher elevations of forest.

In the distance, the large mountain rose. Padre saw a canoe tied to a tree and said, "I bet the river will lead us to Maghali."

"But we'd have some tough paddling to do, me measure," said Asser, hands on his hips. "Good thing we got the horses."

Beside the canoe, a small hill rose and flattened to level dirt that seemed to have been prepared by someone in the past. Some white things were sticking up here and there—with their tops rounded as knobs and fanned out like tree branches.

Jeremiah encouraged his horse and climbed up first. *What is this?* he wondered as he looked about in awe and slid off his horse to look closer. Although there were giant leg bones scattered haphaz-ardly about, they had been arranged to support each other. Standing upright at various angles, the feet of them were planted in the ground. The fully assembled legs towered over him, and the knee joints came at his chest. The strange three-toed feet dwarfed his boots. Like they were placed here, he thought; it was a graveyard—a monument—of bones. He picked through the piles, as did the others, and discovered lots of daggers.

Suddenly, the wind picked up, and the forest swayed with faint whistles surrounding them. Then, from left to right, towards the river, the whistles became shrill cries as something jumped and jumped through the forest, and the horses shied.

"Did anyone see that?" asked Jeremiah, stepping over to take his horse's reins and speak words of calm.

"See what?" asked Asser. "Dreaming things again?"

Eyes wide with fear, Mo clamped down his hat, took longer strides, and said through irregular breaths, "We need to leave."

Images of giant creatures—maybe Mo's relatives—like the bones in the graveyard, crossed Jeremiah's mind.

But Mo doesn't have three-toed feet, he thought.

Whoosh, whoosh—shadows crissed and crossed, darting in and out of the forest.

Whoosh, whoosh—shadows flanked them, merged, then shouted.

Whoosh, whoosh—shadows formed a pack, then attacked.

Whinny, whinny—the horses sounded neighs of panic as Jeremiah's own hair stood on end and he mounted, for safety, as did the others.

Nearby, hideous creatures with dangly clumps of hair, man-beasts short in the legs but long in the torso, dug their gnarled teeth into a deer. The creatures blindly swiped out with long arms and claw-like fingernails to beat off rodents who tried to join the meal. They took no notice of the men and horses.

Almost at the same time, the creatures' heads rose and blood dripped from their mouths onto the deer carcass. They left the meat, and with ears pressed back, sprang to flee. From multiple directions, they fanned out towards the forest, leaving the team alone on the brink of the plateau over the river.

Mo held up a hand to signal "Halt!" in the soft dusk light—he pointed down to where a mammoth mama bear and cubs were catching fish from the river. "To the woods," commanded Mo.

Arrows came, and the cubs scattered. The bear roared and mounted the hill to head for the woods. The shadows crissed and crossed behind her, and the bear shot towards the team, alone in the open.

"Oh no, oh no, oh no, no!" yelled Jeremiah. "We gotta go!"

They kicked their horses, yanked the reins, and turned for the woods themselves. Fast and faster—they trotted, then cantered; breaths quickened, and visions blurred as the horses, having little need of prodding, scattered into different paths of escape.

Jeremiah flew through the trees, as creatures were chasing and flanking him. The bear, just ahead, stopped, slapped her massive paws against the pine forest floor, and growled. She sniffed and chose a direction.

Jeremiah turned his head and saw nothing behind him. *Whew!* He slowed his horse and called tentatively for the team. "Mo!" he cried quietly, then without answer, he shouted and looked around. "Padre! Asser! Where are you?" he called as he saw a body—*no, two!*—falling and heard horses whinnying.

He squeezed his legs against his horse and then kicked and kicked until it galloped. Over bumpier ground, the reins sailed through moist hands as he bounced up and down, up and down in the saddle.

The horse abruptly skidded before hitting a dense stand of trees, and Jeremiah was flung forward off the horse; he released his hands and crashed onto his stomach. He scrambled to his feet and hastily grabbed at the reins, but they slipped. He grabbed again, and before the horse flew away, he pulled at his bags until they fell beside him.

He pulled an arrow from his quiver, readied the bow, and looked about in the dim forest—nothing. The bear had come back into his vicinity and went past him, then stopped. Ears cocked forward, she listened, then turned.

Jeremiah shuffled backwards to hide behind in thicker vegetation. Pulse racing, he began to hyperventilate. Weak legs didn't allow him to run.

Memories flowed fuzzy, but Jameela came into focus.

The bear spotted him, fixed on her target, and in full-tilt speed, ran and lunged at him—but she pulled back, confused, as Jeremiah let out a blood-curdling scream. His primal roar from childhood had returned. She slapped at the ground and swayed among the trees. Rising on hind legs, she growled.

Behind her, arrows still flew and found their mark and landed into horses. The bear swiped the air, fell to all fours, and charged directly for Jeremiah. The ground rumbled, but louder than could be accounted for by the beast's four striking paws. Something else was pounding the dirt.

Arms wobbling, Jeremiah struggled to place an arrow across the middle of the bow, and a heavy layer of sweat broke across his forehead. His heart pulsed furiously, like rapid hammer hits onto an iron chisel. The bear gained speed, and the creatures barreled at him. He steadied his breath and pulled the bowstring to full arc.

But it was too late—another creature knocked him from his feet and landed on him and wound back its hand with razor-sharp nails across the fabric of his cloak.

Charging through the forest like a bull came Mo, who dragged the creature off Jeremiah, giving him a moment to find his feet. Then Mo tackled the bear, drove her to the ground, and repeatedly knifed her in the heart until she relented. Two of the other creatures hissed, redirected their wrath, and pounced for Mo.

Never again! Jeremiah thought.

Fangs extended in slow motion, bared, the creatures flew for their target. In precise succession, Jeremiah shot two arrows, and they dropped, thudding to the ground and shrieking. He lassoed their arms as Louise had taught him, the more able-bodied first, and tied their hands and legs in vine, and ripped the arrows from their legs. Their screams summoned other creatures, and they circled around the pair of men. Jeremiah nocked an arrow, and Mo roared.

A boom blasted through the forest and caused the creatures to disperse for a moment, but they reformed like hyenas waiting to pounce. Mo lowered Jeremiah's bow but raised his own dagger where he stood over the creatures' tied companions. In deep clicks of his tongue, Mo communicated something in the creatures' language.

Their leader, in a flint necklace and peacock feathers fluttering around his boot tops, inched closer and said in English, "This *was* your home in older days. No longer."

"Move, Vozd," he ordered, "or your friends die."

"Giant," their leader said, "we own these woods now."

"Move!" yelled Mo. He lowered his dagger to his captive.

"We do not fear your anger again, giant," said the creature.

"Move!" yelled Mo, and he made a determined gesture with his dagger.

With palms up, the leader said, "Surely, we can negotiate. Like in the past."

Jeremiah let off an arrow, and it buzzed by the leader's head and landed in bark. The leader raised his hand, signaling retreat, and they all stepped back.

"The boat," Jeremiah said. "Their lives for the boat."

The leader considered, then said, "But they may die from their wounds." The wounded yelled in unrecognizable clicks, and their tongues chattered in various tones against their mouths in protest.

"What they'd say, Mo?" asked Jeremiah.

"They're urgin' their chief to agree," said Mo, "because giants are a woody tribe."

"Some medicine for the canoe," said Jeremiah. "We can make it right now."

Their clicks rose in pitch and rapid beats.

"Yes, yes," agreed the chief. He waved a hand. "Heal them in return for the boat—and leave us the bear."

"The ointment," said Jeremiah, still holding his bow. "My bag is near the bear." From the bag, Padre pulled out seeds that he dropped into a bowl, then Mo's hands. Mo pulverized them into flour and mixed them with water from a bottle Aliyah had given Jeremiah— fern dew.

Under Jeremiah's continuing watchful gaze, Mo applied the poultice to the creatures' wounds and tied leaves to keep them in place. Then they released the two wounded ones to their fellows, whose leader nodded grimly and led them all down to the river.

The team tended to Mo's cuts and applied the same ointment. Mo cut a large chunk of the bear's flesh and slung it over his shoulders in a bag. "Ours, Zakari," he growled to the creatures. Asser, meanwhile, had found their horses and removed their tack and baggage, before setting them free in the woods.

Upon joining their attackers down by the river, Jeremiah told the chief, "If you try to attack us, you'll all die." The clicks slowed in beat, and the creatures broke off from the group in concession, traveling in packs deep into the woods.

They untied the canoe and paddled up the river, far enough away to set up camp for the night.

Over roasted bear flesh, Mo shared his history for the first time. The land of giants used to call those woods home but scattered after constant attacks by Zakari, a people originally from the Zakar mountains, a range of mountains south of the Turla River. A peaceful people, the giants moved slowly and deliberately but could kill easily once agitated. Therefore, they protected their tempers.

Mo's wife and children had died many years ago from an unknown illness, but Mo was immune. Lost and depressed, he moved constantly, drinking, searching for a purpose, and changing jobs frequently. He hunted, he fished, he built, and he cut. Using his strength and knowledge of the woods, he started a timber business near the capital, where demand for housing was strong. Business was good, but he yearned for a purpose.

"This journey must be it," said Mo.

"I'm thankful you're with us," Jeremiah assured him with hands out towards the fire, and the others murmured with smiles. Jeremiah remembered his figurines and the names the legends spoke of—the savages and giants. Having learned the local name, Zakari, for savages, he wondered if there was indeed a race of giants, as the legends told— and not just a name for large men.

What about the three-toed creatures in the graveyard?

After feasting, they wrapped up around the small fire. Before falling deeply asleep, Jeremiah reminded himself to ask Mo about the race of giants another day.

TROLLS

They paddled the wooden canoe during the day, camped alongside streams at dusk, and fished at dawn. Maghali loomed and seemed only days away.

One dusk, they spotted a large clearing off the river and decided to camp nearby, in case they could learn of the people of the area from a traveler.

Right at the climax of an Asser tall tale that evening as they sat by the fire, all heads lifted at the sound—pebbles crunched, and water sloshed ahead of them.

"You hear that?" whispered Jeremiah. "Through the woods."

"Must be the wind," said Asser. "Jeremiah, you heard it—you go check it out."

"If it's just the wind, why don't you go?"

"There's no need," said Mo. "Look."

A man, woman, two girls, and a boy, all wearing tall, pointy hats, emerged from the woods and came into the glow of the fire. In indistinct chatter, the man spoke in an unrecognizable language, though it sounded older and lighter, an ancient-sounding accent that rolled off the tongue.

Padre replied, "No, Brother," with open arms, and the man switched to English.

"Please excuse us," he said. "We're passing through and looking for a village near the river."

"Village?" asked Padre. "We haven't seen one, but we can—"

Jeremiah stopped him. "Padre, we don't know them."

"We can help," finished Padre. "They're not a threat, Jeremiah."

"Me don't know, Padre," said Asser. "Should we trust them?"

"Why not?"

Looking them over, Asser said, "Because they're trolls."

"What's wrong with trolls?" asked Padre.

"Me mum told bedtime stories of frightening people living in the forests. Plump and ugly with long, hideous noses and big mouths; big ears; big, bright eyes; and missing teeth. These may be good-looking ones—to fool us."

"Your mum told you fairy tales to scare you from entering the forests alone. But you're not alone, Asser."

Rather than short, plump, and ugly, they were taller than average, slender, with long noses, rounded jaw lines, and small mouths. Tufts of light hair fell against their ears, tucked under the white conical hats crowned with a ball of some fabric or fur.

The man took a step towards Asser and introduced himself, his hand out. "Kristoff," he said. Asser pulled back, and Kristoff shook Padre's hand instead. "And this is my wife, Alaina, my daughters, Camilla and Alexandra, and my son, Erik."

Their dark almond eyes, angled under curved eyebrows, matched the night. The faintest flickers of their eyes twinkled along with reflections from the crackling fire.

"We haven't seen a village," Jeremiah said and, out of habit, patted his tunic pockets, but he remembered the stone was gone.

"But we'll help," said Padre.

Clearing his throat, Jeremiah said, "What are you doing?"

Wrinkles of amusement dashed across Padre's eyes, and he asked the father, "Where'd you come from?"

"We've been on a few weeks' journey from the Dark Sea and Maghali. We followed the river to the first large clearing, and the village should be near. We left our homes in the city to live among extended family."

Extended family, Jeremiah thought. What did that mean? His parents had abandoned him, and he didn't know the reason. "We haven't seen a village. Have a good night," said Jeremiah with a note of sadness. *What would it be like to have such connection with a family?*

"It must be close," Kristoff said, taking the signal. The family lowered their heads and turned back towards the woods.

"Wait!" exclaimed Padre. "Please come back."

Louder, Jeremiah said again, "Padre, what are you doing?"

"Why sleep in the woods when we could find the village and stay with them there? Plus, they can show us the way to Maghali. It appears they're coming from where we're trying to go."

The realization hit him like opening an elixir and drinking from a potion of hope; Jeremiah felt things all over his body he hadn't felt since that first beer at graduation. *Maybe "trolls" do have some power . . . or something else to offer.*

He stood beside Kristoff, feet tapping, as if waiting for the horn to start the race. "Well," Jeremiah said earnestly with what he hoped was an encouraging air, "let's go."

"Thank you, sir," said Kristoff. "Please join us. We won't bite." Looking at the rising moon, he added, "Even on a full moon."

The boy, Erik, howled like a wolf, and Kristoff laughed heartily, the team a bit nervously.

Asser sidled up beside Jeremiah and said, "Maybe Erik can help you wrestle the wolves next time."

"Funny. Shut up, Asser."

They extinguished their fire and walked together on mushy paths along a creek snaking through the woods, until they came into an oval clearing surrounded by trees. Beyond the trees, past rows of plant beds spread across the pasture, shadows hopped, then stopped to join sheep, horses, and chickens standing still, as if waiting for something.

"This must be it," said Kristoff.

"How do you know?" asked Asser.

"Each of our villages looks the same. I will show you around while my family finds our relatives." At that cue, his wife and children sped into the village, chattering with excitement.

Tension flowed out of Jeremiah's body and swept in torrents from his head to his feet as he moved from mush onto mulch. *Why this strange reaction?* But it felt like *home*.

It smelled like his carpentry shop, he thought—the lingering sweet scents, hints of cherry and rose infused into the sawdust, the air whirring rhythmically in soft, constant, and subtle beats. It was a strange familiarity of safety and warmth.

"You have no gate or wall?" Jeremiah asked Kristoff.

"No, our villages don't need them."

Several long, timber houses formed the circumference with thick layers of turf blanketing the roofs. "This is where residents stay," explained Kristoff.

Through a passage between two houses, they followed him to where numerous smaller, conical-shaped, pointy buildings ringed the inner circle. Almost magical, each cone connected to four other cones with passages, the central one in a set of five the tallest. "And this is where guests stay," Kristoff said and swept out a hand and turned, but Jeremiah wandered to a wooden building shaped in a series of stacked pyramids.

"What's that?" asked Jeremiah.

"Our Witen hall."

"May we see?" Jeremiah asked.

"Yes," Kristoff answered politely, "but after dinner. Follow me to our community hall. We've trekked a long way, and my family needs rest."

"Yes, of course," Jeremiah said, and the others followed Kristoff past the first ring, through the passage to the nearest building, a long, rectangular structure.

Kristoff knocked on the wooden door with an arched top. As it opened, he removed his hat and placed a hand across his heart and said, "Peace, Brother."

Lines of age streaked the shorter man's face, and his hair was lighter, more silver than Kristoff's. The family placed their hats on poles beside the spot for shoes.

"Welcome, Brother Kristoff," the shorter one said. "As you can see, your loved ones are already welcomed." He waved to the interior, where the family members had placed their hats on poles and were removing their shoes.

"My name is Kormak. We've been expecting you. A rough journey, I heard?"

"Yes, but this too shall pass."

"This too shall pass," Kormak repeated in a firmer tone.

"We can discuss that later, Brother Kormak. Where's the elder? I have brought guests."

"He'll be back soon."

"Catching the dinner?"

"Yes," Kormak said indifferently, as if this was a usual activity. Going past them, Kormak then went to the porch and rang a bell. Soon, the courtyard teemed with people; from each circle, they closed in and formed a line. "Time for dinner," said Kormak pleasantly.

In the twilight, Jeremiah saw a range of ages, old to young, families and single people, all with conical-shaped hats. A smaller man, about Asser's height, trailed the line with a diamond-shaped fish hanging from his hand.

"This way," said the man, and guided them all.

Through the door, they followed him into the large dining hall with several long tables. The first thing Jeremiah noticed was the contrast. He admired the wooden floor panels and a wooden ceiling arching upwards to a point. Beams of triangles supported the roof, and circular chandeliers darkened the cast brightness against white walls.

Thinking of his shop as a carpenter, he moved closer to the wall to inspect it, and a faint spoiled odor tickled at his nose. *Like a decomposing rabbit*, he thought, remembering his figurines and the rabbit glue he used.

He touched the wall. A light cotton cloth, hemmed in squares, had been pasted to the wood. *Not plaster at all!* The lines of wood grain waved behind the light cloth. He ran a nail against the fabric, peeling back some, revealing the wood underneath, a cross-section of a tree. He turned his head and noticed all four walls colored white. The decomposition smell dissipated here, but another floated closer. It was slightly rancid, smelling fishy.

Though it was a foul odor, Jeremiah felt a warmth, an energy, and a stillness comparable to what he felt when his father took one step into the shop.

Someone suddenly stood shoulder to shoulder with him.

"Good eye," the man said, his voice breaking gently but sharply. The voice had a wet character and was suffused with sweetness and notes of wonder.

Jeremiah turned. A short man, dressed in wet overalls—*the one who led us in here?*

"Like my waders?" the man asked and unhooked a strap from his shoulder.

"Hello, I'm Jeremiah."

"Nice to meet you, Jeremiah," the man said and admired the wall with him. "I'm Munnie, the master elder. How many rings did you count?"

Something else reminded Jeremiah of Elfred—the confidence Munnie carried, the weathered hands, maybe the aura of precision.

"Yes, yes," Jeremiah said and smoothed his hands across the wall. He stopped his hands in the briefest instance of a pause, and his mind flashed to questions about his real father.

"No," he uttered.

"No, what?" asked Munnie kindly.

"Nothing," said Jeremiah. "This wood is a few hundred years old, at least."

"Very good," Munnie said, and invited Jeremiah's gaze with his own.

A deepish blue, almost purple, his eyes sparkled. Set within almond-shaped lenses, the colors seemed fitting for an icon, like those in Padre's office, or in the wild, like a flower.

Bluebells, Jeremiah remembered. *Or the eyes of my dadde when he finished a project,* he thought. However, one major trait contrasted Elfred. Munnie's air of hope had no dash of Elfred's cynicism.

"It's called muslin, my friend," Munnie said with a boyish zest.

"It's from our Eastern friends. Handwoven from fine, handspun yarns. They use it to burp babies, but we'll use it as background for beautiful art on our walls."

Munnie removed his smaller pointed hat and placed it on a pole near the door like the others. His hair was the whitest color Jeremiah had seen—whiter than muslin, whiter than clouds, and whiter than light. It wrapped around his head, several layers thick, and probably would fall to his ankles if unbound.

"Please sit," said Munnie to the whole room. As the troll people were seated, he remained standing at the head of the hall. He sang a blessing, and the hall repeated it. Each side sang a verse, and both sides sang the refrain. After three verses, Munnie closed with thanksgiving.

"Before you eat, I want to recognize Kristoff and his family. They are new to our community. And their friends. Please welcome them," said Munnie.

They clapped and stood to wait in line for food.

Jeremiah and the others followed Kristoff to the serving line. Looking around the hall, Jeremiah noticed a pattern. Younger to older, the hair was colored blond to silver to white. Jeremiah took fish, a big portion of grain, a glass of water, and a shot of something clear the server held out with a smile.

"What's this?" asked Jeremiah.

"Pear liqueur," said Munnie, beside him.

Jeremiah's heart sank, remembering the mead, and he shook his head.

"It's good, Jeremiah. It's from our trees."

It smelled sweet, but bad thoughts lingered. After Asser teased him, though, Jeremiah drank it from where he stood; it tasted fruity and had a long aftertaste.

"That was an after-dinner drink, Jeremiah," said Munnie.

His knees turned inward, and his tray rattled slightly. Jeremiah felt his face grow hot at the gaffe.

"Where are you from?" Munnie asked as they sat.

"Witenberg."

"A far journey. And where are you headed?"

"Master Munnie," said Kristoff, "they're journeying to the Dark Sea and Maghali."

"You don't have too far to go, then."

"Yes, and he's in a hurry—after a lady," said Asser.

"We know our journey ends at the sea and mountain," Jeremiah said and pulled the map from his bag. A rush of panic forked across his neck and strained across his cheeks as his body quickly prepared him for running. *Why? It's a simple question.* "I-I believe we're near here," he said, pointing to the pinch in the river. "But part of the map was damaged."

"Can I see it?" asked Munnie. "The missing section," he said, his voice simple and open, "is likely for Maghali. But no matter. There's a village near the mountain, with a similar setup to ours. Go there and ask. Give them my name."

"But, Constantinople is a large city. She could be anywhere," pressed Jeremiah.

"True, but the village will help. Find the master elder."

"Master," said Kristoff wearily, "Master Harald is dead."

"Why?"

Kristoff's pale skin blotched in red clusters like a rash across his neck. He fanned himself and held Alaina's hand against his cheek when she placed it there to cool him.

The soft planes of Munnie's face sharpened, and his open mouth closed.

"Why?" urged Munnie.

"The Count."

The ball in Munnie's throat bulged, stuck as if he were swallowing something large. "You fled the city, then. Are they following?"

"I don't think so, but—"

Asser interrupted, "Isn't that special?" he said bitterly. "We randomly meet trolls near our campsite, and their village from which they're escaping, let me remind you, is just where we need to go? Doesn't sound right."

"Have faith," Padre scolded him. "Kristoff, please continue."

"Instead of talking about it, let me show you after dinner. Can you pass the bread?"

"Jeremiah," said Munnie, "this lady you're after—is there a reason?"

Jeremiah watched Munnie dip bread into oil and chew patiently, as if he could wait for a reply all night.

The sound of his thoughts went on like piercing barks, a constant beat of desolation. *She stole the stone and my heart.* "Oh," he said slowly, feigning nonchalance, "she's a friend who's gotten into trouble, so my mates and I are going after her."

"A beautiful friend," said Asser. As he described her, Jeremiah squirmed, and Kristoff swirled the liqueur in his glass.

"Hmm," Munnie said and raised his chin. "And you're going to the place from which Kristoff fled?"

"Master," assured Kristoff, "they'll be safe in the village." His eyes glanced towards his family, and he added, looking towards Asser, "We left the city to come here to raise our kids."

"Your people?" asked Asser.

"Trolls."

With arms crossed, Asser beamed. "Me knew it."

"More precisely, Holons," said Munnie. "*Trolls* is the English name our enemies call us."

"Enemies?" asked Asser hoarsely.

Kristoff stood and raised a glass. "I'm ready for the tour."

Munnie's face tightened in annoyance. He stood and raised a glass. "Saints," he said, "dinner has concluded. Please stand." Munnie blessed the evening and gulped the pear liqueur in union with his village.

Kristoff led his family from the community hall to their quarters, then returned and met the team on the community hall porch. "So, Kristoff-on-the-Run Troll Man," rattled Asser, "you have enemies? A nice man like yourself?"

In torchlight, Jeremiah noticed Kristoff had changed clothes. Over his white tunic, he had thrown on a light-blue gown with a hood and a flatter, conical hat than most wore.

"Rabbit fur?" asked Jeremiah. "And a tassel? Are you a professor?"

"Yes, of the natural sciences," answered Kristoff. "Please follow me."

He led them to the stacked-triangle building and its front porch. The entirety was comprised of wood—even the altar in the rear. Behind the altar was a flame with a red glow.

"The eternal flame," Kristoff said as he removed his cap. "A candle is always lit here." Images were carved into various sections of the interior, symbolizing the Holon people, and the gods they used to worship, Kristoff explained.

Padre touched a wooden image with a round head, bulbous ears, and protruding nose, disproportionate to the rest of its body.

That looks more like what I thought a troll was, Jeremiah thought.

"A Holon god of wisdom," said Kristoff.

"Hideous," remarked Asser, "but a nice specimen of a troll."

Lines around Kristoff's mouth showed his annoyance. "Wisdom, Asser," he said, "is inner beauty."

"Go on, please," said Padre.

"Munnie didn't tell the entire story. Our enemies call us trolls, but we called ourselves trolls in the beginning. We converted to Christianity several centuries ago and changed our name to 'Holons,' but in many respects, we've remained in tune with our own original spirituality."

"What do you mean?" asked Jeremiah.

"Love—take care of yourself and each other. Legends say our way of life originated from Moses, and we spread to the western part of the kingdom. We came from a lost tribe of Israel. And here"—he pointed to the benches flanking the edge of the building—"this is where we hold council—our Witen hall."

"Council?" asked Jeremiah. "What kind of council?"

"Though we share the community hall, each family or individual is responsible for its own area and its own house. We believe in private possessions, but the expectation is that those bounties should be shared with neighbors in need."

"You didn't answer the question, Troll Man," said Asser.

"I'm getting there, *Tiny Hands*—heard somebody call you that," Kristoff muttered irritably. He walked them to an altar. "Spontaneous order emerges when each person, each with a unique gift, skill, or talent, does what he or she is supposed to do, and then shares that gift. The system breaks, however, when people become too selfish and too fearful they may suffer lack. There are disputes, of course."

Kristoff paused and winked at Asser. "It's only human nature."

Asser suppressed a laugh and said in harsh tone, "Good one."

"When this happens," continued Kristoff, "we resolve the disputes here. If people can't solve their own problems between neighbors, we bring those disputes to the larger community."

"This only works if the community is small," countered Asser.

"Ah, yes," Kristoff nodded and put on his cap. They exited the building and entered the courtyard. "It can work in larger groups if they follow this structure throughout."

"What do you mean?" asked Jeremiah.

"Certain problems should be handled by the individual. Certain problems should be solved between two people, between two families, between two communities, between two kingdoms, between two empires, and so on. The system becomes unwieldy when those at the top make decisions applicable for all in every area of life."

"Very professorial, Troll Man," said Asser. "Do you normally go on like this?"

"Like how?" asked Kristoff.

"Ignore him," said Jeremiah. "How do you remedy this?"

"We encourage each sect to attend the Althing. It's held every five years. We meet, discuss issues, and vote on ways to solve problems. The Althing is next year, but our enemies—" He broke off abruptly and flinched.

"Can other groups join?" asked Jeremiah.

"Hold on," Asser said and elbowed Jeremiah. "Me want to hear about these enemies."

Jeremiah looked towards Padre and Mo, but it was hard to discern beyond their long stares past the trees.

"We haven't had other groups," said Kristoff. "Perhaps we could vote, but their people and governments would need to approve."

"The altar," Padre said. "Can you show us that again?"

Inside the Witen hall, Kristoff pointed above the altar. "You may have missed this carving."

"Yes, I saw the Dark Sea and Maghali," said Jeremiah.

"See the rings?" asked Kristoff. "And the center building? The layout matches this village."

Mo moved his candle against the wall and said, "And this hourglass. Flip the triangles and stack them—it's the same map symbols."

Jeremiah's mouth fell. "Is that a church or a home?" asked Jeremiah. "Where the symbol is."

"A home," Kristoff said tonelessly, his voice dreary.

"Who lives there?"

"The woman you seek—we helped her move in. We've known her since her childhood. Her dad and I worked together at the university."

Jeremiah gasped and quickly followed with a question. "So, the

Count, those people who chased you, know where she lives?" asked Jeremiah angrily.

"I don't know. I doubt it; they stopped at the border."

"You doubt it?" questioned Asser. "What does that mean?"

"They can't break through our defenses—at least not yet."

"Why didn't you tell us earlier?" barked Jeremiah.

"How could I trust you?" Kristoff said in fast pitch. "I just met you."

"And you're positive it's her?"

"Brown hair, light-brown skin, nose ring. Beautiful. Strong. Yes, there's only one."

Jeremiah's voice suppressed an adolescent squeal. His spirit lifted through the roof, and adrenaline flushed through his body, striking each nerve. "We leave at dawn."

"May you sleep well, then," Kristoff said, his voice lighter. "I'll show you your rooms."

"Wait," said Padre. "How do we get through the defenses?"

"Take your canoe and follow the river. It will bend, and you must paddle upstream and around Maghali. Once there . . . ," Kristoff said and tore a piece of wafer-thin paper from a large roll underneath the altar. He lit what resembled a long match, like a cone of incense, blew out the flame, then used the burning material to write onto the paper.

"When you arrive, take this and give it to the sentinels," Kristoff said to Padre.

"It's blank," said Jeremiah.

"It's not; they'll see the message."

Padre took the paper, and they followed Kristoff to the cluster of tent-like buildings, and he pulled open a curved wooden door. Kristoff struck a match and lit wood inside the central fireplace. "Your rooms will be warm soon."

Around the perimeter Kristoff lit candles, and the vastness of the space surprised Jeremiah. He followed the angled fireplace as it sloped upward to the ceiling and tentacled out to each cone room. Between ribbed vaults hung panels of fabric in various shades of purple.

"The structure is supported by the arches," Kristoff explained and led them through a narrow corridor into another cone and into different bedrooms. Like the arched processional doors on cathedral façades, the windows curved up and around and connected to a point.

"There's a path outside that leads to the stream for washing. The wooden buildings near the stream are privies. There's a handle to aerate the pot, and the pile of wood chips beside the pots is for the smell. Add the chips after you go. Bars of soap and towels should be in the building. If you need anything else, knock on the community hall building, and someone will get me. Good night." He quietly closed the door behind him.

Jeremiah sat cross-legged beside the bed and wrapped Padre's cloak around his shoulders. He tried to pray, but the vastness of the cone mesmerized him. More so his thoughts, the anticipation of seeing her, clouded his mind.

What will she say? "I'm happy to see you"?
No—she stole the stone and ran from me.
Ran.
Like I've been doing.
Why do I want her? Am I blind?
But she could say yes and run into my arms.

No matter what he did to channel them, Jeremiah's thoughts focused on running. Faster and faster. Away from his father and mother, his adopted parents. Running faster, after striking his spiritual father, climbing the mountain, and running to the ledge. Then running down the mountain for mercy.

Who are my real dadde and mum? Do they look like me?
You have two fathers, reminded the voices. *And you rejected both.*

Tingles shot up his left side and landed into his armpit, the target of his rash flares. He looked for an object to keep his hands busy, to stop the wringing. Through his bag he looked—nothing was small enough. Maybe he could build something or get more wood for the fireplace. Or visit the privy.

He tiptoed outside.

Lights blinked.

Many of them—

And moved, flying around.

A number of animals were gathered outside, remaining still as if waiting for something. One hopped, then many followed. They were large rabbits with ears as big as antlers, long whiskers, longer than feathers, and bodies as wide as a boar's. But they looked cuddly. *And I'm sure they're soft,* Jeremiah thought.

Through the blinking lights, Jeremiah saw the woods with bark white as snow, and white as Munnie's hair. Halos of light looked like points with different shades of white and yellow that formed the shape of leaves on the barren trees.

The closer he got, his steps irresistibly drawn towards them, the more distinct the shapes became, and he saw shades of purple and blue in pods that suspended from the air and dangled from the branches. Something else seemed to fill the trees on higher branches. It looked sticky, webbed.

He stopped—two tall figures stood at the forest edge. Beyond was darkness. Moonlight led his eyes to the distance and other trees on the hills. Those trees felt menacing and, like fangs, they sharpened to points. The figures moved with long sticks in their hands. Swords? But they swirled shades of purple, blue, and white.

Jeremiah heard voices and felt another presence—ominous, cold, and shadowy, like the chills that cut into his body when he was on the mountain. It was a different language, harsher in tone and carrying deep. The sound of hooves stopped at the forest edge. *Are they horses or another kind of creature?* he wondered.

The tall figures' swords glowed bright as light, and they began to sing. On the first note, the shadows vanished and rode away from the light with vapors trailing behind them.

Buds began to pop. Like toppling dominoes, pod by pod, they opened, revealing their secrets. Fireflies blinked rapidly and provided continuous light to show the most amazingly colored wings that were of deep purplish blue, a stronger color than bluebells and more radiant than Munnie's eyes.

Hundreds fluttered, then flapped their wings and carried themselves away, past the trees, over the pasture, and over the animals to somewhere south.

Butterflies, Jeremiah concluded.

Village children had been silently watching with him, though he had not seen them. Only now he became aware of their presence as they returned inside, and Jeremiah heard the faintest of sounds coming from open windows. Listening more closely, he understood parents were whistling, "Good night," in melody.

ARREST

A sentinel was not at his post—perhaps patrolling, she thought, but the birds' chirping seemed to call her, inviting her to risk venturing alone past the village. She walked under the ring and followed the birds to the sunflower path at twilight.

As night fell, a burnt-orange light glowed beyond her. The path inclined, and she saw what looked like iron rings spiraling out of the dirt.

The closer she got, the warmer she felt, and she learned the glow came from firelight reflecting off the rings. They were hard, mottled with dirt and colored with iron oxide, the same material in her red dyes. "No, not rings," she said, suddenly remembering a conversation with Jeremiah. "What did Jeremiah call them?"

Walking underneath them felt like she was in a tunnel, the view blocked by thick vegetation, as if it hadn't been trimmed for some time. "But there's a fire," she said, puzzling over what she beheld.

She exited the third ring, and the tunnel continued in sets of three rings. Perhaps the rings continued and wrapped around Maghali, but no one had been that far. Legends told of an impenetrable gate.

Her memory broke in, and she said, "Ellipses!" with a sudden rush of joy. She heard a faint sound with celestial accents—music, a voice, a cry—so gentle she could barely hear it. The sound echoed but quickly vanished, and the singing abruptly stopped.

Then the light went out.

One by one, ring by ring, beginning at Maghali, each fire was choked in what seemed like the pinch of fingers squeezing out candle-light. Notes of music overflowed in violent color, with a deep, guttural sound corkscrewing from the mountain to her ear. She turned and ran back towards home.

The cords in her neck tightened, and an incredible heaviness plunged down upon her, as if the tunnel were collapsing. She ran faster, but her airways constricted, slowing her.

She pushed harder, attempting to break whatever trap enclosed her, but the sinewy material barely stretched.

Do I hide? she thought with panic. *Where?*

She stopped—bewildered, spent.

A hand touched her hand, and she gasped.

It was two village sentinels, dressed in the same armor she had seen Hakon and the other sentinel wear the last time she was here. "Early warning," one said. "Stay here and don't move."

"Is someone after us?" she wheezed.

"Not so loud, or they'll hear us," whispered the other. "We'll be back." They sprinted with their arms out towards the mountain. Suddenly, the trap loosened, and she could breathe.

The sentinels returned. "Listen, you live in the village, correct?"

"Yes," she rushed out.

"We need you to extinguish the fires before they come."

"Who?" she exclaimed. "With what?" She frantically looked for water or something to smother the fire.

"We'll loosen the trap to let you leave, and you can warn the village." A sentinel held her arms, and with a sharp widening of his eyes and urgent emphasis in his voice, he said, "You must extinguish the fires. Understand?"

"Yes."

"This too shall pass," assured the other sentinel. "Use this." He handed her a tube, and then both of them ran towards the mountain.

"Witen," she uttered. "What's this?" she asked and rotated the tube in her hand, and particles of a dry powder moved within. She sprinkled some onto the third ring fire; it dampened down, then roared back.

Aye, she thought, *I need enough to put out each fire.* She used a third of the bottle on the third ring and a third on the second. Moving towards the first ring, she felt the choking sensation return, and she heard two rapid groans. *Where'd that come from?*

"Hurry," she told her hands. Some of the powder spilled.

"Witen!" she cried and poured the rest on the flames. The fire slowed to embers, but one flame still burned. She stomped it with a boot, and as the boot pounded, a louder pounding sounded nearby.

Her spine tingled as the final stomp snuffed the fire.

"Jameela," said two men in unearthly, unison tones. "Come with us."

Her hands and feet were tied, and she was brought to a long, narrow boat, where they left her with another man, who started rowing south along the river. Maghali was behind her, and the city of Kula and its smaller mountains came into focus.

"Who are you?" she asked, finally getting the courage to speak.

The man continued rowing with a long oar. He slowly pushed the water and whistled in steady beats, as if this was a routine activity.

"Who are you?" she demanded, her voice louder.

The tree line broke, and she saw more clearly that he was one of Rohad's men. His legs were wrapped in stretchy wool, his feet were in low boots, and a fitted black bork hat rose high above his head with a metallic emblem in the middle of the forehead area. "I suggest you keep your voice quiet," he said coolly.

"Where are you taking me?"

"Rohad has requested you."

"Why?" she thundered. "Who were those men?"

He stopped whistling as the oar rested against his thigh. "You ask lots of questions," he said.

It had happened in a blur. The fire went out, oddly with no smoke. In complete darkness, the path beneath her feet and the flowers brushing her legs guided her, but a gloved hand had grabbed her shoulder and forcefully turned her. Two men, clothed in masks and dark uniforms, stood there. "You know them," said the rower, with a confident tone in his voice.

"I don't know them," she countered.

"You do," he said calmly, and gently guided the boat into the harbor. He tied the boat and said, "Your appointment, madam."

"Is this a joke? I'm under arrest, right?"

"Madam, please," he begged, "it's been a long night. Get out."

She considered dropping into the water and cutting the ropes against the jagged rocks.

"Madam, please," he repeated and sighed.

She awkwardly shifted to the side of the boat, maneuvering with her bonds hindering her movement, and she cradled her stomach over the rail as she tumbled out. The boatman moved quickly and carried her across the dock to another man, who put her into a carriage.

The horse carriage rode through the still Kula streets and came to a gate, where a guard untied her feet so she could walk. "Come with us," he said and escorted her to the funicular carriage.

She entered the carriage with two guards and sat on the wooden seat. Looking out the window, she saw the lake, dam, and water wheel. A footman outside the carriage shut the door and walked to the lower station. He picked up the cone of parchment hooked to the wall and spoke into it.

"She's a go," the footman said, then exited the lower station and removed a tank under the carriage floor full of water and drained it.

"Glorious system," one guard told the other as he jerked forward a little when the brake disengaged from the rack mounted between the rails. The carriage clicked, clacked, and clicked in a slow chug up the hill, then accelerated when the brakeman at the upper station moved the wooden shaft at the water wheel, and water flowed over it, propelling the wheel, then the cable underneath the carriage faster. Another carriage began its descent and passed Jameela's carriage about halfway up the mountain.

Once the carriage came near the top, the brakeman slowly shifted the wooden shaft to slow the flow of water. The carriage came to a gradual stop, and the brakeman engaged the brake. Guards dragged her from the carriage and out of the station. Below, the bay opened into the grander sea, and she supposed the specks were ships.

She dismissed the thought, and slogged through the suppressed memories that came as she plodded along the paved path with head down. Suddenly a large white albatross emerged and landed on the path several paces ahead; like the birds that swooped overhead, this reminded her of a burden that flew somewhere, close to her, hunting her—that prevented full freedom. *Either set it free or finally kill it*, she ordered in her mind.

ꝺRAGON

reezes blew across the White Sea, and the ship sailed around islands in the archipelago. Richard pulled at his wild hair until he could tie it into a ponytail. Palming his forehead, he told William, "Too much distress makes this damn hairline recede."

"Has something changed, Your Majesty?" asked William.

Richard puffed out his massive chest and flexed his arms, enlarged from strenuous workouts and fed with a ravenous diet of salted meat and ale-soaked porridge. The wind blew harder but remained steady, and the sails could work with that.

"According to legend," Richard said, pointing to the stern, "the dragon heads and tails should have been removed in order to not frighten local nature spirits, but I ordered them to remain."

Protection, he argued to William. Deterrence, he justified. Each dragon part had been painted with vibrant red and black shades to instill maximum fear in all who beheld the ship.

"We'll arrive soon, and I hope no war comes of it. But I know my brother. He won't comply."

"But Adam and Yusuf, Your Highness," said William firmly. "Convince Rohad to hand them over, and we'll prosecute them in Witenberg."

"Will that change anything, William? Rohad's militia will fight; they won't unify around the idea of one kingdom and one God."

William attempted to say something about killing for God, about just war, but his thoughts mocked him, and his breaths caught in hiccups. Stopping one man would be more efficient and more *effective*.

471

Weak sea legs had been strengthened by the exercise the king led, and William kept his feet planted solidly on deck. The bounce and stutter remained, but there was a cold hardness to them, as if months of saltwater had preserved the cold water splashing onto him.

"How about ale and backgammon?" William asked and pushed off the wooden rail and walked to the king's cabin with Richard.

Cookie entered the cabin, plated bread, and poured ale. "My pleasure," he said unprompted and opened the door to leave. "Good day."

Since the second encounter, William's suspicion had remained, and he carried his satchel everywhere. "Have you noticed how he's changed too?" asked William. "I can't place it, but he's been more aloof."

"I don't know, William," said Richard coldly. "Let's play."

Months at sea hadn't dampened William's appetite for vengeance. Rather, he had time to tweak the plan, improve the plan, and perfect the plan. He would enact justice against the man he had spent six years helping to craft a manuscript on misery.

Had the pope experienced pain? Agony? Misery? William doubted it. A spoiled child growing up in Rome, the pope didn't know struggle. He had only read about it, placing his thoughts above others' counsel, thinking he was right and no one else could be.

I dream of beating him at his game, William thought. He was determined to prosecute him at the Roman Rota, the pope's court, his own turf.

"Rohad wants to humiliate you, Your Majesty," he said as he rolled the dice, then moved the checkers.

Richard gulped the beer and said, "And take my throne, but he won't get it. It's mine. That bastard is half the man I am."

"The pope is pushing this—you can counter his move."

"Rachel's argument," the king said smugly.

"Am I forgetting something? You told me months ago to move on. You'll honor her death by refusing the pope's plan, by transforming his plan. Replace Rohad."

"With whom?" asked Richard. He stood and looked out the cabin window over the sea. "John the Short? Robert the Bearded?"

Or Jeremiah, William thought.

That was the biggest shock—that Jeremiah was her son by Rohad.

After weeks of surveilling Cookie's patterns, William would waken and quietly sneak by the sleeping military officers and the Oths. He opened a Bible on deck and pretended to pray. If alone, he pulled out her diary. Richard didn't know about the boy, the plan, and the training. Her letters were detailed, emotional, and gave him context to understand.

When was she planning on telling Richard?

Rachel didn't know everything, but she hated the stone and its power over men. She wanted it destroyed. Several pages had question marks around mentions of the Count and his network, with notes to check with Mati.

"I'm not sure, but you'll figure it out," assured William.

"Perhaps you're right." Richard opened the cabin door and rubbed his hand on the railing and added, "You're smart—not as smart as me, but smart."

"Yes, my king," said William, his tone light but sarcastic.

Richard's right hand gripped letters he had held since the ship departed Witenberg. William assumed they were from Rachel, but he never asked. How he wanted to read them! When caught looking at his hands, William replied with admiration for the king's rings. From their discussion, he'd learned how Rachel and Richard met, the day when Richard had rescued her from raptors in a field of tulips and had fallen in love. William had tried teasing out more details about Rachel, but Richard focused on their love life.

Closer to the Kula shore, black flocks undulated up and down like in a wave, swimming through the clouds, appearing and disappearing.

"What's your favorite—" Richard stopped, as if begging for William to finish the answer.

"My favorite?" asked William.

"Yes, your favorite legend."

William's hands spread and dropped in a gesture of futility. However, he masked the fake concern without breaking contact and took notes as they talked. "My favorite legend," William said and thought while writing. "I don't know, probably about one of the saints. What's yours?"

"Legends tell of a fierce dragon that guards those cliffs out there," Richard said, "one too afraid to face me years ago."

"And why is this dragon so fierce—and so afraid?" William asked, looking at Richard dead in the face.

"Traditional dragons hunt by sight, but it hunts by *smell*. Combined with perfect vision, no one can escape once it locks on."

"Fantastic," said William dryly. "And what of the griffins?" His voice broke low, barely hiding with drips of bitterness as he recalled his mother's contempt of mythology.

"But that dragon is no match for this dragon that taunts me, this one in my hands."

William dropped his shoulders and loosened the pencil in his hands. "In my experience, it's best to open up difficult secrets."

"What do you know of love? Of loss?" Richard asked with a faint bite in his voice.

"You're right, as usual, Your Majesty. I don't know. B-b-but, I've seen you in pain. Would you like me to open that for you?"

Richard stared at the dragon head. "I'm sorry, William. He was your friend."

"Your friend too, my king."

"The serpent is a message, William. 'Open the letters,' it says."

Richard broke the purple seals and skimmed—then stopped and grimaced. "Apologies? More apologies. And more apologies?" he said. Sails whipped and howled; he fumbled with the letters but held on—his cheeks blew.

"I have a son," he read aloud, "and his name is Jeremiah." He looked up, confused, then repeated aloud, "A son? A son! A son . . .

an heir!" The final word shouted through the wind, then Richard remembered something.

"I'm sorry. I wanted to tell you . . . ," he read. He lowered his head and slumped over a little, staring blankly. Stares blanked and lengthened past choppy waters to a distant speck, up the mountain to clouds swallowing long whiskers and a spiked tail whole.

"It was the best decision for the kingdom. . . . Please forgive me . . . it was only one night with him . . . ," he read.

"With him? With him?" Richard shouted as wind shrieked around the masts.

"Rohad knows the son is his. . . . I'm sorry . . . ," he read.

Bells rang. Bells rang . . . again and again and again . . .

"Time for dinner!" yelled Cookie. "Time for dinner!"

Richard crumpled the letters and stuffed them into his pockets.

His hands shot to his ears instinctively. A rumbling sound came beneath them with the shift change. Spars creaked, and the rigging strained. Seamen on deck shouted prayers as they managed the sails.

"Get inside, Your Majesty," William said and tugged his arm. "A storm is coming."

Richard looked to the water—cold, black, and deep. The waves climbed higher, high enough for the ship to heel over.

"Oh! The bells, the bells, the bells!" screamed Richard. He clutched the rails. "A son? An heir?" he babbled. "But Jeremiah is dead . . . Daniel said . . ."

William managed to catch the last utterance and remembered the last time he saw Jeremiah, cowering behind stones in the courtyard of the Mont Church. He closed his eyes and prayed for Jeremiah's soul, with the hope that he and Alfred were together eternally.

Light faded, and night fell.

Stars twinkled, and mist sprinkled.

"So, you mock me?" Richard asked the dragon head. Water splashed from its mouth. "And you spit at me? A bastard son, you tell me?" Fast and faster—he paced the deck furiously, waves rushing and spilling over the deck.

Loud and louder—their clamor and clanging shrieked.

"Oh! The bells, the bells, the bells!" he shouted. "I'm not a coward. I'm not a dry stick!"

Veins strained and popped to the top. He rummaged through a pile of tools on deck until he found an axe. With one swoop, veins popping in his temples and neck as he strained, Richard chopped the dragon's head and launched it into the sea.

"Oh! The bells, the bells, the bells! The bells toll, and ghouls patrol my soul!"

Richard marched to the captain's cabin and told Earl Marshall Stewart he wanted the invasion plan changed. The rain fell in sheets, and William covered his bag as he ran to his room in the officer's cabin.

"I'm sorry, Rachel," he muttered. Standing at the door, he looked for Cookie. Something didn't sound right. The words in the letter— what Richard read.

William opened her diary and read.

"I hated each minute; he made my skin crawl. I soaked and rubbed for weeks to cleanse his filth off me. Please forgive me."

More detailed, he thought. How did the letter get on the floor? Like the thunder that struck around him, thoughts flashed through William's mind. He hastily flipped through the pages. "Someone in his court must know about Jeremiah. Maybe several."

He read on about her intuition and suddenly grasped the probability that the letter was planted. By whom?

ROHAD

The guards passed Jameela through the gate onto the entrance hall of the white castle. She looked from the wall-mounted animal heads to the rugs draped over the balcony railing to the chandelier ornamented by a raptor in low relief against the ceiling.

"Wait here," a guard said, "and I'll get the duke."

She could smell him from across the room as soon as he'd pushed his way in through the door.

"Welcome home," he said. Two massive dogs with broad, square heads followed him. Rohad offered a generous smile, too kind, opening his entire mouth wide to show his missing teeth.

Her heart stopped as he stole a piece of her pulse by undressing her with his eyes. "Olive-green garb and no makeup? Your clients would be upset."

She grinned stiffly, fleetingly, but it faded quickly.

"Yet," he continued, "still beautiful."

"You belong in a forest," said Jameela.

"Thank you for the compliment," he replied. "Pine is the finest musk."

Jameela attempted to shake hands, but he lifted her hand to his mouth and kissed it.

"Beautiful hands," he said, tongue smacking against his lips, "just as I remember. But why this nervous energy, darling?"

Certainly, the vision of Rohad was not of a cupid, but it did grab her attention. Clothed in rough garments, wrapped in a hairy gown and with a hairy beard, everything about Rohad made Jameela shudder.

"Why am I here?" she asked. "I did what we agreed to."

"Yes, of course, my lady," he said and escorted her through a corridor and into the parlor, "but there has been a slight hiccup." He dismissed the guards and told them to wait behind closed doors.

"Why am I here?" she repeated in a coarser tone.

"You don't want to see me?" he asked and winked. He crept around until he was directly behind her and whispered into her ear, "Remember those days?"

Stench wrapped around her, and his warm breaths suffocated her.

"Why would I return to this place?" she asked. "I was perfectly fine in my village."

"Fine?" he scoffed and fluttered his hand away as if dismissing a fly. "A successful woman, a strong woman, a young woman painting all day? No, you have a future."

"A peaceful future that I choose," she countered, "free from dependence, manipulation, and abuse."

"Yes, I distinctly remember," he said crisply. "You wanted out, but a part of you can never fully escape."

Like being poked with a hundred needles, she felt air slowly escaping, deflating her lungs and shallowing her breaths. Normally, she wasn't this nervous around powerful men. She'd been with plenty. But she became skittish around this filth.

"Time has helped, I'm sure, but the pain will always remain a part of you, Jameela." He bade her follow him and maneuvered around strewn birch papers and his dogs' shredded chew toys to reach the window. "See that speck out there, far in the distance?" he asked. "That is a warship, and it will arrive soon."

"A warship? Why?" she asked curtly. Coldness spread through her, and she rubbed her arms. Though she thought them long numbed, war flashbacks scratched at scabs she thought had healed.

"Take a walk with me," he said with an open hand, heading back towards the corridor and entrance hall.

"No, tell me," she said defiantly.

"Jameela, calm down. I'll show you."

She followed him outside, down a slight hill and around the castle through a narrow passageway. Beneath laundry hung over the second-floor railings, wooden floorboards under their feet creaked as they walked.

Soon they moved across the middle and inner baileys.

Ahead, the smell hit her before she saw it. Beds of flowers, between deep purple and light blue—lavender—welcomed them to a cobble-stone courtyard.

The soothing smooth scent washed over her, and, for a moment, pent-up tension released when she breathed in deeply. Instantly, she was transported to her childhood home, remembering her arms and legs spread out in the dirt, watching sunflowers sway and brushing picked lavender wands under her nose.

She followed the mellowing, soothing aroma until Rohad guided her to a small building at the base of the great tower that dwarfed the flanking towers of the garden walls. It was plain, nondescript, but ancient—the small structure seemed Greek-like with its columns and white stones.

At the entrance, cobblestone gave way to larger blocks of stones, weathered over time and older. She pointed to several squares lined in a grid, with writing upon them, and asked, "A child's game? In Hebrew?"

"Close," he responded. "Aramaic. We don't know for certain, but it's believed kids played in this courtyard while their parents wor-shipped in the Jewish temple."

He opened the doors. Unlike most churches she knew, this was very simple. The walls were whitewashed, and there were no statues—a marble altar was in the center of the space. Rays of light reflected off something beyond the altar, but she focused on the pile of fabric beside her feet at the entrance, next to a bowl for washing feet.

"The custom is to remove your boots and cover your head," he said. "But—I don't follow it."

She snorted, then bent and grabbed for a cream-colored scarf with sewn purple tulips. The entire place felt sacred; peace soaked each fiber in her body. She wrapped her head with the soft linen, and it was warm to the cheek, like sun-dried clothes. She longed to stay in the stillness.

Closed eyes.

Deep breaths.

Serene. Carefree. Spiritually high.

Present.

Breaking such silence violated natural law.

But they did.

"Over here," Rohad said. "Beyond the altar. See the rose window?"

Light poured through a round window with four semicircles surrounding the center and a larger circle ringed by eight semicircles.

"Each segment of glass was crafted with different kinds of sand— some from the Dark Sea, some from the Dead Sea, and some from the Sea of Galilee. The combined effect of various yellow and white shades creates a luminescent glow when the sun shines."

"Yes, it is miraculous light," she said. "Heavenly. What's past the altar? A pedestal?" She lifted a hand to her open mouth as she took in the vision. Dazzling white light bounded her heart into knots.

"That, my dear, motivated Adam and Yusuf to travel hundreds of leagues to bring you home."

She paused, and one tear strolled down her cheek. She thought of the journey, of the team, and of her betrayal. Her chest ached, and her nose ran.

"Seems your freedom from servitude was more important than your love for Jeremiah," said Rohad. "But no matter—this suits our larger purpose for you."

Her vision blurred, but the luminescence remained. Holding back tears, she stumbled over the words to ask, "L-love? What-what are you talking about?"

"Yusuf told me about your journey home. That you didn't talk for much of the journey, that you complained about the stone being cold, and that you cried when you learned Alfred was Jeremiah's brother. It's obvious, Jameela. You fell in love with the boy."

"What? No . . . ," she said, her voice barely audible. Her stomach rose and fell with her agitation.

"And that suits your larger purpose."

"What, what's my purpose?"

"This is the stone's original home. It was carved out of a larger stone and formed from millions of years of pressure and heat with the creation of Maghali. Many believe it grants tremendous powers to its owner. Thousands have died over the years in pursuit of it. Its most famous owner? King David—he used it to kill Goliath."

"You believe in this nonsense?" she blurted, the tone rising and falling as quickly as she asked.

"No, of course not."

She gasped and followed with a rise in her voice at a higher pitch. "Then why—then why, in return for my freedom, commission me to find the stone, and send Adam and Yusuf to help. Why do that if you didn't plan to use it for its powers?"

"Stop whining, Jameela. While I don't personally believe in the stone's powers, it's beautiful. But I don't have to believe in it. Many people do."

"Where are the people, then?"

"Ah, you're right. I'm keeping it safe until I'm in power. It's leverage, my dear." He held her glance pompously, making sure he had her and with full attention.

"Leverage?" she asked. "For what?"

"I don't know," he said, exasperated, as if he were upset she hadn't figured it out. "Insurance, a trap—useful for a future exchange."

"So you returned the stone to its original home. Why is there a warship? Why were the knights chasing us? Why did the queen die?"

He turned to leave. "You're not getting it, my dear."

"No, Rohad," she said and stopped him with an outstretched arm. "Apparently not. Tell me. Now."

He sighed and pushed at her arm.

"Jameela, I intend to take power from my brother and become king. A bastard as king." He stopped and laughed. "I enlisted Adam and Yusuf to convince local tribes *I* should be in power, and *I* would allow religious freedom and independence, local law without oppressing rule from the capital."

Leaning against the altar, he continued, "But . . . actually . . . I intend to enforce a heavier hand than Richard's. My brother has been too weak in enforcing decrees. His wife had too much influence on him. She had to go. I knew if I humiliated him and made it seem Adam and Yusuf had killed her, he would go to war with an entire people. The pope has helped, of course."

"Evil," she said, and her stomach acid climbed into her throat.

"In exchange for this arrangement, the pope will be able to instill religious law on the entire kingdom. His Church, his law, his faith. One people, united under his God. More peace, more souls for God. Blah, blah, blah."

She felt herself blanch a few shades.

"Of course," he continued, "we don't need a war to accomplish this. If we make the king the villain, then kill him in front of a crowd, we win hearts and minds. Few will die."

"Evil," she repeated, and her stomach hardened to a rock. Her legs weakened, and she steadied an arm against the pedestal.

He laughed and said in a voice exact and monotonous, "And I know precisely the person to kill him." He imitated a drum roll with his lips and tongue.

"Who?" she asked finally.

"Thank you for asking. His own son, your *lover*," he said.

"My what?"

"The trap is being set as we speak; my men have fanned out throughout Kula and your village. Jeremiah will be here soon."

"You're lying," she said, his false smile raising her alarms. "Your men can't break into my village."

"Oh, how wrong you are, beautiful."

She caught his eyes closing longer than normal. "You don't know."

He laughed. "My sources know how—plus, weren't you arrested outside your village? You ventured too far, my dear."

"Evil," she uttered through shallow breaths.

"Like prostituting yourself for money, for freedom?" he countered.

"I didn't have a choice. Mama dead, Papa dead, brother dead, village in ruin. A slave."

"There are always choices, my dear," he reminded her. "You didn't have faith in your artwork. You abused your gifts, your body you had from God—a temple."

"This gift you're suddenly interested in?" she sneered. "Should I surrender it for a different future?"

"A gift that can be transformed, my dear, to something greater. The Pleasure House promised freedom if you used your body. You knew you could pay your debt sooner by pleasing men."

She knew her veins were popping out on her temples. Poking his chest, she growled, "Don't you dare use fake religiosity on me. Did I have a choice? Did any girl have a choice? NO, the Count forced us."

"Persuaded, my dear."

She dug a finger deeper into his chest and said, "When an opportunity presented itself from you for freedom, I seized it."

He cracked a grin and pushed off from the altar. "We always have choices, Jameela. Out of necessity, we make unwise decisions we later regret, but they seem necessary at the time, to serve the higher purpose."

"And I assume you becoming king serves that purpose?"

"Yes, there's been too much instability over the years. We need a strong hand, a powerful leader from the top to enact justice and guide the market. There's been too much chaos."

"Tyranny," she said strongly.

"People like and respect strong men. People want kings to lead them and take care of them."

"Control them," she corrected.

"People can't be trusted to decide for themselves. They don't want freedom."

His fat jiggled as he moved, and he wheezed. "Come on, we're finished here, but thank you for the debate." He brushed his greasy hand through her hair.

"Get off me," she snapped and slapped his hand.

He chuckled, and they left the church. "I hope you find your accommodations pleasant." To a guard, he ordered, "Take her to the first cell."

"Goodbye for now, beautiful. Your Jeremiah will be here shortly."

She kicked at the guards, and more guards raced to subdue her.

They dragged her up the stairs and towards the prison.

Rohad watched as she glared down at him, then he dramatically turned away, abruptly stopped, paused, and turned back. "Oh, my dear flax-wench," he said and licked his lips, "I believe your name means *sacrifice?*"

"What do you mean?" she shouted.

"No greater love hath any man than this, that a man lay down his life for his friends."

"What?" she barked.

"Your family was a sacrifice—now you'll be a sacrifice. Carrying on the family tradition."

Confusion turned to anger instantly.

"Even at thirteen you were beautiful," he added. "The Count knew you would make money for me at the Pleasure House when you had matured."

Jameela's memory raced to the day she was corralled. *The nightmare is happening again!*

She kicked and screamed and tried to free herself from the guards. They tied her hands and legs, threw her in the prison, and slammed the door.

"Good one, Duke Rohad. 'Flax-wench,'" one guard said with a

shake of his head and a laugh.

Rohad smiled, giggled, then guffawed and chuckled and chuck-led. Jameela could only block out the horrible sounds—creaking wood boards and maniacal laughter—one ear at a time.

RESCUE

"The first bend," Jeremiah said, looking at the map. "Kristoff said we take the first bend, and the river will lead us past Maghali."

The team rowed and pushed their oars to the left as he directed.

"Do we have a plan?" asked Asser. "Or can you smell your girlfriend miles away?"

"Normally, me'd laugh and punch you," Jeremiah mocked in a raspy voice, "but this time, me'll let it go." He smooched his lips and moved closer to Asser. "Because how much of a man me's become."

"Now me know you're mad, Woody," Asser said and playfully punched Jeremiah. "Your loins throbbing?"

"More like his libido hummin'," Mo remarked.

Maghali towered even at a distance, and its peak hid behind clouds.

"Another bend, men," declared Jeremiah, "to the right."

"Me not your horse," mocked Asser. "Tallyho, men!"

Jeremiah ignored him and held the oar in the water, steering the canoe against the current, then rowing past elliptical shapes spiraling out of the ground. The water slowed, and they floated beside a village dock under three rings. The air hung heavy, as if they were in a tunnel, yet it was clear and warm.

A guard resembling a Holon greeted them with a hand across his heart. "Good day, Sentinel," Padre said and handed him the note.

The sentinel reviewed the invisible-ink note and said with a bemused smile, "You too shall pass."

He blew into some sort of horn hanging around his neck and pulled a lever.

The heaviness lifted, and they passed through a gate. "Witen me," said Asser. "The third time me've heard that silly phrase."

"Like your mum's lullaby?" joked Jeremiah. He swung a rope around a pole, and they docked. "Look for the stacked triangles."

Beyond a tent and gazebo, a mousy woman ran to a house colored yellow with a purple door. "Bhakita!" she shouted. "Bhakita, where are you?" cried the mousy woman.

A darker woman stepped onto her porch, with a girl standing in the doorway behind her. "What is it, Nadia?"

"I came from Kula," the mousy woman wheezed, huffing and resting elbows on her knees. Neither woman took note of the visitors.

"Asser, Mo, Padre," said Jeremiah, "over there." He pointed out the same design as they'd seen in their troll lodgings.

They jogged over to the yellow house, and Mo asked, "Is somethin' the matter, lady?"

"Who are you?" asked the darker woman.

"We're Jameela's friends," Jeremiah said sharply and moved in front of Mo. "Who are you?"

"We're her friends too."

After swift introductions, Bhakita said, "Tell me what's wrong."

"Jameela's in prison," said Nadia.

Jeremiah was on instant alert, and his stomach tightened. "How do you know?" he asked, his voice suddenly loud.

"Who are you?" asked Nadia. "Her prince?"

"Me like her already," said Asser.

"We've been chasing—no—we've been following her, no," Jeremiah admitted. "Listen, we've come to help. "Why is she in prison?"

Nadia looked to Bhakita. "They should be safe," Bhakita said, her voice husky. "They got through the gate."

Nadia's petite, wiry frame buzzed around the yard as if she were a fly. "Adam and Yusuf. I overhead them. What will we do?"

"What else did they say?" asked Bhakita.

"Not much—they moved inside when they saw me. But Jameela's intuition was right," explained Nadia hurriedly. "A war's coming. Duke Rohad's men have swarmed the market in full battle uniform."

"My Abba," said Bhakita. "Mercy."

"War? Not war, please," Asser said in rising notes of resignation, then sarcasm: "Good thing we came all this way to die. Let's hurry and find that magic stone, then." He jumped at an angle and clicked his heels.

"Hush, Asser," said Jeremiah. "How do we rescue her, Bhakita?"

"Come in and we can discuss it," said Bhakita. "You look like you've been traveling."

———

That night, over cardamom tea, they plotted. "I'll need wood and tools," Jeremiah told Bhakita.

"And magical weapons," said Asser.

Bhakita threw him a sharp sideways glance. "Come now, child."

"What?" Asser asked and laughed. "Me assumed the village had invisible weapons."

"We'll need dark clothes too," said Jeremiah. "For Padre, we need beggar clothes."

———

Two nights passed until there was a full moon. After a hearty meal, Jeremiah, Asser, and Mo dressed in all black: flat caps, tunics, leggings, and boots. Padre put on a tattered tunic, frayed at the ends, then slid into old sandals.

"Holy sandals," Asser said, pointing to the holes in the sandals.

In lighter tone, Bhakita repeated, "Come now, child." She then laughed, and Mo rumbled with deep chuckles.

"The walking stick too, Padre," Jeremiah said seriously and handed it to him. "Let's go."

Each sheathed their swords and slung sleds over their backs. Other neighbors joined Bhakita and Nadia in pinning them into thicker, black cloaks.

"It's a quick-release brooch," explained Nadia. "Pull, and the cloak comes off easily. Use it if you're chased."

"You mean *when* we're chased?" asked Asser.

"Abba bless," Bhakita and Padre said in unison. Bhakita placed a hand over her heart.

The image of Alf leaving for war popped into Jeremiah's mind. He remembered his brother's mouth had the hint of a smile and his body marched dutifully, yet Jeremiah had wondered whether Alf was nervous.

His muscles seized temporarily, but his heart's longing pulled him forward. Under full light, they carried bags to the dock.

"The navis," Jeremiah said to a man standing on the dock. Jeremiah attempted to pay the man, but the man waved off payment because he was Bhakita's friend. The navalier helped the team load the long, narrow boat, called a navis, with bags and sleds.

No one spoke as they drifted slowly south along a river that flowed to the town of Kula. The navalier guided them to the first bend and a water mill.

"Meet us here at sunrise," Jeremiah told the navalier. They waded through tall reeds into farmland, each man pulling a sled with a bag on top of it. "There it is," said Jeremiah. Atop a small mountain covered with pine trees rose a white castle.

Through the darkness, they followed in single file along a creek trail until it opened into the clearing. "This is the back side," said Jeremiah. An incline of smooth stones buttressed the castle. "Bhakita said we have thirty minutes during the break of the guards. Shift changes begin after the next strike." After unfastening their brooches, they eased the sleds onto the pine floor. They refastened their cloaks and unloaded their bags.

With the full moonlight, Jeremiah methodically assembled

wooden rail pieces on the incline. Midway down, he angled a different track sixty degrees off-center. While he built the track, the team covered pillows with pine needles and positioned them below the ramparts. "Mo," reminded Jeremiah, "wait until the signal."

Sharp strike, sharp strike, sharp strike.
Ring up. Wait.
Long strike. Full circle.
Four rings signify the hour.

The sound of freedom rang.

From a bag, Jeremiah pulled rope and handed it to Asser. Mo stayed, and Jeremiah led Asser and Padre around the mountain as tall as two cathedrals. A massive water wheel became visible atop the mountain, reaching into the skyline. At an angle, lantern glow cut across the spokes so they seemed like slits in serpents' eyes.

The funicular used two parallel straight tracks, four rails, with separate station platforms at both ends for each carriage. Beside one track, water trickled down a wide wooden gutter and emptied into a creek. Beside the other track, steps climbed to the upper station. Forest hid remaining views left and right of the tracks. Atop the lower station hung a cord that stretched up the tracks, supported by poles in the middle and connecting to the upper station.

"Padre," said Jeremiah, "go to the carriage in a moment. Empty the water tank when I give you the signal."

They watched until the footman went inside the lower station. "Too easy," Asser said and picked the lock. The gate slowly opened, and Padre scuttled to the carriage and lowered beside it. Asser started the climb up the steps beside the right track.

Jeremiah ran to the lower station and threw a sharp hook to the footman's jaw. The footman fell immediately, and Jeremiah stuffed a rag into his mouth.

Meanwhile, Jeremiah waited, occasionally stepping outside the station to see Asser's location.

Halfway.

Indistinct chatter came from a cup hooked to a station wall, and Jeremiah sped to it and put his ear to it. "Demir, come in. Demir, are you there?" rushed a voice.

Jeremiah panicked; he looked around the station. The footman started to shuffle and awaken.

Jeremiah stepped outside, but he couldn't see Asser.

He ran back to the cup.

"Demir, Demir, where are you?" asked the voice.

As Jeremiah uttered a response, the man's voice abruptly cut off—moments passed, then a familiar voice spoke into the cup.

"Woody, Woody—over—you there? Me is Master Ash, and me's speaking from the magic cup."

Jeremiah exhaled a huge breath, then stepped outside the station and signaled to Padre with a twirl of his finger. From the castle, two dots of light were approaching the upper station.

Padre emptied the tank of water, and the carriage chugged bit by bit.

"Asser," Jeremiah called into the cup inside the lower station, "hurry—the guards are coming."

Asser pushed the shaft, and water tunneled directly over the wheel and flowed down the wooden gutter. The pulley spun, and cables underneath the platform accelerated the carriage.

Jeremiah caught up to the carriage, and Padre opened the door to let him inside. Minutes later, the carriage passed the other carriage to its left and arrived at the upper platform. Asser applied the brake, and the carriage stopped.

"Stay here, Padre," said Jeremiah, "and play the part."

Jeremiah left the carriage and went to the upper station. Asser opened the door. The brakeman was on the ground, unconscious.

"Ready the rope, Asser. Two guards are coming."

The guards approached with swords drawn. "Careful, Firat," said a taller guard. Padre opened the carriage door with a smile. "Hello," he asked in a frail voice, "can you help me, please? I'm lost."

The guards sheathed their swords, and Firat spoke: "Baris, you forget to lock the brake again?"

"No," said Baris harshly. "Who are you, old man?"

Padre flapped his lips. "I told you I'm lost. My cats are here somewhere." He ambled towards the castle and called different names. "Princess, Bella, where are you?"

"He's mad," said Firat. "Chain him to the carriage."

Baris shook his head and asked, "How long has this damn thing had a ticket in for repair?"

Firat drew in a sharp breath, then said, "Months, I believe."

Padre's face seized, and he pretended to cry. He fell to the ground. "Shut his hole," ordered Firat, "before the duke wakes."

When Baris rushed towards him, Asser threw a rope around his feet. Firat lunged for Asser, but Jeremiah sweep-kicked, then punched him. Jeremiah and Asser each tied a guard to a station platform railing and stuffed rags into their mouths.

Jeremiah cut the strings connected to cups inside the station, then said, "Good work, Padre. We'll meet you on the back side of the mountain. Asser—let's go."

Jeremiah briefly glanced to the parapet where a Night Watcher manned the bell tower. "Head down," he said and used the guards' keys to unlock the front door.

Jeremiah peered inside. A single lantern lit the entrance hall.

"No one," he whispered and waved a hand and moved around a hideous statue into a parlor. Through the parlor and out another door, he walked into a corridor lit by lanterns of soft amber light. Along the wall ran strings. *For communications.*

Jeremiah stopped and raised a fist. "Wait—I hear something."

A thud came, then a soft grunt.

"Asser, where are you?" Jeremiah turned to look.

The parlor door clicked shut.

"Asser," whispered Jeremiah loudly, "be quiet."

"Why didn't you warn me about the evil troll statue?" asked Asser. "Wide feet, ugly nose, white hair," he mumbled.

"Asser, shh."

Below them, a woman sang. Jeremiah rushed one foot forward, but it made a loud squeaking sound.

LOVE OR FREEDOM

Bars of moonlight striped the stone floor. Jameela squirmed with tied hands to search for a sharp object to cut the rope, but she stopped once she heard the floorboards. *How did I get here? I go from slavery to freedom to imprisonment again.*

Before the journey, she had fully participated in the world but as a slave, bound to the man who now literally imprisoned her, though her debt had been paid.

The journey rolled back to the beginning in her mind. She had eagerly accepted the mission from Rohad. A chance for freedom? No longer to be prostituting herself to disgusting men? Yes! It was fortuitous to have found Jeremiah so easily. The mission was simple—find the stone, steal it, and deliver it to Rohad.

The night with Aliyah had loosened her memories; darkness in prison squeezed out more.

+ —— +

She ran to her parents and brother after they left the house. The door opened: the battlefield was littered with strewn bodies, some white and dark, all soaked in crimson.

Frightened, cold, and confused, her heart frantically thumped as she wandered. Where was her family?

Rohad welcomed her: "Come here, my child. All is well." He took her hand and pulled her into his chest. "It will be fine. Let me take you to safety."

Rohad had blocked her view, but she heard their wailing and groaning.

+———+

She shook off more memories, and her entire body ached.

Her thoughts attempted to fix on joyous images—her home, paintings, and Jeremiah; however, memories of Jeremiah brought regret. She closed her eyes to force sleep, but her mind spun. Jeremiah kept reappearing.

+———+

"That's her," whispered Jeremiah. "Wait before we go."

Slow knot by slow knot, he looped a rope around the railing. He lowered his body past a hole to the subfloor and softly landed onto pebbles. He ran his fingers atop the floor joists until he found the gaps, then inserted shims and pulled himself up. "This way," he mouthed to Asser, "the prison is this way."

+———+

I should tell him my mission: that I purposely came for him, intentionally pursued him, so I could steal the stone during a moment when we were close. But my feelings became genuine? When did the lies become truth?

Her eyes brimmed with tears.

No, I can't tell him. It's too much. His love was innocent. I'll tell him I was forced, and it wasn't my choice.

No, I can't tell him! We can't be together. I don't need to explain myself. He'll be fine. He doesn't need to know it was my idea. That I approached Rohad with the proposal, and he agreed.

She vividly recalled the scene. Due to high demand from his top clients, Rohad had requested regular visits to tell her the schedule.

+———+

"Who am I seeing this week?" she asked.

Rohad stumbled from his throne but picked up a pile of letters from the messy floor. "Here, read these for me," he said. "Start there," he slurred, "the ones with the church seals."

She had learned about the pope's plan to reunite east and west Christendom, and his proposal to assist Rohad with becoming king of Witen, if Rohad found and returned the missing stone and allowed his duchy to be staged for Crusades. Queen Rachel had too much influence over King Richard, the pope explained. The knowledge of Rachel's illegitimate son, a carpenter from Witenberg named Jeremiah, could be useful information.

<hr />

She shivered and writhed and pushed off a wall with her boots.
Why'd I fall for Jeremiah? He even looks like Rohad!
No—stop—he's not Rohad. Women end up with men they're familiar with. Right? Men they know?
But Jeremiah is so infinitely better! Must have his mother's traits. But also raised by a loving, adopted family. A man is more than his origins.

<hr />

Midway along the corridor, a string moved, and they heard a voice.

"Witen," said Asser, "there must be a guard."

"Quick," said Jeremiah, "in here." They slid into a narrow gap in the wall and hid. "Stand straight."

<hr />

After several minutes of letting Jameela read the letters, Rohad had garbled, then stammered, "Wh-what do they say?"

A silver wine goblet crashed and clanked to the floor after she read them in totality.

Rohad laughed, then said, "My son—I have a son—with Rachel!"

He scuttled out the door and called for a scribe.

Moments later, a scribe came to the door with a notebook and pencil and asked, "Yes, my lord? You called?"

"This is highly confidential, scribe. Do y-you understand?"

"Fully, my lord," the scribe said, then bowed. "On my life."

"Good," Rohad said. "Send a letter to George of Bath in Witenberg as quickly as possible—use my fastest horse. Tell him to meet with Klara and plan a coup against Richard. Tell him Rachel slept with me, and she has a bastard son named Jeremiah. More correspondence will come after I receive his receipt of the letter."

The scribe bowed, and Rohad dismissed him. "And you too, Jameela. You're dismissed."

Rohad returned to his throne and slouched into the seat. "I said you're dismissed, Jameela."

An opportunity! she had thought.

She cleared her throat and postured with her shoulders back and her hands on her hips. "I'll find the stone and give it to you."

Rohad laughed. "How will you find it? And then steal it? Seduction?"

She raised her eyebrows.

"Never mind," he said and found another goblet. "Yes, of course, you're good at that. And I presume you're asking for something in return?"

She leaned forward eagerly and said with a glow: "Yes. My freedom." She rocked back on her heels, waiting for an answer.

He sat upright, pointed to her, and said, "I'll grant you freedom if you deliver. But I'll send help too. Adam and Yusuf will trail you."

Help for me or for you? she wondered. But *Yes!*

She accepted, and shook his hand, but abruptly pulled back once he smirked at her.

Time to go, she thought. With three steps towards the door, she heard Rohad's heavy breath and wide feet waddling as he lumbered after her.

"Love or freedom?" he asked.

"Sorry?" she asked with her neck bent. Her stomach rolled with nausea.

"Simple question, Jameela. Do you prefer love or freedom?"

She swallowed, but the taste in the back of her throat was sour.

"I don't understand. We-we agreed."

She turned, and his frozen smirk cascaded chills from her throat down to her stomach. She hunched over and applied pressure to her midsection.

"A signal, silly. That's all. A phrase to know when Adam and Yusuf are near."

After she answered, Rohad warned, "Just steal the stone—don't let anyone fall in love with you."

<hr />

A board creaked.

"Missed one," muttered Asser.

Then another.

The sound was louder than Jeremiah's hammering heart.

"Concentrate," whispered Jeremiah.

The sound stopped, and Jeremiah smelled garlic and onions.

Jeremiah slowed his breathing and body. With eyes closed, he focused on his training.

The guard turned left, then right, then left again. "The duke will be upset," he said and continued through the corridor. "I must hurry."

The creaking waned, and the guard strode quietly to the parlor door. "What are you doing?" asked the guard. "Why weren't you answering the call?"

In a scratchy voice, the man said, "Your brakeman is sick. Come quickly."

Asser smiled and said, "Aye, the bonniest priest."

"Let's hope he buys us time," said Jeremiah.

+———+

She had buried the threat about love and left Rohad's presence. She promptly told the madam at the Pleasure House her mission, packed, then left the next day on a horse given to her by order of Rohad.

She was confident she would find the missing stone. She scouted Witenberg, took residence in the bath house for months and eavesdropped on many conversations as she served drinks to men.

After overhearing George speak about the carpenter's son allegedly having the stone, she asked around about the location of the carpentry guild. Information led her to the building and a picture of Jeremiah— he had the resemblance of Rohad.

The bath house buzzed with rumors of a prison escape, and Richard's knights pursuing the convicts. When she learned Jeremiah had escaped prison, she assumed he probably sought refuge in shady pubs, far from the law. If he had the stone, stealing it from him would be easy, she remembered thinking.

+———+

She sighed and sang, "Close your eyes, soothe your sighs. Off to the land of dreams you fly. My dear Assie . . ."

Right, another plan. And I'm in prison. I'm being punished for my sins. I can't make things right with Jeremiah—if we see each other again.

"Calm your whys, don't you cry. Off to the land of dreams you fly. My dear Assie . . . ," she sang, and tears welled up.

The lock to her cell jiggled.

She slid back against the wall.

The lock opened, and the door swung out, letting in a little light from the corridor.

Two men were clad in black tunics and cloaks. One was very short, with small hands. *Tiny Hands!* she thought, and cried tears of joy. She could not speak.

"Jameela, you're free," Jeremiah said as he stepped inside. "But we must hurry."

Love or freedom? she asked herself.

Freedom, she decided.

She hiccupped as he untied her hands and legs. Behind them Padre called out, "Run!"

Two guards were sprinting down the hallway.

"They're closing in!" yelled Asser.

"Under the arches," said Jeremiah quickly. "I'll fall back."

"But the towers," warned Jameela.

The guards came closer.

Jeremiah loosened his brooch and hung the cloak over a lantern on the wall, darkening the hallway.

"We got him," crowed a guard.

Jeremiah exited, then closed the door and ran.

The guards extended their arms in the dark and smacked into the door.

"Quick!" Jameela cried, and led them through the middle and inner baileys.

"Around the chapel," said Jameela. "The wall."

The door opened, and more guards slid around the fallen men. "Shoot!" commanded a guard, and his men rained arrows onto the stone courtyard.

"Behind the chapel," called Jameela in a loud whisper.

The guards ran.

"We have to jump," said Jeremiah. They sprang for the wall, and Jeremiah and Asser clasped on, but Jameela slipped.

"Hurry!" bellowed Asser. Over the wall, he looked to Mo. "Prepare the sleds!"

"Jump, Jameela, and I'll grab you," said Jeremiah.

She jumped up, and their fingertips touched but could not hold.

"Try again," urged Jeremiah. Their fingers slipped, and the guards were closing in. Jeremiah jumped down and knelt just behind her. "Climb up," he ordered.

"They'll get you, Jeremiah," she cautioned.

He grunted and pushed her legs on his shoulders. "Over, Jameela."

He pushed until her chest hung over the wall, and she pulled herself over.

"Get him!" one guard said desperately. "He's the one."

Jameela's eyes met his, and Jeremiah said, "Go."

She hesitated, then jumped with Asser off the wall. Jeremiah heard them land as a guard grabbed his leg. He kicked and jumped, then pushed off the wall and climbed. "Go!" he shouted to the team.

They started their slide as Jeremiah jumped into a cushion of pillows and pine. He moved to a sled and dragged it forward with his hands. He accelerated as the guards panicked, then yelled for something to slide down the wall.

Jeremiah looked behind him.

Two guards had jumped and were now sliding down the wall on what resembled a burlap sack.

The diversion was ahead.

The team was near the bottom.

Left or right? he asked himself. *Left or right?*

The team stopped and looked up. "Go!" hollered Jeremiah.

Asser pulled Jameela's arm, and they ran with Mo into the forest darkness.

Jeremiah steered left and skidded and crashed into a pine pile. The guards landed soon thereafter and quickly subdued him. "We got him!" shouted a guard.

"And we got some fatter bait too" said another guard and laughed. They frog-marched Jeremiah around the mountain to the lower funicular station, where Duke Rohad stood with a bloodied Padre in chains.

"Keep them at the station until I signal," Rohad told the guards.

WAR

L ight from the waxing moon illuminated William's notes. Two questions were circled on the first page.

Who killed Mati? Who killed Rachel?

He drew a line that connected both circles. *They must be connected*, he thought, connected to what Rachel had showed him.

He had drafted a plan to drive the pope mad by using his manuscript arguments against him, and to plant clues to lead the pope on a chase. He wanted to make him feel the same anxiety Mati and Rachel must have felt moments before their deaths.

After Richard chopped the dragon's head, he wouldn't budge. Rohad would pay, the king insisted; Adam and Yusuf next; then their militia and residents as collateral damage, if necessary. The Oths would seek justice against Adam and Yusuf, then find the stone.

The colossal ship was gently guided into the shore harbor. Fog slowly rolled in and formed a blanket over the inlet. "Take this," Richard said and handed William a dagger.

It felt heavy in his hands, like an unwanted burden. He stowed his notes in a bag and calmed his nerves with slow breathing.

Richard assessed the plaza. "There he is," said Richard coldly. "Rohad the Round." He told Earl Marshall Stewart, Daniel, and two additional Oths, "Wait for my signal, men."

"Yes, Your Majesty," they said.

They left the ship and started their walk into the city center.

Disorganized and shapeless, clusters of men were gathered in the plaza. Above him, William heard loud, choking squawks. Sparks from a massive bonfire shot into the night and flashed against ghostly, stocky forms flapping out from their hill roosts and soaring over the sea.

Rohad greeted them, flanked by soldiers. There was no awkward hug, nor handshake, nor smile—merely acknowledgment.

"Hello, Richard."

"Hello, Rohad."

Silence followed.

Rohad smelled of pine, William noticed. He scratched his shaggy beard and tightened his velvet cloak before waddling closer to Richard. "Are you here to make an offer, Brother?"

Richard stood taller than the plumper Rohad. "You've failed at keeping the peace, Rohad. The pope blessed this mission, so through strength, we will subdue this people and fully convert them to one faith and one God. You will help me. If you refuse, then war you shall have."

"Brother, Brother, it's not I who has failed. *You* failed your late wife. She would be so disappointed in you."

Richard blew out his cheeks.

He looked at Rohad dead in the face and said, "What do you know about love, Brother? How many wives have you had? How many young women have you harmed through your sex trade?"

"Harmed?" Rohad's body chuckled at the thought. "Quite the opposite. *Your* war left many young women widowed and without brothers or fathers to financially provide for them. I commissioned Adam and Yusuf to engage in a wonderful business. Those women are now able to live on their own. It's called *empowerment*."

"Adam and Yusuf! You commissioned them!" Richard barked and clenched the shield with his left hand. "Those very devils who killed my wife. Killed my wife!"

With corded neck and rattling mail, Richard unsheathed the sword with his right hand. He pushed the grip before Rohad's nose. "*You* commissioned them to murder Rachel. That was your signature. Your code words."

Rohad read Rachel's name inscribed on the leather grip of the sword and closed his eyes. He swayed his body and licked his lips as if remembering something. He whiffed at the grip and slow-clapped and said, "Very good, Brother. Very good. You must have seen the message."

Waving a finger, Rohad continued, "I always knew you were smarter than most people said. But death wasn't the primary goal. I meant merely to scare her enough to convince you to start another war. To manipulate you, to *humiliate* you. She knew the gift was from me. It spoke truth. But the tapestry must have frightened her so much that she died. You may not have realized it, Richard, but you abandoned your son."

A tapestry scared her to death? William thought. *That doesn't make sense.* He watched Rohad's body language.

Richard balked and clenched the sword tighter. "You're lying. Ever since we were kids, you've done nothing but lie."

Rohad paused, then his face split into a smile. He raised his right hand, and the militia enclosed Richard, Stewart, and the Oths.

Several fighters placed drums about the cluster of Richard's men, and with each beat, they pounded loud and louder and quick and quicker. Others lifted their torches and yelled. Horns joined them.

Earl Marshall Stewart and the Oths inched closer, but Richard raised his shield high. Stewart looked over his shoulder to the ships and signaled.

Rohad raised his voice. "You're right about that. I do lie, but only to protect people. *Your* wife must have kept the secret hidden for many years."

How does he know? William thought.

Rachel was careful; yet someone close must have known about Jeremiah—and told Rohad. *A midwife? A maid? A sentinel?*

Rohad signaled the crowd. Drumming stopped, horns silenced, and hollering halted. Adam swaggered into the circle with a hammer and shield.

Richard squeezed the sword grip tighter and grunted. His eyes glazed over, and William saw the same look, the same cold, empty focus Richard had before he chopped off the dragon's head.

Rohad pressed further, "Oh, I'm sorry. She didn't tell you before her tragic death, did she? I seduced her one night twenty years ago. What can I say?" He massaged his belly. "She couldn't resist my charm. She was embarrassed about it, but you were off looking for the stone. Eventually she would tell you about him, I thought. I guess you didn't know. It was only one night for her. But it was a *good* night."

Where was Rohad during Rachel's pregnancy?

Richard released the shield, leaned forward with his left leg, and drew his sword high with both hands, the point aiming downward at Rohad's throat.

"In a moment, Richard," Rohad continued, his voice full of malicious tones, "you will see Rachel's betrayal—" He began to laugh but choked on his laughter and managed, "You weren't good enough! You couldn't—she planned your succession from my seed!"

"No mercy from the edge of this blade," snarled Richard. "This means war." Richard lunged towards Rohad to strike, but Adam moved forward with his shield. Richard recoiled slightly from the unexpected resistance while Adam laughed, making a half-chuckling, half-sneering sound.

"So embarrassing for a king. And you expect to unify the entire kingdom with bravery the size of a mustard seed?" asked Rohad. He waddled outside the ring and ordered the guards, "Bring Jeremiah and Padre here."

The guards left the plaza and ran towards the castle, stopping at the base of the mountain beside a funicular station.

He's alive? William thought. But Daniel said he had died.

William looked to the square-jawed knight; with less protection than the army had, Daniel's legs were thicker and his chest wider than most soldiers. There was no shock on his face—and William remembered the remarkable ability for each member of the Oths to change from playful comrades to fierce warriors instantly—as fast as turning a key and opening a locked door.

Perhaps Richard had misheard Daniel—or Daniel lied—or Daniel didn't know and misled Richard.

As Daniel stared at Adam, then looked beyond Jeremiah to something flying over the hills, Padre and Jeremiah were dragged into the circle.

FREEDOM

"Your Majesty, we await your command," Daniel said, then staggered his feet, angled them to the side, and raised a rear heel, as if eager to charge towards Adam, who was swinging his hammer in smooth rhythm and rotation.

Richard stabilized into a solid, well-balanced stance, picked up his shield, and said, "Wait."

Jeremiah clenched his jaw, tightened his muscles, and swiveled his head, noticing the ring of soldiers surrounding the king and his men was tightening. One man in Richard's circle seemed out of place with his gaunt and angular frame and a satchel in one hand and a dagger in the other hand. He jiggled his legs and rocked on his toes.

Before Jeremiah could process a nagging suspicion that he knew this man, Rohad tapped his fingers against his tongue and then asked, "Can't an uncle welcome a nephew and his teacher? And oh—" He stopped and growled to mock Jeremiah: "I do like your all-black outfit—an assassin in training, are you?"

Summoning a bit of Asser's combative attitude, Jeremiah moaned, leaned forward, and challenged Rohad: "Gross, you knave. Uncle? You have some resemblance to me, but you, you got the ugly side of the coin."

"I haven't kept up with my appearance like I should," he admitted and patted his humongous belly. "Too much bacon, ale, and wine, I gather, have put on the pounds."

"And the grease. Do you roll around with the pigs too?"

Rohad stroked his finger down Jeremiah's cheek and diagonally across his neck like a blade aiming for the cut. "Oh, you have my humor too. I always love killing the sarcastic ones first. It's so much pleasure."

Jeremiah boiled inside, then hollered, "Piss off, dolt! Woodness, you're pure woodness."

Rohad circled Jeremiah and added, "You didn't know the king was your *real* father, your flesh and blood?"

"He's lying, Jeremiah," Richard said, the words snapping dryly, without breaking eye contact with Rohad.

Jeremiah pulled against the chains that tied his hands.

"Why the God-fearing, lovely man, Padre—he didn't tell you during this long journey?"

"Padre?" asked Jeremiah. "That can't be true, Rohad."

"Are you sure?" asked Rohad. He tilted his head and flashed his eyes.

Jeremiah turned to Padre, who had turned red. Jeremiah squinted, then asked, "Padre? Is this true?"

Padre didn't answer.

"Take Adam and Yusuf," said the slender man wearing a wide-brimmed black hat.

The man's voice punctuated the suspicion Jeremiah had, confirming that this was the same man that searched for the stone during the mead ball. However, the broken bits of thoughts wondering what this man was doing beside the king flew past his attention like the large number of embers being blown by the wind.

"Injustice here is a threat to justice elsewhere in the kingdom," Richard said, his voice precise and monotonous. His pearly eyes fixated on Rohad, and he straightened his back.

"When I heard you had escaped from prison, I thought: 'that's my nephew.' That's the same courage we"—Rohad beat his chest—"in the family possess. I have it, and you have it. Haven't you ever wondered why you look so different from the rest of your family?"

Rohad rested a chestnut-colored cheek against Jeremiah's. "See the resemblance, boys?"

"Why'd you bring us here?" barked Jeremiah.

"I have what you want."

"And what's that?"

"Something you need, something you want, something you love."

"Listen, I don't care about the stone. You can have it. It's powerless, anyway."

"Oh, you misguided boy. The stone does have powers, tremendous powers, but that's not what I'm talking about. You have the power to stop war, a war that stripped your brother of his mind, that forced him to cower before Adam."

Tackle him, pounded the thoughts in Jeremiah's mind. "Adam!" barked Jeremiah. He bared his teeth and pulled at his chains. "You swinish canker-blossom murderer!"

Rohad rubbed his gut and smirked. "How cute—you learned the Witen's English."

"Let me go!"

"Certainly, but you must do one little thing for me."

Jeremiah paused and cooled—slowly. "First, you must hand over Adam and Yusuf to King Richard."

"Oh, he has backbone. I love it." Rohad twirled his knotty hair. "It's not that simple. How can I trust you'll do what I ask?"

"Name it. I'll do it. On my real parents' grave—the grave of my dadde and mum who raised me, who loved me." Jeremiah stopped and recognized this was the first time he had mentioned love and his adopted parents in a long time. *But I said it in the past tense,* he thought.

"Good, very good. Adam," Rohad beckoned, "come here." Rohad signaled to his soldiers, and they promptly subdued Adam and tied his hands and feet.

"Take him to the king's soldiers," ordered Jeremiah.

"Of course, my lord," Rohad said and waved a hand. Cursing and spitting, Adam was pushed into the arms of Earl Marshall Stewart.

As Adam grunted, Daniel slapped him across the face, then punched him in the stomach.

"Tie him, Daniel," said Richard. "We want Yusuf too, Rohad."

"You'll have Yusuf if Jeremiah does another easy task."

"How do I know?" asked Jeremiah.

"Know what?"

"Know Yusuf—is here. I don't see him."

"Trust me."

After a high, cold laugh, Richard said, "Don't trust him, Jeremiah. He's fluent in treachery."

Jeremiah inhaled sharply, then said, his voice sounding earnest, "Show me."

"My pleasure, my lord. Colonel, parade Yusuf."

Soldiers dragged Yusuf across the plaza in chains and handed him over to Stewart. "See, you can trust me."

Turning to Richard, Rohad said, "Isn't this what you wanted? Or, did you want *me*?"

Richard turned towards the ship and raised his shield; sailors ran to different stations, and the sound of metal clinking against metal pierced the plaza.

Soldiers left the ship and assembled on shore, and the shapeless clusters of Rohad's militia organized into tactical formation columns.

After a curt nod, Rohad dropped a stone into Jeremiah's palm.

"Little Jeremiah, meet your father, the man who abandoned you for that stone in your hand. The man who abandoned your mother. Have you noticed your resemblance to Queen Rachel?"

My mother? What?

Suddenly, Jeremiah remembered the pendant and its words. "This too shall pass," he said aloud in the troll's language. That day at the castle. The loving embrace and her long-held glance. *Why didn't she tell me?*

"Stop a war by killing your father," demanded Rohad.

Richard's face had the look of a father who had watched his son go off to war. He looked strong, yet his face held the suggestion of poise containing sorrow about to flood.

Elfred, recalled Jeremiah. His adopted father had such an expression, before he saw one son depart in glory and another retreat in fear.

Rohad's wooly frame symbolized the cannibal of the moment, his sanctimonious, arrogant mouth salivating to devour his prey. All for power. All for control. His words conveyed no war, but his body proclaimed the opposite. He would do *anything* for power.

"Stop a war by killing your father," Rohad reminded, his voice cold and impersonal, commanding deference.

Drums started again, pounded louder, and soldiers hollered.

Richard lowered his shield; their eyes met, and Jeremiah's heart hurt.

An emptiness returned—with a vast and bottomless hole. He looked at the stone and considered. Ice cold, it cooled his flushed skin.

Will killing him prevent war?

Padre's head was pulled back, his mouth gaped, and his body tensed as if he were about to accept a blow.

The plan to make me a man, Jeremiah recalled. *The Evil One,* Louise had taught, *highlights your pain and lures with false hope, encouraging you to give in to your anger. He wants you to transmit the pain onto others.*

"But you're stronger than that," Louise had assured him. "Be a seed of hope."

War is not the answer, persuaded a louder voice. *More will die.*

Rohad removed Jeremiah's chains and pushed him into the ring until he was within stone-striking distance. "Do it, boy!"

Richard calmly commanded, "Come here, Jeremiah, so you can hear me."

Jeremiah studied the battle ring; drums beat to the rhythmic pounding of his heart.

"Do it, boy!" yelled Rohad. "Kill him now!"

Jeremiah stumbled forward with leaden legs and trembling arms. He stopped until a foot before Richard. Their eyes locked; Jeremiah discerned the heart of a strong, yet broken man. The stone wobbled in his hand. From a distance, he heard hoarse screeches.

"What are you doing?" shouted Rohad. "Kill him, you bastard!"

Richard's soldiers bounced on their toes, ready to charge on his order. Rohad's militia drew weapons, ready to charge on his order.

Richard lowered his head to meet Jeremiah's gaze. Jeremiah fumbled; he didn't know Richard—only despised his rule. He tried to dam an outbreak of despair he hadn't permitted himself to release. *My real parents!* he lamented to himself. Palming the stone, he about-faced and declared coldly to Rohad, "I'll do it."

"Good boy!" exclaimed Rohad.

He turned to Rohad and said slowly, intently, "Release Padre, and I'll do it."

"Do as he says," ordered Rohad.

The cuffs came off, and Padre stood motionless for a moment, a glazed look on his face with an utterly blank stare of confusion and disappointment.

The stone wobbled in Jeremiah's hand.

A thin strip of reddish-orange hues, as straight as a line drawn on wood before the cut, coated the Dark Sea. Above it, the sky brightened but darkness still ruled the morning.

A sense of hope flashed as he recalled a similar sunrise during the morning he and Elfred had left home and took the chair to the castle.

Dread quickly returned, however, and the atmosphere was like a coming thunderstorm with the sense of charged and suspended air.

He closed both eyes.

Hoarse screeches came more distinctly—coming in beats of three—and images of Rûah diving and catching a mouse popped into his focus.

As he opened his eyes, voices taunted him: *Rejection! Bastard!* He recalled the time when Marianne rejected him for Harry at the creek and his first response was to throw stones at a tree, pretending Harry's face was the target.

But he had missed Harry's imaginary forehead—he shot high.

He tossed the stone twice into the air, then steadied his stance. *What should I do?*

Drumming stopped, and a ghostly hush dampened sounds as effective as sealing gaps around doors and windows.

He tossed the stone into the air.

A quieter, gentler voice spoke: *Aim high.*

After catching the stone, he wound back and threw it in a powerful, straight line.

Rohad's cry was immediate and had the sound of panic and quality of an automatic reflex. At the sound, Rohad's men rushed to the Oths and pulled Adam and Yusuf to their side.

The stone sailed wide over Richard's head and his raised shield and splashed straight into the sea. At the sound of the splash, he could smell the fear and desperation oozing from Rohad's pores. *That is what abuse of power really looks like*, he thought. An overwhelming sense of agitation filled him, attacking him for intentionally missing. He sensed Rohad was evil and Richard was misguided.

He charged towards Richard, growling like the bear attacking in full sprint, then stopped and said softly to Richard, "A show, Dad."

Richard beamed. "Rachel, your mother, was always right. She was a wonderful woman. Know well that she loved you. Honor her death and my death. Be a servant king."

Richard pulled him closer and showed him a dagger. "Listen to me closely. You'll punch me. I'll charge towards you, and we'll wrestle to confuse them. You'll cut me slightly. I'll roar, and they'll think you killed me. Then you'll run to Rohad's castle. If I don't kill Rohad, you will. Understand?"

"Kill Rohad?" Jeremiah asked. His peripheral vision became cloudy, and his hand shook.

Richard grasped Jeremiah's hand and said, his voice sincere, "I loved Rachel with all my heart, Son. Rohad ordered Adam and Yusuf to kill her. Though I wasn't the best king, I tried. You must believe me."

With tears, Jeremiah accepted. "Yes, yes, I believe you."

"Good. Ready?"

"Yes."

"Aye. Scream and go," said Richard.

Jeremiah roared deeply and landed a strong right hook into Richard's jaw.

"Finally, boy!" yelled Rohad. "The throne is mine! Kill him."

Richard lunged and tackled Jeremiah. Clutched in Richard's arms, he firmed his hand and made a shallow slice on Richard's stomach, under his mail.

Feigning rage, Richard boomed, and his voice must have carried beyond the market into the villages. "Rachel!" he bellowed. His men heeded the order, beat their chests, and repeated the roars. They sounded the horns.

Richard pushed Jeremiah off him. "Go!"

Jeremiah ran, but Rohad's soldiers rushed towards him. "You failed, boy. But I had a backup plan. Don't trust anyone—ever."

"Swinish canker!" Jeremiah yelled as they tied him.

"Lieutenants," said Rohad, "release Yusuf to the hills. Free Adam and give him the hammer."

Adam bared his teeth like a caged animal. He roared as the rope was cut and he was given a war hammer. "Kill Richard, Adam," ordered Rohad. "Colonel, after Richard dies, take Jeremiah to the castle."

Adam ripped at his tunic. Showing his massive chest and broad shoulders, Adam growled. Drumming started again with beats hurried and heavier. Adam swung the war hammer attached to a chain, whirling it about him as if it were a lasso. He released it, and it thudded a foot before Richard, cracking the town square pavement.

"For my people!" barked Adam.

Jeremiah cringed at the stabs of regret.

Daniel and the Oths pulled the sword handles past their hips and held their stances with the long edges down, *in plow position*, Jeremiah remembered, to protect and cover from attack.

Richard ordered the Oths to stand down. "He's mine," he announced. "Fight me, heathen!" Richard charged towards Adam.

Rohad rested his cheek beside Jeremiah's and said, "Watch your dadde die." His laugh came high and raw.

Jeremiah squirmed as Rohad's piney beard bristled against his mouth. He forcefully jerked his head to push Rohad from him and yelled, "Let's go, Your High—" Jeremiah broke off abruptly and swallowed. "Let's go, Dadde!" he cheered.

Adam pulled the hammer out of the pavement and swung it again, but the shield blocked it. Richard released the shield and grabbed the chain, pulling Adam in. Adam kicked, swiped with a dagger, but he barely scratched Richard's mail. Adam regained the hammer and swung with less force but landed a blow right in Richard's gut. The king thundered, recoiled, and slammed backwards.

"Dadde!" shouted Jeremiah. "Get back up."

"Shut his hole," yapped Rohad.

A soldier pushed a rag into Jeremiah's mouth.

As Richard dry-heaved, he stumbled and looked towards Jeremiah. He saw the rag and exploded with rage, then ripped his chain mail cleanly in two halves.

Rohad's militia encircled closer and encouraged Adam with chants. Adam ran with a dagger out and head down like a rhino.

Richard clutched the chain and dragged it to him.

When Adam reached him, Richard dodged the dagger, tackled him, and wrapped the chain around his throat. "For Rachel," Richard said, grimacing. He pulled tighter until Adam breathed his last breath.

Adam's body limped and crumpled to the ground, and Richard's body fell too, from exhaustion. He fell on his knees, and he closed Adam's eyes.

"For Rachel," Richard mumbled.

The crowd hushed, and drums stopped.

"Witen," grumbled Rohad. "Colonel, take Jeremiah and follow

me." As Jeremiah was pulled into a run, he witnessed the carnage around him.

From the hills, archers released arrows and lit pigs that had been fitted with torches. Friendly fire rained down and killed many of Rohad's men. Flaming war boars squealed, broke loose, and bolted down the mountain in terror. Some ran into the sea and some trampled the combatants.

Rohad's lieutenants tried to control the mess, but most scattered. Arrows continued to strike flesh and thud into stone.

Richard stood and yelled out with arms extended—this time the signal ordered the release of crossbow fires from his ship. With Richard leading, Daniel and the Oths charged, and the man in the black hat panicked.

Jeremiah turned his head continuously, seeing Richard attacking with his sword, then picking up a bow and arrow.

Padre weaved and ducked around swords, then ran towards the ship, but men were quickly gaining on him.

Daniel fought off the men chasing Padre, then protected him with a shield until retreating beyond the city plaza and closer to the ship.

"William," yelled Daniel during the run, "return to the ship!"

Once Padre was safe in the ship, Daniel charged two men attacking William, and with a swish and thrust of his sword, killed two men easily. William went to the ship, and Daniel ran farther into the city.

Closer to the funicular station, Jeremiah saw archers falling from the cliffs and plunging into the sea. Some survivors fled; others pushed boulders down the mountain, and the rest ran down the hills to join the clash in the square.

The flaming arrows and pigs ignited the forested hills; the conflagration began to devour the parched mountain, but the fog blanket dampened some of the flames.

Birds multiplied; flocks swarmed from multiple directions to feast on the roasted swine and bloodied carcasses of men.

Meanwhile, the Royal Army hurtled towards the soldiers with

shields and all fury and valor. After spears flew, the two armies collided and echoed against the mountains to create a cacophony of terror. Swords struck down maces, hammers, and axes. They sliced through armored flesh and crushed the militia with irresistible strength.

"To the rail," wheezed Rohad. "Colonel, stay here with your men and guard the gate." Rohad pushed Jeremiah into the carriage and motioned to the footman. He yelled into the cup, "Brakeman, start the ride!"

No response came, and Jeremiah spat out the rag. Rohad smacked the cup with his hand. "Somebody, start this damn rail!"

The only response was Jeremiah's cackling. "It won't work," he said, his voice biting. "We cut the strings."

"Ugh!" growled Rohad. He stopped and caught his breath. "This way, you bastard." They climbed the steps beside the track. Below them, men groaned their last, and Rohad surveyed his militia in a glance. Richard and his army had killed scores of them.

"Rohad!" roared Richard, looking up at his brother on the steps. "Let him go."

Forest burned around them, and half-eaten hogs lay prostrate in flames. Other birds scattered when the albatrosses soared, but one familiar hawk circled through the smoke. Breathless and dragging, Rohad said, "I've had too much wine over the years, dear brother."

Richard pulled an arrow from a quiver around his back, placed it in the bow and aimed for Rohad's head, but Jeremiah was in the way. "It's finished, Rohad," the king said. "Surrender. Let him go."

"Never, Brother. I will have what is rightfully mine."

Yusuf emerged from the hills and shot arrows towards Richard.

"Yusuf, thank God," struggled Rohad. "Finish him. Avenge Adam's death and this destruction. Kill the king."

Jeremiah tried to break free but couldn't. Squawking, Rûah zoomed around flames and under snapping tree branches.

"Rûah!" shouted Jeremiah. "Good girl!"

She flew past Rohad's head, and he stumbled up the steps. She looped around and came back for Rohad, screeching, then flew into the hills.

Rohad pushed Jeremiah and chugged up the hill. Richard shot at Rohad but missed as he had to keep blocking Yusuf's arrows with another shield.

Yusuf skipped and jumped downward off rocks. He somersaulted onto flat land and flung two daggers that found their mark in Richard's neck.

After the impact, Richard immediately sucked for air. He grabbed his throat and fell to his knees. Jeremiah furiously rubbed the rope against a rock, loosened it, and yelled, "No!"

Yusuf spat on Richard. "For my people," he said, then climbed the tracks.

Richard struggled to speak, but he managed to say, "I'm sorry, Tulip. I love you. I'll always love you."

His eyelids flipped rapidly like he was dreaming. "I'll be with you soon," he said. Jeremiah, loose, raced to him and propped up his head. Richard opened his eyes, clenched Jeremiah's shoulder, and said, "By my authority, I declare you King of Witen."

Richard sucked air, and after a long breath, he mumbled, "Be a servant king."

Richard died, and Jeremiah increased swallowing in spasms. He turned his head to search the steps for Rohad, but he couldn't move with Richard in his arms. He grimaced at his own indecision, yet he remembered Richard's command. He carefully lay Richard down and said, "I'll return."

He surveyed the funicular tracks. He couldn't go to the front of the castle. He hopped over thicket and swerved around trees as he climbed the mountain and came to a curtain wall flanked with towers, where guards with arrows searched for intruders.

"Witen," snapped Jeremiah. *How would Rohad escape? Where would he go?* he wondered.

Overhead, Rûah circled.

Through the forest, the sound of another person was running.

He held his breath.

The brush opened to reveal Louise, and in the light of dawn, she shone brilliantly, resembling his imagined figurine, clad in armor and wielding two mighty swords on her back.

"Your pack, Jeremiah," she said gaily. "We're here."

He looked at her silently, shocked.

She pulled both swords and gave one to him. "You don't get to have all the fun."

"We need to find Rohad," he told her. "But the guards," he said and pointed.

"Have faith, Jeremiah." She whistled through her fingers, and Rûah shed altitude. "Something I taught her while you were away."

Rûah dove towards the towers and harassed the guards. They fired but missed as she maneuvered in and out, then flew around the towers. One guard fell, and another guard raced down the stairs.

"Our chance," she said. "Lift me."

He hoisted her over the wall. She lowered her arm, and he jumped. He held on as she pulled, and he kicked his legs up the wall.

They landed in grass on the other side and hid behind the nearest building. "What's our plan?" she asked him.

"Justice," he said, gritting his teeth.

She drew in a long breath, then smacked his thigh as she had done with the ruler.

"Capture, then, Sister," he confirmed after a brief pause and thought of Richard. "That is our plan."

"Good, let's move."

"Wait," he mouthed and tilted his head, listening. Guards had entered the courtyard with bags.

"Rohad must be packing," she said. "Quick, through here."

She quickly picked the lock and opened a door.

They entered.

Serenity and power resided in this space. Twilight shone through a mosaic stained-glass window and spotlighted a small area behind the altar with a free-standing, cylindrical marble column, about waist high.

He went to the pedestal, and there was a stone.

Wait.

He stopped.

He had already used the stone. *Was it a replica or the real one?*

Compelled to touch it, he pressed and rotated his right thumb into each indentation. Its power rang through him and electrified each nerve. Blood rushed to his brain, and his eyelids batted uncontrollably.

Images blurred like a fast flip-book through his mind; he watched the vanquishing of Goliath and a dragon. When he removed his thumb, the moving images reversed. He sat on a nearby bench and deeply exhaled.

All the times I touched the stone and never . . .

He remembered the cipher commission: "'Slay the lies. Learn King, Sage, Warrior, Lover.'"

He palmed the stone, then uncurled his fingers. Twilight highlighted the speckles of broken white shells inside its crevices. A kaleidoscope of sunflower spirals twirled on the floor.

Jeremiah marveled at the brilliance.

Through the window, he saw a figure that threw a shadow into the church. The shadow figure moved towards the front door.

I should keep the stone for now—to protect it.

He touched the marble throne, but he pulled back and stuffed the stone inside his tunic pocket.

"We must go," Jeremiah said and darted out the back door.

Near the wall, they stopped. An arrow missed them and hit the grass near his foot.

"Jeremiah, my boy!" Rohad said with false cheer and wobbled into the courtyard. "I believe you have what is mine."

"What are you talking about, knave?" barked Jeremiah. He looked left and right, but Rohad's men had closed in.

"Get him, boys," ordered Rohad.

Guards charged towards them with swords drawn. Louise held off the initial blow as Jeremiah sprang for Rohad.

Swords clanked, and she thrust her sword into a guard's armor, back-kicked, and swiped another's chest mail. She ran into the middle bailey and fought more guards. "Alive!" she shouted.

Rohad turned and retreated towards the castle. Behind him, Jeremiah thought he heard footsteps, but he saw a passing shadow. Down the wooden floorboards he ran and entered the parlor after Rohad.

"Rohad," said Jeremiah, "you can't escape. Come with me to Witenberg."

"And be tortured?" retorted Rohad. "I don't think so." He ran through the entrance hall, but Yusuf stood there, a towering figure clad in black.

"Yusuf," gasped Rohad, "thank God you're here. You have impeccable timing. Kill him."

Lantern light showed the steel glints in Yusuf's eyes. He threw Rohad to the floor and ordered, "Wait here, bastard. I want you to watch." Yusuf locked the door, and Rohad cowered in the corner.

Yusuf attacked Jeremiah with a sword, but Jeremiah moved aside, and it slashed the wall maps. "*I* will have the stone."

Jeremiah danced around the hall, remembering his training with Louise, and returned hits with his sword, but his arms grew tired.

"She won't love you," Yusuf said and front-kicked him. Jeremiah stumbled into the parlor, and Yusuf charged. The front door burst open, and Rohad shrieked. Yusuf turned, and in that brief instance, Jeremiah ran.

"Get him, Yusuf!" said a man robed in brown.

"No, please, no," cried Rohad. "You don't understand."

"What don't I understand?" asked the man gruffly. "How long have you kept the stone from our master?"

"A short time," Rohad muttered as he weaseled into the parlor.

"Too long for him," said the man.

Jeremiah crouched behind a large oak coffer and looked around the room. The door was in reach, but how many guards were there?

Louise, he wondered, *where are you?*

"No, no, please no," cried Rohad. "What does he want? I have money. He can have the castle."

"The stone," fumed the man. He rotated his neck, and it cracked loudly. "Goodbye, you bumbling fool." The man raised his sword high and punched it sharply into Rohad's chest.

"Yusuf," the man said as he retracted his sword. "Where's Jeremiah?"

"Who are you?" asked Yusuf.

"Your best friend. Now find Jeremiah."

Jeremiah looked through the glass parlor door; there he saw a glittering eye, and joy erupted inside him. She held a finger to her mouth.

Louise opened the door and shot two arrows, one into each man's leg. Jeremiah bolted for the door. "I know a way out," he said.

They ran through the baileys, jumped for the ledge, and stood atop the wall. "Bloody good work," said Jeremiah, noticing the bodies strewn across the grass.

"Bloody, yes," she quipped, "but not deadly."

"You stunned them," he concluded, and his lips held the hints of a smile.

They jumped onto a pile of pine and pillows. "Get a cloak," he said, indicating the pile they'd left earlier.

The first one she grabbed and put on swallowed her. "No, Sister," he said and laughed. "It goes on under your bottom."

He handed her a smaller cloak, and he used Mo's. They flew down the chute, and then ran through the forest.

Louise called in high-pitched beats of three, and Rûah swooped, slowed, and landed on her gloved arm.

LOVE

Jeremiah shared the journey with Louise during their fast trek through the woods. They came to the first bend of the river and the water mill.

"Your friends are safe in the village," said the navalier.

"All of them?" asked Jeremiah. "Padre too—the older man?"

"Yes, all of them."

Jeremiah and Louise boarded the long, narrow boat and sat. Jeremiah unfolded a note he had tucked away for most of the journey.

It was his poem—but not the poem to Marianne—that was destroyed instantly in the mead-ball fire, he remembered. It felt like so long ago, but he hoped she was happy.

I was in love with her.

"A note?" asked Louise.

"Yes, Sister, for Jameela. I wrote it during the long winter after my brother's death. I almost forgot how to write, but I recalled the feelings I had had with Marianne. And the Holy Spirit inspired."

"Jameela?" she asked.

"Yes, the woman my heart longed for," he said.

Like the rising sun, Jeremiah's heart ballooned with warmth as his warm blood galloped through each vessel. "I can't wait to see her."

He folded the note in two and then tore it. He stowed the bottom half in his tunic pocket and held the top half in his hand. They gazed upon the shimmering dawn light along the river as the navis came to the second bend and around Maghali towards the Dark Sea.

"Rings?" asked Louise, pointing to shapes spiraling out of the landscape for a few miles.

"Ellipses," said Jeremiah. "The village is beyond the ellipses, but we must enter by the sea." They came to a dock and a sentinel. Jeremiah recited Rachel's prayer to the sentinel.

"This too shall pass," the sentinel said and allowed passage through the gate. Before leaving the dock, he saw arms waving wildly from her house.

Having had no rest, all Jeremiah wanted was to fall over and sleep this nightmare away. But at first glance, he sprang back to life. Her beauty radiated; her hair, skin, and eyes glistened against the Dark Sea's waters and Maghali's snowcapped peaks.

There was slight hesitation, then running—both of them. As if filled with a thousand candles, his heart ignited and glowed. From his sparkles, he hoped that, like arrows, his love was shooting towards her.

They met in the middle and kissed briefly. Then, as if on cue, her sneeze broke the embrace. After sneezing in fits of three, she cradled him in a hug. The aroma of honeysuckle and bluebonnets filled her hair. Jeremiah dreamed of staying in her arms—for that moment never to end—to rest in her scent and hug her for eternity.

She pulled back. The emotion and fatigue nearly collapsed him, but he managed to pull out the note. "For you," he said. "I missed you, Jameela."

"I missed you too, Jeremiah," she said and bit her lip.

"Open it!" he exclaimed.

She unfolded the note and read.

A flush crept across her cheeks; she squirmed but steadied herself to skim the rest. She hastily folded the note. In the distance, a black flock undulated up and down like in a wave, up and down, swimming through the clouds, appearing and disappearing, coming closer. She dragged her feet back a step.

"Like it?" he asked.

"Yes, yes, very much so." She extended arms for a light hug; her limbs shook as she looked up.

"Are you all right?"

"Yes," she said and lowered her gaze down and to the side. "I'm sorry, Jeremiah."

Sorry? He massaged his rolling stomach with suddenly cold fingers. She took another step back.

"Sorry?" he asked, his voice full of contempt and confusion. "I thought you'd love the note," he said.

"Yes," she said and turned and ran towards her home, "but I must use the privy."

His knees buckled, but Louise steadied him. "She'll be fine, Jeremiah," said Louise. "Look, it's your friends."

Asser, Mo, and Padre ran towards him.

"Miah!" Padre exclaimed, then buried him in a hug.

"Welcome home. Good to see you're not dead," joked Asser.

Mo smiled and said, "Keeping shinin', my brother. Shine on."

"My Lord will always be Christ, but," Padre said and bowed, "but I hope you are a virtuous, earthly king."

"King?" mocked Asser. "God help us."

"Yes, bow to your new king," said Padre.

"Where are Richard and Rohad?" asked Asser.

"Dead," Jeremiah said flatly and shared more details.

Louise handed Rûah to Jeremiah, and his face glowed.

"Shall we celebrate?" asked Louise. She grabbed Padre's arm, and they two-stepped around the yard. She broke from Padre's twirl and ran to the purple house, where Bhakita and a girl were standing on the porch. "I'll invite them and get Jameela," assured Louise. "And we'll drink!"

"Aye, King Jeremiah of the Wood," said Asser. "Me measure it has a nice ring to it." He jumped and clicked his heels. "But me prefer King Woody."

"Think Jameela has Jeremiah Mead in her house?" asked Jeremiah.

"Not a chance, Woody."

Mo rubbed his great paw against Jeremiah's head and sang deep from his diaphragm,

I say, roll, Miah, roll. Roll, Miah, roll.
Your soul arise, oh, my Lord! Roll, Miah, roll.

Asser bleated like a goat. "Me have a better one, Mo."

He clapped his hands and sang:

"Hop on ya left, and hop on ya right. That's it," said Asser. "And clap your hands."

"Asser," Jeremiah said lightly and dragged the "Ass." He clapped his hands and said, "This is so stupid. Ohhhh," he sang, and his voice rose in pitch. "My dear Assie . . ."

EPILOGUE

After Daniel left William at the ship and returned to the battlefield, William went to his room in the officer's cabin and saw that the cupboards were open. Utensils and papers were spread across the floor.

He went to the king's cabin and saw a similar mess—like someone had been searching for something.

On deck, sailors continued to shoot large arrows with crossbows. Through the fog of war, William saw two men, robed in brown, running towards the hills.

He left the ship and followed them through the forest. They came to a castle gate, and someone let them in.

William retraced his steps and came to the base of the mountain. After spying the lower funicular station and seeing it empty, he climbed the steps.

The upper station was also deserted, so he crouched beneath the windows. Minutes after bells struck on the quarter hour, the sounds of cracking popped.

He slowly raised his head.

The sun shone over the wheel, and the beams hit him in the eyes. *What is that?* he wondered as he peaked above a window.

A body was being dragged across the castle's front plaza. A man in brown hobbled on one foot and disrobed. *That man,* William thought and ducked quickly.

He caught a glimpse of the man's body: broad shoulders and a long, mangy mane. The man turned before entering the carriage, and a wedge of light fell across his face. He brushed cork from his beard.

Cracky?

From the carriage, the man shot daggers at William.

"Witen," uttered William.

Beyond the wheel, a bell rang.

Sharp strike, sharp strike, sharp strike.

Ring up. Wait.

Long strike. Full circle.

Six rings signify the hour.

CHARACTER LIST

In order of appearance

CHARACTERS   **ROLE**

Prologue

Matia Virdis   Archbishop of Witenberg

Part One

Jeremiah   Carpenter
Elfred   Jeremiah's father
Asser   Witenberg bailiff
Sarah   Jeremiah's mother
Aubrey de Vere   King Richard's chamberlain
Harold   Witenberg sheriff
Stewart   Earl Marshall/Commander of Royal Army
William   Investigator for the Church
Harry   Lord Harold's son
Rachel   Queen of Witen
James Eames   Abbot of Rose Abbey
Adolphus   Elder of the Order of Night Watchers
Stinky Feet   Brother at Rose Abbey
Cracky   Brother at Rose Abbey
Pius   Brother at Rose Abbey
Marianne   Jeremiah's friend
Alfred   Jeremiah's brother

CHARACTER LIST

In order of appearance

CHARACTERS	ROLE
Martin	Jeremiah's grandfather
Padre	Jeremiah's friend/Pastor of Our Lady Church
Richard	King of Witen
Elena	Queen Rachel's maid
Isabella	Princess of Witen/daughter of Richard and Rachel
Klara	Princess Isabella's maid
Charles	Chief of Witen Parliament
Charlotte	Marianne's mother
George of Bath	Merchant guild master
Robert the Bearded	Prince of Anjou
Lothar of Segni	Cardinal/later elected as Pope Innocent III
John the Short	Richard's brother

Part Two

Thèrèse	Alfred's wife
Maren	Alfred's daughter
Inanna	Tailor
Atticus	Marianne's father
Olga	Folk dancer
Helga	Folk dancer

CHARACTER LIST

In order of appearance

CHARACTERS	ROLE
Gwyn	Asser's friend
Maurice	Giant
Misty	Prostitute
Scarlet	Prostitute
Jameela	Artist from Kula Duchy
Cyrus	Villager
Marcus	Fisherman
Count	Banker
Smith	High Constable of Royal Army
Daniel	Knight
Charlie	Knight
Bailey	Farmer
Ashlyn	Farmer
Yusuf	Kula Duchy Ambassador
Adam	Kula Duchy Ambassador
Francis	Brother at Rose Abbey
Madelyn	Princess Isabella's daughter
Aliyah	Padre's friend
Emma	Villager

CHARACTER LIST

In order of appearance

CHARACTERS   **ROLE**

Part Three

Characters	Role
Louise	Nun
Cookie	Cook
Simone	Villager
Bhakita	Villager
Riona	Villager
Haider	Jameela's brother
Masha	Jameela's mother
Abbas	Jameela's father
Kristoff	Troll/Professor
Alaina	Kristoff's wife
Camilla	Kristoff's daughter
Alexandra	Kristoff's daughter
Erik	Kristoff's son
Kormak	Troll
Munnie	Elder of troll village
Rohad	Duke of Kula Duchy/ Richard's half-brother
Nadia	Villager
Firat	Kula guard
Baris	Kula guard

ACKNOWLEDGMENTS

Dear Readers,

This book was a labor of love, and I am eternally grateful for those who walked with me as I journeyed through the lands of deep depression, panic disorder, suicidal ideation, and post-traumatic stress from October 2018 until December 2020.

———

During this writing journey, my writing coach and friend, Robyn Campbell, passed away. Though she emphasized that writing is the greatest teacher, she helped me build the foundation for writing a novel. This book was not possible without her.

———

Another person who has been with me from the beginning is my friend Courtney Woodley. The wife of a great friend who served with me during war, she became a sister-in-arms as I battled my internal demons. She held me accountable, encouraged me, and collaborated with me on the book as my alpha reader.

———

Thank you to the professionals at Reedsy who edited and designed this book: Cindy Marsch, Lynn Post, and David Provolo. Your expertise guided this debut novel to publication.

———

Thank you to the many I asked to read the book and provide constructive feedback. From friends and family to beta readers and the strangers I met along the way, thank you for taking the time to read and suggest changes. The book became much better because of your feedback.

＋————＋

Lastly, to the readers, thank you for reading!

Want to connect with me?

I am @michaelpaulauthor on Instagram.

Or visit my website @ https://michaelpaulauthor.com/

I would love to see your posts or just chat about the book.

Could you please leave a review? It can be positive or constructive or somewhere in between—leaving reviews is one of the best ways you can support independent authors you love.

https://www.goodreads.com/review/edit/58417132

http://www.amazon.com/review/create-review?&asin=B-098CDS9XX

I look forward to the next steps along the journey as I continue writing…

Sincerely,

Michael Paul

ABOUT ME

When **Michael Paul** is not writing, he works for the United States Air Force as an intelligence officer. After six years of active duty service, he transitioned to the Air Force Reserve. He worked as a procurement professional at Caterpillar for eight years, then left in November 2019 to pursue his dream of writing novels.

CPSIA information can be obtained
at www.ICGtesting.com
Printed in the USA
LVHW091905220921
698481LV00010B/139/J

9 781737 166061